W9-BVK-042

Dear Reader,

Once upon a time, back when I was a fledgling romance author, I wanted to write a miniseries of connected books, and I did some brainstorming with my good friend Eric, searching for a unique hook to tie these books together.

In Eric's travels, he happened across a *Newsweek* article about the Navy SEAL BUD/S (Basic Underwater Demolition SEALs) "Hell Week" of training. He immediately called me and announced, "I have found your miniseries hook!"

I remember running to the library (this was pre-internet), reading that article and getting goosebumps because I knew Eric was right. Navy SEALs make great romance heroes. And with my lifelong admiration for the men and women of the U.S. Military, I knew I would be able to do them justice. (And I'd love doing the research, along the way....)

And so my Tall, Dark & Dangerous series about U.S. Navy SEAL Team Ten came to be. The book you're holding includes two installments—*Harvard's Education* and *Hawken's Heart* (originally published with the holiday title *It Came Upon A Midnight Clear*)— first published by Silhouette Books.

Don't miss the recently reissued *Tall, Dark and Dangerous* (*Prince Joe* and *Forever Blue*), and *Tall, Dark and Fearless* (*Frisco's Kid* and *Everyday, Average Jones*). And visit www.eHarlequin.com or my website, www.SuzanneBrockmann.com, for more information about upcoming releases and reissues!

Happy reading,

Suz Brockmann

SUZANNE BROCKMANN

TALL, DARK AND DEVASTATING

HQN™

ISBN-13: 978-0-373-77518-7

TALL, DARK AND DEVASTATING

Copyright © 2010 by Harlequin Books S.A.

The publisher acknowledges the copyright holder of the individual works as follows:

HARVARD'S EDUCATION
Copyright © 1998 by Suzanne Brockmann

HAWKEN'S HEART
Copyright © 1998 by Suzanne Brockmann

Recycling programs
for this product may
not exist in your area.

CONTENTS

HARVARD'S EDUCATION

* * * *

For my fearless pointman, Ed.

ACKNOWLEDGMENTS

Special thanks to Candace Irvin—friend, fellow writer
and unlimited source of U.S. Navy information.

Thanks also to the helpful staff at the UDT SEAL Museum
in Fort Pierce, Florida, and to Vicki Debock,
who told me about it.

Thanks to my swim buddy Eric Ruben for suggesting
I write a book with a Navy SEAL hero!
(I owe it all to you, baby!)

Thanks to the Harvard Project volunteers from the
Team Ten list
(http://groups.yahoo.com/group/teamten/)
for their proofreading skills: Group Captain
Rebecca Chappell, Vi Dao, Kellie Jones, Amy Madden,
Claire Madden, Lynn McCrea, Heather McCormack-
McHugh, Debbie Meiers and Kelly Shand.
Hooyah, gang! Thanks for helping to make
the TDD world as typo-free as possible.

Thanks to the real teams of SEALs, and to all the
courageous men and women in the U.S. military
(especially the Marines! Forgive me for including the
banana joke as an example of the healthy rivalry
between the Navy and the Marines!), who sacrifice
so much to keep America the land of the free
and the home of the brave.

Last but not least, a heartfelt thank-you to the wives,
husbands, children and families of these
real-life military heroes and heroines.
Your sacrifice is deeply appreciated.

Any mistakes I've made or liberties I've taken
in writing this book are completely my own.

CHAPTER ONE

THIS WAS WRONG. It was all wrong. Another few minutes, and this entire combined team of FInCOM agents and Navy SEALs was going to be torn to bits.

There was a small army of terrorists out there in the steamy July night. The Ts—or tangos, as the SEALs were fond of calling them—were waiting on their arrival with assault rifles that were as powerful as the weapon P. J. Richards clutched in her sweating hands.

P.J. tried to slow her pounding heart, tried to make the adrenaline that was streaming through her system work for her rather than against her as she crept through the darkness.

FInCOM Agent Tim Farber was calling the shots, but Farber was a city boy—and a fool, to boot. He didn't know squat about moving through the heavy underbrush of this kind of junglelike terrain. Of course, P.J. was a fine one to be calling names. Born in D.C., she'd been raised on concrete and crumbling blacktop—a different kind of jungle altogether.

Still, she knew enough to realize that Farber had to move more slowly to listen to the sounds of the night around him. And as long as she was criticizing, the fact that four FInCOM agents and three SEALs were occupying close to the same amount of real estate along this narrow trail made her feel as if she were part of some great big Christmas package, all wrapped up with a ribbon on top, waiting under some terrorist's tree.

"Tim." P.J. spoke almost silently into the wireless radio

headset she and the rest of the CSF team—the Combined SEAL/FInCOM Antiterrorist team—had been outfitted with. "Spread us out and slow it down."

"Feel free to hang back if we're moving too fast for you." Farber intentionally misunderstood, and P.J. felt a flash of frustration. As the only woman in the group, she was at the receiving end of more than her share of condescending remarks.

But while P.J. stood only five feet two inches and weighed in at barely one hundred and fifteen pounds, she could run circles around any one of these men—including most of the big, bad Navy SEALs. She could outshoot nearly all of them, too. When it came to sheer, brute force, yes, she'd admit she was at a disadvantage. But that didn't matter. Even though she couldn't pick them up and throw them any farther than she could spit, she could outthink damn near anyone, no sweat.

She sensed more than heard movement to her right and raised her weapon.

But it was only the SEAL called Harvard. The brother. His name was Daryl Becker and he was a senior chief—the naval equivalent of an army sergeant. He cut an imposing enough figure in his street clothes, but dressed in camouflage gear and protective goggles, he looked more dangerous than any man she'd ever met. He'd covered his face and the top of his shaved head with streaks of green and brown greasepaint that blended eerily with his black skin.

He was older than many of the other SEALs in the illustrious Alpha Squad. P.J. was willing to bet he had a solid ten years on her at least, making him thirty-five—or maybe even older. This was no green boy. This one was one-hundred-percent-pure grown man—every hard, muscled inch of him. Rumor had it he'd actually attended Harvard University and graduated *cum laude* before enlisting in Uncle Sam's Navy.

He hand-signaled a question. "Are you all right?" He mouthed the words as well—as if he thought she'd already forgotten the array of gestures that allowed them to communicate silently. Maybe Greg Greene or Charles Schneider had forgotten, but she remembered every single one.

"I'm okay," she signaled to him as tersely as she could, frowning to emphasize her disapproval.

Damn, Harvard had been babying her from the word go. Ever since the FInCOM agents had first met the SEALs from Alpha Squad, this man in particular had been watching her closely, no doubt ready to catch her when she finally succumbed to the female vapors and fainted.

P.J. used hand signals to tell him what Tim Farber had ignored. *Stop. Listen. Silent. Something's wrong.*

The woods around them were oddly quiet. All the chirping and squeaking and rustling of God only knows *what* kinds of creepy crawly insect life had stopped. Someone else was out there, or they themselves were making too much racket. Either possibility was bad news.

Tim Farber's voice sounded over the headphones. "Raheem says the campsite is only a quarter mile ahead. Split up into groups."

About time. If *she* were the AIC—the agent in charge— of the operation, she would have broken the group into pairs right from the start. Not only that, but she would have taken what the informant, Raheem Al Hadi, said with a very large grain of salt instead of hurtling in, ill-informed and half-cocked.

"Belay that." Tim's voice was too loud in her ears. "Raheem advises the best route in is on this path. These woods are booby-trapped. Stay together."

P.J. felt like one of the redcoats, marching along the trail from Lexington to Concord—the perfect target for the rebel guerrillas.

She had discussed Raheem with Tim Farber before

they'd left on this mission. Or rather, she'd posed some thought-provoking questions to which he'd responded with off-the-cuff reassurances. Raheem had given information to the SEALs before. His record had proven him to be reliable. Tim had reassured her, all right—he'd reassured her that he was, indeed, a total fool.

She'd found out from the other two FInCOM agents that Farber believed the SEALs were testing him to see if he trusted them. He was intending to prove he did.

Stay close to me, Harvard said with his hands.

P.J. pretended not to see him as she checked her weapon. She didn't need to be babysat. Annoyance flooded through her, masking the adrenaline surges and making her feel almost calm.

He got right in her face. *Buddy up,* he signaled. *Follow me.*

No. You follow me. She shot the signal back at him. She, for one, was tired of blindly following just anyone. She'd come out here in these wretched, bug-infested, swampy woods to neutralize terrorists. And that was exactly what she was going to do. If G.I. Joe here wanted to tag along, that was fine by her.

He caught her wrist in his hand—Lord, he had big hands—and shook his head in warning.

He was standing so close she could feel body heat radiating from him. He was much taller than she was, more than twelve inches, and she had to crane her neck to glare at him properly.

He smiled suddenly, as if he found the evil eye she was giving him behind her goggles amusing. He clicked off his lip mike, pushing it slightly aside so that he could lean down to whisper in her ear, "I knew you'd be trouble, first time I saw you."

It was remarkable, really, the way this man's smile transformed his face, changing him from stern, savage warrior to intensely interested and slightly amused potential lover. Or maybe he was just mildly interested and highly amused, and her too vivid imagination had made up the other parts.

P.J. pulled her hand away, and as she did, the world exploded around her, and Harvard fell to the ground.

He'd been shot.

Her mind froze, but her body reacted swiftly as a projectile whistled past her head.

She brought her weapon up as she hit the ground, using her peripheral vision to mark the positions of the tangos who had crept up behind them. She fired in double bursts, hitting one, then two, then three of them in rapid succession.

All around her, weapons were being fired and men were shouting in outrage and in pain. From what she could see, the entire CSF team was completely surrounded—except for the little hole she'd made in the terrorists' line of attack.

"Man down," P.J. rasped, following FInCOM procedure as she crawled on knees and elbows toward Harvard's body. But he'd taken a direct hit. She knew from one glance there was no use pulling him with her as she moved outside the kill zone.

"Backup—we need backup!" She could hear Tim Farber's voice, pitched up an octave, as she moved as silently as possible toward the prone bodies of the terrorists she'd brought down.

"By the time help arrives—" Chuck Schneider's voice was also very squeaky "—there'll be nothing left here to back up!"

Yeah? Not if *she* could help it.

There was a tree with low branches just beyond the terrorists' ambush point. If she could get there and somehow climb up it…

She was a city girl, an urban-street agent, and she'd never climbed a tree in her life. She absolutely *hated* heights, but she knew if she could fire from the vantage point of those branches, the tangos wouldn't know what hit them.

P.J. moved up and onto her feet in a crouching run and headed for the tree. She saw the tango rising out of the bushes at the last possible second and she fired twice, hitting him squarely in the chest. He fell, and only then did she see the man behind him.

She was dead. She knew in that instant that she was dead. She fired anyway, but her aim was off.

His wasn't.

The force of the double impact pushed her back, and she tripped and went down. She felt her head crack against something, a rock, the trunk of a tree—she wasn't sure what, but it was granite hard. Pain exploded, stars sparking behind her tightly closed eyes.

"Code eighty-six! Eighty-six! Cease and desist!"

Just like that, the gunfire stopped. Just like that, this particular training exercise was over.

P.J. felt bright lights going on all over the area, and she struggled to open her eyes, to sit up. The movement made the world lurch unappealingly, and she desperately fought the urge to retch, curling instead into a tight little ball. She prayed she'd somehow find her missing sense of equilibrium before anyone noticed she was temporarily out for the count.

"We need a hospital corpsman," the voice over her headset continued. "We've got an agent down, possible head injury."

P.J. felt hands touching her shoulder, her face, unfastening her goggles. So much for no one noticing.

"Richards, yo. You still with me, girl?" It was Harvard, and his voice got harsher, louder as he turned away from her. "Where the hell is that corpsman?" Softer again, and sweeter, like honey now. "Richards, can you open your eyes?"

She opened one eye and saw Harvard's camouflaged

face gazing at her. His chin and cheeks were splattered with yellow from the paint ball that had hit him in the center of his chest.

"I'm fine," she whispered. She still hadn't quite regained her breath from the paint ball that had caught her directly in the midsection.

"Like hell you're fine," he countered. "And I should know. I saw you doing that George of the Jungle imitation. Right into that tree, headfirst…"

One Harvard became two—and Lord knows one was more than enough to deal with. P.J. had to close her eyes again. "Just give me another minute…."

"Corpsman's on the way, Senior Chief."

"How bad's she hurt, H.?" P.J. recognized that voice as belonging to Alpha Squad's commanding officer, Captain Joe Catalanotto—Joe Cat, as his men irreverently called him.

"I don't know, sir. I don't want to move her, in case she's got a neck injury. Why the *hell* didn't one of us think about the danger of firing a paint ball at someone this girl's size? What is she? A hundred, hundred and five pounds at the most? How the hell did this get past us?"

The breathlessness and dizziness were finally fading, leaving a lingering nausea and a throbbing ache in her head. P.J. would have liked a few more minutes to gather her senses, but Harvard had just gone and called her a girl.

"This is no big deal," P.J. said, forcing her eyes open and struggling to sit up. "I was moving when the projectile hit me—the force caught me off balance and I tripped. There's no need to turn this into some kind of a national incident. Besides, I weigh one-fifteen." On a good day. "I've played paint-ball games before with no problem."

Harvard was kneeling next to her. He reached out, caught her face between his hands and lightly touched the back of her head with the tips of his fingers. He skimmed an incredibly sore spot, and she couldn't help but wince.

He swore softly, as if it hurt him, as well. "Hurts, huh?"

"I'm—"

"Fine," he finished for her. "Yes, ma'am, you've made that clear. You've also got a bump the size of Mount Saint Helens on the back of your head. Odds are, you've got a concussion to go along with that bump."

P.J. could see Tim Farber standing in the background, all but taking notes for the report she knew he was going to file with Kevin Laughton. *I recommend from now on that Agent Richards's role in this antiterrorist unit be limited to dealing with administrative issues....* Some men couldn't abide working in the field alongside a woman. She glanced at Harvard. No doubt *he'd* be first in line to put his initials right next to Farber's recommendation.

She silently composed her own note. *Hey, Kev, I fell and I landed wrong—so sue me. And before you pull me off this team, prove that no male FInCOM agent ever made a similar mistake and... Oh, wait, what's that I'm remembering? A certain high-level AIC who shall remain nameless but whose initials are K.L. doing a rather un-graceful nosedive from a second-story window during a training op back about a year and a half ago?*

P.J. focused on the mental image of Laughton grinning ruefully as he rubbed the newly healed collarbone that still gave him twinges of pain whenever it rained. That picture made Farber's lofty smirk easier to bear.

No way was Kevin Laughton pulling her from this assignment. He had been her boss for two years, and he knew she deserved to be right here, right through to the end, come hell or high water *or* Tim Farber's male chauvinist whining.

The corpsman arrived, and after he flashed a light into

P.J.'s eyes, he examined the bump on the back of her head a whole lot less gently than Harvard had.

"I want to take you over to the hospital," the corpsman told her. "I think you're probably fine, but I'd feel better if we got an X-ray or two. You've got a lot of swelling back there. Any nausea?"

"I had the wind knocked out of me, so it's hard to tell," P.J. said, sidestepping the question. Harvard was shaking his head, watching her closely, and she carefully made a point not to meet his gaze.

"Can you walk or should we get a stretcher?"

P.J. was damned if she was going to be carried out of these woods, but truth was, her legs felt like rubber. "I can walk." Her voice rang with false confidence as she tried to convince herself as well as everyone else.

She could feel Harvard watching as she pushed herself unsteadily to her feet. He moved closer, still looking to catch her if she fell. It was remarkable, really. Every other woman she knew would've been dying for a good-looking man like Senior Chief Daryl Becker to play hero for them.

But she wasn't every other woman.

She'd come this far on her own two feet and she wasn't about to let some silly bump on the head undermine her tough-as-nails reputation.

It was hard enough working at FInCOM, where the boys only grudgingly let the girls play, too. But for eight weeks, she was being allowed access to the absolutely-no-women-allowed world of the U.S. Navy SEALs.

For the next eight weeks, the members of SEAL Team Ten's invincible Alpha Squad were going to be watching her, waiting for her to screw up so they could say to each other, *See, this is precisely why we don't let women in.*

The SEALs were the U.S. Navy's special operations units. They were highly trained warriors with well-earned reputations for being the closest things to superheroes this side of a comic book.

The acronym came from sea, air and land, and SEALs were equally comfortable—and adept—at operating in all of those environments.

They were smart, they were brave and they were more than a little crazy—they had to be to make it through the grueling sessions known as BUD/S training, which included the legendary Hell Week. From what P.J. had heard, a man who was still in the SEAL program after completing Hell Week had every right to be cocky and arrogant.

And the men of Alpha Squad at times could be both.

As P.J. forced herself to walk slowly but steadily away, she could feel all of Alpha Squad's eyes on her back.

Especially Senior Chief Harvard Becker's.

CHAPTER TWO

HARVARD DIDN'T KNOW what the hell he was doing here.

It was nearly 0100. He should have gone back to his apartment outside the base. He should be sitting on his couch in his boxers, chillin' and having a cold beer and skimming through the past five days' videotapes of *The Young and the Restless* instead of making a soap opera out of his own life.

Instead, he was here in this allegedly upscale hotel bar with the rest of the unmarried guys from Alpha Squad, making a sorry-assed attempt to bond with FInCOM's wunderkinder.

Steel guitars were wailing from the jukebox—some dreadful song about Papa going after Mama and doing her in because of her cheatin' heart. And the SEALs—Wes and Bobby were the only ones Harvard could see from his quick scan of the late-night crowd—were sitting on one side of the room, and the three male FInCOM agents were on the other. Not much bonding going down here tonight.

Harvard didn't blame Wes and Bob one bit. FInCOM's fab four didn't have much in common with the Alpha Squad.

It was amazing, really. There were something like seventy-three-hundred agents in the Federal Intelligence Commission. He'd have thought the Chosen Four would have come equipped with superhero capes and a giant *S* emblazoned on the fronts of their shirts at the very least.

Timothy Farber was FInCOM's alleged golden boy. He

was a fresh-faced, college-boy type, several years shy of thirty, with a humorless earnestness that was annoying as hell. He was a solid subscriber to the FInCOM my-way-or-the-highway way of thinking. This no doubt worked when directing traffic to allow clear passage for the President's convoy, but it wouldn't do him quite as well when dealing with unpredictable, suicidal, religious zealots.

No, in Harvard's experience, a leader of a counterter-rorist team needed constantly to adjust his plan of attack, altering and revising as unknown variables become known. A team leader needed to know how to listen to others' opinions and to know that sometimes the other guy's idea might be the best idea.

Joe Cat had consulted with Alan "Frisco" Francisco—one of the best BUD/S training instructors in Coronado—and had purposely put blustery Tim Farber in command of the very first training scenario in an attempt to knock him off his high horse. A former member of the Alpha Squad who was off the active duty list because of a per-manent injury to his knee, Frisco had duties that kept him in California, but he was in constant contact with both Alpha Squad's captain and Harvard.

Still, judging from the way Farber was holding court at the bar, surrounded by his two fellow agents, it was obvious to Harvard that Frisco's ploy hadn't worked. Farber was totally unperturbed by his failure.

Maybe tomorrow, when Alpha Squad reviewed the exer-cise, the fact would finally sink in that Farber had person-ally created this snafu, this grand-scale Charlie Foxtrot.

But somehow Harvard doubted it.

As Harvard watched, Farber drew something on a napkin, and the two other FInCOM agents nodded seriously.

Greg Greene and Charles Schneider were around Har-vard's age, thirty-five, thirty-six, maybe even older. They'd spent most of the preliminary classroom sessions looking bored, their body language broadcasting "been there, done that." But in the field, during the evening's exercise, they'd shown little imagination. They were standard issue FInCOM agents—finks, as the SEALs were fond of calling them. They didn't make waves, they followed the rule book to the last letter, they waited for someone else to take the lead and they looked good in dark suits and sunglasses.

They'd looked good smeared with yellow paint from the terrorists' weapons, too. They'd followed Tim Farber's command without question, and in the mock ambush that had resulted, they'd been rather messily mock killed.

Still, they hadn't seemed to learn that following Farber unquestioningly might've been a mistake, because here they were, following Farber still. No doubt because someone higher up in FInCOM had told them to follow him.

Only one of the four superfinks out there tonight had openly questioned Farber's command decisions.

P. J. Richards.

Harvard glanced around the bar again, but he didn't see her anywhere. She was probably in her room, having a soak in the tub, icing the bruise on the back of her head.

Damn, he could still see her, flung backward like some rag doll when that paint ball hit her. He hadn't gone to church in a long time, but he'd silently checked in with God as he'd called for the training session to halt, asking for divine intervention, praying that P.J. hadn't hit that tree with enough force to break her pretty neck.

Men died during training. The risk was part of being a SEAL. But P. J. Richards was neither man nor SEAL, and the thought of her out there with them, facing the dangers they so casually faced, made Harvard's skin crawl.

"Hey, Senior Chief. I didn't expect to see *you* here." Lucky O'Donlon was carrying a pitcher of beer from the bar.

"I didn't expect to see you here, either, O'Donlon. I was

sure you'd be heading out to see that girlfriend of yours at warp speed."

Harvard followed Lucky to the table where Bobby and Wes were sitting. He nodded a greeting to them—the inseparable twins of Alpha Squad. Unidentical twins. Bobby Taylor came close to Harvard's six foot five, and he gave the impression of being nearly as wide around as he was tall. If he hadn't wanted to become a SEAL, he would have had a serious future as a professional football linebacker. And Wes Skelly was Alpha Squad's version of Popeye the sailor man, short and wiry and liberally tattooed. What he lacked in height and weight, he more than made up for with his extremely big mouth.

"Renee had a meeting tonight for the state pageant." Lucky sat down at the table and then kicked out a chair for Harvard to join them. He filled first Bobby's mug from the pitcher, then poured some beer for Wes. "You want me to get you a glass?" he asked Harvard.

"No, thanks." Harvard shook his head as he sat down. "What's that title Renee just won? Miss Virginia Beach?"

"Miss East Coast Virginia," Lucky told him.

"Pretty girl. *Young* girl."

Lucky flashed his movie-star-perfect grin as if the fact that his girlfriend probably hadn't yet celebrated her nineteenth birthday was something to be proud of. "Don't I know it."

Harvard had to smile. To each his own. Personally, he liked women with a little more life experience.

"Hey, Crash," Wes called in his megaphone voice. "Pull up a chair."

William Hawken, Alpha Squad's newest temporary member, sat across from Harvard, meeting his eyes and nodding briefly. Hawken was one spooky individual, dark and almost unnaturally quiet, seemingly capable of becoming invisible upon demand. At first glance, he was not particularly tall, not particularly well-built, not particularly handsome.

But Harvard knew better than to go by a first glance. The man had been nicknamed Crash for his ability to move soundlessly in any circumstance, under any condition. Crash was anything but average. On closer examination, his eyes were a steely shade of blue with a sharpness to them that seemed almost to cut. Crash didn't so much look around a room—he absorbed it, memorized it, recorded it, probably permanently. And beneath his purposely loose-fitting clothes, his body was that of a long-distance runner—lean and muscular, without an extra ounce of fat anywhere.

"Grab a glass and have a beer," Lucky told Crash.

He shook his head. "No, thanks," he said in his deceptively quiet voice. "Beer's not my drink. I'll wait for the waitress."

Harvard knew that Crash was part of this FInCOM project at Captain Catalanotto's special request. He was in charge of organizing all the "terrorist" activities the Combined SEAL/FInCOM team would be running into over the next eight weeks. He'd been the strategical force behind tonight's paint-ball slaughter. The score so far was Crash—one, CSF team—zero.

Harvard didn't know him very well, but Hawken's reputation was close to legendary. He'd been part of the SEALs' mysterious Gray Group for years. And apparently he'd been involved in countless black operations—highly covert, hush-hush missions that were as controversial as they were dangerous. SEALs were allegedly sent into other countries to perform tasks that even the U.S. Government claimed to know nothing about—neutralization of drug lords, permanent removal of political and military leaders preaching genocide and so on. The SEALs were forced to play God, or at least take on the roles of judge, jury and hangman combined. It was not a job Harvard would have relished doing.

If the SEALs on a black op succeeded at their mission, they'd get little or no recognition. And if they failed, they were on their own, possibly facing espionage charges, with no chance of the government stepping forward and accepting the responsibility.

No wonder Crash didn't drink beer. He probably had an ulcer the size of an aircraft carrier from the stress.

He'd no doubt come here tonight in an attempt to better get to know the SEALs who made up Alpha Squad—the men he'd be working with for the next eight weeks.

Which reminded Harvard of why *he'd* come here. He glanced at the three FInCOM agents sitting at the bar. Still no sign of P.J. "Has anyone tried to make friends with the finks tonight?"

"Besides you trying to get close to P. J. Richards, you mean? Trying to hold her hand out in the woods?" Wes Skelly laughed at his miserable joke. "Jeez, Senior Chief, only time in *my* memory that you were the first man down in a paint-ball fight."

"That was my paint ball that hit you, H.," Lucky drawled. "I hope it didn't hurt too badly."

"Hey, it's about time he found out what it feels like just being hit," Bobby countered in his sub-bass-woofer voice.

"I couldn't resist," Lucky continued. "You were such a great, big, perfect target, standing there like that."

"I think Harvard let you shoot him. I think he was just trying to score some sympathy from P.J.," Wes said. "Is she hot or is she hot?"

"She's a colleague," Harvard said. "Show a little respect."

"I am," Wes said. "In fact, there are few things I respect more than an incredibly hot woman. Look me in the eye,

H., and tell me that you honestly don't think this lady is a total babe."

Harvard had to laugh. Wes could be like a pit bull when he got hold of an idea like this. He knew if he didn't admit it now, Wes would be on him all night until he finally caved in. He met Crash's amused gaze and rolled his eyes in exasperation. "All right. You're right, Skelly. She's hot."

"See? Harvard was distracted," Bobby told Lucky. "That's the only reason you were able to hit him."

"Yeah, his focus was definitely not where it should have been," Lucky agreed. "It was on the lovely Ms. Richards instead." He grinned at Harvard. "Not that I blame you, Senior Chief. She *is* a killer."

"Are you gonna go for her?" Wes asked. "Inquiring minds want to know. You know, she's short, but she's got really great legs."

"And a terrific butt."

Wes smiled blissfully, closing his eyes. "And an incredible set of—"

"Well, this is really fun." Harvard looked up to see P. J. Richards standing directly behind him. "But aren't we going to talk about Tim and Charlie and Greg's legs and butts, too?" Her big brown eyes were open extra wide in mock innocence.

Silence. Dead, total silence.

Harvard was the first to move, pushing back his chair and standing up. "I have to apologize, ma'am—"

The feigned curiosity in her eyes shifted to blazing hot anger as she glared at him from her barely five-foot-two-inch height.

"No," she said sharply. "You don't have to apologize, Senior Chief Becker. What you have to do is learn not to make the same disrespectful mistakes over and over and over again. What you as men have to do is learn to stop dissing women by turning them into nothing more than sex objects. Great legs, a terrific butt and an incredible set of what, Mr. Skelly?" She turned her glare to Wesley. "I have to assume you weren't about to compliment me on my choice of encyclopedias, but were instead commenting on my breasts?"

Wes actually looked sheepish. "Yeah. Sorry, ma'am."

"Well, you get points for honesty, but that's *all* you get points for," P.J. continued tartly. She looked from Wes to Bobby to Lucky. "You were the first three tangos I shot out there tonight, weren't you?" She turned to Crash. "Exactly how many members of your team were hit tonight, Mr. Hawken?"

"Six." He smiled slightly. "Four of whom you were responsible for."

"Four out of six." She shook her head, exhaling in a short burst of disbelief as she glared at the SEALs. "I beat you at your own game, and yet you're not talking about my skills as a shooter. You're discussing my butt. Don't you think there's something *really* wrong with this picture?"

Lucky looked at Bobby, and Bobby glanced at Wes.

Bobby seemed to think a response was needed, but didn't know quite what to say. "Um…"

P.J. still had her hands on the hips in question, and she wasn't finished yet. "Unless, of course, you think maybe my ability to hit a target was just dumb luck. Or maybe you think I wouldn't have been able to hit you if I had been a man. Maybe it was my very femaleness that distracted and stupefied you, hmm? Maybe you were stunned by the sight of my female breasts—which, incidentally, boys, are a meager size thirty-two B and can barely be noticed when I'm wearing my combat vest. We're not talking heavy cleavage here, gang."

Harvard couldn't hide his smile.

She turned her glare to him. "Am I amusing you, Senior Chief?"

Damn, this woman was *mad*. She was funny as hell, too, but he wasn't going to make things any better by laughing.

Harvard wiped the smile off his face. "Again, I'd like to apologize to you, Ms. Richards. I assure you, no disrespect was intended."

"Maybe not," she told him, her voice suddenly quiet, "but disrespect was given."

As he looked into her eyes, Harvard could see weariness and resignation, as if this had happened to her far too many times. He saw physical fatigue and pain, too, and he knew that her head was probably still throbbing from the blow she'd received earlier that evening.

Still, he couldn't help thinking that despite everything she'd said, Wesley was right. This girl *was* smoking hot. Even the loose-fitting T-shirt and baggy fatigues she wore couldn't disguise the lithe, athletic and very female body underneath. Her skin was smooth and clear, like a four-year-old's, and a deep, rich shade of chocolate. He could imagine how soft it would feel to his fingers, how delicious she would taste beneath his lips. Her face was long and narrow, her chin strong and proud, her profile that of African royalty, her eyes so brown the color merged with her pupils, becoming huge dark liquid pools he could drown in. She wore her hair pulled austerely from her face in a ponytail.

Yeah, she was beautiful. Beautiful and very, very hot.

She stepped around him, heading toward the bar. Harvard caught up with her before she was halfway across the room.

"Look," he said, raising his voice to be heard over the cowboy music blaring from the jukebox. "I don't know how much of that conversation you overheard—"

"Enough. Believe me."

"The truth is, you *were* a distraction out there tonight. To me. Having you there was extremely disconcerting."

She had her arms folded across her chest, one eyebrow raised in an expression of half-disdain, half-disgust. "And the point of your telling me this is…?"

He let his eyelids drop halfway. "Oh, it's not a come-on line. You'd know for sure if I were giving you one of those."

Her gaze faltered, and she was the first to look away. What do you know? She wasn't as tough as she was playing.

Harvard pressed his advantage. "I think it's probably a good idea for you to know that I believe there's no room in this kind of high-risk joint FInCOM/military endeavor for women."

P.J. gave him another one of those you've-lost-your-mind laughs. "It's a good thing you weren't on the FInCOM candidate selection committee, then, isn't it?"

"I have no problem at all with women holding jobs in both FInCOM and in the U.S. military," he continued. "But I believe that they—that *you*—should have low-risk sup-porting roles, doing administrative work instead of taking part in combat."

"I see." P.J. was nodding. "So what you're telling me is that despite the fact that I'm the best shooter in nearly all of FInCOM, you think the best place for me is in the *typing pool?*"

Her eyes were shooting flames.

Harvard stood his ground. "You *did* prove yourself an expert shooter tonight. You're very good, I'll grant you that. But the fact is, you're a woman. Having you on my team, out in the field, in a combat situation, would be a serious distraction."

"That's *your* problem," she said, blazing. "If you can't keep your pants zipped—"

"It has nothing to do with that, and you know it. It's a protectiveness issue. How can my men and I do our jobs when we're distracted by worrying about you?"

P.J. couldn't believe what she was hearing. "You're tell-ing me that because *you're* working with a Stone Age men-tality, because *you're* the one with the problem, *I* should be the one to adapt? I don't think so, Jack. You're just going to have to stop thinking of me as a woman, and then we'll get along just fine."

It was his turn to laugh in disbelief. "That's not going to happen."

"Try counseling, Senior Chief, because I'm here to stay."

His smile was nowhere to be seen, and without it, he looked hard and uncompromising. "You know, it's likely that the only reason you're here is to fill a quota. To help someone with lots of gold on their sleeves be PC."

P.J. refused to react. "I could fire those exact same words right back at you—the only black man in Alpha Squad."

He didn't blink. He just stood there, looking at her.

Lord, he was big. He'd changed into a clean T-shirt, but he still wore the camouflage fatigue pants he'd been wearing earlier tonight. With his shirt pulled tight across his mile-wide shoulders and broad chest, with his shaved head gleaming in the dim barroom light, he looked impossibly dangerous. And incredibly handsome in a harshly masculine way.

No, Harvard Becker was no pretty boy, *that* was for sure. But he *was* quite possibly the most handsome man P.J. had ever met. His face was angular, with high cheekbones and a strong jaw. His nose was big, but it was the right length and width for his face. Any smaller, and he would have looked odd. And he had just about the most perfect ears she'd ever seen—just the right size, perfectly rounded and streamlined. Before the war game, he'd taken off the diamond stud he always wore in his left ear, but he'd since put it back in, and it glistened colorfully, catching snatches of the neon light.

But it was Harvard's eyes that P.J. had been aware of right from the start. A rich, dark golden-brown, they were the focal point of his entire face, of his entire being. If it were true that the eyes were the window to the soul, this man had one powerfully intense soul.

Yeah, he was the real thing.

As a matter of fact, more than one or two of the other patrons in the bar, both men and women, were sneaking looks at the man. Some were wary, some were nervous, and some were flat-out chock-full of pheromones.

Without even turning around, Harvard could have snapped his fingers and three or four women—both black and white—would've been pushing their way to his side.

Well, maybe she was exaggerating a little bit. But only a little bit.

This man could have any woman he wanted—and he knew it. And even though P.J. could still hear an echo of his rich voice saying yes, he thought she was hot, she knew the last thing he needed was any kind of involvement with her.

Hell, he'd made it more than clear he didn't even want to be friends.

P.J. refused to feel regret, pushing the twinges of emotion far away from her, ignoring them as surely as she ignored the dull throb of her still-aching head. Because the last thing she needed was any kind of involvement with him—or with anyone, for that matter. She'd avoided it successfully for most of her twenty-five years. There was no reason to think she couldn't continue to avoid it.

He was studying her as intently as she was looking at him. And when he spoke, P.J. knew he hadn't missed the fatigue and pain she was trying so hard to keep from showing in her face. His voice was surprisingly gentle. "You should call it a night—get some rest."

P.J. glanced toward the bar, toward Tim Farber and the other FInCOM agents. "I just thought I'd grab a nightcap before I headed upstairs." Truth was, she'd wanted nothing more than to drag herself to her room and throw herself into a warm tub. But she felt she had to come into the bar, put in an appearance, prove to the other agents and to any of the SEALs who might be hanging around that she was as tough as they were. Tougher. She could go from a hospital X-ray table directly to the bar. See? She wasn't really hurt. See? She could take damn near anything and come back ready for more.

Harvard followed her as she slid onto a bar stool several seats away from the other agents. "It wasn't even a concussion," she said. She didn't bother to raise her voice—she knew Farber was listening.

Harvard glanced at the FInCOM agents. "I know," he said, leaning against the stool next to her. "I stopped in at the hospital before heading over here. The doctor said you'd already been checked over and released."

"Like I said before, I'm fine."

"Whoops, I'm getting paged." Harvard took his pager from his belt and glanced at the number. As the bartender approached, he greeted the man by name. "Hey, Tom. Get me my usual. And whatever the lady here wants."

"I'm paying for my own," P.J. protested, checking her own pager out of habit. It was silent and still.

"She's paying for her own," Harvard told Tom with a smile. "Mind if I use the phone to make a local call?"

"Anytime, Senior Chief." The bartender plopped a telephone in front of Harvard before looking at P.J. "What can I get you, ma'am?"

Iced tea. She truly wanted nothing more than a tall, cool glass of iced tea. But big, tough men didn't drink iced tea, so she couldn't, either. "Give me a draft, please, Tom."

Beside her, Harvard was silent, listening intently to whoever was on the other end of that telephone. He'd pulled a small notebook from one of his pockets and was using the stub of a pencil to write something down. His smile was long gone—in fact, his mouth was a grim line, his face intensely serious.

"Thanks, Joe," he said, then he hung up the phone. Joe.

He'd been talking to Joe Catalanotto, Alpha Squad's CO. He stood up, took out his wallet and threw several dollar bills onto the bar. "I'm sorry, I can't stay."

"Problem at the base?" P.J. asked, watching him in the mirror on the wall behind the bar. For some reason, it was easier than looking directly at him.

He met her eyes in the mirror. "No, it's personal," he said, slipping his wallet into his pants.

She instantly backed down. "I'm sorry—"

"My father's had a heart attack," Harvard told her quietly. "He's in the hospital. I've got to go to Boston right away."

"I'm sorry," P.J. said again, turning to look directly at him. His father. Harvard actually had a *father*. Somehow she'd imagined him spawned—an instant six-and-a-half-foot-tall adult male. "I hope he's all right…."

But Harvard was already halfway across the room.

She watched him until he turned the corner into the hotel lobby and disappeared from view.

The bartender had set a frosty mug of beer on a coaster in front of her. And in front of the bar stool that Harvard had been occupying was a tall glass of iced tea. His usual.

P.J. had to smile. So much for her theory about big, tough men.

She pushed the beer aside and drank the iced tea, wondering what other surprises Harvard Becker had in store for her.

CHAPTER THREE

"HE LOOKS AWFUL."

"He looks a great deal better than he did last night in that ambulance." His mother lowered herself carefully onto the deck chair, and Harvard was aware once again of all the things he'd noticed for the first time in the hospital. The gray in her hair. The deepening lines of character on her slightly round, still pretty face. The fact that her hip was bothering her yet again—that she moved stiffly, more slowly each time he saw her.

Harvard's father *had* looked awful—a shriveled and shrunken version of himself, lying in that hospital bed, hooked up to all those monitors and tubes. His eyes had been closed when Harvard had come in, but the old man had roused himself enough to make a bad joke. Something about how he'd gone to awfully extreme lengths this time just to make their wayward son come to visit.

The old man. Harvard had called his father that since he was twelve. But now it was true.

His parents were getting old.

The heart attack had been relatively mild, but from now on Dr. Medgar Becker was going to have to stop joking about how he was on a two-slices-of-cheesecake-per-day diet and really stick to the low-fat, high-exercise regimen his doctor had ordered. He was going to have to work to cut some of the stress out of his life, as well. But God knows, as the head of the English department at one of New England's most reputable universities, that wasn't going to be an easy thing to do.

"We're selling the house, Daryl," his mother told him quietly.

Harvard nearly dropped the can of soda he'd taken from the refrigerator on his way through the kitchen. "You're *what?*"

His mother lifted her face to the warmth of the late afternoon sunshine, breathing in the fresh, salty air. "Your father was offered a part-time teaching position at a small college in Phoenix. It'll be fewer than a third of the hours he currently has, and far less responsibility. I think we've been given a sign from the Almighty that it's time for him to cut back a bit."

He took a deep breath, and when he spoke, his voice was just as calm as hers had been. "Why didn't you tell me about this before?"

"Medgar wasn't sure he was ready to make such a big change," his mother told him. "We didn't want to worry you until we knew for sure we were going to make the move."

"To Phoenix. In Arizona."

His mother smiled at the skepticism in his voice. "We'll be near Kendra and Robby and the kids. And Jonelle and her bunch won't be too far away in Santa Fe. And we'll be closer to you, too, when you're in California. It'll be much easier for you to come and visit. There's a fine community theater there—something I'm truly looking forward to. And last time we were out there, we found the perfect little house within walking distance of the campus."

Harvard leaned against the railing on the deck, looking out over the grayish-green water of Boston Harbor. His parents had lived in Hingham, Massachusetts, in this house near the ocean, for nearly thirty years. This had been his home from the time he was six years old.

"I've read that the housing market is really soft right now," he said. "It might be a while before you find a buyer willing to meet your asking price."

"We've already got a buyer—paying cash, no less. I called this morning from the hospital, accepted his offer. Closing date's scheduled for two weeks from Thursday."

He turned to face her. "That soon?"

His mother smiled sadly. "I knew that out of all the children, you would be the one to take this the hardest. Five children—you and four girls—and *you're* the sentimental one. I know you always loved this house, Daryl, but we really don't have a choice."

He shook his head as he sat next to her. "I'm just surprised, that's all. I haven't had any time to get used to the idea."

"We're tired of shoveling snow. We don't want to fight our way through another relentless New England winter. Out in Arizona, your father can play golf all year long. And this house is so big and empty now that Lena's gone off to school. The list of pros is a mile long. The list of cons has only one item—my Daryl will be sad."

Harvard took his mother's hand. "I get back here twice a year, at best. You've got to do what's right for you and Daddy. Just as long as you're sure it's really what you want."

"Oh, we're sure." Conviction rang in his mother's voice. "After last night, we're *very* sure." She squeezed his fingers. "We've been so busy talking about Medgar and me, I haven't had the chance to ask about you. How are you?"

Harvard nodded. "I'm well, thanks."

"I was afraid when I called last night you'd be off in some foreign country saving the world or whatever it is that you Navy SEAL types do."

He forced a smile. His parents were moving from this house in just a few weeks. This was probably going to be the very last time he sat on this deck. "Saving the world just about sums it up."

"Have you told that captain of yours it ticks your

mother off that you can't freely talk about all these awful, dangerous assignments you get sent on?"

Harvard laughed. "Right now we're temporarily stationed in Virginia. We're helping train some FInCOM agents in counterterrorist techniques."

"That sounds relatively safe."

P. J. Richards and her blazing eyes came to mind. "Relatively," he agreed. "But it's going to keep me tied up over the next seven and a half weeks. I won't be around to help you pack or move or anything. Are you sure you're going to be able to handle that—especially with Daddy laid up?"

"Lena's home for the summer, and Jonelle's volunteered to help out, too."

Harvard nodded. "Good."

"How's that young friend of yours—the one that just got married and had himself a son, although not quite in that order?"

"Harlan Jones." Harvard identified the friend in question.

His mother frowned. "No, that's not what you usually call him."

"His nickname's Cowboy."

"That's right. Cowboy. How could I forget? How's that working out for him? He had to grow up really fast, didn't he?"

"It's only been a few months, but so far so good. He's on temporary assignment with SEAL Team Two out in California. He had the chance to be part of a project he couldn't turn down."

"A project you can't tell me anything about, no doubt."

Harvard had to smile. "Sorry. You'll like this irony, though. Cowboy's swim buddy from BUD/S training—a guy named William Hawken—is temporarily working with Alpha Squad."

"That's that small world factor again," his mother

proclaimed. "Everyone's connected in some way—some more obviously than others." She leaned forward. "Speaking of connections—what's the chance you'll bring a girlfriend with you when you come to the new house for Thanksgiving?"

He snorted. "We're talking negative numbers—no chance at all. I'm not seeing anyone in particular right now."

"Still tomcatting around, huh? Gettin' it on without getting involved?"

Harvard closed his eyes. "Mom."

"Did you really think your mother didn't know? I know you're a smart man, so I won't give you my safe-sex speech—although in my opinion, the only sex that's truly safe is between a man and his wife." She pushed herself out of her chair. "Okay, I'm done embarrassing you. I'm going to go see about getting lunch on the table."

"Why don't you let me take you out somewhere?"

"And miss the chance to make sure you get at least one home-cooked meal this month? No way."

"I'll be in in a sec to help."

She kissed the top of his head. "You know, you were *born* with hair. You have exceptionally *nice* hair. I don't see why you insist on shaving it all off that way."

Harvard laughed as she headed inside. "I'll try to grow it in for Thanksgiving."

He'd already reserved a few days of leave to spend the holiday at home with his parents.

Home.

It was funny, but he still thought of this place as home. He hadn't lived here in more than fifteen years, but he'd always considered this house his sanctuary. He could come here anytime he needed to, and he could center himself. It was the one place he could come back to that he'd foolishly thought would always remain the same.

The sweet smell of cookies baking in his mother's kitchen. The scent of his father's pipe. The fresh ocean air.

It was weird as hell to think that within less than two weeks his home would belong to strangers.

And he would be spending Thanksgiving far from the ocean at his parents' new house in Arizona.

"Excuse me, Senior Chief Becker! I've been looking for you!"

Harvard turned to find P. J. Richards bearing down on him, eyes shooting fire.

He turned and kept walking. He didn't need this right now. Damn it, he was tired, he was hungry, he was wearing the same clothes he'd had on when he'd left here close to forty-eight hours ago, he hadn't been able to grab more than a combat nap on the flight from Boston to Virginia, and he'd had to stand on the crowded bus back to the base.

On top of the annoying physical inconveniences, there were seven different items that had crash-landed on his desk while he was gone that needed his—and only his— immediate and undivided attention.

It was going to be a solid two hours before he made his way home and reintroduced himself to his bed.

And that was if he was lucky.

P.J. ran to catch up with him. "Did you give the order to restrict my distance for this and yesterday morning's run to only three miles?"

Harvard kept walking. "Yes, I did."

She had to keep trotting to match the length of his stride. "Even though the rest of the team was required to go the full seven miles?"

"That's right."

"How *dare* you!"

She was nearly hopping up and down with anger, and Harvard swore and turned to face her. "I don't have time for this." He spoke more to himself than to her, but of course, she had no way of knowing that.

"Well, you're going to have to *make* time for this."

Damn, she was pretty. And so thoroughly passionate. But if his luck continued in its current downward spiral, he stood only a blind man's chance in a firing range of ever getting a taste of that passion any way other than her hurling angry words—or maybe even knives—in his direction.

"I'm sorry if my very existence is an inconvenience," she continued hotly, "but—"

"My order was standard procedure," he told her tightly.

She wasn't listening. "I will file a formal complaint if this coddling continues, if I am not treated completely the same as—"

"This coddling is by the book for any FInCOM agent who has received an injury sufficient to send him—or her—to the hospital."

She blinked at him. "What did you say?"

Well, what do you know? She *was* listening. "According to the rule book set up for this training session, if a fink goes to the hospital, said fink gets lighter physical training until it's determined that he—or she—is up to speed. Sorry to disappoint you, Ms. Richards, but you were treated no differently than anyone else would have been."

The sun was setting, streaking the sky with red-orange clouds, giving the entire base a romantic, fairy-tale look. Everything was softer, warmer, bathed in diffused pink light. Back home in Hingham, it would have been the perfect kind of summer evening for a long, lazy walk to the local ice-cream stand, flirting all the way with his sister's friends, strutting his seventeen-year-old stuff while they gazed at him adoringly.

The woman in front of him was gazing at him, but it sure as hell wasn't adoringly. In fact, she was looking at him as if he were trying to sell her a dehumidifier in the desert. "*Rule* book?"

Harvard glanced in the direction of his office, wishing he was there so he could, in turn, soon go home. "No doubt one of your bosses was afraid that Alpha Squad was going to hurt you and keep on hurting you. There's a list of ground rules for this training session."

"I wasn't shown any rule book."

Harvard snorted, his patience flat-out gone. He started walking again, leaving her behind. "Yeah, you're right, I'm making all this up."

"You can't blame me for being wary!" P.J. hurried to keep pace. "As far as I know, there's never been this kind of a rule book before. Why should FInCOM start now?"

"No doubt someone heard about BUD/S Hell Week—about the sleep deprivation and strenuous endurance tests that SEALs undergo at the end of phase-one training. I bet they were afraid we'd do something similar to the finks with this counterterrorist deal. And they were right. We would have, if we could. Because in real life, terrorists don't pay too much attention to time-out signals."

P.J. was back to glaring at him, full power. "I'll have you know that I find 'fink' to be an offensive term."

"It's a nickname. A single syllable versus four. Easier to say."

"Yeah, well, I don't like it."

"There's not much you *do* like, is there?" Including him. Maybe *especially* him. Harvard pushed open the door to the Quonset hut that housed Alpha Squad's temporary offices. "My father's going to be fine. I'm sure you were dying to know."

"Oh, God, I'm so sorry I didn't ask!"

His mistake was turning to look at her.

She looked stricken. She looked completely, thoroughly horrified, all her anger instantly vanished. He almost felt bad for her—and he didn't want to feel bad for her. He didn't want to feel bad for anyone, especially not himself.

He'd been off balance since he'd gotten that phone call from Joe Cat telling him about his father's heart attack. His entire personal life had been turned on its side. His parents were succumbing to age and his home was no longer going to be his home.

And then here came P. J. Richards, getting in his face, making all kinds of accusations, reminding him how much easier this entire assignment would be were it not for her female presence.

"Please forgive me—I didn't mean to be insensitive. I was rude not to have asked earlier. Is he really going to be all right?"

As Harvard gazed into P.J.'s bottomless dark eyes, he knew he was fooling himself. He hadn't been off balance since that phone call came in about his father. Damn, he'd been off balance from the moment this tiny little woman had stepped out of the FInCOM van and into his life. He'd liked her looks and her passion right from the start, and her ability to face up to her mistakes made him like her even more.

"Yeah," he told her. "He should be just fine in a few weeks. And his long-term prognosis is just as good, provided he stays with his diet." He nodded at her, hoping she'd consider herself dismissed, wishing he could pull her into his arms and kiss that too-vulnerable, still-mortified look off her face. Thank God he wasn't insane enough to try *that*. "If you'll excuse me, Ms. Richards, I have a great deal of work to do."

Harvard went inside the Quonset hut, forcing himself to shut the door tightly behind him, knowing that starting something hot and heavy with this woman was the dead last thing he should do but wanting it just the same.

Damn, he wanted it, wanted her.

He wanted to lose this unpleasant sensation he had

of being adrift, to temporarily ground himself in her sweetness.

He took a deep breath and got to work.

His father was going to be fine in a few weeks, but he suspected his own recovery was going to take quite a bit longer.

P.J. had never done so much shooting in her life. They were going on day fourteen of the training, and during every single one of those days she'd spent a serious chunk of time on the firing range.

Before she'd started, she could outshoot the three other FInCOM agents, as well as some of the SEALs in Alpha Squad. And after two weeks of perfecting her skill, she was at least as good as the quiet SEAL with the thick Southern accent, the XO or executive officer of Alpha Squad, the one everyone called Blue. And *he* was nearly as good as Alpha Squad's CO, Joe Cat. But, of course, nobody even came close to Harvard.

Harvard. P.J. had managed successfully to avoid him since that day she'd been so mad she'd forgotten even the most basic social graces. She still couldn't believe she hadn't remembered to ask him about his father's health. Her anger was a solid excuse, except for the fact that *that* degree of rudeness was inexcusable.

Lord, she'd made one hell of a fool out of herself that evening.

But as much as she told herself she was avoiding any contact with Harvard out of embarrassment, that wasn't the only reason she was avoiding him.

The man was too good at what he did. How could she not respect and admire a man like that? And added onto those heaping double scoops of respect and admiration was a heady whipped topping of powerful physical attraction. It was a recipe for total disaster, complete with a cherry on top.

She'd learned early in life that her own personal success and freedom hinged on her ability to turn away from such emotions as lust and desire. And so she was turning away. She'd done it before. She could do it again.

P.J. went into the mess hall and grabbed a tray and a turkey sandwich. It turned out the food they'd been eating right from the start wasn't standard Uncle Sam fare. This meal had been catered by an upscale deli downtown, as per the FInCOM rule book. Such a list of rules did exist. Harvard had been right about that.

She felt his eyes following her as she stopped to pour herself a glass of iced tea.

As usual, she'd been aware of him from the moment she'd walked in. He was sitting clear across the room, his back against the far wall. He had two plates piled on his tray, both empty. He was across from the quiet SEAL called Crash, his feet on a chair, nursing a mug of coffee, watching her.

Harvard watched her all the time. He watched her during physical training. He watched her during the classroom sessions. He watched her on the firing range.

You'd think the man didn't have anything better to do with his time.

When he wasn't watching her, he was nearby, always ready to offer a hand up or a boost out of the water. It was driving her insane. He didn't offer Greg Greene a boost. Or Charlie Schneider.

Obviously, he didn't think Greg or Charlie needed one.

P.J. was more than tempted to carry her tray over to Harvard, to sit herself down at his table and to ask him how well she was doing.

Except right now, she knew exactly how well she was doing.

The focus of this morning's classroom session had been on working as a team. And she and Tim Farber and Charlie and Greg had totally flunked Teamwork 101. P.J. had read the personnel files of the other three agents, so when asked, she'd at least been able to come up with such basic facts as where they were from. But she hadn't been able to answer other, more personal questions about her team members. She didn't know such things as what they perceived to be their own strengths and weaknesses. And in return, none of them knew the first little teeny thing about her. None of them were even aware that she hailed from Washington, D.C.—which, apparently, was as much her fault as it was theirs.

And it was true. She hadn't made any attempts to get to know Tim or Charlie or Greg. She'd stopped hanging out in the hotel bar after hours, choosing instead to read over her notes and try to prepare for the coming day's assignments. It had seemed a more efficient use of her time, especially since it included avoiding Harvard's watching eyes, but now she knew she'd been wrong.

P.J. headed for the other FInCOM agents, forcing her mouth into what she hoped was a friendly smile. "Hey, guys. Mind if I join you?"

Farber blinked up at her. "Sorry, we were just leaving. I've got some paperwork to do before the next classroom session."

"I'm due at the range." Charlie gave her an insincere smile as he stood.

Greg didn't say anything. He just gathered his trash and left with Charlie.

Just like that, they were gone, leaving P.J. standing there, holding her tray like an idiot. It wasn't personal. She *knew* it wasn't personal. She'd arrived late, they had already eaten, and they all had things that needed to get done.

Still, something about it felt like a seventh-grade shunning all over again. She glanced around the room, and this time Harvard wasn't the only one watching her. Alpha Squad's captain, Joe Catalanotto, was watching her, too.

She sat and unwrapped her sandwich, praying that both men would leave her be. She took a bite, hoping her body language successfully broadcast, "I want to be alone."

"How you doing, Richards?" Joe pulled out the chair next to hers, straddled it and leaned his elbows on the backrest.

So much for body language. Her mouth was full, so she nodded a greeting.

"You know, one of my biggest beefs with FInCOM has to do with their refusing to acknowledge that teams just can't be thrown together," he said in his husky New York accent. "You can't just count down a line, picking, say, every fourth guy—or woman—and automatically make an effective team."

P.J. swallowed. "How do the SEALs do it?"

"I handpicked Alpha Squad," Joe told her, his smile making his dark brown eyes sparkle. It was funny. With his long, shaggy, dark hair, ruggedly handsome face and muscle-man body, this man could pull off sitting in a chair in that ridiculously macho way. He made it look both comfortable and natural. "I've been with Blue McCoy, my XO, for close to forever. Since BUD/S—basic training, you know?"

She nodded, her mouth full again.

"And I've known Harvard just as long, too. The rest of the guys, well, they'd developed reputations, and when I was looking for men with certain skills... It was really just a matter of meeting and making sure personalities meshed before I tapped 'em to join the squad." He paused. "Something tells me that FInCOM wasn't as careful about compatible personalities when they made the selections for this program."

P.J. snorted. "That's the understatement of the year."

Joe absentmindedly twisted the thick gold wedding band he wore on his left hand. P.J. tried to imagine the kind of woman who'd managed to squeeze vows of fidelity from this charismatic, larger-than-life man. Someone unique. Someone very, very special. Probably someone with the brains of a computer and the body of a super model.

"What FInCOM *should* have done," he told her, "if they wanted a four-man team, was select a leader, have that leader choose team members they've worked with before—people they trust."

"But if they'd done that, there's no way I would be on this team," she pointed out.

"What makes you so sure about that?"

P.J. laughed.

Joe laughed along with her. He had gorgeous teeth. "No, I'm serious," he said.

P.J. put down her sandwich. "Captain, excuse me for calling you crazy, but you're crazy. Do you really think Tim Farber would have handpicked me for his team?"

"Call me Joe," he said. "And no, of course Farber wouldn't have picked you. He's not smart enough. From what I've seen, out of the four of you, he's not the natural leader, either. He's fooled a lot of people, but he doesn't have what it takes. And the other two…" He shrugged. "I'm not particularly impressed. No, out of the four of you, this assignment should've been yours."

P.J. couldn't believe what she'd just heard. She wasn't sure what to say, what to do, but she *did* know that knocking over her iced tea was *not* the correct response. She held tightly onto the glass. "Thank you…Joe," she somehow managed to murmur. "I appreciate your confidence."

"You're doing all right, P.J.," he said, standing in one graceful movement. "Keep it up."

As he walked away, P.J. closed her eyes. God, it had been so long since she'd been given any words of encouragement, she'd almost forgotten how important it was to hear praise. Someone else—in this case, the commanding officer of Alpha Squad—recognized that she was doing her job well. He thought *she* was the one who should lead the team.

Out of the four FInCOM agents…

P.J. opened her eyes, realizing with a flash of clarity that the captain's compliment hadn't been quite as flattering as she'd first believed. She was the best candidate for team leader—compared to Farber, Schneider and Greene.

Still, it was better than being told that women had no place on a team like this one.

She wrapped her half-eaten sandwich and threw it in the trash on her way out of the mess hall, aware of Harvard glancing up to watch her go.

CHAPTER FOUR

"BLUE CALLED TO SAY HE'S RUNNING LATE. He'll be here in about a half hour." Joe Catalanotto closed the door behind Harvard, leading him through the little rented house.

"He went home first, didn't he?" Harvard shook his head in amused disgust. "I *told* the fool not to stop at home." Blue McCoy's wife, Lucy, had come into town two days ago. After spending a month and a half apart, Harvard had no doubt exactly what was causing Blue's current lateness.

And now Blue was going to show up for this meeting at Joe Cat's house grinning like the Cheshire cat, looking relaxed and happy, looking exactly like what he was—a man who just got some.

Damn, it seemed everyone in Alpha Squad had that little extra swing in their steps these days. Everyone but Harvard.

Joe's wife was with him in Virginia, too. Lucky O'Donlon was living up to his nickname, romancing Miss East Coast Virginia. Even Bobby and Wes had hooked up with a pair of local women who were serving up more than home-cooked meals.

Harvard tried to remember the last time he'd gone one on one with a member of the opposite sex. June, May, April, March… Damn, it had been February. He'd been seeing a woman named Ellen off and on for a few months. It was nothing serious—she'd call him, they'd go out and wind up at her place. But he hadn't noticed when she'd stopped phoning. He couldn't call up a clear picture of her face.

Every time he tried, he kept seeing P. J. Richards's big brown eyes.

"Hello, Harvard." Joe's wife, Veronica, was in the kitchen. As usual, she was doing three different things at once. A pile of vegetables was next to a cutting board, and a pot of something unidentifiable was bubbling on the stove. She had paperwork from her latest consulting assignment spread out across the kitchen table and one-and-a-half-year-old Frankie in his high chair, where he was attempting rather clumsily to feed himself his dinner.

"Hey, Ron," Harvard said as Joe stopped to pull several bottles of beer from the refrigerator. "What's up?"

"I'm teaching myself to cook," she told him in her crisp British accent. Her red hair was loose around her shoulders, and she was casually dressed in shorts and a halter top. But she was the kind of super classy woman who, no matter what she wore, always looked ready to attend some kind of state function. Just throw on a string of pearls, and she'd be ready to go. "How's your father?"

"Much better, thanks. Almost back to one hundred percent."

"I'm so glad."

"Moving day's coming. My mother keeps threatening to pack *him* in a box if he doesn't quit trying to lift things she perceives as being too heavy for him."

Joe looked up from his search for a bottle opener. "You didn't tell me your parents were moving."

"No?"

He shook his head. "No."

"My father's taking a position at a school out in Arizona. In Phoenix. Some little low-key private college."

"It sounds perfect," Veronica said. "Just what he needs—a slower pace. A change of climate."

"Yeah, it's great," Harvard said, trying to mean it. "And they found a buyer for the house, so…"

Joe found the bottle opener and closed the drawer with his hip, still gazing at Harvard. "You okay about that?"

"Yeah, yeah, sure," Harvard said, shrugging it off.

Veronica turned to the baby. "Now, Frank, *really*. You're supposed to use the *other* end of the spoon."

Frankie grinned at her as he continued to chew on the spoon's handle.

"He inherited that smile from his father," Veronica told Harvard, sending a special smile of her own in Joe Cat's direction. "And he knows when he uses it, he can get away with anything. I swear, I'm doomed. I'm destined to spend the rest of my life completely manipulated by these two men."

"That's right," Joe said, stopping to kiss his wife's bare shoulder before he handed Harvard an opened bottle of beer. "I manipulated her into allowing me to refinish the back deck two weeks ago. We don't even own this place, and yet I managed to talk her into letting me work out there in the hot sun, sanding it down, applying all those coats of waterproofing…."

"It was fun. Frank and I helped," Veronica said.

Joe just laughed.

"Can I convince you to stay for dinner?" she asked Harvard. "I'm making a stew. I hope."

"Oh, no, Ron, I'm sorry," Harvard said, trying hard to sound as if he meant it. "I have other plans." Plans such as eating digestible food. Veronica may have been one of the sweetest and most beautiful women in the world, but her cooking skills were nonexistent.

"Really? Do you have a date?" Her eyes lit up. "With what's her name? The FInCOM agent? P.J. something?"

Harvard nearly choked on his beer. "No," he said. "No, I'm not seeing her socially." He shot a look at Joe Cat. "Who told you that I was?"

Joe was shaking his head, shrugging and making not-me faces.

"Just a guess. I saw her the other day." Veronica stirred the alleged stew. "While I was dropping something off at the base. She's very attractive."

No kidding.

"So what's the deal?" Veronica asked, leaning against the kitchen counter. "Has Lucky O'Donlon already staked his claim three feet in every direction around her?"

Lucky and P.J.? Of course, now that Harvard was thinking about it, Lucky *had* been circling P.J.—albeit somewhat warily—for the past few days. No doubt Miss East Coast Virginia was starting to cling. Harvard knew of nothing else that would send Lucky so quickly into jettison mode— and put him back on the prowl again. He had to smile, thinking of the way P.J. would react to Lucky's less-than-subtle advances.

His smile faded. Unless it was only Harvard she was determined to keep her distance from.

"P.J.'s not seeing anyone, Ron," Joe told his wife as he slid open the door to the back deck. "She's working overtime trying to be one of the guys. She's not going to blow that just because Lucky gives her a healthy dose of the O'Donlon charm."

"Some women find heart-stoppingly handsome blond men like Lucky irresistible," Veronica teased. "Particularly heart-stoppingly handsome blond men who look as if they've stepped off the set of *Baywatch*."

"There's no rule against a SEAL getting together with a FInCOM agent." Harvard managed to keep his voice calm. "I have no problem with it, either. As long as the two of them are discreet." The minute he got back to base, he was going to track down O'Donlon and… What? Beat him up? Warn him off? He shook his head. He had no claim on the girl.

"Ronnie, would you please send Blue out here after

he gets here?" Joe asked his wife as he led Harvard onto
the deck.

As Harvard closed the door behind him, he looked
closely at his longtime friend. The captain of Alpha Squad
looked relaxed and happy. The undercurrent of tension
that seemed to surround the man like an aura was down
to a low glow. And that was amazing, since the meeting
tonight was to discuss the fact that the frustration levels
regarding this FInCOM training mission were about to go
off the chart.

At least Harvard's were.

"You're not really that bothered by all the interference
we're getting from FInCOM and Admiral Stonegate, are
you?" Harvard asked.

Joe shrugged and leaned both elbows on the deck railing. "You know, H., I knew this program was a lost cause
the day I met FInCOM's choices for the team. To be honest,
I don't think there's anything we can do to get those four
working effectively together. So we do what we do, and
then we recommend—emphatically—that FInCOM stay
the hell out of counterterrorist operations. We suggest—
strongly—that they leave that to the SEALs."

"If you're quitting, man, why not just detonate the
entire program right now? Why keep on wasting our time
with—"

"Because I'm being selfish." Joe turned to look at him,
his dark eyes serious. "Because Alpha Squad runs at
two-hundred-and-fifty percent energy and efficiency one
hundred percent of the time, and the guys need this down
time. *I* need this down time. I'm telling you, H., it's tough
on Ronnie with me always leaving. She never knows when
we sit down to dinner at night if that's the last time I'm
going to be around for a week or for a month or—God
forbid—forever. She doesn't say anything, but I see it
in her eyes. And that look's not there right now because
she knows I'm leading this training drill for the next six

weeks. She's got another six weeks of reprieve, and I'm not taking that away from her. Or from any of the other wives, either."

"I hear you," Harvard said. "But it rubs the wrong way. Doing all this for nothing."

"It's not for nothing." Joe finished his beer. "We've just got to revise this mission's goal. Instead of creating a Combined SEAL/FInCOM counterterrorist team, we're creating a FInCOM counterterrorist expert. We're giving this expert all of the information she can possibly carry, and you know what she's gonna do?"

"She?"

"She's gonna take that expertise back to Kevin Laughton, and she's gonna tell him and all of the FInCOM leaders that the best thing they can do in a terrorist situation is to step back and let SEAL Team Ten do the job."

Harvard swore. *"She?"*

"Yes, I'm referring to P. J. Richards." Joe grinned. "You know, you should try talking to her sometime. She doesn't bite."

Harvard scowled. "Yes, she does. And I have the teeth marks to prove it."

Joe's eyebrows went up. "Oh, really?"

Harvard shook his head. "I didn't mean it that way."

"Oh, yeah, that's right. I almost forgot—you have no problem with her hooking up with Lucky O'Donlon as long as the two of them are discreet." Joe snorted. "Why do I foresee a temporary transfer for O'Donlon crossing my desk in the near future?"

"You know I wouldn't do that."

"Well, maybe you should."

Harvard clenched his teeth and set his barely touched bottle of beer on the deck railing. "Cat, I'm trying to be professional here."

"What happened, she turn you down?"

Harvard pushed himself off the rail and walked toward

the sliding doors, then stopped and walked toward the captain. "What exactly do you envision her role at FInCOM to be?"

"You're purposely changing the subject."

"Yes, I am."

"I can't believe you haven't at least *tried* to get friendly with this woman. If I weren't a happily married man, I'd be pulling some discreet moves myself. I mean, she's smart, she's beautiful, she's—"

"What exactly do you envision her role at FInCOM to be?" Harvard enunciated very clearly.

"All right," Joe said with a shrug. "Be that way." He drew in a deep breath, taking the time to put his thoughts into words. "Okay, I see her continuing to climb FInCOM's career ladder and moving into an upper-level position—probably onto Kevin Laughton's staff. She's worked with him before. He was the one who insisted she be part of this program in the first place."

Kevin Laughton and P.J. Now Harvard had to wonder about *that* relationship. Inwardly, he rolled his eyes in disgust. Everything became more complicated when women were thrown into the equation. Suddenly sex became an issue, a motivation, a factor.

A possibility.

Damn, why couldn't P.J. just stay in the FInCOM office, safe and sound and out of sight—a distraction for after hours?

"I see her as being the voice of reason and being right there, on hand, so that when a terrorist situation like that incident at the Athens airport comes up again, she can tell Laughton to get the SEALs involved right from the start instead of waiting a week and a half and getting five agents and ten civilians killed.

"The U.S. has a no-negotiation policy with terrorists," Joe Cat went on. "We need to go one step further and consistently deliver an immediate and deadly show of force.

Tangos take over another airport? FInCOM snaps to it, and boom, SEAL Team Ten is there within hours. The first CNN report doesn't bring attention to the bastards' cause—instead it's an account of how quickly the Ts were crushed. It's a report on the number of body bags needed to take the scum out of there. Tangos snatch hostages? Same thing. Boom. We go in, we get them out. No standing around wringing our hands. And eventually the terrorists will realize that their violent action causes a swift and deadly reaction from the United States every single time."

"And you think P. J. Richards will really reach a point in FInCOM where her opinion is that important?" Harvard let his skepticism ring in his voice. "Where she can say, 'Call in the SEALs,' and have anyone listen to her?"

"On her own? Probably not," Joe said baldly. "She's a woman *and* she's black. But I *do* think Kevin Laughton's going all the way to the top. And I think P. J. Richards will be close by when he gets there. And I'm betting when she says, 'Call in the SEALs,' *he's* going to listen."

Harvard was silent. Damn, but he hated politics. And he hated the image of Laughton with P.J. by his side.

"So since our goal has changed," Harvard asked, crossing his arms and trying to stay focused, "do we still try to convince FInCOM to let us run training ops that extend past their current ten-hour limit? And what about our request to go out of the country with the finks? If you'd prefer to just stay here in Virginia—"

"No," Joe said. "I think it would create more of an impression on P.J. if we put on a real show—you know, let her feel the impact of being in a strange country for these longer exercises."

"But you just said Veronica—"

"Ronnie will be fine if I go out of town for a few days for something as safe as a FInCOM training exercise. And I can't stress enough the importance of convincing P.J. that the creation of a CSF team is *not* the way to go," Joe told him. "And the way I think we can do that is to set up and run two different forty-eight-hour exercises either in the Middle East or somewhere in Southeast Asia. We'd let the finks take part in the first operation. And then, after they fail miserably again, I'd like to set P.J. up as an observer as Alpha Squad does a similar training op—and succeeds. I want her to see exactly how successfully a SEAL team like Alpha Squad can operate, but I want her to get a taste of just how hard it is first."

"We'll need to make a formal request to Admiral Stonegate's office."

"It's already sent. They're pretty negative. I think they're afraid we're somehow going to hurt the finks."

Harvard smiled. "They're probably right. God only knows what will happen if the finks don't get their beauty sleep."

"I've also put in a call to Laughton's office," Joe told him. "But I'm having trouble reaching the man. So far, his staff has been adamant that the rules stand as is."

The door slid open and Blue stepped onto the deck. "Sorry I'm late."

Harvard looked at Joe. "He look sorry to you?"

"He's trying."

"He's not succeeding. Look at that smile he can't keep off his face."

Blue sat down. "Okay, okay, I'm not sorry. I admit it. So what are we talking about? P. J. Richards? Her test scores are off the scale. And I assume you're both aware she's an expert-level sharpshooter?"

"Yeah, we've already voted her in as Wonder Woman," Harvard told him.

"What we've got to do now," Joe said, "is make sure she's got the same warm fuzzy feelings about us that we have about her. We want her going back to Laughton and telling him, 'These guys are the best,' not 'Whatever you do, stay away from those nasty SEALs.' She's been kind of aloof, but then again, we haven't exactly welcomed her with open arms."

"Consider that about to change," Blue said. "I heard Lucky talking before I left the base. P.J.'s having dinner with him—the Alpha Squad's ambassador of open arms—right this very moment."

Joe swore. "That's not what I had in mind. You'd better go and intercept that," he said, turning toward Harvard.

But Harvard was already running for his car.

P.J. punched her floor number into the hotel elevator. Well, *that* had been a joke.

She'd finally decided to take some action. Over the past few days, she'd come to the conclusion that she had to attempt to make friends with one of the SEALs. She needed an ally—because it was more than obvious that these big, strong men were scared to death of her.

She needed just one of them to start looking at her as if she were an equal. All it would take was one, and that one would, by example, teach the others it *could* be done. She *could* be accepted as a person first, a woman second.

But that special chosen one wasn't going to be the SEAL nicknamed Lucky, that was for sure.

He had a nice smile and an even nicer motorcycle, but his intentions when he'd asked her to join him for dinner hadn't been to strike up a friendship. On the contrary, he'd been looking for some action.

A different kind of action than the kind she was looking for.

He'd fooled her at first. They had a common interest in motorcycles, and he let her drive his from the base to the restaurant. But when he rode behind her, he'd held her much too tightly for the tame speeds they were going.

And so she'd told him bluntly between the salad and the main course that she wasn't interested in anything other than a completely nonsexual friendship. By the time coffee arrived, she'd managed to convince him. And although he wasn't as forthright as she had been, from the way he kept glancing at his watch she knew that he wasn't interested in anything other than a sexual relationship.

Which left her back at square one.

The doors opened, and P.J. stepped into the small sitting area by the elevators. She searched through her belt pack for her key card. She almost didn't see Harvard Becker sitting in the shadows.

And when she did see him, she almost kept going. If she'd had any working brains in her head, she *should* have kept going. But in her surprise, she stopped short, gaping at him like an idiot. He was the dead last person she'd expected to see sitting in the hallway on the soft leather of the sofa, waiting for her.

Harvard nodded a greeting. "Ms. Richards."

She had to clear her throat so her voice wouldn't come out in an undignified squeak. "Were you looking for me? Am I needed on base? You could have paged me."

"No." He stood up—Lord, he was tall. "Actually, I was looking for Luke O'Donlon."

"He's not here."

"Yes, I can see that."

P.J. started for her room, afraid if she didn't move, her anger would show. Who was he checking up on and trying to protect? Her or Lucky? Either way, it was damned insulting. She unlocked her door with a vicious swipe of the key card.

"Do you happen to know where he was headed?"

"Back to the base," she said shortly. She wanted to slam the door behind her, but she forced herself to turn and face him.

"I'm sorry to have bothered you," he said quietly.

"Was there anything else you wanted?" She knew as

soon as the sarcastic words were out of her mouth it was the wrong thing to say.

Undisguised heat flared in his eyes, heat tinged with an awareness that told her he knew quite well his attraction was extremely mutual. He wanted her. The message was right there in his gorgeous brown eyes. But all he did was laugh, a soft chuckle that made her heart nearly stop beating and the hair stand up on the back of her neck.

All she had to do was step into her room and hold open that door, and he would come inside and...

And what? Mess up her life beyond repair, no doubt.

He was not on her side. He'd flatly admitted that he didn't like working with her, he didn't *want* to work with her.

P.J. moistened her dry lips, holding her head high and trying to look as if she were totally unaffected by the picture he made standing there. "Good night, Senior Chief."

She closed the door tightly behind her and drew in a deep breath.

Dear God, how on earth was she going to make it through another six weeks? She needed an ally, and she needed one bad.

CHAPTER FIVE

HARVARD KNEW THE MOMENT P.J. walked into the bar. He turned and sure enough, there she was, looking everywhere but at him, pretending he didn't exist.

Today had been a classroom day for the finks, and Harvard had had other business to take care of. He'd gone to the mess hall at lunchtime, hoping for...what? He wasn't sure. But when he got there, Wes told him P.J. had gone to the firing range.

The afternoon had passed interminably slowly, the biggest excitement being when he spoke to Kevin Laughton's assistant's assistant, who had told him there was no way the FInCOM rule book was going to be altered to allow for two- or three-day-long exercises. And hadn't they already compromised on this issue? And no, Mr. Laughton *couldn't* come to the phone, he was far too busy with *important* matters.

Harvard had wheedled and cajoled, reasoned and explained, but he'd hung up the phone without any real hope that Laughton would call him or Joe Cat. He'd cheered himself up some by calling the friend of a friend of a friend who worked at the Pentagon and who faxed him the layout of FInCOM headquarters, where Kevin Laughton's office was housed. He'd spent his coffee break pinpointing the areas of FInCOM HQ that would be most vulnerable to a direct assault by a small, covert group of SEALs. He'd managed to put a smile on his face by imagining the look on Laughton's face when he walked into his high-level security office and found Harvard and Joe Cat sitting there, feet up on his desk, waiting to talk to him.

Harvard headed for an empty table in the bar, keeping P.J. securely in his peripheral vision, trying to figure out the best strategy for approaching her.

It was funny. He'd never had to work at approaching a woman before. Usually women fell right in his lap. But P.J. wasn't falling anywhere. She was running—hard—in the opposite direction.

The only other woman he'd ever pursued was Rachel.

Damn, he hadn't thought about Rachel in years. He'd met her during a training op in Guam. She was a marine biologist, part of a U.S. Government survey team housed in the military facilities. She was beautiful—part African American, part Asian and part Hawaiian—and shyly sweet.

For a week or two, Rachel had had Harvard thinking in terms of forever. It was the only time in his life he'd been on the verge of crossing that fine line that separated sex from love. But then he'd been sent to Desert Shield, and while he was gone, Rachel had reconciled with her ex-husband.

He could still remember how that news had sliced like a hot knife into his quick. He could still remember that crazily out-of-control feeling of hurt and frustration—that sense of being on the verge of despair. He hadn't liked it one bit, and he'd worked hard since then to make sure he'd never repeat it.

He glanced at P.J. and met her eyes. She quickly looked away, as if the spark that had instantly ignited had been too hot for her to handle.

Hot was definitely the key word here.

Yes, he was the pursuer, but he wasn't in any real danger of going the Rachel route with this girl.

She was nothing like Rachel, for one thing.

For another, this thing, this *current* between him and P.J.

came from total, mindless, screaming animal attraction. Lust. Pure, sizzling sex. Two bodies joined in a quest for heart-stopping pleasure.

That wasn't what his relationship with Rachel had been about. He'd been so careful with her. He'd held back so much.

But when he looked into P.J.'s eyes, he saw them joined in a dance of passion that had no civilities. He saw her legs locked around him as he drove himself into her, hard and fast, her back against the wall, right inside the doorway of her hotel room.

Oh, yeah. It was going to be amazingly good, but no one was going to cry when it was over.

Harvard smiled at himself, at his presumption that such a collaboration was, indeed, going to happen.

First thing he had to do was figure out how to get this girl to quit running away for long enough to talk to her. Only then could he start to convince her they'd gotten off to a bad start.

He should have been cooler last night.

He'd stood there outside her hotel room and he hadn't been able to think of anything besides how good she looked and how badly he wanted her and how damn glad he was that she hadn't been bringing Lucky back to her room with her.

He wasn't sure he would have been able to make small talk even if he'd tried. But he hadn't tried. He'd just stood there, looking at her as if she were the gingerbread girl and he was the hungry fox.

At least he hadn't drooled.

He caught the waitress's eye as he sat down. "Iced tea, no sugar," he ordered, then glanced again at P.J.

This time, she was looking straight at him and smiling. Damn, she had an incredible smile. On a scale from one to ten, it was an even hundred. He felt his mouth curve into an answering smile. He couldn't explain what caused her sudden change of heart, but he wasn't going to complain.

"Hey," she said, walking toward him. "What are *you* doing here?"

As she moved closer, Harvard realized she wasn't looking at him at all. Her focus was behind him. He turned and saw that Joe Cat had come into the bar through the back door.

"I thought I'd stop in tonight before going home," the captain said to P.J. "What's shaking?"

"Not much," Harvard heard P.J. say as she gave Joe Cat another of those killer smiles. "Everyone's glued to the TV, watching baseball." She rolled her eyes in mock disgust.

Excuse me, Harvard felt like standing up and saying, *but everyone isn't watching baseball.* The waitress put his drink on the table in front of him, and P.J. still didn't glance in his direction.

Joe shrugged out of his jacket. "You're not a baseball fan?"

"Nuh-uh. Too slow for me. The batter wiggles around, getting all ready for the pitch, and the pitcher does his thing, getting ready for the pitch, and I'm sitting there thinking, 'Just throw the ball!'" She laughed. She had musical-sounding laughter. "And then the ball is fired over the plate so fast that they've got to play it back in slo-mo just so I can *see* it."

"You're probably not into football, either, then. Too many breaks in the play."

"You got that right," P.J. said. "Do you have time to sit down? Can I buy you a beer?"

"I'd love it," Joe said.

"Then grab us a table. I'll be right back."

P.J. headed toward the bar.

"If you don't sit with me, sir, I may have to seriously damage you," Harvard said to his friend.

Joe Cat laughed and pulled out a chair at Harvard's

table. "You didn't think I couldn't see you lurking here, eavesdropping, did you?"

"Of course, she may not want to chill with you after she comes back and sees the excess company," Harvard pointed out. "She's been running from me all day—she's bound to keep it up."

"Nah, she's tougher than that."

Harvard gave a short laugh of disbelief as he squeezed the lemon into his iced tea. "Wait a minute. Suddenly you're the authority on this girl?"

"I'm trying to be," Joe said. "I spent about two hours with her today at the range. She just happened to show up while I was there. You know, H., she's really good. She's got a real shooter's instinct. And a natural ability to aim."

Harvard didn't know what to say. P.J. had just happened to show up…. He took a sip of his drink.

"She's funny, too," Joe added. "She has a solid sense of humor. She's one very sharp, very smart lady."

Harvard found his voice. "Oh, yeah? What's Veronica think about that?" He was kidding, but only half kidding.

Joe didn't miss that. And even though P.J. was coming toward them carrying two mugs filled with frothy beer, he leaned closer to Harvard. "It's not about sex," he said, talking fast. "Yes, P.J.'s a woman, and yes, she's attractive, but come on, H., you know me well enough to know I'm not going to go in that direction. Ever. I love Ronnie more than you will ever know. But I'm married, I'm not dead. I can still appreciate an attractive woman when I see one. And being friendly to this particular attractive woman is going to get us further than shutting her out. She approached me. She's clearly trying to make friends. This is exactly what we wanted."

Harvard saw P.J. glance over and see him sitting with

Joe. He saw her falter, then square her shoulders and keep coming.

She nodded at him as she set the mugs on the table. "Senior Chief Becker," she said coolly, managing not to meet his eyes. "If I'd known you'd be joining us, I'd have offered to get you a drink, as well."

He wasn't aware they sold hemlock in this bar. "You can catch me on the next round," he said.

"I've got a lot of reading to do. I may not be able to stay for a next round. It might have to be some other time." She sat as far from him as possible and took a sip of her beer.

The temperature in that corner of the room had definitely dropped about twenty degrees.

"Basketball," Joe said to P.J. "I bet you like basketball."

She smiled, and the temperature went up a bit. "Good guess."

"Do you play?"

"I'm a frustrated player," she admitted. "I have certain... height issues. I never really spent enough time on the court to get any good."

"Have you had a chance to check out that new women's professional basketball league?" Harvard asked, attempting to be part of the conversation.

P.J. turned to him, her eyes reminiscent of the frozen tundra. "I've watched a few games." She turned to Joe Cat. "I don't spend much time watching sports—I prefer to be out there playing. Which reminds me, Tim Farber mentioned that you're something of a wizard on the handball court. I was wondering if you play racquetball. There's a court here in the hotel, and I'm looking for an opponent."

Harvard shifted in his seat, clenching his teeth to keep from speaking.

"I've played some," Joe told her.

"Hmm. Now, in my experience, when people say they've

played *some,* that really means they're too humble to admit that if you venture onto the court with them, they're going to thoroughly whip your butt."

Joe laughed. "I guess that probably depends on how long you've been playing."

P.J.'s smile returned. "I've played some."

She was flirting with Joe. P.J. was sitting right there, directly in front of him, flirting with the captain. What was this girl up to? What was she trying to pull?

Joe's pager went off. He looked at Harvard. "You getting anything?"

Harvard's pager was silent and still. "No, sir."

"That's a good sign. I'll be right back."

As Joe headed toward the bar and a telephone, P.J. pretended to be fascinated by the architectural structure of the building.

Harvard knocked on the table. Startled, she looked at him.

"I don't know what your deal is," he said bluntly. "I don't know what you stand to gain by getting tight with the captain—whether it's some career thing or just some personal power trip—but I'm here to tell you right now, missy, hands off. Didn't your research on the man include the fact that he's got a wife and kid? Or maybe you're the kind that gets off on things like that."

As Harvard watched, the permafrost in P.J.'s eyes morphed into volcanic anger. "How dare you?" she whispered.

The question was rhetorical, but Harvard answered it anyway. "I dare because Cat is my friend—and because you, little Miss Fink, are temptation incarnate. So back off."

She was looking at him as if he were something awful she'd stepped in, something disgusting that had stuck onto the bottom of her shoe. "You're such a...man," she said, as if that were the worst possible name she could call him.

"The captain is the only person in this entire program who's even bothered to sit down and talk to me. But if you're telling me that all he's doing is dogging me, despite having a wife and kid at home—"

"He's not dogging you, baby, *you're* dogging *him*."

"I am *not*."

"You just *happen* to head over to the firing range while Cat's scheduled to be there. He walks into this bar, and you all but launch yourself at him."

She flushed, unable to deny his accusations. "You really have no idea what it's like, do you?"

"Poor baby, all alone, far away from home. Is this where the violins start to play? Tell me, do you go for the married men because there's less of a chance of actually becoming involved?"

She was seething, her eyes all but shooting sparks. "I was only trying to be friends!"

"Friends?"

"You know, people who hang out together, share meals occasionally, sometimes get together for a game of cards or Scrabble?"

"Friends." Harvard let skepticism drip from his voice. "You want to be Cat's *friend*."

P.J. stood. "I knew you wouldn't understand. You've probably never had a friend who was a woman in your entire life."

"I'm ready to learn—a willing and able volunteer with the added bonus of being unattached. I'm wicked good at Scrabble. Among other things."

She snorted. "Sorry. From where I stand, you're the enemy."

"I'm *what?*"

"You heard me. You want me gone from this training op on pure principle. You think women have no place out in the field, in the line of fire. You're judging me not as an individual, but based only on the fact that I don't have a penis. What's the deal with that? Do you use your penis to aim your rifle better? Does it help you dodge bullets or run faster?"

This woman could really piss him off, but at the same time, she could really make him laugh. "Not that I know of."

"Not that *I* know of, either. You're a bigot, Senior Chief, and I have no desire to spend even a minute more in your company."

Harvard stopped laughing. A *bigot?* "Hey," he said.

But P.J. was already walking away, her beer barely touched.

Harvard had never been called a bigot before. A bigot was someone narrow-minded who believed unswervingly that he and his opinions were inarguably right. But the fact is, he *was* right. Women did *not* belong on combat missions, carrying—and firing—weapons and being shot at. It was not easy to stare down the sight of a rifle at a human being and pull the trigger. And countless psych reports stated that women, God bless 'em, had a higher choke factor. When the time came to pull that trigger, after all those tax dollars had been spent on thousands of hours of training, most women couldn't get the job done.

God knows that certainly was the truth when it came to women like his mother and sisters and Rachel. He couldn't picture Rachel holding an MP5 automatic weapon. And his sisters... All four of them were card-carrying pacifists who spouted make-love-not-war-type clichés whenever he was around.

Still, after his sister Kendra had gotten married and started a family, she'd attached an addendum to her non-violent beliefs. "Except if you threaten or hurt my kids." Harvard could still see the light of murder in his sister's eyes as the former president of Students Against Violence proclaimed that if anyone, *anyone* threatened her precious children, she would rip out their lungs with her bare hands.

Put an MP5 in that girl's hands and tell her her children were in danger, and she'd be using up her ammo faster than any man.

But on the other hand, you'd never be able even to *get* a weapon into his father's hands. The old man would gently push the barrel toward the floor and start lecturing on the theme of war in modern American literature.

Harvard could imagine what P.J. would say about that. He could hear her husky voice as clearly as if she were standing right behind him. *Just because your father and men like him don't make good soldiers doesn't mean that all* men *shouldn't be soldiers. And in the same way, women like me shouldn't be lumped together with softer women like Rachel or your mother.*

Damn, maybe he *was* a bigot.

Joe returned to the table. "I don't suppose P.J.'s in the ladies' room?"

Harvard shook his head. "No, I, uh…let's see." He counted on his fingers. "I totally alienated her, I incensed her, and last but not least, I made her walk away in sheer disgust."

Joe pursed his lips, nodding slowly. "All that in only six minutes. Very impressive."

"She called me," Harvard said, "a bigot."

"Yeah, well, you've got to admit, you've been pretty narrow-minded when it comes to P.J.'s part in this exercise."

Damn, Joe Cat thought he was a bigot, too.

Joe finished his beer. "I've got to go. That was Ronnie who paged me. Frankie's had an ear infection over the past few days, and now he's throwing up the antibiotic. I'm meeting them at the hospital in fifteen minutes."

"Is it serious?"

"Nah, the kid's fine. I keep telling Ronnie, babies barf. It's what they do. She's just not going to sleep tonight until she hears a doctor say it, too." Joe rolled his eyes. "Of course, she probably won't even sleep then. I keep telling her it's the *baby* who's supposed to wake the mother up at night, not the other way around. But she has a friend who lost a kid to SIDS. I'm hoping by the time Frank turns two, Veronica will finally sleep through the night." Joe picked up his jacket from the back of the chair he'd thrown it over.

"You sure there's nothing I can do to help?"

The captain turned to look at him. "Yeah," he said. "There *is* something you can do. You can stay away from P. J. Richards after hours. It's clear you two aren't ever going to be best friends."

There was that word again. *Friends.*

"If there's one thing I've learned as a commander," Joe continued, "it's that you can't force people to like each other."

The stupid thing was, Harvard did like P.J. He liked her a lot.

"But it's not too much to ask that you and she work together in a civil manner," Joe continued.

"I've been civil," Harvard said. "She's the one who walked away in a huff."

Joe nodded. "I'll speak to her about that in the morning."

"No, Cat…" Harvard took a deep breath and started again. "With your permission, Captain, allow me to handle the situation." He wasn't a bigot, but he *was* guilty of generalizing without noting that there was, of course, a minuscule amount of the population that was an exception to the rule. And maybe P. J. Richards was in that tiny percentage.

Joe Cat looked at Harvard and grinned. "She drives you crazy, but you can't stay away from her, can you? Aw, H., you're in trouble, man."

Harvard shook his head. "No, Captain, you've got it wrong. I just want to be the lady's friend."

They both knew he was lying through his teeth.

CHAPTER SIX

"THAT'S AN APOLOGY?" P.J. laughed. "You say, 'Yes, I'm guilty of being small-minded when it comes to my opinions about women, but oh, by the way, I still think I'm right'?"

Harvard shook his head. "I didn't say that."

"Yes, you did. I'm paraphrasing, but that is the extent of the message you just delivered."

"What I said was that I think women who have the, shall we say, aggressive tendencies needed to handle frontline pressures are the exception rather than the rule."

"They're few and far between, was what you said." P.J. crossed her arms. "As in practically nonexistent."

Harvard turned away, then turned back. He was trying hard to curb his frustration, she had to give him that much. "Look, I didn't come here to argue with you. In fact, I want us to try to figure out a way we can get along over the next six weeks. Joe Cat's aware that we're having some kind of personality clash. I want him to be able to look over, see us working side by side without this heavy cloud of tension following us around. Do you think we can manage to do that?"

"The captain knows?" Every muscle in P.J.'s body ached, and she finally gave in to the urge to sit on the soft leather of the lobby couch.

Harvard sat across from her. "It's not that big a deal. When you're dealing with mostly alpha personalities, you've got to expect that sometimes the fit won't work." He gazed at her steadily, leaning slightly forward, his elbows resting on his knees. "But I think that transferring out of this particular program isn't an option for either of us. Both of us want to be here badly enough to put in a little extra effort, am I right?"

"You are." She smiled. "For once."

Harvard smiled, too. "A joke. Much better than fighting."

"A half a joke," she corrected him.

His smile widened, and she saw a flash of his perfect white teeth. "That's a start," he told her.

P.J. took a chance and went directly to the bottom line. "Seriously, Senior Chief, I need you to treat me as an equal."

She was gazing at him, her pretty face so somber. She'd changed out of her uniform shirt and into a snugly fitting T-shirt boasting the logo, Title Nine Sports. She had put on running shorts, too, and Harvard forced his gaze away from the graceful shape of her bare legs and back to her eyes. "I thought I had been."

"You're always watching me—checking up on me as if I were some little child, making sure I haven't wandered away from the rest of the kindergarten class."

Harvard shook his head. "I don't—"

"Yeah," she said, "you *do*. You're always looking to see if I need some help. 'Is that pack too heavy for you, Ms. Richards?' 'Careful of your step, Ms. Richards.' 'Let me give you a boost into the boat, Ms. Richards.'"

"I remember doing that," Harvard admitted. "But I gave Schneider and Greene a boost, too."

"Maybe so, but you didn't announce it to the world, the way you did with me."

"I *announced* it with you because I felt it was only polite to give you a proper warning before I grabbed your butt."

She gazed steadily into his eyes, refusing to acknowledge the embarrassment that was heating her cheeks.

"Well, it just so happens that I didn't need a boost. I'm plenty strong enough to pull myself into that boat on my own."

"It's harder than it looks."

"I didn't get a chance to find that out, did I?"

She was right. She may indeed have found that she couldn't pull herself into the boat without a boost, but she hadn't had that opportunity, and so she *was* right. Harvard did the only thing he could do.

"I'm sorry," he said. "I shouldn't have assumed. It's just that women tend not to have the upper body strength necessary—"

"*I* do." She cut him off. "It's one of the times my size works to my advantage. I can probably do more chin ups than you, because I'm lifting less than you."

"I'll grant that you weigh less because you're smaller, but everything's smaller. Your arms are smaller."

"That doesn't mean I don't have muscles." P.J. pushed up the sleeve of her T-shirt and flexed her biceps. "Check this out. Feel this. That's one solid muscle."

She actually wanted him to touch her.

"Check it out," she urged him.

Harvard was so much bigger than she was, he could have encircled her entire upper arm with one hand—flexed biceps and all. But he knew if he did that, she would think he was mocking her. Instead, he touched her lightly, his fingers against the firmness of her muscle, his thumb against the inside of her arm. Her skin was sinfully soft, impossibly smooth. And as he moved his fingers, it was more like a caress than a test of strength.

His mouth went dry, and as he looked up, he knew everything he was thinking was there in his eyes, clear as day, for her to see. He wanted her. No argument, no doubt. If she said the word *go*, he wouldn't hesitate even a fraction of a second.

P.J. pulled her arm away as if she'd been burned. "Bad

idea, *bad* idea," she said as if she were talking to—and scolding—herself. She stood up. "I need to go to bed. You should, too. We both have to be up early in the morning."

Harvard slouched on the couch, drawing in a deep breath and letting it out in a rush of air. "Maybe *that's* a way to relieve some of the tension between us."

She turned to look at him, her beautiful eyes wary. "What is?"

"You and me," Harvard said bluntly. "Going to bed together—getting this attraction thing out of our systems."

P.J. crossed her arms. "Now, how did I *know* you were going to suggest that?"

"It's just a thought."

She looked at him, at the way he was sitting, the way he was trying to hide the fact that he'd gotten himself totally turned on just from touching her that little tiny bit. "Somehow I think it's more than just a thought."

"Just say the word and it changes from a good idea to hard reality." His eyes were impossibly hot as he looked at her. "I'm more than ready."

P.J. had to clear her throat before she could speak. "It's not a good idea. It's a bad idea."

"Are you sure?"

"Absolutely."

"You know it'd be great."

"No, I don't," she told him honestly.

"Well, *I* know it would be better than great." He looked as if he were ready to sit there all night and try to tease her into getting with him.

But no matter how determined he was, she was more so. "I can't do this. I can't be casual about something so important." Lord, if he only knew the whole truth…. She turned toward her room, and he stood up, ready to follow her.

"I'm not just imagining this," he asked quietly, his

handsome face serious, "am I? I mean, I know you feel this thing between us, too. It's damn powerful."

"There's a definite pull," she admitted. "But that doesn't mean we should throw caution to the wind and go to bed together." She laughed in disbelief, amazed their conversation should have come this far. "You don't even *like* me."

"Not so," Harvard countered. "You're the one who doesn't like *me*. I would truly like us to be friends."

She snorted. "Friends who have sex? What a novel idea. I'm sure you're the first man who's ever come up with *that*."

"You want it platonic? I can keep it platonic for as long as you want."

"Well, *there's* a big word I didn't think you knew."

"I graduated with high honors from one of the toughest universities in the country," he told her. "I know lots of big words."

P.J. desperately wanted to pace, but she forced herself to stand still, not wanting to betray how nervous this man made her feel.

"Look," she said finally. "I have a serious problem with the fact that you've been treating me as if I'm a child or—a substandard man." She forced herself to hold his gaze, willed herself not to melt from the magmalike heat that lingered in his eyes. "If you really want to be my friend, then try me," she said. "Test me. Push me to the edge—see just how far I *can* go before you set up imaginary boundaries and fence me in." She laughed, but it wasn't because it was funny. "Or out."

Harvard nodded. "I can't promise miracles. I can only promise I'll try."

"That's all I ask."

"Good," Harvard said. He held out his hand for her to shake. "Friends?"

P.J. started to reach for his hand, but quickly pulled away.

"Friends," she agreed, "who will stay friends a whole lot longer if we keep the touching to an absolute minimum."

Harvard laughed. "I happen to disagree."

P.J. smiled. "Yeah, well, old buddy, old pal, that's not the first time we've not seen eye to eye, and I'm willing to bet it's not going to be the last."

"Yo, Richards—you awake?"

"I am now." P.J. closed her eyes and sank onto her bed, telephone pressed against her ear.

"Well, good, because it's too early to be sleeping."

She opened one eye, squinting at the clock radio on the bedside table. "Senior Chief, it's after eleven."

"Yeah, like I said, it's too early to crash." Harvard's voice sounded insufferably cheerful over the phone. "We don't have to be on base tomorrow until ten. That means it's playtime. Are you dressed?"

"No."

"Well, what are you waiting for? Get shakin', or they're gonna start without us. I'm in the lobby, I'll be right up."

"Start what?"

But Harvard had already disconnected the line. P.J. hung up the phone without sitting up. She'd gone to bed around ten, planning to get a solid ten hours of sleep tonight. Lord knows she needed it.

Bam, bam, bam. "Richards, open up!"

Now the fool was at the door. P.J. closed her eyes a little tighter, hoping he'd take a hint and go away. Whatever he wanted, she wanted to sleep more.

The past week had been exhausting. True to his word, the Senior Chief had stopped coddling her. She'd gotten no more helpful boosts, no more special treatment. She was busting her butt, but she was keeping up. Hell, she was out front, leading the way. Of course, the FInCOM agents were being trained at a significantly lower intensity than the SEALs normally operated. This was a walk in the park for Alpha Squad. But P.J. wasn't trying to be a SEAL. That wasn't what this was about. She was here to learn from them—to try to understand the best way not just FInCOM but the entire United States of America could fight and win the dirty war against terrorism.

Harvard hadn't stopped watching her, but at least now when she caught him gazing in her direction, there was a glint of something different in his eyes. It may not quite have been approval, but it was certainly awareness of some kind. She was doing significantly better than Farber, Schneider and Greene without Harvard's help, and he knew it. He'd nod, acknowledging her, never embarrassed that she caught him staring.

She liked seeing that awareness. She liked it a lot. She liked it too damn much.

"Oh, man, Richards, don't wimp out on me now."

P.J. opened her eyes to see Harvard standing next to her bed. He looked impossibly tall. "How did you get in here?" she asked, instantly alert, sitting up and clutching her blanket to her.

"I walked in."

"That door was locked!"

Harvard chuckled. "Allegedly. Come on, we got a card game to go to. Bring your wallet. Me and the guys aim to take your paycheck off your hands tonight."

A card game. She pushed her hair out of her face. To her relief, she was still mostly dressed. She'd fallen asleep in her shorts and T-shirt. "Poker?"

"Yeah. You play?"

"Gambling's illegal in this state, and I'm a FInCOM agent."

"Great. You can arrest us all—but only after we get to Joe Cat's. Let's get there quickly, shall we?" He started toward the door.

"First I'm going to arrest you for breaking and entering," P.J. grumbled. She didn't want to go out. She wanted to curl up in the king-size bed. She would have, too, if Harvard hadn't been there. But sinking back into bed with him watching was like playing with fire. He'd get that hungry look in his eyes—that look that made her feel as if everything she did, every move she made, was personal and intimate. That look that she liked too much.

P.J. pushed herself off the bed. It would probably be best to get as far away from the bed as possible with Harvard in the room.

"Those electronic locks are ridiculously easy to override. Getting past 'em doesn't really count as breaking." He looked at the ceiling, squinting suddenly. "Damn, I can feel it. They're starting without us."

"How does the captain's poor wife feel about being dropped in on at this time of night?"

"Veronica loves poker. She'd be playing, too, except she's in New York on business. Come on, Richards." He clapped his hands, two sharp bursts of sound. "Put on your sneakers. Let's get to the car—double time!"

"I've got to get dressed."

"You *are* dressed."

"No, I'm not."

"You're wearing shorts and a T-shirt. Not exactly elegant, but certainly practical in this heat. Come on, girl, get your kicks on your feet and—"

"I can't go out wearing this."

"What, do you want to change into your Wonder Woman uniform?" Harvard asked.

"Very funny."

He grinned. "Yeah, thanks. I thought it was, too. Sometimes I'm so funny, I crack myself up."

"I don't want to look too—"

"Relaxed?" he interrupted. "Approachable? Human? Yeah, you know, right now you actually look almost human, P.J. You're perfectly dressed for hanging out and playing cards with friends." He was still smiling, but his eyes were dead serious. "This was what you wanted, remember? A little platonic friendship."

Approachable. Human. God knows in her job she couldn't afford to be too much of either. But she also knew she had a tendency to go too far to the other extreme.

As she looked into Harvard's eyes, she knew he'd set this game of cards up for her. He was going to go into Joe Cat's house tonight and show the rest of Alpha Squad that it was okay to be friends with a fink. With this fink in particular.

P.J. wasn't certain the Senior Chief truly liked her. She knew for a fact that even though she'd proved she could keep up, he still only tolerated her presence. Barely tolerated.

But despite that, he'd clearly gone out of his way for her tonight.

She nodded. "I thank you for inviting me. Just let me grab a sweatshirt and we can go."

This wasn't a date.

It sure as hell felt like a date, but it wasn't one.

Harvard glanced at P.J., sitting way, way over on the other side of the big bench seat of his pickup truck.

"You did well today," he said, breaking the silence.

She'd totally rocked during an exercise this afternoon. The FInCOM team had been given Intel information pinpointing the location of an alleged terrorist camp which was—also allegedly—the site of a munitions storage facility.

P.J. smiled at him. Damn, she was pretty when she smiled. "Thanks."

She had used the computer skillfully to access all kinds of information on this particular group of tangos. She'd dug deeper than the other agents and found that the terrorists rarely kept their munitions supplies in one place for more than a week. And she'd recognized from the satellite pictures that the Ts were getting ready to mobilize.

All three of the other finks had recommended sitting tight for another week or so to await further reconnaissance from regular satellite flybys.

P.J. had written up priority orders for a combined SEAL/FInCOM team to conduct covert, on-site intelligence. Her orders had the team carrying enough explosives to flatten the munitions site if it proved to be there. She'd also put in a special request to the National Reconnaissance Office to reposition a special KeyHole Satellite to monitor and record any movement of the weapons pile.

There was only one thing Harvard would have done differently. He wouldn't have bothered with the CSF team. He would have sent the SEALs in alone.

But if Joe Cat's plan worked, by the time P. J. Richards completed this eight-week counterterrorist training session, she would realize that adding FInCOM agents to the Alpha Squad would be like throwing a monkey wrench into the SEALs' already perfectly oiled machine.

Harvard hoped that was the case. He didn't like working with incompetents like Farber. And Lord knows, even though he'd been trying, he couldn't get past the fact that P.J. was a woman. She was smart, she was tough, but she *was* a woman. And God help him if he ever had to use her as part of his team. Somebody would probably end up getting killed—and it would probably be him.

Harvard glanced at P.J. as he pulled up in front of Joe Cat's rented house.

"Do you guys play poker often?" she asked.

"Nah, we usually prefer statue tag."

She tried not to smile, but she couldn't help it as she pictured the men of Alpha Squad running around on Joe Cat's lawn, striking statuesque poses. "You're a regular stand-up comic tonight."

"Can't be a Senior Chief without a sense of humor,"

he told her, putting the truck in Park and turning off the engine. "It's a prerequisite for the rank."

"Why a chief?" she asked. "Why not a lieutenant? How come you didn't take the officer route? I mean, if you really went to Harvard..."

"I really went to Harvard," he told her. "Why a chief? Because I wanted to. I'm right where I want to be."

There was a story behind his decision, and Harvard could see from the questions in P.J.'s eyes that she wanted to know why. But as much as he liked the idea of sitting here and talking with her in the quiet darkness of the night, with his truck's engine clicking softly as it cooled, his job was to bring her into Joe's house and add to the shaky foundation of friendship they'd started building nearly a week ago.

Friends played cards.

Lovers sat in the dark and shared secrets.

Harvard opened the door, and bright light flooded the truck's cab. "Let's get in there."

"So *do* you guys play often?" P.J. asked as they walked up the path to the front door.

"No, not really," Harvard admitted. "We don't have much extra time for games."

"So this game tonight—this is for my benefit, huh?" she asked perceptively.

He gazed into her eyes. Damn, she was pretty. "I think it's for all of our benefit," he told her honestly. He smiled. "You should be honored. You're the first fink we've ever set up a poker party for."

"I hate it when you call me that," she said, her voice resigned to the fact that he wasn't going to stop. "And this isn't really any kind of honor. This is calculated bonding, isn't it? For some reason, you've decided you need me as a part of the team." Her eyes narrowed speculatively. "It's in Alpha Squad's best interest to gain me as an ally. But why?"

She *was* pretty, but she wasn't half as pretty as she was smart.

Harvard opened Joe's front door and stepped inside. "You've been doing that spooky agent voodoo for too many years. This is just a friendly poker game. No more, no less."

She snorted. "Yeah, sure, whatever you say, Senior Chief."

CHAPTER SEVEN

P.J. WAS LATE.

A truck had jackknifed on the main road leading to the base, and she'd had to go well out of her way to get there at all.

She grabbed her gym bag from the back of her rental car and bolted for the field where SEALs and FInCOM agents met to start their day with an eye-opening run.

They were all waiting for her.

Farber, Schneider and Greene had left the hotel minutes before she had. She'd seen them getting into Farber's car and pulling out of the parking lot as she'd ridden down from her room in the glass-walled elevator. They must've made it through moments before the road had been closed.

"Sorry I'm late," she said breathlessly. "There was an accident that shut down route—"

"Forget it. It doesn't matter," Harvard said shortly, barely meeting her eyes. "We ready to go? Let's do it."

P.J. stared in surprise as he turned away from her, as he broke into a run, leading the group toward the river.

To Harvard, tardiness was the original sin. There was no excuse for it. She'd fully expected him to lambaste her good-naturedly, to use her as yet another example to get his point about preparedness across. She'd expected him to point out in his usual effusive manner that she should have planned ahead, should have given herself enough time, should have factored in the possibility of Mr. Murphy throwing a jackknifed truck into her path.

She'd even expected him to imply that a man wouldn't have been late.

But he hadn't.

What was up with him?

In the few days since the poker game, P.J. had enjoyed the slightly off-color, teasing friendship of the men she'd played cards with. Crash had been there, although she suspected he was as much a stranger to the other men as she was. And the quiet blond lieutenant called Blue. The team's version of Laurel and Hardy had anted up, as well—Bobby and Wes. And the captain himself, with his angelic-looking baby son asleep in a room down the hall, had filled the seventh seat at the table.

P.J. had scored big. As the dealer, she'd chosen to play a game called Tennessee. The high-risk, high-penalty, high-reward nature of the game appealed to the SEALs, and they'd played it several times that evening.

P.J. had won each time.

Now she tossed her bag on the ground and followed as Joe Cat hung back to wait for her. The other men were already out of sight.

"I'm really sorry I was late," she said again.

"I pulled in about forty-five seconds before you." The captain pulled his thick, dark hair into a ponytail as they headed down the trail. "I guess H. figured he couldn't shout at you after he didn't shout at me, huh?"

They were moving at a decent clip. Fast but not too fast—just enough so that P.J. had to pay attention to her breathing. She didn't want to be gasping for air and unable to talk when they reached their destination. "Does the Senior Chief shout at *you?*" she asked.

"Sometimes." Joe smiled. "But never in public, of course."

They ran in silence for a while. The gravel crunching under their feet was the only sound.

"Is his father all right?" P.J. finally asked. "I didn't see

Harvard at all yesterday, and today he seems so preoccupied. Is anything wrong?" She tried to sound casual, as if she were just making conversation, as if she hadn't spent a good hour in bed last night thinking about the man, wondering why he hadn't been at dinner.

They'd only gone about a mile, but she was already soaked with perspiration. It was ridiculously humid today. The air clung to her, pressing against her skin like a damp blanket.

"His father's doing well," Joe told her. He gave her a long, appraising look. "H. has got some other personal stuff going on, though."

P.J. quickly backpedaled. "I didn't mean to pry."

"No, your question was valid. He was uncharacteristically monosyllabic this morning," he said. "Probably because it's moving day."

She tried not to ask, but she couldn't stop herself. "Moving day?"

"H.'s parents are moving. I don't want to put words in his mouth, but I think he feels bad that he's not up there helping out. Not to mention that he's pretty thrown by the fact that they're leaving Massachusetts. For years his family lived in this really great old house overlooking the ocean near Boston. I went home with him a few times before his sisters started getting married and moving out. He has a really nice family—really warm, friendly people. He grew up in that house—it's gotta hold a lot of memories for him."

"He lived in *one* house almost his entire life? God, I moved five times in one year. And that was just the year I turned twelve."

"I know what you mean. My mother and I were pros at filling out post office change of address cards, too. But H. lived in one place from the time he was a little kid until he left for college. Wild, huh?"

"And on top of that his parents are both still alive and together." P.J. shook her head. "Doesn't he know how lucky he is? Unless he's got some deep, dark, dysfunctional secret that I don't know about."

"I don't think so, but I'm not exactly qualified to answer that one. I think it's probably best if Harvard got into those specifics with you himself, you know?"

"Of course," she said quickly. "I wasn't looking to put you on the spot."

"Yeah, I know that," he said easily. "And I didn't mean to make it sound as if I was telling you to mind your own business. Because I wasn't."

P.J. had to laugh. "Whew—I'm glad we got *that* settled."

"It's just… I'm speculating here. I don't want to mislead you in any way."

"I know—and you're not." As he glanced at her again, P.J. felt compelled to add, "The Senior Chief and I are just friends."

Joe Catalanotto just smiled.

"I've known H. almost as long as I've known Blue," he told her after they'd run another mile or so in silence.

"Yeah, you told me you and Blue—Lieutenant McCoy—went through BUD/S together, right?" P.J. asked.

"Yeah, we were swim buddies."

Swim buddies. That meant Joe Cat and Blue had been assigned to work together as they'd trained to become SEALs. From what P.J. knew of the rigorous special operations training, they'd had to become closer than blood brothers, relying on one man's strengths to counter the other's weaknesses, and vice versa. It was no wonder that after all those years of working side by side, the two men could communicate extensively with a single look.

"H. was in our graduating class," Joe told her. "In fact, he was part of our boat team during Hell Week. A vital part."

Funny, they were talking about Harvard again. Not that P.J. particularly minded.

"Who was *his* swim buddy?"

"Harvard's swim buddy rang out—he quit—right before it was our turn to land our IBS on the rocks outside the Hotel Del Coronado."

"IBS?"

"Inflatable Boat, Small." Joe smiled. "And the word *small* is relative. It weighs about two hundred and fifty pounds and carries seven men. The boat team carries it everywhere throughout Hell Week. By the time we did the rock portage, we were down to only four men—all enlisted—and that thing was damn heavy. But we all made it through to the end."

Enlisted? "You and Blue didn't start out as officers?"

Joe picked up the pace. "Nope. We were both enlisted. Worked our way up from the mail room, so to speak."

"Any idea why Harvard didn't take that route?" she asked. She quickly added, "I'm just curious."

The captain nodded but couldn't hide his smile. "I guess he didn't want to be an officer. I mean, he *really* didn't want to. He was approached by OCS—the Officer's Candidate School—so often, it got to be kind of a joke. In fact, during BUD/S, he was paired with a lieutenant, I think in an attempt to make him realize he was prime officer material."

"But the lieutenant quit."

"Yeah. Harvard took that pretty hard. He thought he should've been able to keep his swim buddy—Matt, I think his name was—from quitting. But it was more than clear to all of us that H. had been carrying this guy right from the start. Matt would've been out weeks earlier if he hadn't been teamed up with H."

"I guess even back then, Harvard was a team player," P.J. mused. The entire front of her T-shirt was drenched with sweat, and her legs and lungs were starting to burn, but the captain showed no sign of slowing down.

"Exactly." Joe wasn't even slightly winded. "He hated

feeling like he was letting Matt down. Except the truth was, Matt had been doing nothing but letting H. down from day one. Swim buddies have to balance out their strengths and weaknesses. It doesn't work if one guy does all the giving and the other does nothing but take. You know, even though Harvard saw Matt's ringing out as a personal failure, the rest of us recognized it for the blessing it was. God knows it's hard enough to get through BUD/S. But it's damn near impossible to do it with a drowning man strapped to your back."

She could see Harvard way up ahead on the trail, still in the lead. He'd taken off his T-shirt, and his powerful muscles gleamed with sweat. He moved like a dancer, each step graceful and sure. He made running look effortless.

As Joe Cat cranked their speed up another few notches, P.J. found that it was getting harder to talk and run at the same time.

The captain kept his mouth tightly shut as they raced past first Schneider and Greene, then Tim Farber, but it wasn't because he couldn't talk. Once out of the other agents' earshot, he turned to grin at her.

"My *grandmother* could outrun those guys."

"How far are we going today?" P.J. asked as they passed the five-mile mark. Her words came out in gasps.

"However far H. wants to take us."

Harvard didn't look as if he were planning on stopping anytime soon. In fact, as P.J. watched, he punched up the speed.

"You know, I used to be faster than H.," Joe told her. "But then he went and shaved his head and cut down on all that wind resistance."

P.J. had to laugh.

"So I asked Ronnie, what do you think, should I shave *my* head, too, and she tells me no way. I say, why not? She's always talking about how sexy Harvard is—about how women can't stay away from him, and I'm thinking maybe

I should go for that Mr. Clean look, too. So she tells me she likes my hair long, in what she calls romance-cover-model style. But I can't stop thinking about that wind resistance thing, until she breaks the news to me that if *I* shaved my head, I wouldn't look sexy. I'd look like a giant white big toe."

P.J. cracked up, trying to imagine him without any hair and coming up with an image very similar to what his wife had described.

Joe was grinning. "Needless to say, I'm keeping my razor securely locked in the medicine cabinet."

Harvard heard the melodic burst of P.J.'s laughter and gritted his teeth.

It wasn't that it sounded as if she were flirting with Joe Cat when she laughed that way. It wasn't that he was jealous in any way of the special friendship she seemed to have formed with Alpha Squad's captain. It wasn't even so much that he was having one bitch of a bad day.

But then she laughed again, and the truth of the matter smacked him square in the face.

She *did* sound as if she were flirting with Joe Cat. Harvard was jealous not only of that, but of any kind of friendship she and the captain had formed, and he couldn't remember ever having had a worse day in the past year, if not the past few years. Not since that new kid who transferred from SEAL Team One had panicked during a HALO training op. The cells of his chute hadn't opened right, and he hadn't fully cut free before pulling the emergency rip cord. That second chute had gotten tangled with the first and never opened. The kid fell to his death, and Harvard had had to help search for his remains. That had been one hell of a bad day.

He knew he should count his blessings. No one had died today. But thinking that way only made him feel worse. It made him feel guilty on top of feeling lousy.

He took a short cut to the base, knowing he could run forever today and it wouldn't make him feel any better. He ran hard and fast, setting a pace he knew would leave the three male finks in the dust.

He had no doubt that P.J. would keep up. Whenever she ran, she got that same look in her eye he'd seen in many a determined SEAL candidate who made it through BUD/S to the bitter end. Like them, she would have to be dead and buried before she would quit. If then.

It was almost too bad she was a woman. As she'd pointed out to him, she *was* one of the best shooters in all of FInCOM. She was good, she was tough, but the fact was, she was a girl. Try as he might, he couldn't accept that there was a place for females in combat situations. The sooner she got promoted up and out of the field, the better.

He ran faster, and as they reached the home stretch, Lucky was cursing him with every step. Bobby and Wes were complaining in stereo by the time Harvard slowed to a stop. Even Blue and Joe Cat were out of breath.

P.J. was trying not to look as if she were gasping for air, but she doubled over, head down, hands on her knees.

Harvard backtracked quickly, hoisting her into a more vertical position by the back of her T-shirt. "You know better than to stick your head down lower than your heart after running like that," he said sharply.

"Sorry," she gasped.

"Don't apologize to me," he said harshly. "I'm not the one whose reputation is going to suffer when you live up to everyone's expectations by blacking out and keeling over like some fainthearted little miss."

Her eyes sparked. "And I'm not the great, huge, stupid he-man who had to prove some kind of macho garbage by running the entire team as hard as he possibly could."

"Believe me, baby, that wasn't even half as hard as I can get." He smiled tightly to make sure she caught the double entendre, then lowered his voice. "Just say the word, and I'll give you a private demonstration."

Her eyes narrowed, her mouth tightened, and he knew he'd gone too far. "What's up with you today?"

He started to turn away, but she stopped him with a hand on his arm, unmindful of the fact that his skin was slick with sweat. "Are you all right, Daryl?" she asked quietly. Beneath the flash of anger and impatience in her eyes, he could see her deep concern.

He could handle fighting with her. He *wanted* to fight with her. The soft warmth of her dark brown eyes only made him feel worse. Now he felt bad, topped with guilt for feeling bad, and he also felt like a certified fool for lashing out at her.

Harvard swore softly. "Sorry, Richards, I was way out of line. Just…go away, okay? I'm not fit to be around today."

He looked up to find Joe Cat standing behind him. "I'm going to give everyone the rest of the morning free," the captain told him quietly. "Let's meet at the Quonset hut after lunch."

Harvard knew Joe was giving them free time because of him. Joe knew Harvard needed a few hours to clear his head.

He shouldn't have needed it—he was too experienced, too much of a professional to become a head case at this stage of his life. But before Harvard could argue, Joe Cat walked away.

"You want to take a walk?" P.J. asked Harvard.

He didn't get a chance to answer before she tugged at his arm. "Let's go," she said, gesturing with her chin toward the path they'd run along. She grabbed several bottles of water from her gym bag and handed one to him.

Damn, it was hot. Rivers of perspiration were running down his chest, down his legs, dripping from his chin, beading on his shoulders and arms. He opened the bottle and took a long drink. "What, you want to psychoanalyze me, Richards?"

"Nope. I'm just gonna listen," she said. "That is, if you want to talk."

"I don't want to talk."

"Okay," she said matter-of-factly. "Then we'll just walk."

They walked in silence for an entire mile, then two. But right around the three-mile marker, she took the boardwalk right-of-way that led to the beach. He followed in silence, watching as she sat in the sand and began pulling off her sneakers.

She looked at him. "Wanna go for a swim?"

"Yeah." He sat next to her and took off his running shoes.

P.J. pulled off her T-shirt. She was wearing a gray running bra underneath. It covered her far better than a bathing suit top would have, but the sight of it, the sight of all that smooth, perfect skin reminded him a hundredfold that he wasn't taking a walk with one of the boys.

"Look at this," P.J. said. "I can practically wring my shirt out."

Harvard tried his best to look. He purposely kept his gaze away from the soft mounds of her breasts outlined beneath the thick gray fabric of her running top. She wasn't overly endowed, not by any means, but what she had sure was nice.

Her arms and her stomach glistened with perspiration as she leaned forward to peel off her socks. It didn't take much imagination to picture her lying naked on his bed, her gleaming dark skin set off by the white cotton of his sheets, replete after hours of lovemaking. He tried to banish the image instantly. Thinking like that was only going to get him into trouble.

"Come on," she said, scrambling to her feet. She held out her hand for him, and he took it and let her pull him up.

He wanted to hold on to her, to lace their fingers together, but she broke away, running fearlessly toward the crashing surf. She dove over the breakers, coming up to float on top of the swells beyond.

Harvard joined her in that place of calm before the breaking ocean. The current was strong, and there was a serious undertow. But P.J. had proven her swimming skills many times over during the past few weeks. He didn't doubt her ability to hold her own.

She pushed her hair out of her face and adjusted her ponytail. "You know, up until last year, I didn't know how to swim."

Harvard was glad the water was holding him up, because otherwise, he would have fallen over. "You're kidding!"

"I grew up in D.C.," she told him matter-of-factly. "In the inner city. The one time we moved close enough to the pool at the Y, it was shut down for repairs for eight months. By the time it opened again, we were gone." She smiled. "When I was really little, I used to pretend to swim in the bathtub."

"Your mother and father never took you to the beach in the summer to stay cool?"

P.J. laughed as if something he'd said was extremely funny. "No, I never even saw the ocean until I went on a class trip to Delaware in high school. I meant to take swimming lessons in college, but I never got around to it. Then I got assigned to this job. I figured if I were going to be working with Navy SEALs, it'd be a good idea if I knew how to swim. I was right."

"I learned to swim when I was six," Harvard told her. "It was the summer I…"

She waited, and when he didn't go on, she asked, "The summer you what?"

He shook his head.

But she didn't let it go. "The summer you decided you were going to join the Navy and become a SEAL," she guessed.

The water felt good against his hot skin. Harvard let himself float. "No, I was certain right up until the time I finished college that I was going to be an English lit professor, just like my old man."

"Really?"

"Yeah."

She squinted at him. "I'm trying to picture you with glasses and one of those jackets with the suede patches on the elbows and maybe even a pipe." She laughed. "Somehow I can't manage to erase the M-16 that's kind of permanently hanging over your shoulder, and the combination is making for quite an interesting image."

"Yeah, yeah." Harvard treaded water lazily. "Laugh at me all you want. Chicks dig guys who can recite Shakespeare. And who knows? I might decide to get my teaching degree some day."

"The M-16 will certainly keep your class in line."

Harvard laughed.

"We're getting off the subject here," P.J. said. "You learned to swim when you were six and it was the summer you also made your first million playing the stock market? No," she answered her own question, "if you had a million dollars gathering interest from the time you were six, you wouldn't be here now. You'd be out on your yacht, commanding your own private navy. Let's see, it must've been the summer you got your first dog."

"Nope."

"Hmm. The summer you had your first date?"

Harvard laughed. "I was *six*."

She grinned at him. "You seem the precocious type."

They'd come a long way, Harvard realized. Even though there was still a magnetic field of sexual tension surrounding them, even though he still didn't want her in the CSF team and she damn well knew it, they'd managed to work around those issues and somehow become friends.

He liked this girl. And he liked talking to her. He would've liked going to bed with her even more, but he knew women well enough to recognize that when this one shied away from him, she wasn't just playing some game. As far as P. J. Richards was concerned, *no* didn't mean *try a little harder.* No meant no. And until that no became a very definite yes, he was going to have to be content with talking.

But Harvard liked to talk. He liked to debate. He enjoyed philosophizing. He was good with words, good at verbal sparring. And who could know? Maybe if he talked to P.J. for long enough, he'd end up saying something that would start breaking through her defenses. Maybe he'd begin the process that would magically change that no to a yes.

"It was the summer you first—"

"It was the summer my family moved to our house in Hingham," Harvard interrupted. "My mother decided that if we were going to live a block away from the ocean, we all had to learn to swim."

P.J. was silent. "Was that the same house your parents are moving out of today?" she finally asked.

He froze. "Where did you hear about that?"

She glanced at him. "Joe Cat told me."

P.J. had been talking to Joe Cat about him. Harvard didn't know whether to feel happy or annoyed. He'd be happy to know she'd been asking questions about him. But he'd be annoyed as hell if he found out that Joe had been attempting to play matchmaker.

"What, the captain just came over to you and said, guess what? Hot news flash—Harvard's mom and pop are moving today?"

"No," she said evenly. "He told me because I asked him

if he knew what had caused the great big bug to crawl up your pants."

She pushed herself forward to catch a wave before it broke and bodysurfed to shore like a professional—as if she'd been doing it all of her life.

She'd asked Joe. Harvard followed her out of the water feeling foolishly pleased. "It's no big deal—the fact that they're moving, I mean. I'm just being a baby about it."

P.J. sat in the sand, leaned back against her elbows and stretched her legs out in front of her. "Your parents lived in the same house for, what? Thirty years?"

"Just about." Harvard sat next to her. He stared at the ocean in an attempt to keep from staring at her legs. Damn, she had nice legs. It was impossible not to look, but he told himself that was okay, because he was making damn sure he didn't touch. Still, he wanted to.

"You're not being a baby. It *is* a big deal," she told him. "You're allowed to have it be a big deal, you know."

He met her eyes, and she nodded. "You *are* allowed," she said again.

She was so serious. She looked as if she were prepared to go into mortal combat over the fact that he had the right to feel confused and upset over his parents' move. He felt his mouth start to curve into a smile, and she smiled, too. The connection between them sparked and jumped into high gear. Damn. When they had sex, it was going to be great. It was going to be *beyond* great.

But it wasn't going to be today. If he were smart he'd rein in those wayward thoughts, keep himself from getting too overheated.

"It's just so stupid," he admitted. "But I've started having these dreams where suddenly I'm ten years old again, and I'm walking home from school and I get home and the front door's locked. So I ring the bell and this strange lady comes to the screen. She tells me my family has moved, but she doesn't know where. And she won't let me in, and I just feel so lost, as if everything I've ever counted on is gone and... It's stupid," he said again. "I haven't actually lived in that house for years. And I know where my parents are going. I have the address. I already have their new phone number. I don't know why this whole thing should freak me out this way."

He lay back in the sand, staring at the hazy sky.

"This opportunity is going to be so good for my father," he continued. "I just wish I could have taken the time to go up there, help them out with the logistics."

"Where exactly are they moving?" P.J. asked.

"Phoenix, Arizona."

"No ocean view there."

He turned to face her, propping his head on one hand. "That shouldn't matter. I'm the one who liked the ocean view, and I don't live with them anymore."

"Where *do* you live?" she asked.

Harvard couldn't answer that without consideration. "I have a furnished apartment here in Virginia."

"That's just temporary housing. Where do you keep your stuff?"

"What stuff?"

"Your bed. Your kitchen table. Your stamp collection. I don't know, your *stuff.*"

He lay down, shaking his head. "I don't have a bed or a kitchen table. And I used the last stamp I bought to send a letter to my little sister at Boston University."

"How about your books?" P.J. ventured. "Where do you keep your books?"

"In a climate-controlled self-storage unit in Coronado, California." He laughed and closed his eyes. "Damn, I'm pathetic, aren't I? Maybe I should get a sign for the door saying Home Sweet Home."

"Are you sure you ever really moved out of your parents' house?" she asked.

"Maybe not," he admitted, his eyes still closed. "But if that's the case, I guess I'm moving out today, huh?"

P.J. hugged her legs to her chest as she sat on the beach next to the Alpha Squad's Senior Chief.

"Maybe that's why I feel so bad," he mused. "It's a symbolic end to my childhood." He glanced at her, amusement lighting his eyes. "Which I suppose had to happen sooner or later, considering that in four years I'll be forty."

Harvard Becker was an incredibly beautiful-looking man. His body couldn't have been more perfect if some artisan had taken a chisel to stone and sculpted it. But it was his eyes that continued to keep P.J. up at night. So much was hidden in their liquid brown depths.

It had been a bold move on her part to suggest they go off alone to walk. With anyone else, she wouldn't have thought twice about it. But with everyone else, the boundaries of friendship weren't so hard to define.

When it came to this man, P.J. was tempted to break her own rules. And that was a brand-new feeling for her. A dangerous feeling. She hugged her knees a little tighter.

"There was a lot wrong with that house in Hingham," Harvard told her. "The roof leaked in the kitchen. No matter how many times we tried to fix it, as soon as it stormed, we'd need to get out that old bucket and put it under that drip. The pipes rattled, and the windows were drafty, and my sisters were *always* tying up the telephone. My mother's solution to any problem was to serve up a hearty meal, and my old man was so immersed in Shakespeare most of the time he didn't know which century it was."

He was trying to make jokes, trying to bring himself out of the funk he'd been in, trying to pretend it didn't matter.

"I couldn't wait to move out, you know, to go away to school," he said.

He was trying to make it hurt less by belittling his

memories. And there was no way she was going to sit by and listen quietly while he did that.

"You know that dream you've been having?" she asked. "The one where you get home from school and your parents are gone?"

He nodded.

"Well, it didn't happen to me exactly like that," she told him. "But one day I came home from school and I found all our furniture out on the sidewalk. We'd been evicted, and my mother was gone. She'd vanished. She'd dealt with the bad news not by trying to hustle down a new apartment, but by going out on a binge."

He pushed himself into a sitting position. "My God…"

"I was twelve years old," P.J. said. "My grandmother had died about three months before that, and it was just me and Cheri—my mom. I don't know what Cheri did with the rent money, but I can certainly guess. I remember that day like it was yesterday. I had to beg our neighbors to hold on to some of that furniture for us—the stuff that wasn't already broken or stolen. I had to pick and choose which of the clothing we could take and which we'd have to leave behind. I couldn't carry any of my books or toys or stuffed animals, and no one had any room to store a box of my old junk, so I put 'em in an alley, hoping they'd still be there by the time I found us another place to live." She shot him a look. "It rained that night, and I never even bothered to go back. I knew the things in that box were ruined. I guess I figured I didn't have much use for toys anymore, anyway."

She took a deep breath. "But that afternoon, I loaded up all that I could carry of our clothes in shopping bags and I went looking for my mother. You see, I needed to find her in order to get a bed in the shelter that night. If I tried to go on my own, I'd be taken in and made a ward of the state. And as bad as things were with Cheri, I was afraid that would be even worse."

Harvard swore softly.

"I'm not giving you the 411 to make you feel worse." She held his gaze, hoping he would understand. "I'm just trying to show you how really lucky you were, Daryl. How lucky you *are*. Your past is solid. You should celebrate it and let it make you stronger."

"Your mother..."

"Was an addict since before I can remember," P.J. told him flatly. "And don't even ask about my father. I'm not sure my mother knew who he was. Cheri was fourteen when she had me. And *her* mother was sixteen when she had *her*. I did the math and figured out if I followed in my family's hallowed tradition, I'd be nursing a baby of my own by the time I was twelve. That's the childhood *I* climbed out of. I escaped, but just barely." She raised her chin. "But if there's one thing I got from Cheri, it's a solid grounding in reality. I am where I am today because I looked around and I said no way. So in a sense, I celebrate my past, too. But the party in my head's not quite as joyful as the one you should be having."

"Damn," Harvard said. "Compared to you, I grew up in paradise." He swore. "Now I really feel like some kind of pouting child."

P.J. looked at the ocean stretching all the way to the horizon. She loved knowing that it kept going and going and going, way past the point where the earth curved and she couldn't see it anymore.

"I've begun to think of you as a friend," she told Harvard. She turned to look at him, gazing directly into his eyes. "So I have to warn you—I only have guilt-free friendships. You can't take anything I've told you and use it to invalidate your own bad stuff. I mean, everyone's got their own luggage, right? And friends shouldn't set their personal suitcase down next to someone else's, size them both up and say, hey, mine's not as big as yours, or hey, mine's bigger and fancier so yours doesn't count." She smiled. "I'll tell you right now, Senior Chief, I travel with an old refrigerator box, and it's packed solid. Just don't knock it over, and I'll be all right. Yours, on the other hand, is very classy Masonite. But your parents' move made the lock break, and now you've got to tidy everything up before you can get it fixed and sealed up tight again."

Harvard nodded, smiling at her. "That's a very poetic way of telling me don't bother to stage a pissing contest, 'cause you'd win, hands down."

"That's right. But I'm also telling you don't jam yourself up because you feel sad about your parents leaving your hometown," P.J. said. "It makes perfect sense that you'll miss that house you grew up in—that house you've gone home to for the past thirty years. There's nothing wrong with feeling sad about that. But I'm also saying that even though you feel sad, you should also feel happy. Just think—you've had that place to call home and those people to make it a good, happy home for all these years. You've got memories, good memories you'll always be able to look back on and take comfort from. You know what having a home means, while most of the rest of the people in the world are just floating around, upside down, not even knowing what they're missing but missing it just the same."

He was silent, so she kept going. She couldn't remember the last time she'd talked so much. But this man, this new friend with the whiskey-colored eyes, who made her feel like cheating the rules—he was worth the effort.

"You can choose to have a house and a family someday, kids, the whole nine yards, like your parents did," she told him. "Or you can hang on to those memories you carry in your heart. That way, you can go back to that home you had, wherever you are, whenever you want."

There. She'd said everything she wanted to say to him.

But he was so quiet, she began to wonder if she'd gone too far. She was the queen of dysfunctional families. What did *she* know about normal? What right did she have to tell him her view of the world with such authority in her voice?

He cleared his throat. "So where do *you* live now, P.J.?"

She liked it when Harvard called her P.J. instead of Richards. It shouldn't have mattered, but it did. She liked the chill she got up her spine from the heat she could sometimes see simmering in his eyes. And she especially liked knowing he respected her enough to hold back. He wanted her. His attraction was powerful, but he respected her enough to not keep hammering her with come-on lines and thinly veiled innuendos. Yeah, she liked that a lot.

"I have an apartment in D.C., but I'm hardly ever there." She picked up a handful of sand and let it sift through her fingers. "See, I'm one of the floaters. I still haven't unpacked most of my boxes from college. I haven't even bought furniture for the place, although I *do* have a bed and a kitchen table." She shot him a rueful smile. "I don't need extensive therapy to know that my nesting instincts are busted, big-time. I figure it's a holdover from when I was a kid. I learned not to get attached to any one place because sooner or later the landlord would be kicking us out and we'd be living somewhere else."

"If you could live anywhere in the world," he asked, "where would you live?"

"Doesn't matter where, as long as it's not in the middle of a city," P.J. answered without hesitation. "Some cute little house with a little yard—doesn't have to be big. It just has to have some land. Enough for a flower garden. I've never lived anywhere long enough to let a garden grow," she added wistfully.

Harvard was struck by the picture she made sitting there. She'd just run eight miles at a speed that had his men cursing, then walked three miles more. She was sandy, she was sticky from salt and sweat, her hair was less than perfect, her makeup long since gone. She was tough, she was driven, she was used to not just getting by but getting ahead in a man's world, and despite all that, she was sweetly sentimental as all get out.

She turned to meet his gaze, and as if she could somehow read his mind, she laughed. "God, I sound like a sap." Her eyes narrowed. "If you tell *anyone* what I said, you're a dead man."

"What, that you like flowers? Since when is that late-breaking piece of news something you need to keep hidden from the world?"

Something shifted in her eyes. "*You* can like flowers," she told him. "*You* can read Jane Austen in the mess hall at lunch. *You* can drink iced tea instead of whiskey shots with beer chasers. You can do what you want. But if *I'm* caught acting like a woman, if I wear soft, lacy underwear instead of the kind made from fifty percent cotton and fifty percent sandpaper, I get looked at funny. People start to wonder if I'm capable of doing my job."

Harvard tried to make her smile. "Personally, I stay away from the lacy underwear myself."

"Yeah, but you *could* wear silk boxers, and your men would think, 'Gee, the Senior Chief is really cool.' I wear silk, and those same men start thinking with a nonbrain part of their anatomy."

"That's human nature," he argued. "That's because you're a beautiful woman and—"

"You know, it always comes down to sex," P.J. told him crossly. "Always. You can't put men and women in a room together without something happening. And I'm not saying it's entirely the men's fault, although men *can* be total dogs. Do you know that I had to start fighting off my mother's boyfriends back when I was ten? *Ten.* They'd come over, get high with her, and then when she passed out, they'd start sniffing around my bedroom door. My grandmother was alive then, and she'd give 'em a piece of her mind, chase 'em out of the house. But after she died, when I was twelve, I was on my own. I grew up fast, I'll tell you that much."

When Harvard was twelve, he'd had a paper route. The toughest thing he'd had to deal with was getting up early every morning to deliver those papers. And the Doberman on the corner of Parker and Reingold. That mean old dog had been a problem for about a week or two. But in time, Harvard had gotten used to the early mornings, and he'd made friends with the Doberman.

Somehow he doubted P.J. had had equally easy solutions to her problems.

She gazed at the ocean, the wind moving a stray curl across her face. She didn't seem to feel it, or if she did, she didn't care enough to push it away.

He tried to picture her at twelve years old. She must've been tiny. Hell, she was tiny now. It wouldn't have taken much of a man to overpower her and—

The thought made him sick. But he had to know. He had to ask. "Did you ever... Did they ever..."

She turned to look at him, and he couldn't find any immediate answers in the bottomless darkness of her eyes.

"There was one," she said softly, staring at the ocean. "He didn't back off when I threatened to call my uncle. Of course, I didn't really have any uncle. It's possible he knew that. Or maybe he was just too stoned to care. I had to go out the window to get away from him—only in my panic, I went out the wrong window. I went out the one without the fire escape. Once I was out there, I couldn't go back. I went onto the ledge and I just stood there, sixteen stories up, scared out of my mind, staring at those little toy cars on the street, knowing if I slipped, I'd be dead, but certain if I went back inside I'd be as good as dead." She looked at Harvard. "I honestly think I would've jumped before I would've let him touch me."

Harvard believed her. This man, whoever he'd been, may not have hurt P.J. physically, but he'd done one hell of a job on her emotionally and psychologically.

He had to clear his throat before he could speak. "I don't suppose you remember this son of a bitch's name?" he asked.

"Ron something. I don't think I ever knew his last name."

He nodded. "Too bad."

"Why?"

Harvard shrugged. "Nothing important. I was just thinking it might make me feel a little better to hunt him down and kick the hell out of him."

P.J. laughed—a shaky burst of air that was part humor and part surprise. "But he didn't hurt me, Daryl. I took care of myself and...I was okay."

"Were you?" Harvard reached out for her. He knew he shouldn't. He knew that just touching her lightly under the chin to turn her to face him would be too much. He knew her skin would be sinfully soft beneath his fingers, and he knew that once he touched her, he wouldn't want to let go. But he wanted to look into her eyes, so he did. "Tell me this—are you still afraid of heights?"

She didn't need to answer. He saw the shock of the truth in her eyes before she pulled away. She stood up, moved toward the water, stopping on the edge of the beach, letting the waves wash over her feet.

Harvard followed, waiting for her to look at him again.

P.J.'s head was spinning. Afraid of heights? Terrified was more like it.

She couldn't believe he'd figured that out. She couldn't believe she'd told him enough to give herself away. Steeling herself, she looked at him. "I can handle heights, Senior Chief. It's not a problem."

She could tell from the look on his face he didn't believe her.

"It's not a problem," she said again.

Damn. She'd told him too much.

It was one thing to joke around about her dream house. But telling him about her problem with heights was going way too far.

It would do her absolutely no good to let this man know her weaknesses. She had to have absolutely no vulnerabilities to coexist in his macho world. She could not be afraid of heights. She *would* not be. She could handle it—but not if he made it into an issue.

P.J. rinsed her hands in the ocean. "We better get back if we want to have any lunch."

But Harvard blocked the way to where her sneakers and T-shirt were lying on the sand. "Thanks for taking the time to talk to me," he said.

She nodded, still afraid to meet his eyes. "Yeah, I'm glad we're friends."

"It's nice to be able to talk to someone in confidence— and know you don't have to worry about other people finding out all your deep, dark secrets," Harvard told her.

P.J. did look at him then, but he'd already turned away.

CHAPTER EIGHT

"Man, it's quiet around here today," Harvard said as he came into the decaying Quonset hut that housed Alpha Squad's office.

Lucky was the only one around, and he looked up from one of the computers. "Hey, H.," he said with a cheerful smile. "Where've you been?"

"There was a meeting with the base commander that I absolutely couldn't miss." Harvard rolled his eyes. "It was vital that I go with the captain to listen to more complaints about having the squad temporarily stationed here. This base is regular Navy, and SEALs don't follow rules. We don't salute enough. We drive too fast. We make too much noise at the firing range. We don't cut our hair." He slid his hand over his cleanly shaved head. "Or we cut our hair too short. I tell you, there's no pleasing some folks. Every week it's the same, and every week we sit there, and I take notes, and the captain nods seriously and explains that the noise at the firing range occurs when we discharge our weapons and he's sorry for the inconvenience, but one of the reasons Alpha Squad has the success record it does is that each and every one of us takes target practice each day, every day, and that's not going to change. And then the supply officer steps forward and informs us that the next time we want another box of pencils, we've got to get 'em from Office Max. We appear to have used up our allotted supply." He shook his head. "We got lectured on *that* for ten minutes."

"Ten minutes? On *pencils?*"

Harvard grinned. "That's right." He turned toward his office. "Joe's right behind me. He should be back soon—unless he gets cornered into sticking around for lunch."

Lucky made a face. "Poor Cat."

"This is what *you* have to look forward to, O'Donlon," Harvard said with another grin. "It's only a matter of time before you make an oh-six pay grade and get your own command. And then you'll be rationing pencils, too." He laughed "It's not just a job—it's an adventure."

"Gee, thanks, H. I'm all aquiver with anticipation."

Harvard pushed open his office door. "Do me a favor and dial the captain's pager number. Give him an emergency code. Let's get him out of there."

Lucky picked up the phone and quickly punched in a series of numbers. He dropped the receiver into the cradle with a clatter.

"So where's everyone this afternoon?" Harvard called as he took off his jacket and hung it over the chair at his desk. "I stopped by the classroom on my way over, but it was empty. They're not all still at lunch, are they?"

"No, they're at the airfield. I'm heading over there myself in about ten minutes." Lucky raised his voice to be heard through the open door.

Harvard stopped rifling through the files on his desk. "They're where?"

"At the field. It's jump day," Lucky told him.

"Today?" Harvard moved to the door to stare at the younger SEAL. "No way. That wasn't scheduled until next week."

"Yeah, everything got shifted around, remember? We had to move the jump up a full week."

Harvard shook his head. "No. No, I don't remember that."

Lucky swore. "It must've been the day you went to Boston. Yeah, I remember you weren't around, so Wes took care of it. He said he wrote a memo about it. He said he left it on your desk."

Harvard's desk was piled high with files and papers, but he knew exactly what was in each file and where each file was in each pile. It may have looked disorganized, but it wasn't. He'd cleared his In basket at least ten times since he'd taken that day of personal leave. He'd caught up on everything he'd missed. There was no memo from Wesley Skelly on that desk.

Or was there?

Underneath the coffee mug with a broken handle that held his pens and some of those very pencils the base supply officer had been in a snit about, Harvard could see a flash of yellow paper. He lifted the mug and turned the scrap of paper over.

This was it.

Wes had written an official memo on the inside of an M&M's wrapper. It was documentation of the rescheduled jump date, scribbled in barely legible pencil.

"I'm going to kill him," Harvard said calmly. "I'm going to find him, and I'm going to kill him."

"You don't have to look far to find him," Lucky said. "He's with the finks in the classroom at the main hangar. He's helping Blue teach 'em the basics of skydiving."

Harvard shook his head. "If I'd known the jump was today, I would've made arrangements to skip this morning's meeting. I wanted to be here to make it clear to the finks that participating in this exercise is optional." He looked sharply at O'Donlon. "Were you there when Blue gave his speech? Do they understand they don't have to do this?"

Lucky shrugged. "Yeah. They're all up for it, though. It's no big deal."

But it was a big deal. Harvard knew that for P.J. it had to be a very, very big deal.

When he'd figured out yesterday that she was afraid of heights, he'd known about the skydiving jump, but he'd thought it was a week away. If he'd known otherwise, he would've warned her then and there. He could've told her that choosing not to participate didn't matter one bit in the big picture.

The purpose of the exercise was not to teach the finks to be expert skydivers. There was no way they could do that with only one day and only one jump. When they'd set up the program, the captain had thought a lesson in skydiving would give the agents perspective on the kind of skills the SEALs needed to succeed as a counterterrorist team.

It was supposed to underscore the message of the entire program—let the SEALs do what they do best without outside interference.

Harvard looked at his watch. It was just past noon. "O'Donlon, is the jump still scheduled for thirteen-thirty?"

"It is," Lucky told him. "I'm going over to help out. You know me, I never turn down an opportunity to jump."

Harvard took a deep breath. More than an hour. Good. He still had time. He could relax and take this calmly. He could change out of this blasted dress uniform instead of screaming over to the airfield in a panic.

The phone rang. It had to be Joe Cat, answering his page.

Harvard picked it up. "Rescue squad."

Joe covered a laugh by coughing. "Sit rep, please." The captain was using his officer's voice, and Harvard knew that wherever he was, he wasn't alone.

"We're having a severe pencil shortage, Captain," Harvard said rapidly, in his best imitation of a battle-stressed officer straight from Hollywood's Central Casting. "I think you better get down here right away to take care of it."

Joe coughed again, longer and louder this time. "I see."

"So sorry to interrupt your lunch, sir, but the men are in tears. I'm sure the commander will understand."

Joe's voice sounded strangled. "I appreciate your calling."

"Of course, if you'd prefer to stay and dine with the—"

"No, no. No, I'm on my way. Thank you very much, Senior Chief."

"I love you, too, Captain," Harvard said and hung up the phone.

Lucky was on the floor, laughing. Harvard nudged him with his toe and spoke in his regular voice. "I'm changing out of this ice-cream suit. Don't you dare leave for the airfield without me."

The half of a chicken-salad sandwich P.J. had forced down during lunch was rolling in her stomach.

Lieutenant Blue McCoy stood in front of the group of SEALs and FInCOM agents, briefing them on the afternoon's exercise.

P.J. tried to pay attention as he recited the name of the aircraft that would take them to an altitude from which they'd jump out of the plane.

Jump *out* of the plane.

P.J. took a deep breath. She could do this. She knew she could do this. She was going to *hate* it, but just like going to the dentist, time would keep ticking, and the entire ordeal would eventually be over and done with.

"We'll be going out of the aircraft in teams of two," Blue said in his thick Southern drawl. "You will stay with your jump buddy for the course of the exercise. If you become separated during landing, you must find each other immediately upon disposing of your chute. Remember, we'll be timing you from the moment you step out of that plane to the moment you check in at the assigned extraction point. If you reach the extraction point without your partner, you're automatically disqualified. Does everyone understand?"

P.J. nodded. Her mouth was too dry to murmur a reply.

The door opened at the back of the room, and Blue paused and smiled a greeting. "About time you boys got here."

P.J. turned to see Harvard closing the door behind him. He was wearing camouflage pants tucked securely into black boots and a snugly fitting dark green T-shirt. He was looking directly at her from under the brim of his cap. He nodded just once, then turned his attention to McCoy.

"Sorry to interrupt," he said. It wasn't until he moved toward the front of the room that P.J. noticed Lucky had been standing beside him. "Have you worked up the teams yet, Lieutenant?"

Blue nodded. "I have the list right here, Senior Chief."

"Mind doing some quick revising so I can get in on the action?"

"'Course not," Blue replied. He looked at the room. "Why don't y'all take a five-minute break?"

P.J. wasn't the only one in the room who was nervous. Greg Greene went to the men's room for the fourth time in half an hour. The other men stood and stretched their legs. She sat there, wishing she could close her eyes and go to sleep, wishing that when she woke up it would be tomorrow morning and this day would be behind her, most of all wishing Harvard had given her some kind of warning that today's challenge would involve jumping out of an airplane thousands of feet above the earth.

As she watched, Harvard leaned against the table to look at the list. He supported himself with his arms, and his muscles stood out in sharp relief. For once, she let herself look at him, hoping for a little distraction.

The man was sheer perfection. And speaking of distractions, his shirt wasn't the only thing that fit him snugly. His camouflage pants hugged the curve of his rear end sinfully well. Why on earth anyone would want to camouflage that piece of art was beyond her.

He was deep in discussion with Blue, then both men paused to glance at her, and she quickly looked away. What was Harvard telling the lieutenant? It was clear they were talking about her. Was Harvard telling McCoy all she'd let slip yesterday at the beach? Were they considering the possibility that she might freeze with fear and end up putting more than just herself in danger? Were they going to refuse to let her make the jump?

She glanced at them, and Harvard was still watching her, no doubt taking in the cold sweat that was dampening her shirt and beading on her upper lip. She knew she could keep her fear from showing in her eyes and on her face, but she couldn't keep from perspiring, and she couldn't stop her heart from pounding and causing her hands to shake.

She was scared to death, but she was damned if she was going to let anyone tell her she couldn't make this jump.

As she watched, Harvard spoke again to Blue. Blue nodded, took out a pen and began writing on the paper.

Harvard came down the center aisle and paused next to her chair.

"You okay?" he asked quietly enough so that no one else could hear.

She was unable to hold his gaze. He was close enough to smell her fear and to see that she was, in fact, anything but okay. She didn't bother to lie. "I can do this."

"You don't have to."

"Yes, I do. It's part of this program."

"This jump is optional."

"Not for me, it's not."

He was silent for a moment. "There's nothing I can say to talk you out of this, is there?"

P.J. met his gaze. "No, Senior Chief, there's not."

He nodded. "I didn't think so." He gave her another long look, then moved to the back of the room.

P.J. closed her eyes, drawing in a deep breath. She wanted to get this over with. The waiting was killing her.

"Okay," Blue said. "Listen up. Here're the teams. Schneider's with Greene, Farber's with me. Bobby's with Wes, and Crash is with Lucky. Richards, you're with Senior Chief Becker."

P.J. turned to look at Harvard. He was gazing at her, and she knew this was his doing. If he couldn't talk her out of the jump, he was going to go with her, to babysit her on the way down.

"Out in the other room, you'll find a jumpsuit, a helmet and a belt pack with various supplies," Blue continued. "Including a length of rope."

Farber raised his hand. "What's the rope for?"

Blue smiled. "Just one of those things that might come in handy," he said. "Any other questions?"

The room was silent.

"Let's get our gear and get to the plane," Blue said.

Harvard sat next to P.J. and fastened his seat belt as the plane carrying the team went wheels up.

Sure enough, P.J. was a white-knuckle flyer. She clung to the armrests as if they were her only salvation. But her head was against the seat, and her eyes were closed. To the casual observer, she was totally relaxed and calm.

She'd glanced at him briefly as he sat down, then went back to studying the insides of her eyelids.

Harvard took the opportunity to look at her. She was pretty, but he'd had his share of pretty women before, many of them much more exotic-looking than P.J.

It was funny. He was used to gorgeous women throwing themselves at his feet, delivering themselves up to him like some gourmet meal on a silver platter. They were always the ones in pursuit. All he'd ever had to do was sit back and wait for them to approach him.

But P.J. was different. With P.J., he was clearly the one doing the chasing. And every time he moved closer, she backed away.

It was annoying—and as intriguing as hell.

As the transport plane finally leveled off, she opened her eyes and looked at him.

"You want to review the jump procedure again?" he asked her quietly.

She shook her head. "There's not much to remember. I lift my feet and jump out of the plane. The static line opens the chute automatically."

"If your chute tangles or doesn't open right," Harvard reminded her, "if something goes wrong, break free and make sure you're totally clear before you pull the second rip cord. And when you land—"

"We went over all this in the classroom," P.J. interrupted. "I know how to land."

"Talking about it isn't the same as doing it."

She lowered her voice. "Daryl, I don't need you holding my hand."

Daryl. She'd called him Daryl again. She'd called him that yesterday, too. He lowered his voice. "Aren't you just even a *little* bit glad I'm here?"

"No." She held his gaze steadily. "Not when I know the only reason you're here is you don't think I can do this on my own."

Harvard shifted in his seat to face her. "But that's what working in a team is all about. You don't have to do it on your own. You've got an issue with this particular exercise. That's cool. We can do a buddy jump—double harness, single chute. I'll do most of the work—I'll get us to the ground. You just have to close your eyes and hold on."

"No. Thank you, but no. A woman in this business can't afford to have it look as if she needs help," she told him.

He shook his head impatiently. "This isn't about being a woman. This is about being *human*. Everybody's got *some*thing they can't do as easily or as comfortably as the next man—*person*. So you've got a problem with heights—"

"Shh," she said, looking around to see if anyone was listening. No one was.

"When you're working in a team," Harvard continued, speaking more softly, "it doesn't do anybody any good for you to conceal your weaknesses. I sure as hell haven't kept mine hidden."

P.J.'s eyes widened slightly. "You don't expect me to believe—"

"Everybody's got something," he said again. "When you have to, you work through it, you ignore it, you suck it up and get the job done. But if you've got a team of seven or eight men and you need two men to scale the outside of a twenty-story building and set up recon on the roof, you pick the two guys who are most comfortable with climbing instead of the two who can do the job but have to expend a lot of energy focusing on not looking down. Of course, it's not always so simple. There are lots of other things to factor in in any given situation."

"So what's yours?" P.J. asked. "What's your weakness?" From the tone of her voice and the disbelief in her eyes, she clearly didn't think he had one.

Harvard had to smile. "Why don't you ask Wes or O'Donlon? Or Blue?" He leaned past P.J. and called to the other men, "Hey, Skelly. Hey, Bob. What do I hate more than anything?"

"Idiots," Wes supplied.

"Idiots with rank," Bobby added.

"Being put on hold, traffic jams and cold coffee," Lucky listed.

"No, no, no," Harvard said. "I mean, yeah, you're right, but I'm talking about the teams. What gives me the cold sweats when we're out on an op in the real world?"

"SDVs," Blue said without hesitation. At P.J.'s

questioning look, he explained. "Swimmer Delivery Vehicles. We sometimes use one when a team is being deployed from a nuclear sub. It's like a miniature submarine. Harvard pretty much despises them."

"Getting into one is kind of like climbing into a coffin," Harvard told her. "That image has never sat really well with me."

"The Senior Chief doesn't do too well in tight places," Lucky said.

"I'm slightly claustrophobic," Harvard admitted.

"Locking out of a sub through the escape trunk with him is also a barrel of laughs," Wes said with a snort. "We all climb from the sub into this little chamber—and I mean little, right, H.?"

Harvard nodded. "*Very* little."

"And we stand there, packed together like clowns in a Volkswagen, and the room slowly fills with water," Wes continued. "Anyone who's even a little bit funny about space tends to do some serious teeth grinding."

"We just put Harvard in the middle," Blue told P.J., "and let him close his eyes. When it's time to get going, when the outer lock finally opens, whoever's next to him gives him a little push—"

"Or grabs his belt and hauls him along if his meditation mumbo jumbo worked a little too well," Wes added.

"Some people are so claustrophobic they're bothered by the sensation of water surrounding them, and they have trouble scuba diving," Harvard told her. "But I don't have that issue. Once I'm in the water, I'm okay. As long as I can move my arms, I'm fine. But if I'm in tight quarters with the walls pressing in on me…" He shook his head. "I *really* don't like the sensation of having my arms pinned or trapped against my body. When that happens, I get a little tense."

Lucky snickered. "A little? Remember that time—"

"We don't need to go into that, thank you very much,"

Harvard interrupted. "Let's just say, I don't do much spelunking in my spare time."

P.J. laughed. "I never would have thought," she said. "I mean, you come across as Superman's bigger brother."

He smiled into her eyes. "Even old Supe had to deal with kryptonite."

"Ten minutes," Wes announced, and the mood in the plane instantly changed. The men of Alpha Squad all became professionals, readying and double-checking the gear.

Harvard could feel P.J. tighten. Her smile faded as she braced herself.

He leaned toward her, lowering his voice so no one else could hear. "It's not too late to back out."

"Yes, it is."

"How often does your job require you to skydive?" he argued. "Never. This is a fluke—"

"Not never," she corrected him. "Once. At least once. This once. I can do this. I know I can. Tell me, how many times have you had to lock out of a sub?"

"Too many times."

Somehow she managed a smile. "I only have to do this once."

"Okay, you're determined to jump. I can understand why you want to do it. But let's at least make this a single-chute buddy jump—"

"No." P.J. took a deep breath. "I know you want to help. But even though you think that might help me in the short term, I know it'll harm me in the long run. I don't want people looking at me and thinking, 'She didn't have the guts to do it alone.' Hell, I don't want you looking at me and thinking that."

"I won't—"

"Yes, you will. You already think that. Just because I'm a woman, you think I'm not as strong, not as capable. You think I need to be protected." Her eyes sparked. "Greg

Greene's sitting over there looking like he's about to have a heart attack. But you're not trying to talk him out of making this jump."

Harvard couldn't deny that.

"I'm making this jump alone," P.J. told him firmly, despite the fact that her hands were shaking. "And since we're being timed for this exercise, do me a favor. Once we hit the ground, try to keep up."

P.J. couldn't look down.

She stared at the chute instead, at the pure white of the fabric against the piercing blueness of the sky.

She was moving toward the ground faster than she'd imagined.

She knew she had to look down to pinpoint the landing zone—the LZ—and to mark in her mind the spot where Harvard hit the ground. She had little doubt he would come within a few dozen yards of the LZ, despite the strong wind coming from the west.

Her stomach churned, and she felt green with nausea and dizziness as she gritted her teeth and forced herself to watch the little toy fields and trees beneath her.

It took countless dizzying minutes—far longer than she would have thought—for her to locate the open area that had been marked as their targeted landing zone. And it *had* been marked. There was a huge bull's-eye blazed in white on the brownish-green of the cut grass in the field. It was ludicrously blatant, and despite that, it had been absorbed by the pattern of fields and woods, and she nearly hadn't seen it.

What would it be like to try to find an unmarked target? When the SEALs went on missions, their landing areas weren't marked. And they nearly always made their jumps at night. What would it be like to be up here in the darkness, floating down into hostile territory, vulnerable and exposed?

She felt vulnerable enough as it was, and no one on the ground wanted to kill her.

The parachute was impossible for her to control. P.J. attempted to steer for the bull's-eye, but her arms felt boneless, and the wind was determined to send her to another field across the road.

The trees were bigger now, and the ground was rushing up at her—at her and past her as a gust caught in the chute's cells and took her aloft instead of toward the ground.

A line of very solid-looking trees and underbrush was approaching much too fast, but there was nothing P.J. could do. She was being blown like a leaf in the wind. She closed her eyes and braced herself for impact and…jerked to a stop.

P.J. opened her eyes—and closed them fast. Dear, dear sweet Lord Jesus! Her chute had been caught by the branches of an enormous tree, and she was dangling thirty feet above the ground.

She forced herself to breathe, forced herself to inhale and exhale until the initial roar of panic began to subside. As she slowly opened her eyes again, she looked into the branches above her. How badly was her chute tangled? If she tried to move around, would she shake herself free? She definitely didn't want to do that. That ground was too far away. A fall from this distance could break her legs—or her neck.

She felt the panic return and closed her eyes, breathing again. Only breathing. A deep breath in, a long breath out. Over and over and over.

When her pulse was finally down to ninety or a hundred, she looked into the tree again. There were big branches with leaves blocking most of her view of the chute, but what she could see seemed securely entangled.

Sweat was dripping from her forehead, from underneath her helmet, and she wiped at it futilely.

There were quick-release hooks that would instantly

cut her free from the chute. They were right above her shoulders, and she reached above them, tugging first gently, then harder on the straps.

She was securely lodged in the tree. She hoped.

Still looking away from the ground, she brought one hand to her belt pack, to the length of lightweight rope that was coiled against her thigh. The rope was thin, but strong. And she knew why she had it with her. Without, she would have to dangle here until help arrived or risk almost certain injury by making the thirty-foot leap to the ground.

She uncoiled part of the rope, careful to tie one end securely to her belt. This rope wouldn't do her a whole hell of a lot of good if she went and dropped it.

She craned her neck to study the straps above her head. Her hands were shaking and her stomach was churning, but she told herself over and over again—as if it were a mantra—that she would be okay as long as she didn't look down.

"Are you all right?"

The voice was Harvard's, but P.J. didn't dare look at him. She felt a rush of relief, and it nearly pushed her over an emotional cliff. She took several deep, steadying breaths, forcing back the waves of emotion. God, she couldn't lose it. Not yet. And especially not in front of this man.

"I'm dandy," she said with much more bravado than she felt when she finally could speak. "In fact I'm thinking about having a party up here."

"Damn, I thought for once you'd honestly be glad to see me."

She was. She was thrilled to hear his voice, if not to actually *see* him. But she wasn't about to tell *him* that. "I suppose as long as you're here, you might as well help me figure out a way to get down to the ground." Her voice shook despite her efforts to keep it steady, giving her away.

Somehow he knew to stop teasing her. Somehow he knew that she was way worse off than her shaking voice had revealed.

"Tie one end of the rope around your harness," he told her calmly, his velvet voice soothing and confident. "And toss the rest of the rope up and over that big branch near you. I'll grab the end of the rope, anchoring you. Then you can release your harness from the chute and I'll lower you to the ground."

P.J. was silent, still looking at the white parachute trapped in the tree.

"You've just got to be sure you tie that rope to your harness securely. Can you do that for me, P.J.?"

She was nauseous, she was shaking, but she could still tie a knot. She hoped. "Yes." But there was more here that had to be removed from the tree than just herself. "What about the chute?" she asked.

"The chute's just fine," he told her. "Your priority—and my priority—is to get *you* down out of that tree safely."

"I'm supposed to hide my chute. I don't think leaving it here in this tree like a big white banner fits Lieutenant McCoy's definition of *hide*."

"P.J., it's only an exercise—"

"Throw your rope up to me."

He was silent. P.J. had to go on faith that he was still standing there. She couldn't risk a look in his direction.

"Throw me your rope," she said again. "Please? I can tie your rope around the chute, and then once I'm on the ground, we can try to pull it free."

"You're going to have to look at me if you want to catch it."

She nodded. "I know."

"Tie your rope around your harness first," he told her. "I want to get you secure before we start playing catch."

"Fair enough."

P.J.'s hands were shaking so badly she could barely tie

a knot. But she did it. She tied three different knots, and just as Harvard had told her, she tossed the coil of the rope over a very sturdy-looking branch.

"That's good," Harvard said, approval heating his already warm voice. "You're doing really well."

"Throw me your rope now. Please."

"You ready for me?"

She had to look at him. She lowered her gaze, and the movement of her head made her swing slightly. The ground, the underbrush, the rocks and leaves and Harvard seemed a terrifyingly dizzying distance away. She closed her eyes. "Oh, God, oh, God, oh, God, oh, God..."

"P.J., listen to me." Harvard's voice cut through. "You're safe, do you understand? I'm tying the end of your rope around my waist. I've got you. I *will not* let you fall."

"These knots I tied—they could slip."

"If they do, I swear, I'll catch you."

P.J. was silent, trying desperately to steady her breathing and slow her racing heart. Her stomach churned.

"Did you hear me?" Harvard asked.

"You'll catch me," she repeated faintly. "I know. I know that."

"Unhook your harness from the chute and let me get you down from there."

God, she wanted that. She wanted that so badly. "But I need your rope first."

Harvard laughed in exasperation. "Damn, woman, you're stubborn! This exercise is not that important. It's not that big a deal."

"Maybe not to you, but it is to me."

As Harvard gazed at her, the solution suddenly seemed so obvious. "P.J., you don't have to catch my rope. You don't have to look down. You don't even have to open your eyes. I can tie mine onto the end of yours, and you can just pull it up."

She laughed. It was a thin, scratchy, hugely stressed-out

laugh, but it was laughter just the same. "Well, duh," she said. "Why didn't *I* think of that?"

"It'll only work if you feel secure enough up there without me holding on to my end of your rope."

"Do it," she said. "Just do it, so I can get down from here."

Harvard quickly tied the coiled length of his rope to the end of P.J.'s. "Okay," he called. "Pull it up."

He shaded his eyes, watching as P.J. tugged on the rope that was tied to her harness. She wrapped her rope around her arm between her elbow and her wrist as she took up the slack. He had to admire her control—she was able to think pretty clearly for someone who had been close to panic mere moments before.

She worked quickly and soon tossed the ends of both ropes to the ground.

Harvard looped the rope tied to her harness around his waist and tugged on it, testing the strength of the branch that would support P.J.'s weight.

"Okay, I'm ready for you," he called to her.

This wasn't going to be easy for her. She was going to have to release herself from the chute. She had to have absolute faith that he wouldn't let her fall.

She didn't move, didn't speak. He wasn't sure she was breathing.

"P.J., you've got to trust me," he said quietly, his voice carrying in the stillness of the afternoon.

She nodded. And reached up and unfastened the hooks.

P.J. weighed practically nothing, even with all her gear. He lowered her smoothly, effortlessly, gently, but when her feet hit the ground, her knees gave out and she crumpled, for a moment pressing the front of her helmet to the earth.

He moved quickly toward her as she pushed herself onto her knees. She looked at him as she took off her helmet, and the relief and emotion in her eyes were so profound, Harvard couldn't stop himself. He reached for her, pulling her into his arms and holding her close.

She clung to him, and he could feel her heart still racing, hear her ragged breathing, feel her trembling.

Harvard felt a welling of indescribable emotion. It was an odd mix of tenderness and admiration and sheer, bittersweet longing. This woman fit too damn well in his arms.

"Thank you," she whispered, her face pressed against his shoulder. "Thank you."

"Hey," he said, pulling back slightly and tipping her chin so she had to meet his eyes. "Don't thank me. You did most of that yourself. You did the hard part."

P.J. didn't say anything. She just looked at him with those gigantic brown eyes.

Harvard couldn't help himself. He lowered his mouth the last few inches that separated them and he kissed her.

He heard her sigh as his lips covered hers, and it was that little breathless sound that shattered the very last of his resistance. He deepened the kiss, knowing he shouldn't, but no longer giving a damn.

Her lips were so soft, her mouth so sweet, he felt his control melt like butter in a hot frying pan. He felt his knees grow weak with desire—desire and something else. Something big and frighteningly powerful. He closed his eyes against it, unable to analyze, unable to do anything but kiss her again and again.

He kissed her hungrily now, and P.J. kissed him back so passionately he nearly laughed aloud.

She was like a bolt of lightning in his arms—electrifying to hold. Her body was everything he'd imagined and then some. She was tiny but so perfect, a dizzying mix of firm muscles and soft flesh. He could cover one of her breasts completely with the palm of his hand—he could, and he did.

And she pulled back, away from him, in shock.

"Oh, my God," she breathed, staring at him, eyes wide, breaking free from his arms, moving away from him, scuttling back in the soft dirt on her rear end.

Harvard sat on the ground. "I guess you were a little glad to see me after all, huh?" He meant to sound teasing, his words a pathetic attempt at a joke, but he could do little more than whisper.

"We're late," P.J. said, turning away from him. "We have to hurry. I really screwed up our time."

She pushed herself to her feet, her fingers fumbling as she unbuckled the harness and stepped out of the jumpsuit she wore over her fatigues and T-shirt. As Harvard watched, she took the rope attached to the chute and tried to finesse the snagged fabric and lines out of the tree.

Luck combined with the fact that her body weight was no longer keeping the chute hooked in the branches, and it slid cooperatively down to the ground, covering P.J. completely.

By the time Harvard stood to help her, she'd wrestled the parachute silk into a relatively small bundle and secured both it and her flight suit beneath a particularly thick growth of brambles.

She swayed slightly as she consulted the tiny compass on her wristwatch. "This way," she said, pointing to the east.

Harvard couldn't keep his exasperation from sounding in his voice. Exasperation and frustration. "You don't really think you're going to walk all the way to the extraction site."

"No," she said, lifting her chin defiantly. "I'm not going to walk, I'm going to run."

P.J. stared at the list of times each of the pairs of SEALs and FInCOM agents had clocked during the afternoon's exercise.

"I don't see what the big deal is," Schneider said with a nonchalant shrug.

P.J. gave him an incredulous look. "Crash and Lucky took fourteen and a half minutes to check in at the extraction site—fourteen and a half minutes from the time they stepped out of the airplane to the time they arrived at the final destination. Bobby and Wes took a few seconds longer. You don't see the big difference between those times and the sixty-nine big, fat minutes you and Greene took? Or how about the forty-four minutes it took Lieutenant McCoy because he was saddled with Tim Farber? Or my score—forty-eight embarrassingly long minutes, even though I was working with the Senior Chief? Don't you see a pattern here?"

Farber cleared his throat. "Lieutenant McCoy was not *saddled* with me—"

"No?" P.J. was hot and tired and dizzy and feeling as if she might throw up. Again. She'd had to take a forced time-out during the run from the LZ to the check-in point. Her chicken-salad sandwich had had the final say in their ongoing argument, and she'd surrendered to its unconditional demands right there in the woods. Harvard had gotten out his radio and had been ready to call for medical assistance, but she'd staggered to her feet and told him to put the damn thing away. No way was she going to quit—not after she'd come so far. Something in her eyes must have convinced him she was dead serious, because he'd done as she'd ordered.

She'd made it all the way back—forty-eight minutes after she'd stepped out of that plane.

"Look at the numbers again, Tim," she told Farber. "I know for a fact that if the Senior Chief had been paired with Lieutenant McCoy, they would have a time of about fifteen minutes. Instead, their time was not just doubled but *tripled* because they were saddled with inexperienced teammates."

"That was the first time I've ever jumped out of a plane," Greg Greene protested. "We can't be expected to perform like the SEALs without the same extensive training."

"But that's exactly the point," P.J. argued. "There's no way FInCOM can provide us with the kind of training the Navy gives the SEAL teams. It's insane for them to think something like this Combined SEAL/FInCOM team could work with any efficiency. These numbers are proof. Alpha Squad can get the job done better and faster—not just twice as fast but three times faster—without our so-called help."

"I'm sure with a little practice—" Tim Farber started.

"We might only slow them down half as much?" P.J. interjected. She looked up to see Harvard leaning against a tree watching her. She quickly looked away, afraid he would somehow see the heat that instantly flamed in her cheeks.

She'd lost her mind this afternoon, and she'd let him kiss her.

No, correction—she hadn't merely let him kiss her. She'd kissed him just as enthusiastically. She could still feel the impossibly intimate sensation of his hand curved around her breast.

Dear Lord, she hadn't known something as simple as a touch could feel so good.

As Farber and the twin idiots wandered away, clearly not interested in hearing any more of her observations, Harvard pushed himself up and away from the tree. He took his time to approach her, a small smile lifting the corners of his lips. "You up for a ride to your hotel, or do you intend to run back?"

Her lips were dry, and when she moistened them with the tip of her tongue, Harvard's gaze dropped to her mouth and lingered there. When he looked into her eyes, she could see an echo of the flames they'd ignited earlier that day.

His smile was gone, and the look on his face was pure predator.

She didn't stand a chance against this man.

The thought popped into her head, but she pushed it far away. That was ridiculous. Of course she stood a chance. She'd been approached and hit on and propositioned and pursued by all types of men. Harvard was no different.

So what if he was taller and stronger and ten times more dangerously handsome than any man she'd ever met? So what if a keen intelligence sparkled in his eyes? So what if his voice was like velvet and his smile like a sunrise? And so what if he'd totally redefined the word *kiss*—not to mention given new meaning to other words she'd ignored in the past, words like *desire* and *want*.

Part of her wanted him to kiss her again. But the part of her that wanted that was the same part that had urged her, at age eleven, to let fourteen-year-old Jackson Porter steal a kiss in the alley alongside the corner market. It was the same part of her that could so easily have followed her mother's not quite full-grown footsteps. But P.J. had successfully stomped that impractical, romantically, childishly foolish side of her down before. Lord knows she could do it again.

She wasn't sure she was ready yet to risk her freedom—not even for a chance to be with a man like Daryl Becker.

"Come on." Harvard took her arm and led her toward the road. "I confiscated a jeep. You look as if you could use about twelve straight hours with your eyes shut."

"My car's at the base."

"You can pick it up tomorrow morning. I'll give you a lift back."

P.J. glanced at him, wondering if she'd imagined the implication of his suggestion—that he would still be with her come morning.

He opened the door of the jeep and would probably have

lifted her onto the seat if she hadn't climbed in. She closed the door before he could do that for her.

He smiled, acknowledging her feminist stance, and she had to look away.

As Harvard climbed into the jeep and turned the key in the ignition, he glanced at her again. P.J. braced herself, waiting for him to say something, waiting for him to bring up the subject of that incredible, fantastic and absolutely inappropriate kiss.

But he was silent. He didn't say a word the entire way to the hotel. And when he reached the driveway, he didn't park. He pulled up front, beneath the hotel overhang, to drop her off.

P.J. used her best poker face to keep her surprise from showing. "Thanks for the ride, Senior Chief."

"How about I pick you up at 0730 tomorrow?"

She shook her head. "It's out of your way. I can arrange to get to the base with Schneider or Greene."

He nodded, squinting in the late-afternoon sunlight as he gazed out the front windshield. "It's not that big a deal, and I'd like to pick you up. So I'll be here at 0730." He turned to look at her. "What I'd *really* like is to *still* be here at 0730." He smiled slightly. "It's not too late to invite me in."

P.J. had to look away, her heart pounding almost as hard as it had been when she was hanging in that tree. "I can't do that."

"That's too bad."

"Yeah," she agreed, surprising herself by saying it aloud. She unlatched the door. She had to get out of there. God knows what else she might say.

"I'll see you at 0730," he said. "Right here."

P.J. nodded. She didn't want to give in, but it seemed the easiest way to get him to take his bedroom eyes and those too-tempting lips and drive away. "All right."

She pulled her aching body from the jeep.

"I was really proud to know you today, Richards," Harvard said softly. "You proved to me that you can handle damn near anything. There're very few men—except for those in the teams—I can say *that* about."

She looked at him in surprise, but he didn't stop. "You've done one hell of a good job consistently from day one," Harvard continued. "I have to admit, I didn't think a woman could cut it, but I'm glad you're part of the CSF team."

P.J. snorted, then laughed. Then laughed even harder. "Wow," she said when she caught her breath. "You must *really* want to sleep with me."

A flurry of emotions crossed his face. For the briefest of moments, he looked affronted. But then he smiled, shaking his head in amused resignation. "Yeah, I haven't given you much to work with here, have I? There's no real reason you should believe me." But he caught and held her gaze, his eyes nearly piercing in their intensity. "But I meant what I said. It wasn't some kind of line. I was really proud of you today, P.J."

"And naturally, whenever you're proud of one of your teammates, you French kiss 'em."

Harvard laughed at her bluntness. "No, ma'am. That was the first time I've ever had *that* experience while on an op."

"Hmm," she said.

"Yeah, what's that supposed to mean? *Hmm?*"

"It means maybe you should think about what it would be like to be in my shoes. You just told me you think I'm more capable than most of the men you know, didn't you?"

He held her gaze steadily. "That's right."

"Yet you can't deal with me as an equal. You're impressed with me as a person, but that doesn't fit with what you know about the world. So you do the only thing you can do. You bring sex into the picture. You try to dominate and control. You may well be proud of me, brother, but you don't want those feelings to last. You want to put me back in my nice, safe place. You want to slide me into a role you can deal with—a role like lover, that you understand. So *hmm* means you should think about the way that might make *me* feel." P.J. closed the door to the jeep.

She didn't give him time to comment. She turned and walked into the hotel.

She didn't look back, but she felt his eyes on her, watching her, until she was completely out of his line of sight.

And even then, she felt the lingering power of Harvard's eyes.

CHAPTER NINE

HARVARD DIDN'T CATCH UP TO P.J. until after lunch. She'd
left messages on his voice mail—both at home and in the
office—telling him not to bother giving her a ride to the
base in the morning. She was going in early, and it worked
for her to catch a ride with Chuck Schneider.

He'd tried phoning her back, but the hotel was holding
her calls.

Harvard had thought about everything she said to him as
she got out of the jeep last night. He'd thought hard about
it well into the early hours of the morning. And he thought
about it first thing when he woke up, as well.

But it wasn't until they were both heading to a meeting
at the Quonset hut after lunch that he was able to snatch a
few seconds to talk to her.

"You're wrong," he said without any ceremony, without
even the civility of a greeting.

P.J. glanced at him, then glanced at Farber, who was
walking alongside Joe Cat. The two men were a few yards
ahead of her. She slowed her pace, clearly not wanting
either of them to overhear.

But there was nothing to overhear. "Now's not the time
to get into this discussion," Harvard continued. "But I just
wanted you to know that I've thought—very carefully—
about everything you said, and my conclusion is that you're
totally off base."

"But—"

He opened the door to the Quonset hut and held it for
her, gesturing for her to go in first. "I'd be more than happy

to sit down with you this evening, maybe have an iced tea or two, and talk this through."

She didn't answer. She didn't say yes, but she didn't give him an immediate and unequivocal no, either.

Harvard took that as a good sign.

The main room in the Quonset hut had been set up as a briefing area.

Harvard moved to the front of the room to stand next to Joe Cat and Blue. He watched as P.J. took a seat. She made a point not to look at him. In fact, she looked damn near everywhere *but* at him.

That was, perhaps, *not* such a good sign.

P.J. paid rapt attention to Joe Cat as he outlined the exercise that would take place over the next few days. Day one would be preparation. The CSF team would receive Intel reports about a mock hostage situation. Day two would be the first phase of the rescue—location and reconnaissance of the tangos holding the hostages. Day three would be the rescue.

Harvard looked at the four finks sitting surrounded by the men of Alpha Squad. Schneider and Greene looked perpetually bored, as usual. Farber looked slightly disattached, as if his thoughts weren't one hundred percent on the project being discussed. And P.J.... As the captain continued to talk, P.J. looked more and more perplexed and more and more uncomfortable. She shifted in her seat and glanced at Farber and the others but got no response from them. She risked a glance in Harvard's direction.

There were about a million questions in her eyes, and he suspected he knew exactly what she wanted answered.

She finally raised her hand. "Excuse me, Captain, I'm not sure I understand."

"I'm afraid I can't go into any specifics at this time," Cat told her. "In order for this training op to run effectively, I can't give you any further information than I already have."

"Begging your pardon, sir," P.J. said, "but it seems to me that you've already given us too much information. That's what I don't understand. You've tipped us off as to the nature of this exercise. And what's the deal with giving us an entire day to prepare? In a real-life scenario, we'll have no warning. And everything I've learned from you to date stresses the importance of immediate action. Sitting around with an entire day of prep time doesn't read as immediate in my book."

Joe Cat moved to the front of the desk he'd been standing behind, sat on the edge and looked at P.J. He didn't speak for several long moments. "Anything else bothering you, Richards?" he finally asked.

As Harvard watched, P.J. nodded. "Yes, sir. I'm wondering why the location of the terrorists and the rescue attempt will take place over the course of two individual days in two different phases of activity. That also doesn't gel with a realistic rescue scenario. In the real world," she said, using the SEAL slang for genuine real-life operations, "we wouldn't go back to our hotel for a good night's sleep in the middle of a hostage crisis. I don't understand why we're going to be doing that here."

The captain glanced first at Blue and then at Harvard. Then he turned to the other finks. "Anyone else have the same problems Ms. Richards is having?" he asked. "Mr. Farber? You have any problems with our procedure?"

Farber straightened up, snapping to attention. As Harvard watched, he saw the FInCOM agent study the captain's face, trying to read from Joe's expression whether he should agree or disagree.

"He's looking for your *opinion,* Mr. Farber," Harvard indicated. "There's no right answer."

Farber shrugged. "Then I guess I'd have to say no. A training exercise is a training exercise. We go into it well aware that it's make-believe. There're no real hostages, and there's no real danger. So there's no real point to working around the clock to—"

"Wrong," Harvard interrupted loudly. "There's no right answer, but there *are* wrong answers, and you're wrong. There's a list of reasons longer than my—" he glanced at P.J. "—arm as to why it's vitally necessary to train under conditions that are as realistic as possible."

"Then why are we wasting our time with this half-baked exercise?" P.J. interjected.

"Because FInCOM gave us a rule book," Joe explained, "that outlined in pretty specific detail exactly what we could and could not subject the CSF agents to. We're limited to working within any given ten-hour period. We can't exceed that without providing you with a minimum of eight hours downtime."

"But that's absurd," P.J. protested. "With those restrictions, there's no way we're going to be able to set up a scenario that has any basis in reality. I mean, part of the challenge of dealing with the stress of a hostage crisis is coping with little or no sleep, of being on the job forty-eight or seventy-two or—God!—ninety hours in a row. Of catching naps in the back of a car or in the middle of the woods or... This is ludicrous." She gestured toward herself and the other FInCOM agents. "We're big boys and girls. We've all been on assignments that have required us to work around the clock. What's the deal?"

"Someone upstairs at FInCOM is afraid of the SEAL teams," Joe said. "I think *they* think we're going to try to drag you through some version of BUD/S training. We've tried to assure them that's not possible or even desirable. We've been actively trying to persuade FInCOM to revise that restrictive rule for weeks now. Months."

"This is just plain stupid." P.J. wasn't mincing words. "I can't believe Kevin Laughton would agree to this."

Harvard stepped forward again. "We haven't been able

to reach Laughton," he told her. "Apparently the man has dropped off the face of the earth."

P.J. looked at her watch, looked at the *Baywatch* calendar that was pinned to the wall near Wesley's computer. "Of course you haven't been able to reach him. Because he's on vacation," she said. "He's got a beach house on Pawley's Island in South Carolina." She stood. "Captain, if you let me use your office, I can call him right now—at least make him aware of the situation."

"You have the phone number of Laughton's vacation house?" Harvard couldn't keep from asking. P.J. and Laughton. There was that image again. He liked it even less today.

P.J. didn't answer. Joe had already led her into his office, shutting the door behind her to give her privacy.

Harvard turned to the finks and SEALs still sitting in rows. "I think we're done here for now," he said, dismissing them.

He turned to find the captain and Blue exchanging a long look.

"How well does she know Laughton, anyway?" Joe murmured.

Blue didn't answer, but Harvard knew exactly what both men were thinking. If she knew her boss well enough to have his home phone number, she knew him pretty damn well.

The call came within two hours.

Harvard was surfing the net, wondering how long he'd have to wait before he could head over to P.J.'s hotel, wondering if she'd agree to have a drink with him or if she'd hide in her room, not answer the phone when he called from the lobby.

Wondering exactly what her connection to Kevin Laughton was.

The phone rang, and Wes scooped it up. "Skelly." He

sat a little straighter. "Yes, sir. One moment, Admiral, sir." He put the call on hold. "Captain, Admiral Stonegate on line one."

Joe went into his office to take the call. Blue went in with him, closing the door tightly behind them both.

"That was too quick." Lucky was the first to speak, looking up from his computerized game of golf. "He's either not calling about the FInCOM project or he's calling to say no."

"How well does P.J. know Kevin Laughton?" Bobby put down his book to voice the question they all were thinking.

"How well do you have to know a girl before you give her the phone number of your beach house?" Wes countered.

"I don't have a beach house," Bobby pointed out.

"Suppose that you did."

"I guess it would really depend on how much I liked the girl."

"And what the girl looks like," Lucky added.

"We know what the girl looks like," Wes said. "She looks like P.J. *Exactly* like P.J. She *is* P.J."

"For P.J., I'd consider going out and buying a beach house, just so I could give her my number there," Bobby decided.

Harvard spun around in his chair, unable to listen to any more inane speculation. "The girl is a *woman* and her ears are probably ringing with all this talk about her. Show a little respect here. So she had her boss's phone number. So what?"

"The Senior Chief is probably right," Wes said with a grin. "Laughton probably gives his vacation phone number to all the agents he works with—not just the beautiful female agents he's sleeping with."

Crash spoke. He'd been so quiet, Harvard had almost forgotten he was in the room. "I've heard that Laughton just got married. He doesn't seem to be the kind of man who would cheat on his wife—let alone a bride of less than a year."

"And P.J.'s not the kind of woman who would get with a married man," Harvard added, trying to convince himself, as well. He'd come to know P.J. well over the past few weeks. He shouldn't doubt her, but still, there was this tiny echo of a voice that kept asking, *Are you sure?*

"I'm friends with a guy who's working for the San Diego police," Lucky said, opening the wrapper of a granola bar. "He said working with women in the squad adds all kinds of craziness to the usual stress of the job. If you're working a case with a female partner and there's any kind of attraction there at all, it can easily get blown out of proportion. Think about it. You know how everything gets heightened when you're out on an op."

Harvard kept his face carefully expressionless. He knew firsthand what that was about. He'd experienced it yesterday afternoon.

The captain came out of his office, grinning. "We got it," he announced. "Permission to trash the rule book *and* permission to take our little finks out of the country for some on-location fun and games. We're going west, guys—so far west, it's east. Whatever P.J. said to Kevin Laughton—it had an impact."

"There's your proof," Lucky said. "She calls Laughton, two hours later, major policies are changed. She's doin' him. Gotta be."

Harvard had had enough. He stood up, the wheels of his chair rattling across the concrete floor. "Has it occurred to you that Laughton *might* have responded so quickly because he respects and values P.J.'s opinion as a member of his staff?"

Lucky took another bite of his granola bar, thinking for a moment while he chewed. "No," he said with his mouth full. "She's not interested in any kind of new relationship—she told me that herself. She doesn't want a *new* relationship because she's already got an *old* relationship. With Kevin Laughton."

Harvard laughed in disbelief. "You're speculating." He turned to the captain. "Why are we talking about this? P.J.'s relationship with Laughton is none of our damned business—whatever it may be."

"Amen to that," Joe Cat said. "The exercise start date has been pushed back two days," he announced. "Anyone on the CSF team should take a few days of leave, get some rest." He looked at Crash. "Sorry, Hawken. I know you're going to be disappointed, but apparently there are a few Marines who've been working with the locals, and they're going to be our terrorists for this exercise. You're going to have to go along as one of the good guys."

Crash's lips moved into what might have been a smile. "Too bad."

The captain looked at Harvard. "We're going to have to notify P.J. and the other finks—let 'em know we're heading to Southeast Asia."

"I'll take care of that," Harvard said.

Joe Cat smiled. "I figured you'd want to."

"Make sure you tell 'em to put their wills and personal effects in order," Wes said with a grin that dripped pure mischief. "Because from now on, there're no rules."

P.J. finished the steak and baked potato she'd ordered from room service and set the tray in the hall outside her room. She showered and pulled on a clean T-shirt and a pair of cutoff sweatpants and then, only then, did she phone the hotel desk and ask them to stop holding her calls.

There was a message on her voice mail from Kevin, telling her he'd managed to pull the necessary strings. The CSF team project would be given the elbow room it needed, without interference.

There was also a message from Harvard—"Call me. It's important." He'd left his beeper number.

P.J. wrote the number down.

She knew he wanted to talk to her, to try to convince her he didn't want to have sex with her in an attempt to dominate and put her securely in her place as first and foremost a woman. No, his feelings of desire had grown out of the extreme respect he had for her, and from his realization that gender didn't matter in the work she did.

Yeah, right.

Of course, he might have asked her to call so he could give her some important work-related information. Kevin's message meant there was bound to be some news.

As much as she didn't want to—and she didn't want to call Harvard, she told herself—she was going to have to.

But first she had more important things to do, such as checking in with the weather channel, to see if Mr. Murphy was going to send a tropical depression into their midst on the days they were scheduled to battle the steely-eyed Lieutenant William Hawken and his merry band of mock terrorists.

The phone rang before she'd keyed up the weather channel with the remote control.

P.J. hit the mute button and picked up the call. "Richards."

"Yo, it's H. Did you just page me?"

P.J. closed her eyes. "No. No, not yet. I was going to, but—"

"Good, you got my message, at least. Why don't you come down to the bar and—"

P.J. forced herself to sound neutral and pleasant. "Thanks, but no. I'm ready for bed—"

"It's only twenty hundred." His voice nearly cracked in disbelief. "You can't be serious—"

"I'm very serious. We've got some tough days ahead of

us, starting tomorrow," she told him. "I intend to sleep as much now as I possibly—"

"Starting tomorrow, we've got two days of leave," he interrupted her.

Of all the things she'd expected him to say, that wasn't on the list. "We do?"

"We'll be boarding a plane for Southeast Asia on Thursday. Until then we've got a break."

"Southeast Asia?" P.J. laughed, tickled with delight. "Kevin really came through, didn't he? What a guy! He deserves something special for this one. I'm going to have to think long and hard."

On the other end of the line, Harvard was silent. When he finally spoke, his voice sounded different. Stiffer. More formal. "Richards, come downstairs. We really have to talk."

Now the silence was all hers. P.J. took a deep breath. "Daryl, I'm sorry. I don't think it's—"

"All right. Then I'll be right up."

"No—"

He'd already hung up.

P.J. swore sharply, then threw the phone's handset into the cradle with a clatter. Her bed was a rumpled mess of unmade blankets and sheets, her pillow slightly indented from her late-afternoon nap.

She didn't want to make her bed. She wasn't going to make her bed, damn it. She'd meet him at the door, and they'd step outside into that little lobby near the elevators to talk. He'd say whatever it was he had to say, she'd turn him down one more time, and then she'd go back into her room.

He knocked, and P.J. quickly rifled through the mess on the dresser to find her key card. Slipping it into the pocket of her shorts, she went to the door. She peeked out the peephole. Yeah, it was definitely Harvard. She opened the door.

He wasn't smiling. He was just standing there, so big and forbidding. "May I come in?"

P.J. forced a smile. "Maybe we should talk outside."

Harvard glanced over his shoulder, and she realized there were people sitting on the sofa and chairs by the elevators. "I would prefer the privacy of your room. But if you're uncomfortable with that…"

Admitting she had a problem sitting down and talking to Harvard in the intimate setting of her hotel room would be tantamount to admitting she was not immune to his magnetic sexuality. Yes, she *was* uncomfortable. But her discomfort was not because she was afraid he would try to seduce her—that was a given. Her discomfort came from her fear that once he started touching her, once he started kissing her, she wouldn't have the strength to turn him down.

And God help her if *he* ever realized that.

"I just want to talk to you," he said, searching her eyes. "Throw on a pair of shoes and we can go for a walk. I'll wait for you by the elevator," he added when she hesitated.

It was a good solution. She didn't have to change out of her shorts and T-shirt to go to the bar, but she didn't have to let him into her room, either.

"I'll be right there," P.J. told him.

It took a moment to find her sandals under the piles of dirty clothes scattered around the room. She finally slipped her feet into them and, taking a deep breath, left her room.

Harvard was holding an elevator, and he followed her in and pushed the button for the main floor of the big hotel complex. He was silent all the way down, silent as she led the way out of the hotel lobby and headed toward the glistening water of the swimming pool.

The sky was streaked with the colors of the setting sun, and the early evening still held the muggy heat of the day. A family—mother, father, two young children—were in

the pool, and several couples, one elderly, the other achingly young, sat in the row of lounge chairs watching the
first stars of the evening appear.

Harvard was silent until they had walked to the other
side of the pool.

"I have a question for you," he finally said, leaning
against the railing that overlooked the deep end. "A
personal question. And I keep thinking, this is not my
business. But then I keep thinking that in a way, it *is* my
business, because it affects me and…" He took a deep
breath, letting it out in a burst of air. "I'm talking all around
it, aren't I? I suppose the best way to ask is simply to ask
point-blank."

P.J. could feel tension creeping into her shoulders and
neck. He wanted to ask a personal question. Was it possible
he'd somehow guessed? He was, after all, a very perceptive
man. Was it possible he'd figured it out from those kisses
they'd shared?

She took a deep breath. Maybe it was better that he
knew. On the other hand, maybe it wasn't. Maybe he'd
take it—and her—as some kind of a challenge.

"You can ask whatever you want," she told him, "but I
can't promise I'm going to answer."

He turned toward her, his face shadowed in the rapidly fading light. "Is the reason you've been pushing me
away—"

Here it came.

"—because of your relationship with Kevin
Laughton?"

P.J. heard the words, but they were so different from
the ones she'd been expecting, it took a moment for her to
understand what he'd asked.

Kevin Laughton. Relationship. *Relationship?*

But then she understood. She understood far too well.

"You think because I have Kevin's home number, because I have direct access to the man when he's on vacation,

that I must be getting it on with him, don't you?" She shook her head in disgust, moving away from him. "I should've known. With men like you, everything always comes down to sex."

Harvard followed her. "P.J., wait. Talk to me. Are you saying no? Are you saying there's nothing going on between you and Laughton?"

She turned to face him. "The only thing going on between me and Kevin—besides our highly exemplary work relationship—is a solid friendship. Kind of like what I *thought* you and I had going between us. The man is married to one of my best friends from college, a former roommate of mine. I introduced them because I like Kevin and I thought Elaine would like him even more, in a different way. I was right, and they got married last year. The three of us continue to be good friends. I've spent time at the beach house on Pawley's Island with the two of them. Does that satisfy your sordid curiosity?"

"P.J., I'm sorry—"

"Not half as sorry as I am. Let me guess—the whole damned Alpha Squad is speculating as to how many different times and different ways I've had to get it on with Kevin in order to get his home phone number, right?" P.J. didn't give him a chance to answer. "But if I were a man, everyone would've just assumed I was someone who had earned Kevin Laughton's trust through hard work."

"You're right to be upset," Harvard said. "It was wrong of me to think that way. I was jealous—"

"I bet you were," she said sharply. "You were probably thinking it wasn't fair—Kevin getting some, you not getting any."

She turned to walk away, but he moved quickly, blocking her path. "I'd be lying if I said sex didn't play a part in the way I was feeling," Harvard said, his voice low. "But there's so much more to this thing we've got going—this *friendship,* I guess I'd have to call it for lack of a better name. In a lot of ways, the relationship you have with Laughton is far more intimate than any kind of casual sexual fling might be. And I'm standing here feeling even more jealous about that. I know it's stupid, but I like you too much to want to share you with anyone else."

The edge on P.J.'s anger instantly softened. This man sure could talk a good game. And the look in his eyes was enough to convince her he wasn't just slinging around slick, empty words. He was confused by having a real friendship with a woman, and honest enough to admit it.

"Friends don't own friends," she told him gently. "In fact, I thought the entire issue of people owning other people was taken care of a few hundred years ago."

Harvard smiled. "I don't want to own you."

"Are you sure about that?"

Harvard was silent for a moment, gazing into her eyes. "I want to be your lover," he told her. "And maybe your experiences with other men have led you to believe that means I want to dominate and control—as you so aptly put it the other day. And while I'd truly love to make you beg, chances are if we ever get into that kind of…position, you're going to be hearing *me* do some begging, too."

He was moving closer, an inch at a time, but P.J. was frozen in place, pinned by the look in his eyes and the heat of his soft words. He touched the side of her face, gently skimming the tips of his fingers across her cheek.

"We've played it your way, and we're friends, P.J.," he said softly. "I like being your friend, but there's more that I want to share with you. Much more.

"We can go into this with our eyes open," he continued. "We can go upstairs to your room, and you can lend yourself to me tonight—and I'll lend myself to you. No ownership, no problems." Harvard ran his thumb across her lips. "We can lock your door and we don't have to come out for two whole days."

He lowered his head to kiss her softly, gently. P.J. felt

herself sway toward him, felt herself weakening. Two whole days in this man's arms… Never in her life had she been so tempted.

"Let's go upstairs," he whispered. He kissed her again, just as sweetly, as if he'd realized that gentle finesse would get him further than soul-stealing passion.

But then he stepped away from her, and P.J. realized that all around the pool, lights were going on. One went on directly overhead, and they were no longer hidden by the shadows of the dusk. Harvard still held her hand, though, drawing languorous circles on her palm with his thumb.

He was looking at her as if she were the smartest, sexiest, most desirable woman on the entire planet. And she knew that she was looking at him with an equal amount of hunger in her eyes.

She wanted him.

Worst of all, despite her words, she knew she wanted to own him. Heart, body and soul, she wanted this incredible man for herself and herself alone, and that scared her damn near witless.

She turned away, pulling from his grasp, pressing the palms of her hands against the rough wood of the railing, trying to rid herself of the lingering ghost of his touch.

"This is a really bad idea." She had to work hard, and even then her voice sounded thin and fluttery.

He stepped closer, close enough so she could feel his body heat but not quite close enough to touch her. "Logically, yes," he murmured. "Logically, it's insane. But sometimes you've got to go with your gut—and I'm telling you, P.J., every instinct I've got is screaming that this is the best idea I've had in my entire life."

All *her* instincts were screaming, too. But they were screaming the opposite. *This may well be the right man, but was* so *the wrong time.*

Those treacherous, treasonous feelings she was having—the crazy need to possess this man—had to be stomped down, hidden away. She had to push these thoughts far from her, and even though she was by no means an expert when it came to intimate relationships, she knew that getting naked with Harvard Becker would only make things worse.

She had to be able to look at him, to work with him over the next few weeks and be cool and rational.

She wasn't sure she could spend two days making love to him and then pretend there was nothing between them. She wasn't that good an actor.

"Daryl, I can't," she whispered.

He'd been holding his breath, she realized, and he let it out in a rush that was half laughter. "I would say, give me one good reason, except I'm pretty sure you've got a half a dozen all ready and waiting, reasons I haven't even thought of."

She *did* have half a dozen reasons, but they were all reasons she couldn't share with him. How could she tell him she couldn't risk becoming intimate because she was afraid of falling in love with him?

But she did have one reason she knew he would understand. She took a deep breath. "I've never been with… anyone."

Harvard didn't understand what P.J. meant. He knew she was telling him something important—he could see that in her eyes. But he couldn't make sense of her words. Never been where?

"You know, I've always hated the word virgin," P.J. told him, and suddenly what she'd said clicked. "I came from a neighborhood where eleven-year-old girls were taunted by classmates for still being virgins."

Harvard couldn't help laughing in disbelief. "No way. Are you telling me you're—" Damn, he couldn't even say the word.

"A virgin."

That was the word. Turning her to face him and

searching her eyes, he stopped laughing. "My God, you're serious, aren't you?"

"I used to lie about it," she told him, pulling away to look out over the swimming pool. "Even when I went to college where, you know, you'd expect people to be cool about whatever personal choices other people make in their lives, I had to lie. For some reason, it was okay to be celibate for—well, you name the reason—taking time off from the dating scene, or concentrating on grades for a while, or finding your own space—but it was only okay if you'd been sexually active in the past. But as soon as people found out you were a virgin, God, it was as if you had some disease you had to be cured of as soon as possible. Forget about personal choice. I watched other girls get talked into doing things they didn't really want to do with boys they didn't really like, and so I just kept on lying."

She turned to face him then. "But I didn't want to lie to you."

Harvard cleared his throat. He cleared it again. "I'm, um…"

She smiled. "Look at you. I've managed to shock Alpha Squad's mighty Senior Chief."

Harvard found his voice. "Yes," he said. "Shocked is a good word for it."

She was standing there in front of him, waiting. For what? He wasn't quite sure of the protocol when the woman he'd been ferociously trying to seduce all evening admitted she'd never been with a man before.

Some men might take her words as a challenge. Here was a big chance to boldly go where no man had gone before. The prospect could be dizzyingly exciting—until the looming responsibility of such an endeavor came lumbering into view.

This woman had probably turned down dozens, maybe even *hundreds* of men. The fact that she clearly saw him as a major temptation was outrageously flattering, but it was frightening, too.

What if he *could* apply the right amount of sweet talk and pressure to make her give in? What if he *did* go up to her room with her tonight? This would not be just another casual romantic interlude. This would be an important event. Was he ready for that? Was he ready for this woman to get caught up in the whirlwind of physical sensations and mistake a solid sexual encounter for something deeper, like love?

Harvard looked into P.J.'s eyes. "What I want to know is what drives a person to keep one very significant part of her life locked up tight for so many years," he said. "An incredible, vibrant, *passionate* woman like you. It's not like you couldn't have your pick of men."

"When I was a little girl, no more than five or six years old," she told him quietly, "I decided I was going to wait to find a man who would love me enough to marry me first, you know? I didn't really know too much about sex at the time, but I knew that both my grandmother and my mother *hadn't waited*—whatever that meant. I saw all these girls in the neighborhood with their big expanding bellies— girls who hadn't waited. It was always whispered. Priscilla Simons hadn't waited. Cheri Richards hadn't waited. I decided I was going to wait.

"And then when I *did* start to understand, I was all caught up in the books I read. I was hooked on that fairy-tale myth—you know, waiting on Prince Charming. That carried me through quite a few years."

Harvard stayed quiet, waiting for her to go on.

P.J. sighed. "I still sometimes wish life could be that simple, though I'm well aware it's not. I may never have been with a man, but I'm no innocent. I know that no man in his right mind is going to be foolish enough to marry a woman without taking her for a test drive, so to speak. And no woman should do that, either. Sexual compatibility is important in a relationship. I do believe that. But deep inside, I've got this little girl who's just sitting there, quietly waiting." She laughed, shaking her head. "I see that nervous look in your eyes. Don't worry. I'm not hinting for a marriage proposal or anything. Being tied down is the *last* thing I want or need. See, as I got older, I saw more and more of the pitiful samples of men my mother collected, and I started to think maybe marriage *wasn't* what I wanted. I mean, who in her right mind would want to be permanently tied to one of these losers? Not me."

Harvard found his voice. "But not all men are losers."

"I know that. As I got older, my scope of experience widened, and I met men who weren't drug dealers or thieves. I made friends with some of them. But only friends. I guess old habits die hard. Or maybe I never really trusted any of them. Or maybe I just never met anyone I've wanted to get with." *Until now.* P.J. didn't say the words aloud, but they hung between them as clear as the words in a cartoon bubble.

"I'm not telling you this to create some kind of challenge for you," she added, as if she'd been able to read his mind. "I'm just trying to explain where I'm coming from and why now probably isn't the best time for me and you."

Probably isn't wasn't the same as just plain *isn't*. Harvard knew that if he was going to talk her into inviting him upstairs, now was the time. He should move closer, touch the side of her face, let her see the heat in his eyes. He should talk his way into her room. He should tell her there was so much more for them to say.

But he couldn't do it. Not without really thinking it through. Instead of reaching for her, he rested his elbows on the railing. "It's okay," he said softly. "I can see how this complicates things—for me as well as for you."

The look in her eyes nearly killed him. She managed to look both relieved *and* disappointed.

They stood together in silence for several long moments. Then P.J. finally sighed.

Harvard had to hold tightly to the railing to keep from following her as she backed away.

"I'm, uh, I guess I'm going to go back up. To my room. Now."

Harvard nodded. "Good night."

She turned and walked away. He stared at the reflected lights dancing on the surface of the swimming pool, thinking about the life P.J. had had as a child, thinking about all she'd had to overcome, thinking about how strong she must've been even as a tiny little girl, thinking about her up there in that tree, getting the job done despite her fears, thinking about the sweet taste of her kisses….

And thinking that having a woman like that fall in love with him might not be the worst thing in the world.

CHAPTER TEN

THE FIRST RING jarred her out of a deep sleep.

The second ring made P.J. roll over and squint at the clock.

She picked up the phone on the third ring. "It's five forty-five, I've got my first morning off in more than four weeks. This better be notification from the lottery commission that I've just won megabucks."

"What if I told you I was calling with an offer that was better than winning megabucks?"

Harvard. It was Harvard.

P.J. sat up, instantly awake. She had been so certain her blunt-edged honesty had scared him to death. She'd been convinced her words had sent him running far away from her as fast as his legs could carry him. She'd spent most of last night wondering and worrying if the little news bomb she'd dropped on him had blown up their entire friendship.

She'd spent most of last night realizing how much she'd come to value him as a friend.

"I was positive you'd be awake," he said cheerfully, as if nothing even the slightest bit heavy had transpired between them. "I pictured you already finishing up your first seven-mile run of the day. Instead, what do I find? You're still studying the insides of your eyelids! You're absolutely unaware that the sun is up and shining and that it is a perfect day for a trip to Phoenix, Arizona."

"I can't believe you woke me up at five forty-five on one of only two days I have to sleep late for the next four weeks," P.J. complained, trying to play it cool. She was afraid to acknowledge how glad she was he'd called even to herself, let alone to *him*.

But she hadn't scared him away. They were still friends. And she was very, very glad.

"Yeah, I know it's early," he said, "but I thought the idea of heading into the heart of the desert during the hottest part of the summer would be something you'd find irresistible."

"Better than winning megabucks, huh?"

"Not to mention the additional bonus—the chance to see my parents' new house."

"You are *such* a chicken," P.J. said. "This doesn't have anything to do with me wanting to see the desert. This is all about *you* having to deal with seeing your parents' new house for the first time. Poor baby needs someone to come along and hold his hand."

"You're right," he said, suddenly serious. "I'm terrified. I figure I could either do this the hard way and just suck it up and go, or I could make it a whole hell of a lot easier and ask you to come along."

P.J. didn't know what to say. She grasped at the first thing that came to mind. "Your parents have barely moved in. They couldn't possibly be ready for extra houseguests."

"I don't know how big their house is," Harvard admitted. "I figured you and I would probably just stay in a hotel. In separate rooms," he added.

P.J. was silent.

"I know what you're thinking," he said.

"Oh, yeah, what's that?"

"You're thinking, the man is dogging me because he wants some."

"The thought *has* crossed my mind—"

"Well, you're both wrong and right," Harvard told her. "You're right about the fact that I want you." He laughed softly. "Yeah, you're real right about that. But I'm not going to chase or pressure you, P.J. I figure, when you're ready, *if* you're ever ready, you'll let me know. And until then, we'll play it your way. I'm asking you to come to Phoenix with me as friends."

P.J. took a deep breath. "What time is the flight?"

"Would you believe in forty-five minutes?"

P.J. laughed. "Yes," she said. "Yes, I'd believe that."

"Meet me out front in ten minutes," he told her. "Carry-on bag only, okay?"

"Daryl!"

"Yeah?"

"Thanks," P.J. said. "Just…thanks."

"I'm the one who should be thanking you for coming with me," he said, just as quietly. He took a deep breath. "Okay," he added much more loudly. "We all done with this heartfelt mushy stuff? Good. Let's go, Richards! Clock's ticking. Downstairs. Nine minutes! Move!"

"I always think about wind shear."

Harvard looked over to find P.J.'s eyes tightly shut as the huge commercial jet lumbered down the runway. She had her usual death grip on the armrests. "Well, don't," he said. "Hold my hand."

She opened one eye and looked at him. "Or I think about the improbability of something this big actually making it off the ground."

He held out his hand, palm up, inviting her to take it. "You want to talk physics, I can give you the 411, as you call it, complete with numbers and equations, on why this sucker flies," he said.

"And then," she said, as if she hadn't heard him at all, "when I hear the wheels retract, I think about how awful it would be to fall."

Harvard pried her fingers from the armrest and placed her hand in his. "I won't let you fall."

She smiled ruefully, pulling her hand free. "When you say it like that, I can almost believe you."

He held her gaze. "It's okay if you hold my hand."

"No, it's not."

"Friends can hold hands."

P.J. snorted. "Yeah, I'm sure you and Joe Cat do it all the time."

Harvard had to smile at that image. "If he needed me to, I'd hold his hand."

"He'd never need you to."

"Maybe. Maybe not."

"Look, I'm really okay with flying," P.J. told him. "It's just takeoff that gets me a little tense."

"Yeah," Harvard said, looking at her hands gripping the armrests. "Now that we're in the air, you're really relaxed."

She had small hands with short, neat, efficient-looking nails. Her fingers were slender but strong. They were good hands, capable hands. She may not have been able to palm a basketball, but neither could most of the rest of the world. He liked the way his hand had engulfed hers. He knew he'd like the sensation of their fingers laced together.

"I *am* relaxed," she protested. "You know, all I'd have to do is close my eyes, and I'd be asleep in five minutes. Less."

"That's not relaxed," he scoffed. "That's defensive unconsciousness. *You* know you're stuck in this plane until we land in Phoenix. There's no way out, so your body just shuts down. Little kids do it all the time when they get really mad or upset. I've seen Frankie Catalanotto do it— he's getting into that terrible-two thing early. One second he's screaming the walls down because he can't have another cookie, and the next he's sound asleep on the living room rug. It's like someone threw a switch. It's a defense mechanism."

"I love it when you compare me to a child going through the terrible twos."

"You want me to buy you a beer, little girl?"

She gave him something resembling a genuine smile. "On a six-thirty-in-the-morning flight…?"

"Whatever works."

"I usually bring my Walkman and a book on tape," P.J. told him. "And I listen to that while I catch up on paperwork. Can't do too many things and maintain a high level of terror all at the same time."

Harvard nodded. "You cope. You do what you have to do when you have no choice. But every now and then you can let yourself get away with holding on to someone's hand."

P.J. shook her head. "I've never felt I could afford that luxury." She looked away, as if she knew she might have said too much.

And Harvard was suddenly aware of all the things he didn't know about this woman. She'd told him a little—just a little—about her wretched childhood. He also knew she had huge amounts of willpower and self-control. And drive. She had more drive and determination than most of the SEAL candidates he saw going through BUD/S training in Coronado.

"Why'd you join FInCOM?" he asked. "And I'm betting it wasn't to collect all those frequent-flyer miles."

That got him the smile he was hoping for. P.J. had a great smile, but often it was fleeting. She narrowed her eyes as she caught her lower lip between her teeth, pondering his question.

"I don't really know why," she told him. "It's not like I wanted to be a FInCOM agent from the time I was five or anything like that. I went to college to study law. But I found that achingly boring. I had just switched to a business program when I was approached by a FInCOM recruitment team. I listened to what they had to say, taking all the glory and excitement they told me about with a grain of salt, of course, but…"

She shrugged expressively. "I took the preliminary tests kind of as a lark. But each test I passed, each higher level I progressed to, I realized that maybe I was onto something here. I had these instincts—this was something I was naturally good at. It was kind of like picking up a violin and realizing I could play an entire Mozart concerto. It was cool. It wasn't long before I really started to care about getting into the FInCOM program. And then I was hooked."

She looked at him. "How about you? Why'd you decide to join the Navy? You told me you were planning to be some kind of college professor right up until the time you graduated from Harvard."

"English lit," Harvard told her. "Just like my daddy."

She was leaning against the headrest of her seat, turned slightly to face him, legs curled underneath her. She was wearing a trim-fitting pair of chinos and a shirt that, although similar to the cut of the T-shirts she normally wore, was made with some kind of smooth, flowing, silky material. It clung to her body enticingly, shimmering very slightly whenever she moved. It looked exotically soft, decadently sensuous. Harvard would have given two weeks' pay just to touch the sleeve.

"So what happened?" she asked.

"You really want to know?" he asked. "The real story, not the version I told my parents?"

He had her full attention. She nodded, eyes wide and waiting.

"It was about a week and a half after college graduation," Harvard told her. "I took a road trip to New York City with a bunch of guys from school. Brian Bradford's sister Ashley was singing in some chorus that was appearing at Carnegie Hall, so he was going down to see that, and Todd Wright was going along with him because he was perpetually chasing fair Ashley. Ash only got two comps, so the rest of us were going to hang at Stu Waterman's father's place uptown. We were going to spend two or three days camping out on Waterman's living room rug, doing the city. We figured we'd catch a show or two, do some club-hopping, just breathe in that smell of money down on Wall Street. We were Harvard grads and we owned the world. Or so I thought."

"Uh-oh," P.J. said. "What happened?"

"We pulled into town around sundown, dropped Bri and Todd off near Carnegie Hall, you know, cleaned 'em up a little, brushed their hair and made sure they had the Watermans' address and their names pinned to their jackets. Stu and Ng and I got something to eat and headed over to Stu's place. We knew Todd and Brian weren't going to be back until late, so we decided to go out. I saw in the paper that Danilo Perez's band was playing at a little club across town. He's this really hot jazz pianist. He'd gotten pretty massive airplay on the jazz station in Cambridge, but I'd never seen him live, so I was psyched to go. But Stu and Ng wanted to see a movie. So we split up. They went their way, I went mine."

P.J.'s eyes were as warm as the New York City night Harvard had found himself walking around in all those years ago.

"The concert was out of this world," he told her. "What happened after it wasn't, but I'll never regret going out there. I stayed until they shut the bar down, until Danilo stopped playing, and even then I hung for a while and talked to the band. Their jazz was so fresh, so happening. You know, with some bands, you get this sense that they're just ghosts—they're just playing what the big boys played back in the thirties. And other bands, they're trying so hard to be out there, to be on the cutting edge, they lose touch with the music."

"So what happened after you left the club?" P.J. asked.

Harvard laughed ruefully. "Yeah, I'm getting to the nasty part of the story, so I'm going off on a tangent— trying to avoid the subject by giving you some kind of lecture on jazz, aren't I?"

She nodded.

He touched her sleeve with one finger. "I like that shirt. Did I tell you I like that shirt?"

"Thank you," she said. "What happened when you left the club?"

"All right." He drew in a deep breath and blew it out through his mouth. "It's about two-thirty, quarter to three in the morning, and I'd put in a call to Stu at around two, and he'd told me no sweat, they were still up, take my time heading back, but I'm thinking that a considerate house-guest doesn't roll in after three. I figure I better hurry, catch a cab. I try, but after I leave the club, every taxi I see just slows, checks me out, then rolls on by. I figure it's the way I'm dressed—jams and T-shirt and Nikes. Nothing too out there, but I'm not looking too fresh, either. I don't look like a Harvard grad. I look like some black kid who's out much too late.

"So okay. Cab's not gonna stop for me. It ticks me off, but it's not the end of the world. It's not like it's the first time that ever happened. Anyway, I'd spent four years on the Harvard crew team, and I'm in really good shape, so I figure, it's only a few miles. I'll run."

Harvard could see from the look in P.J.'s eyes that she knew exactly what he was going to say next. "Yeah," he said. "That's right. You guessed it. I haven't gone more than four blocks before a police car pulls up alongside me, starts pacing me. Seems that the sight of a black man running in that part of town is enough to warrant a closer look."

"You didn't grow up in the city," P.J. said. "If you had, you would have known not to run."

"Oh, I knew not to run. I may have been a suburb boy, but I'd been living in Cambridge for four years. But these streets were so empty, I was sure I'd see a patrol car coming. I was careless. Or maybe I'd just had one too many beers. Anyway, I stop running, and they're asking me who I am, where I've been, where I'm going, why I'm running. They get out of the squad car, and it's clear that they don't believe a single word I'm saying, and I'm starting to get annoyed. And righteous. And I'm telling them that the only reason they even stopped their car was because I'm an African-American man. I'm starting to dig in deep to the subject of the terrible injustice of a social system that could allow such prejudice to occur, and as I'm talking, I'm reaching into my back pocket for my wallet, intending to show these skeptical SOBs my Harvard University ID card, and all of a sudden, I'm looking down the barrel of not one, but two very large police-issue handguns.

"And my mind just goes blank. I mean, I've been stopped and questioned before. This was not the first time that had happened. But the guns were new. The guns were something I hadn't encountered before.

"So these guys are shouting at me to get my hands out of my pockets and up where they can see them, and I look at them, and I see the whites of their eyes. They are terrified, their fingers twitching and shaking on the triggers of handguns that are big enough to blow a hole in me no surgeon could ever stitch up. And I'm standing there, and I think, damn. I think, this is it. I'm going to die. Right here, right now—simply because I am a black man in an American city.

"I put my hands up and they're shouting for me to get onto the ground, so I do. They search me—scrape my face on the concrete while they're doing it—and I'm just lying there thinking, I have a diploma from Harvard University, but it doesn't mean jack out here. I have an IQ that could gain me admission to the damn Mensa Society, but that's not what people see when they look at me. They can't see any of that. They can only see the color of my skin. They see a six-foot-five black man. They see someone they think might be armed and dangerous."

He was quiet, remembering how the police had let him go, how they'd let him off with a warning. They'd let *him* off. They hadn't given him more than a cursory apology. His cheek was scraped and bleeding and they'd acted as if he'd been the one in the wrong. He had sat on the curb for a while, trying to make sense of what had just happened.

"I'd heard about the SEALs. I guess I must've seen something about the units on TV, and I'd read their history—about the Frogmen and the Underwater Demolition Teams in World War II. I admired the SEALs for all the risks involved in their day-to-day life, and I guess I'd always thought maybe in some other lifetime it might've been something I would like to have done. But I remember sitting there on that sidewalk in New York City after that patrol car had pulled away, thinking, damn. The average life expectancy for a black man in an American city is something like twenty-three very short years. The reality of that had never fully kicked in before, but it did that night. And I thought, hell, I'm at risk just walking around.

"It was only sheer luck I didn't pull my wallet out of my back pocket when those policemen were shouting for me to put my hands in the air. If I had done that, and if one of those men had thought that wallet was a weapon, I would've been dead. Twenty-two years old. Another sad statistic.

"I thought about that sitting there. I thought, yeah, I could play it safe and not go out at night. Or I could do what my father did and hide in some nice well-to-do suburb. Or I could join the Navy and become a SEAL, and at least that way the risks I took day after day would be worth something."

Harvard let himself drown for a few moments in P.J.'s

eyes. "The next morning, I found a recruiting office, and I joined my Uncle Sam's Navy. The rest, as they say, is history."

P.J. reached across the armrest and took his hand.

He looked at her fingers, so slender and small compared to his. "This for me or for you?"

"It's for you *and* me," she told him. "It's for both of us."

Harvard's mother smelled like cinnamon. She smelled like the fragrant air outside the bakery P.J. used to walk past on her way to school in third grade, before her grandmother died.

The entire house smelled wonderful. Something incredible was happening in the kitchen. Something that involved the oven and a cookbook and lots of sugar and spice.

Ellie Becker had P.J. by one hand and her son by the other, giving them a tour of her new house. Boxes were stacked in all the rooms except the huge kitchen, which was pristine and completely unpacked.

It was like the kitchens P.J. had seen on TV sitcoms. The floor was earth-tone-colored Mexican tile. The counters and appliances were gleaming white, the cabinets natural wood. There was an extra sink in a workstation island in the center of the room, and enough space for a big kitchen table that looked as if it could seat a dozen guests, no problem.

"This was the room that sold us on this house," Ellie said. "This is the kitchen I've been dreaming about for the past twenty years."

Harvard looked exactly like his mother. Oh, he was close to a foot and a half taller and not quite as round in certain places, but he had her smile and the same sparkle in his eyes.

"This is a beautiful house," P.J. told Ellie.

It *was* gorgeous. Brand-new, with a high ceiling in the

living room, with thick-pile carpeting and freshly painted walls, it had been built in the single-story Spanish style so popular in the Southwest.

Ellie was looking at Harvard. "What do *you* think?"

He kissed her. "I think it's perfect. I think I want to know if those are cinnamon buns I smell baking in the oven, and if the chocolate chip cookies cooling on the rack over there are up for grabs."

She laughed. "Yes and yes."

"Check *this* out," Harvard said, handing P.J. a cookie.

She took a bite.

Harvard's mother actually baked. The cookies were impossibly delicious. She didn't doubt the cinnamon buns in the oven would taste as good as they smelled.

Harvard's mother did more than bake. She smiled nearly all the time, even when she wept upon seeing her son. She was the embodiment of joy and warmth, friendly enough to give welcoming hugs to strangers her son dragged home with him.

P.J. couldn't wait to meet Harvard's father.

"Kendra and the twins will be coming for dinner," Ellie told Harvard. "Robby can't make it. He's got to work." She turned to P.J. "Kendra is one of Daryl's sisters. She is going to be *so* pleased to meet you. *I'm* so pleased to meet you." She hugged P.J. again. "Aren't you just the sweetest, cutest little thing?"

"Careful, Mom," Harvard said dryly. "That sweet, cute little thing is a FInCOM field operative."

Ellie pulled back to look at P.J. "You're one of the agents being trained for this special counterterrorist thingy Daryl's working on?"

"Yeah, she's one of the special four chosen to be trained as counterterrorist thingy agents," Harvard teased.

"Well, what would *you* call it? You have nicknames for everything—not to mention all those technical terms and acronyms. LANTFLT, and NAVSPECWARGRU, and...oh, I can never keep any of that Navy-speak straight."

Harvard laughed. "Team, Mom. The official technical Navy-speak term for *this* thingy is counterterrorist *team*."

Ellie looked at P.J. "I've never met a real FInCOM agent before. You don't look anything like the ones I've seen on TV."

"Maybe if she put on a dark suit and sunglasses."

P.J. gave him a withering look, and Harvard laughed, taking another cookie from the rack and holding it out to her. She shook her head. They were too damn good.

"Do you have a gun and everything?" Ellie asked P.J.

"It's called a weapon, Mom. And not only does she have one," Harvard told her, his mouth full of cookie, "but she knows how to use it. She's the best shooter I've met in close to ten years. She's good at all the other stuff, too. In fact, if the four superfinks were required to go through BUD/S training, I'm sure P.J. would be the last one standing."

Ellie whistled. "For him to say that, you must be good."

P.J. smiled into those warm brown eyes that were so like Harvard's. "I am, thank you. But I wouldn't be the last one standing. I'd be the last one running."

"You go, girl!" Ellie laughed in delight. She looked at Harvard. "Self-confident and decisive. I like her."

"I knew you would." Harvard held out another handful of cookies to P.J. She hesitated only briefly before she took one, smiling her thanks, and he smiled back, losing himself for a moment in her eyes.

This was okay. This wasn't anywhere near as hard as he'd dreaded it would be. This house was a little too squeaky clean and new, with no real personality despite the jaunty angle to the living room ceiling, but his mother was happy here, that much was clear. And P.J. was proving to be an excellent distraction. It was hard to focus on the fact that Phoenix, Arizona, was about as different from Hingham, Massachusetts, as a city could possibly be when he was expending so many brain cells memorizing the way P.J.'s silken shirt seemed to flow and cling to her shoulders and breasts.

There was a ten-year-old boy inside him ready to mourn the passing of an era. But that boy was being shouted down by the thirty-six-year-old full-grown man who, although desperately wanting sheer, heart-stopping, teeth-rattling sex, was oddly satisfied and fulfilled by just a smile.

He couldn't wait until the flight back tomorrow afternoon. If he played his cards right, maybe P.J. would hold his hand again.

The absurdity of what he was thinking—that he was wildly anticipating holding a woman's hand—made him laugh out loud.

"What's so funny?" his mother asked.

"I'm just…glad to be here." Harvard gave her a quick hug. "Glad to have a few days off." He looked at P.J. and smiled. "Just glad." He turned to his mother. "Where's Daddy? It's too hot for him to be out playing golf."

"He had a meeting at school. He should be back pretty soon—he's going to be *so* surprised to see you." The oven timer buzzed, and Ellie peeked inside. Using hot mitts, she transferred the pan of fragrant buns to a cooling rack. "Why don't you bring your bags in from the car?"

"We were thinking we'd get a couple hotel rooms," Harvard told her. "You don't need the hassle of houseguests right now."

"Nonsense." She made a face at him. "We've got plenty of space. As long as you don't mind the stacks of boxes…"

"I wasn't sure you'd have the spare sheets unpacked." Harvard leaned against the kitchen counter. "And even if you did, you surely don't need the extra laundry. I think you've probably got enough to do around here for the next two months."

"Don't you worry about that." His mother glanced quickly from him to P.J. and back. "Unless you'd rather stay at a hotel."

Harvard knew the words his mother hadn't said. *For privacy.* He knew she hadn't missed the fact that he'd said they'd get hotel *rooms,* plural. And he knew she hadn't missed the fact that he'd introduced P.J. to her as his *friend*—the prefix *girl* intentionally left off. But he also knew for damn sure his mother hadn't missed all those goofy smiles he was sending in P.J.'s direction.

There were a million questions in his mother's eyes, but he trusted her not to ask them in front of P.J. She could embarrass and tease him all she wanted when they were alone, but she was a smart lady and she knew when and where to draw the line.

"Hey, whose car is in the drive?"

Harvard couldn't believe the difference between the old man he'd seen in the hospital and the man who came through the kitchen door. His father looked fifteen years younger. The fact that he was wearing a Chicago White Sox baseball cap and a pair of plaid golfing shorts only served to take another few years off him.

"Daryl! Yes! I was hoping it was you!"

Harvard didn't even bother to pretend to shake his father's hand. He just pulled the old man in close for a hug as he felt his eyes fill with tears. He'd been more than half afraid that, despite his mother's optimistic reports, he'd find his father looking old and gray and overweight, like another heart attack waiting to happen. Instead, he looked more alive than he had in years. "Daddy, damn! You look *good!*"

"I've lost twenty pounds. Thirty more to go." His father kissed him on the cheek and patted him on the shoulder, not having missed the shine of emotion in Harvard's eyes. "I'm all right now, kid," the elder Becker said quietly to his son. "I'm following the doctor's orders. No more red meat, no more pipe, no more bacon and eggs, lots of exercise—although not as much as you get, I'm willing to bet, huh? You're looking good, yourself, as usual."

Harvard gave his father one more hug before pulling away. P.J.'s eyes were wide, and she quickly glanced away, as if she suddenly realized that she'd been staring.

"Dad, I want you to meet P. J. Richards. She's with FInCOM. We've been working together, and we've become pretty good friends. We got a couple days of leave, so I dragged her out here with me. P.J., meet my dad, Medgar Becker."

Dr. Becker held out his hand to P.J. "It's very nice to meet you—P.J. is it?"

"That's right," P.J. said. "But actually, believe it or not, Dr. Becker, we've met before." She looked accusingly at Harvard. "You never told me your father was Dr. Medgar Becker."

He laughed. "You know my father?"

"Oh!" Ellie said. "It's the small-world factor kicking in! Everyone's connected somehow. You've just got to dig a little bit to find the way."

"Well, you don't have to dig very far for this connection," P.J. said with a smile. She looked at Dr. Becker, who was still holding her hand, eyes narrowed slightly as he gazed at her. "You probably don't recall—"

"Washington, D.C.," he said. "I *do* remember you. We got into a big debate over *Romeo and Juliet.*"

"I can't believe you remember that!" she said with a laugh.

"I've done similar lectures for years, but you're the only student who's asked a question and then stood there and vehemently disagreed with me after I gave my answer."

Harvard's father kissed P.J.'s hand. "I never knew your name, kiddo, but I certainly remember you."

"Dr. Becker was a guest lecturer at our university," P.J. explained to Harvard. "One of my roommates was an English lit major, and she, um, persuaded me to come along to his lecture."

"I remember thinking, 'This one's going to *be* somebody someday,'" Dr. Becker said.

"Well, thank you," P.J. said gracefully.

"You know, I've been thinking about everything you said for years, about wanting the language of the play to be updated and modernized," Dr. Becker said, pulling P.J. with him toward his office, "about how the play was originally written for the people, and how because the language we speak and understand has changed so much since it was written, it's lost the audience that would relate to and benefit from the story the most."

Harvard stood with his mother and watched as P.J. glanced at him and smiled before his father pulled her out of sight.

"I love her smile." He wasn't aware he'd spoken aloud until his mother spoke.

"Yeah, she's got a good one." She chuckled, shaking her head at the sound of her husband's voice, still lecturing from the other end of the house. "You know, he's been acting a little strange lately. I've chalked it up to his having a near-death experience and then losing all that weight. It's as if he's gotten a second wind. I like it. Most of the time. But I might be a little worried about his interest in that girl of yours—if it wasn't more than obvious that she's got it *way* bad for you."

"Oh, no," Harvard said. "We're friends. That's all. She's not mine—I'm not looking for her to become mine, either."

"Bring your bags in from the car," Ellie said. "You two can have the rooms with the connecting bath." She smiled conspiratorially. "Sometimes these things need a little help."

"I don't need any help," Harvard said indignantly. "And I especially don't need any help from my *mother*."

CHAPTER ELEVEN

P.J. FOUND HARVARD standing on the deck, elbows on the railing, looking at the nearly full moon.

She closed the sliding doors behind her.

"Hey," Harvard said without turning.

"Hey, yourself," she said, moving to stand next to him. The night was almost oppressively hot. It was an odd sensation, almost like standing in an oven. Even in the sweatbox that D.C. became in the summer, there was at least a hint of coolness in the air after the sun went down. "I've been wanting to ask you about what you said tonight to your sister—to Kendra?"

He looked at her. "You mean when she was making all that noise about how dangerous your job must be?"

P.J. nodded. Kendra had made such a fuss over the fact that P.J.'s job put her into situations where bad guys with weapons sometimes fired those weapons at her. Her arguments why women shouldn't have dangerous jobs were the same ones Harvard had fired off at P.J. the first few times they'd gone head-to-head. But to P.J.'s absolute surprise, Harvard had stepped up to defend her.

He'd told his sister in no uncertain terms that P.J. was damn good at what she did. He'd told them all that she was tougher and stronger than most men he knew. And then he'd made a statement that had come close to putting P.J. into total shock.

Harvard had announced he would pick P.J. as his partner over almost any man he knew.

"Did you really mean that?" P.J. asked him now.

"Of course, I meant it. I said it, didn't I?"

"I thought maybe you were just, you know…"

"Lying?"

She could see the nearly full moon reflected in his eyes. "Being polite. Being chivalrous. I don't know. I didn't know what to think."

"Yeah, well, I meant what I said. I like you and I trust you."

"You trust me. Enough to really believe that I'm not someone you need to protect?"

He wanted to tell her yes. She could see it in his eyes. But she could also see indecision. And he didn't try to pretend he wasn't sure.

"I'm still working on that," he told her. "I'll tell you this much, though—I'm looking forward to the next few days. It's going to be fun going into the field with you—even if it's only for a training scenario."

P.J. met his gaze steadily, warmed by the fact that he'd been honest with her. She was also impressed that he'd confronted his prejudices about working a dangerous job alongside a woman and had managed to set his preconceived notions aside. His opinion on the subject had turned a complete one-eighty.

"Senior Chief, I'm honored," she told him.

Senior Chief.

The title sat between them as if it were a barricade. She'd used it purposely, and she knew from the way he smiled very slightly that he knew it.

The moonlight, the look in his eyes, the heat of the night and the way she was feeling were all way too intense.

She looked over the railing. The Beckers' small backyard abutted a golf course. The gently rolling hills looked alien and otherworldly in the moonlight. The distant sand traps reflected the light and seemed to glitter.

"They gave up an ocean view for this," Harvard said

with a soft laugh. "There's still a part of me that's in shock."

"You know, I spent about forty minutes in the garage tonight with your father, and he didn't mention Shakespeare once. He spent the entire time showing off his new golf clubs." P.J. turned to look at him. "I suspect he likes this view much better than the view of the ocean he had in Massachusetts. And I *know* your mother loves having those adorable nieces of yours within a short car ride."

"You're right." Harvard sighed. "I'm the one who loves the…ocean. My father just tolerated it. My father." He shook his head. "God—I can't believe how good he looks. Last time I saw him, I was sure we'd be burying him within the next two years. But now he looks like he's ready to go another sixty."

P.J. glanced at him, thinking about the way his eyes had filled with tears when his father had walked in this afternoon. She hadn't believed it at first. Tears. In Senior Chief Becker's eyes.

She remembered how surprised she'd been when she'd found out Harvard had a family. A father. A mother. Sisters.

He'd come across as so stern and strong, so formidable, so completely in charge. But he was more than that. He listened when other people spoke. His confidence was based on intelligence and experience, not conceit, as she'd first believed. He was funny and smart and completely, totally together.

And one of the things that had helped him become this completely, totally together man was his family's love and affection.

It was a love and affection Harvard returned unconditionally.

What would it have been like to grow up with that kind of love? What would it be like to be loved that way now?

P.J. knew Harvard wanted her physically. But what if—what if he wanted more?

The thought was both exhilarating and terrifying.

But totally absurd. He'd told her point-blank he wanted friendship. Friendship, with some sex on the side. Nothing that went any further or deeper.

"Your family is really great," she told him.

He glanced at her, amusement dancing in his eyes. "Kendra's ready to join with Mom and Daddy and become co-presidents of your official fan club. After she came at you with her antigun speech, you know, after she said the only time she could ever imagine picking up a gun was to defend her children, and then you said, 'That's what I do.'" He imitated her rather well. "'Every day when I go to work, I pick up my gun because I'm helping to defend *your* children.' After that, Kendra pulled me aside and gave me permission to marry you."

P.J.'s heart did a flip-flop in her chest. But he was teasing. He was only teasing. He was no more interested in getting married than she was. And she was not interested.

She kept her voice light. "I'm too old for adoption. The way I see it, marrying you is the only way I'm going to get into this family, so watch out," she teased back. "If I could only find the time, I might consider it."

Harvard laughed as he glanced over his shoulder in mock fear. "We better not joke about this too loudly. If my mother overhears, she's liable to take us seriously. And then, by this time tomorrow, our engagement picture will be in the newspaper. She'll be finalizing the guest list with one hand, signing a contract with a caterer with the other and 'helping' you pick out a wedding gown all at the same time—and by helping, I mean she'll really be trying to pick it out *for* you."

P.J. played along. "As long as it's cut so I can wear my shoulder holster."

"The bride wore Smith & Wesson. The groom preferred

an HK MP5 room broom. It was a match made in hardware heaven."

She laughed. "They spent their wedding night at the firing range."

"No, I don't *think* so." Something in his voice had changed, and as P.J. glanced at Harvard, the mood shifted. Laughter still danced in his eyes, but there was something else there, too. Something hot and dangerous. Something that echoed the kiss they'd shared on jump day. Something that made her want to think, and think long and hard, about her reasons for avoiding intimate relationships.

Wedding night. God, she hadn't been thinking clearly. If she had, she certainly wouldn't have brought *that* up.

She cleared her throat. "Your mother told me to tell you she and your dad were heading to bed," she said. "She wanted me to ask you to lock up and turn out the lights when you come in."

Harvard glanced at his watch as he turned to face her, one elbow still on the railing. With his other hand he reached out and lightly touched the sleeve of her shirt, then the bare skin of her arm. "It's after twenty three hundred. You want to go to bed?"

It was an innocent enough question, but combined with the warmth in his eyes and the light pressure of his fingers on her arm, it took on an entirely more complicated meaning.

He trailed his hand down to her hand and laced their fingers together. "I know—I promised no pressure," he continued, "and there is no pressure. It just suddenly occurred to me that I'd be a fool not to check and see if somehow between last night and tonight you've maybe changed your mind."

"Nothing's changed," she whispered. But everything *had* changed. This man had turned her entire world upside down. More than just a tiny part of her wanted to be with him. A great deal more. And if they'd been anywhere in the world besides his mother and father's house, she might well be tempted to give in, and God knows that would be a major mistake.

She couldn't let herself become involved with this man—at least not until the training mission was over. At the very least, she couldn't afford to have anyone believe she'd succeeded in the intensively competitive program because she'd slept with Alpha Squad's Senior Chief.

Including herself.

And after this project was over, she'd have to search long and hard within herself to find out what it was she truly wanted.

Right now, she was almost certain what she wanted was him. Almost certain.

"Nothing's changed," she said again, louder, trying to make herself believe it, too. *Almost* wasn't going to cut it.

Harvard nodded, and then he leaned toward her.

P.J. knew he was going to kiss her. He took his time. He even stopped halfway to her lips, searched her eyes and smiled before continuing.

And she—she didn't stop him. She didn't back away. She didn't even say anything like, "Hey, Holmes, you better not be about to kiss me." She just stood there like an idiot, waiting for him to do it.

His first kiss was one of those sweet ones he seemed to specialize in—the kind that made her heart pound and her knees grow weak. But then he kissed her again, longer, deeper, possessively, sweeping his tongue into her mouth as if it were his mouth, his to do with what he pleased. He pulled her into his arms, holding her close, settling his lips over hers as if he had no intention of leaving anytime soon.

P.J. would have been indignant—but the truth was, she didn't want his mouth to be anywhere but where it was right that moment. She wanted him to kiss her. She loved the feel of his arms around her. His arms were so big, so powerful, yet capable of holding her so tenderly.

So she stood there, in the Arizona moonlight, on the back deck of his parents' new house, and she kissed him, too.

Harvard pulled away first, drawing in a deep breath and letting it out fast. "Oh, boy. That wasn't meant to be any kind of pressure," he told her. He sounded as out of breath as she felt. "That was just supposed to be a friendly reminder—like, hey, don't forget how good we could be together."

"I haven't forgotten." P.J.'s mouth went dry as she looked at him, and she nervously wet her lips.

"Oh, damn," he breathed, and kissed her again.

This time she could taste his hunger. This time he inhaled her, and she drank him in just as thirstily.

She pulled him close, her arms around his shoulders, his neck—God, there was so much of him to hold on to. She felt his hands sliding down her back, felt the taut muscles of his powerful thighs against her legs as she tried to get even closer to this man she'd come to care so much about.

"Oh, God," she gasped, pulling his head down for another soul-shattering kiss when he would have stopped. She didn't care anymore. She didn't care about the fact that they were here, at his mother's house. She didn't care about the potential damage to her reputation. She didn't care that she was taking an entire lifetime of caution and restraint and throwing it clear out the window.

She shook as he trailed his mouth down her neck, as his hand cupped her breast, as sensations she'd never dreamed possible made her lose all sense of coherent thought.

"We should stop," Harvard murmured, kissing P.J. again. But she didn't pull away. She opened herself to him, welcoming his kisses with an ardor that took his breath away. She was on fire, and he was the man who'd started the blaze.

But even as he shifted his weight slightly, subtly maneuvering his thigh between her legs, even as he ran his hands across her perfect body, he knew he shouldn't. He should be backing off, not driving this highly explosive situation dangerously close to the point of no return.

But she tasted like the mocha-flavored coffee they'd shared with his parents just a short time ago, after his sister and the twins had left. And he could feel her heat through the thin cotton of her chinos as she pressed herself against his thigh.

Harvard swept her into his arms, and he could see a myriad of emotions in her eyes. Fear swirled together with anticipation, both fueled powerfully by desire.

She wanted him. She might be scared, but she truly wanted him.

He glanced at his watch again. There was time. They still had enough time.

He could carry her into the house, take her into his parents' guest room, and he could become her first lover.

She could have had anyone, but she'd picked him to be her first.

That knowledge was a powerful aphrodisiac, and it made a difficult decision even harder to carry out.

But the truth was, he had no choice.

Yeah, he could have her tonight. He could continue to sweep her off her feet, to seduce her, with her own desire and need working as his ally. She would come willingly to his bed, and he could show her everything she'd been missing all these years.

He kissed her again, then set her gently in one of the deck chairs and walked all the way to the other side of the porch.

Or he could keep the promise that he'd made to her this morning.

"I wasn't playing fair," he said. His voice came out a husky growl—part man, part beast. "I knew if I kissed you long enough and hard enough and deeply enough, you'd go up in flames. I'm sorry."

He heard her draw in a long, deep, shaky breath. She let it out in a burst of air. "That was…" She stopped, started again. "I was…" Another pause. "I wanted…" A longer pause. "I thought… I'm really confused, Daryl. What just happened here? You don't really want to be with me?"

Harvard turned toward her, shocked she could think that. "No! Damn, woman, *look* at me. Look at just how much I allegedly don't want to be with you!"

She looked.

He stepped closer, and she looked again, her gaze lingering on the front of his fatigues. His erection made an already snug pair of pants even tighter. And the fact that she was looking with such wide eyes made it even worse.

"I'm trying to be a hero here," Harvard told her, his voice cracking slightly. "I'm trying to do the right thing. I want to make love to you more than you will ever know, but you know what? There's something I want even more than that. I want to be sure that when we *do* make love, you're gonna wake up in the morning and not have one single, solitary regret."

She looked away from him, guilt in her eyes, and he knew—as hard as this was—that he *was* doing the right thing.

"I'm not sure I'll ever be able to give you those kind of guarantees," she said quietly.

"I think you will," he countered. "And I've got time. I'm willing to wait." He laughed softly. "Hopefully, it won't take you another twenty-five years."

She glanced at him, then her eyes dropped again to the front of his pants. She laughed nervously. "I've never known a man well enough before to ask him this, but… doesn't that hurt?"

Harvard sat carefully in the other deck chair. "It's uncomfortable, that's for damn sure."

"I'm sorry."

"Like hell you are. I see you over there, laughing at me."

"It just seems so embarrassingly inconvenient. I mean, what happens if you're in a meeting with some admiral and you start thinking about—"

"You don't," Harvard interrupted.

"But what if you forget and just start daydreaming or something and, oops, there you are. Larger than life, so to speak."

Harvard ran his hands down his face. "Then I guess you quickly start doing calculus problems in your head. Or you sit down fast and hope no one noticed your...situation."

Her smoky laughter wrapped around him in the moonlight. He could see her watching him. She'd curled up on her side in the chair, one hand beneath her face, her legs tucked up to her chest.

He could have had her. He could have carried her inside and he would be with her in his bedroom right now. That same moonlight would be streaming in through the window, caressing her naked body as he held her gaze and slowly filled her.

Harvard drew in a deep breath. He couldn't let himself think about that. Not tonight. It wasn't going to happen tonight. But it *was* going to happen. He was going to make damn sure of that.

"May I ask you something else?" she asked.

"Yeah, as long as you don't ask me to kiss you again. I think I can only be strong like this once a night."

"No, this is another penis question."

Harvard cracked up. "Oh, good, because, you know, penis questions are my specialty."

"Promise you won't laugh at me?"

"I promise."

"You're laughing right now," she accused him.

"I'm stopping. See? I'm serious. I'm ready for this really serious penis question." He snorted with laughter.

"Fine. Laugh at me." She sat up. "It's a stupid question anyway, and if I weren't so damned repressed, I'd have already learned the answer through experience."

"Lady, you're not repressed. Overly cautious, maybe, but definitely not repressed."

"It's about the size thing," she told him, and he realized she wasn't joking. "I mean, I know about sex. I know a *lot* about sex. I mean, I may be inexperienced, but I'm not exactly innocent. I know the mechanics—I've seen movies, I've read books, I've heard talk, I've certainly *thought* about it enough. And, you know, everyone always says size doesn't matter, but I think they're talking about when a man is small, and that's definitely not the issue here. Obviously. But I've seen small women and large men together all the time, so I know it must work, but how on earth…" She trailed off.

She was serious. Harvard knew he should say something, but he wasn't sure what.

"I'm only five-one-and-a-half," she continued. "I lied. I round up to make it five-two. I buy my clothes from the petite rack in the store. And petite is not the word I'd use to describe anything about you. You're huge. All of you."

Harvard couldn't keep from chuckling.

She laughed, too, covering her face with her hands. "Oh, God, I knew it. You're laughing at me."

"I'm laughing because I love the fact that you think of me that way. I'm laughing because this conversation is doing nothing to help reduce my, um, current tension. In fact, I think I have to go inside now so I can fill out my official application for sainthood."

"Yeah, go on. Duck out. You just don't want to answer my question."

He met her gaze and held it. "It's one of those things that's easier to show than tell and— You are really pushing me to the wall tonight, lady. I can't even stand next to you without getting turned on, and here we are, talking about making love. If I didn't know better, I would think you were some kind of tease, getting an evil kick out of watching me squirm."

Her tentative smile vanished instantly. "Daryl, I would never do that. I—"

"Whoa," Harvard said, holding up his hands. "Yo, Ms. Much Too Serious, take a deep breath and relax. I was kidding. A joke. Ha, ha. Out of all the two hundred sixty-seven billion women in the world, I'm well aware that you rate two hundred sixty-seven billionth when it comes to being a tease. Which is why I know when you start asking questions about size—" he couldn't hold back his giggle "—it's because you seriously want to know." He giggled again.

She shook her head. "You know, I've seen *Beavis and Butthead,* and I thought it was just some warped fictional exaggeration of male immaturity, but I can see now that the show is based on you."

"Hey, I can't help it. The P word is a funny word. It's a friendly, happy, just plain silly word. And add on top of that the absurdity of us sitting here and discussing the additional absurdity of whether or not I would fit inside you… Damn!" He had to close his eyes at the sudden vivid visual images his words brought to mind. He had to grit his teeth as he could almost feel himself buried deep inside her satin-smooth heat. Never before had sheer paradise been so close and yet so far away.

"Yes." He opened his eyes and looked straight at her. "I would. Fit. Inside you. Perfectly. You've got to trust me on this one, P.J. As much as I'd love to go into the house and prove it to you, you're just going to have to take my word for it. I've been with women who are small—maybe not as skinny as you, but close enough. It works. Nature in action, you know? When—if—when… When we get to the point where we actually get together, you don't have to worry about me hurting you—not that way."

"I know it's going to hurt the first time," she told him. "At least a little bit."

"Some women don't have a problem with that," he told her. "It's not uncommon for a woman's…maidenhead to be already broken—"

She laughed. "Maidenhead? Have you been reading Jane Austen again?"

"It's better than cherry. Or hymen. Damn, who came up with *that* name?"

"Dr. Hymen?"

Harvard laughed. "Hell of a way to gain immortality." He felt his smile soften as he gazed at her. She was sexy and bright and funny. He wanted this night to go on forever.

She met his gaze steadily. "Unlike a Jane Austen heroine, I haven't had the opportunity to have many horseback riding accidents. In fact, I've been to the doctor, and at last inventory, everything's still…intact."

Harvard took a deep breath. "Okay. When you're ready, we'll do it fast. I promise it won't hurt a lot, and I promise that it'll feel a whole lot better real soon after. If you only believe one thing I say, believe that, okay?"

She was silent for a moment, and then she nodded. "Okay."

Harvard sat back in his chair in relief. "Thank God. Now can we move on to some safer topic like birth control or safe sex."

"Hmm…"

"I was kidding," he said quickly. "No more penis questions of any kind, okay? At least not until tomorrow." He looked at his watch: 2340.

"What I really want to ask you now," P.J. said, her chin in the palm of her hand, elbow on the deck chair armrest as she gazed at him, "is more personal."

"More personal than…"

"You know who I've been with. I'm curious about you. How many of those two hundred sixty-seven billion women in the world have you taken to bed?"

"Too many when I was younger. Not enough over the past few years. When I turned thirty, I started getting really picky." Harvard shifted in his seat. "I haven't been in a relationship since this past winter. I was with a woman—Ellen—for about four months. If you can call what we had a relationship."

"Ellen." P.J. rolled the name off her tongue, as if trying it out. "What was she like?"

"Smart and upwardly mobile. She was a lawyer at some big firm in D.C. She didn't have time for a husband—or even a real boyfriend, for that matter. She was totally in love with her career. But she was pretty, and she was willing—when she found the time. It was fun for a while."

"So you've been with, what? Forty women? Four hundred women? More?"

He laughed. "I haven't kept a count or cut notches into my belt or anything like that. I don't know. There was only one that ever really mattered."

"Not Ellen."

"Nope."

"Someone who tragically broke your heart."

Harvard smiled. "It seemed pretty tragic at the time."

"What was her name? Do you mind talking about her?"

"Rachel, and no, I don't mind. It was years ago. I thought she was The One—you know, capital T, capital O—but her husband didn't agree."

P.J. winced. "Ouch." She narrowed her eyes. "What were you doing, messing with a married woman?"

"I didn't know," Harvard admitted. "I mean, I knew she was separated and filing for a divorce. What I didn't realize was that she was still in love with her ex. He cheated on her, and she left him and there I was, ready to take up the slack. Looking back, it's so clear that she was using me as a kind of revenge relationship. It was ironic, really. First time in my life I actually get involved, and it turned out she's using me to get back at her husband."

He shook his head. "I'm making her sound nasty, but she was this really sweet girl. I don't think she did any of it on purpose. She used me to feel better, and she ended up in this place where she could forgive him." He smiled, because for the first time since it had happened, he was talking about it, and it didn't hurt. "I was clueless, though. Alpha Squad got called to the Middle East—this was during Desert Shield. I didn't even get to say goodbye to her. When I came home months later, she'd already moved back in with Larry. Talk about a shock. Needless to say, the entire relationship had a certain lack of closure to it. It took me a while to make any sense of it."

"Some things just never make sense."

"It makes perfect sense now. If I'd hooked up with Rachel, I wouldn't be here with you."

P.J. looked at her sneakers for a moment before meeting his gaze again. "You're good at sweet talk, aren't you?"

"I've never had a problem with words," he admitted.

"You can fly a plane. You can operate any kind of boat that floats, you jump out of planes without getting tangled in trees, you run faster and shoot better than anyone I've ever met, you graduated from Harvard at the top of your class, you're a Senior Chief in the Navy SEALs, *and* you're something of a poet, to boot. Is there anything you *can't* do?"

He thought about it for only a moment. "I absolutely cannot infiltrate a camp of Swedish terrorists."

P.J. stared at him. And then she started to laugh. "Larry must be something else if Rachel gave up you for him."

Harvard looked at his watch, then stood and crossed the deck toward her. He pushed her legs aside with his hips as he sat on her chair, pinning her into place with one hand on either armrest. "It's nearly midnight, Cinderella," he said. "That means I can kiss you again without worrying about it going too far."

Her eyes were liquid brown. "What? I don't under—"

"Shh," he said, leaning forward to capture her lips with his.

He could taste her confusion, feel her surprise. But she hesitated for only half a second before meeting his tongue with equal fervor, before melting into his arms.

And his pager went off.

Hers did, too.

P.J. pulled away from him in surprise, reaching for her belt, pulling the device free and shutting off the alarm.

"Both of us," she said. "At once." She searched his eyes. "What is it?"

He stood up, adjusting his pants. "We have to call in to find out for sure. But I think our leave is over early."

P.J. stood, too, and followed him into the kitchen. "Did you know about this?"

"Not exactly."

"You knew something, didn't you? You've been checking your watch all evening. That's why you kissed me," she accused, "because it was almost midnight and you knew we were going to get beeped!"

"I didn't know exactly when." He keyed the number that had flashed on both their beepers into the kitchen telephone from memory. He grinned at her. "But I guessed. I know Joe Cat pretty well, and I figured he'd try to catch as many of us off guard as he possibly could. It seemed right up his alley to give us all forty-eight hours of leave, then call us in after only twenty-four. I figured it was either going to be midnight or sometime around oh-two-hundred." He held up one hand, giving her the signal to be quiet.

P.J. watched Harvard's eyes as he spoke to Captain Catalanotto on the other end of the line. He caught her staring, and a smile softened his face. He put his arm around her waist and pulled her close.

She closed her eyes, resting her head against his shoulder, breathing in his scent. She could smell the freshness of soap and the tangy aroma of some he-man brand of deodorant. Coffee. A faint whiff of the peppermint gum he sometimes chewed. His already familiar, slightly musky and very male perfume.

She still couldn't believe it was Harvard—and not her—who had kept them from making love tonight.

She'd never met a man who'd say no to sex out of consideration for what *she* might feel.

"Yeah," he said to Joe Cat. "We'll go directly to California, meet the rest of you there. I'm going to need my boots and some clothes. And, Captain? Remember the time I saved your neck, baby? I'm cashing in now. I'm going to tell you something that's for your ears only. P.J. is with me. Consider this her check-in, too."

He paused, listening to Joe. "No," he said. "No, no—we're here visiting my parents. Mom and Daddy. I swear, this whole trip has been completely innocent and totally rated G, but if anyone finds out, they're going to think…" He laughed. "Yeah, we're not talking real mature. Here's the problem, boss. P.J.'s going to need some clothes and her boots. I know you don't have much time yourself, but could you maybe send Veronica out to the hotel to pack up some of her things?"

"Oh, God." P.J. cringed. "My room is a mess."

Harvard looked at her, pulling the phone away from his mouth. "Really?"

She nodded.

"Cool." He kissed her quickly before he spoke into the receiver again. "She wants you to warn Ronnie that her room is a mess. Tell Ron just to grab her boots. We'll get P.J. whatever else she needs in Coronado. We'll be there before you."

Another pause, then Harvard laughed. P.J. could hear it rumbling in his chest. "Thanks, Joe. Yeah, we're on our way."

He hung up the phone and kissed her hard on the mouth. "Time to wake up Mom and Daddy and tell them we're out of here. And no more kissing," he said, kissing her again and then again. "It's time to go play soldier."

CHAPTER TWELVE

HARVARD COULD FEEL P.J. watching him as he stood at the front of the briefing room of the USS *Irvin,* the Navy destroyer steaming toward their destination.

They'd taken an Air Force flight all the way to South Korea. Now, by sea, they were approaching the tiny island nation where their training op was to take place.

P.J. had slept on the plane. Harvard had, too, but his dreams had been wildly erotic and unusually vivid. He could have sworn he still tasted the heated salt of her skin on his lips when he awoke. He could hear the echo of her cries of pleasure and her husky laughter swirl around him. He could still see the undisguised desire in her eyes as she gazed at him, feel the heart-stopping sensation as he sank into the tightness of her heat.

He took a deep breath, exhaling quickly, well aware he had to stop thinking about his dream—and about P.J.— before he found himself experiencing the same discomfort he'd been in when he awoke. He held his clipboard low, loosely clasped in both hands, trying to look casual, relaxed. He was just a guy holding a clipboard—not a guy using a clipboard to keep the world from noticing that he was walking around in a state of semiarousal.

When he glanced at P.J. again, she was trying hard not to smile, and he knew he hadn't managed to fool her.

The captain, meanwhile, was giving a brief overview of their mission. "There's a group of six jarheads—U.S. Marines—who've been doing FID work with the locals, trying to form a combined military and law-enforcement task force to slow drug trafficking in this part of the world. Apparently, this island is used as a major port of call for a great deal of Southeast Asia's heroin trade. Lieutenant Hawken has spent more time in-country than any of us, and he'll fill us all in on the terrain and the culture in a few minutes, after we go over the setup of this op.

"The jarheads are going to play the part of terrorists who've taken a U.S. official hostage. The hostage will also be played by a Marine." Joe Cat sat on the desk at the front of the room as he gazed at the FInCOM agents and the SEALs from Alpha Squad. "This CSF team's job is to insert onto the island at dawn, locate the terrorists' camp, enter the installation and extract the hostage. All while remaining undetected. We'll have paint-ball weapons again, but if the mission is carried out successfully, we won't have an opportunity to use them.

"The Marines have planned and set up this entire exercise. It will not be easy. These guys are going to do their best to defeat us. In case you finks haven't heard, there's an ongoing issue of superiority between the Marines and the SEALs."

"I can clear that issue up right now," Wes called out. "SEALs win, hands down. We're superior. No question in my mind."

"Yeah," Harvard said, "and somewhere right now some Marines are having this exact same conversation, and they're saying Marines win, hands down." He grinned. "Except, of course, in their case, they're wrong."

The other SEALs laughed.

"In other words, they don't like us," the captain went on, "and they're going to do everything they can—including cheat—to make sure we fail. In fact, it wouldn't surprise me to find out that the hostage has turned hostile. We've got to be prepared for him to raise an alarm and give us away."

Tim Farber lifted his hand. "Why are we bothering to

do this if they're going to cheat—if they're not going to follow the rules?"

Harvard stepped forward. "Do you honestly think real terrorists don't cheat, Mr. Farber? In the real world, there *are* no rules."

"And it's not unheard-of for a hostage to be brainwashed into supporting the beliefs of the men who have taken him captive. Having a hostile hostage is a situation we've always got to be prepared for," Blue added.

"Alpha Squad's done training ops against the Marines before," Lucky told the FInCOM agents. "The only time I can remember losing is when they brought in twenty-five extra men and ambushed us."

"Yeah, they work better in crowds. You know that old joke? Why are Marines like bananas?" Bobby asked.

"Because they're both yellow and die in big bunches," Wes said, snickering.

"The comedy team of Skelly and Taylor," Joe said dryly. "Thank you very much. I suggest when you take your powerhouse stand-up act on the road, you stay far from the Marine bases." He looked around the room. "Any questions so far? Ms. Richards, you usually have something to ask."

"Yes, sir, actually, I do," she said in that cool, professional voice Harvard knew was just part of her act. "How will we get from the ship to the island? And how many of us will actually participate in this exercise, as opposed to observe?"

"Everyone's going to participate in some way," the captain told her. "And—answering your questions out of order—we'll be inserting onto the island in two inflatable boats at oh-four-hundred. Just before dawn."

"Going back to your first answer…" P.J. shifted in her seat. "You said everyone would participate in some way. Can you be more specific?"

Harvard knew exactly what she wanted to know. She

was curious as to whether she was going to be in the field with the men or behind lines, participating in a more administrative way. He could practically see the wheels turning in her head as she wondered if she was going to be the one chosen to stay behind.

"We're breaking the CSF team into four sub-teams," Joe Cat explained. "Three teams of three will approach the terrorist camp, and one team of two will remain here on the ship, monitoring communications, updating the rest of us on any new satellite Intel and just generally monitoring our progress."

"Like Lieutenant Uhura on the *Starship Enterprise*." P.J. nodded slowly. Harvard could see resignation in her eyes. She was so certain it was going to be her that was left behind. "'Keeping hailing frequencies open, Captain,' and all that."

"Actually," Blue McCoy cut in with his soft Southern drawl, "I'm part of the team staying on board the *Irvin*. It'll be my voice you hear when and if there's any reason to call a cease and desist. I'll have the ultimate power to pull the plug on this training op at any time." He smiled. "Y'all can think of me as the voice of God. I say it, you obey it, or there'll be hell to pay."

"Crash, why don't you share with us what you know about the island?" Joe suggested.

P.J. was quiet as Lieutenant Hawken stepped forward. She was trying her best to hide her disappointment, but Harvard could see through her shield. He knew her pretty damn well by now. He knew her well enough to know that, disappointed or not, she would do her best—without complaining—wherever she was assigned.

Crash described the island in some detail. It was tropical, with narrow beaches that backed up against inactive volcanic mountains. The inland roads were treacherous, the jungle dense. The most common method of transport was the goat cart, although some of the island's more wealthy residents owned trucks.

He opened a map, and they all came around the desk as he pointed out the island's three major cities, all coastal seaports.

The lieutenant spoke at some length about the large amounts of heroin that passed through the island on the way to London and Paris and Los Angeles and New York. The political situation in the country was somewhat shaky. The United States had an agreement with the island—in return for U.S. aid, the local government and military were helping in the efforts to stop the flow of drugs.

But drug lords were more in control of the country than the government. The drug lords had private armies, which were stronger than the government's military forces. And when the drug lords clashed, which they did far too frequently, they came close to starting a commercially instigated civil war.

Harvard found himself listening carefully to everything Crash said, aware of his growing sense of unease. It was an unusual sensation, this unsettling wariness. This was just a training op. He'd gone into far more dangerous situations in the past without blinking.

He had to wonder if he'd feel this concern if P.J. weren't along for the ride. He suspected he wouldn't worry at all if she'd stayed stateside.

Harvard knew he could take care of himself in just about any situation. He wanted to believe P.J. could do the same. But the truth was, her safety had become far too important to him. Somehow he'd gotten to the point where he cared too much.

He didn't like the way that felt.

"Any questions?" Crash asked.

"Yeah," Harvard said. "What's the current situation between the two largest hostile factions on the island?"

"According to Intel, things have been quiet for weeks," Joe answered.

P.J. couldn't keep silent any longer. "Captain, what *are* the team assignments?"

"Bobby and Wes are with Mr. Schneider," Joe told her. "Lucky and I are with Mr. Greene."

Harvard was watching, and he saw a flicker of disappointment in her eyes. Once again, she hid it well. In fact, she was damn near a master at hiding her emotions.

"I'm with the Senior Chief and Lieutenant Hawken, right?" Tim Farber asked.

"Nope, you're with me, Timmy boy," Blue McCoy said with a grin. "Someone's got to help me mind the store."

Across the room, P.J. didn't react. She didn't blink, she didn't move, she didn't utter a single word. Apparently, she was even better at hiding her pleasure than she was at hiding her disappointment.

Farber wasn't good at hiding anything. "But you can't be serious. Richards should stay behind. Not me."

Joe Cat straightened up. "Why's that, Mr. Farber?"

The fink realized he had blundered hip-deep into waters that reeked of political incorrectness. "Well," he started. "It's just… I thought…."

P.J. finally spoke. "Just say it, Tim. You think I should be the one to stay behind because I'm a woman."

Harvard, Joe Cat and Blue turned to look at P.J.

"My God," Harvard said, slipping on his best poker face. "Would you look at that? Richards *is* a woman. I hadn't realized. We better make her stay behind, Captain. She might get PMS and go postal."

"We could use that to our advantage," Joe Cat pointed out. "Put a weapon in her hands and point her in the right direction. The enemy will run in terror."

"She can outshoot just about everyone in this room." Blue couldn't keep a smile from slipping out. "She can outrun 'em and outreason 'em, too."

"Yeah, but I bet she throws like a girl," Harvard said. He grinned. "Which, in this day and age, means she's just about ready for the major leagues."

"Except she doesn't like baseball," Joe Cat reminded him.

P.J. was laughing, and Harvard felt a burst of pure joy. He loved the sound of her laughter and the shine of amusement and pleasure in her eyes. He pushed away all the apprehension he'd been feeling. Working with her on this mission was going to be fun.

And after the mission was over...

Farber was less than thrilled. "Captain, this is all very amusing, but you know as well as I do that the military doesn't fully approve of putting women in scenarios that could result in frontline action."

Harvard snapped out of his reverie and gave the man a hard look. "Are you questioning the captain's judgment, Mr. Farber?"

"No, I'm merely—"

"Good." Harvard cut him off. "Let's get ready to get this job done."

P.J. felt like an elephant crashing through the underbrush.

She was nearly half the size of Harvard, yet compared to her, he moved effortlessly and silently. She couldn't seem to breathe without snapping at least one or two twigs.

And Crash... He seemed to have left his body behind on the USS *Irvin*. He moved ethereally, like a silent wisp of mist through the darkness. He was on point—leading the way—and he disappeared for long minutes at a time, scouting out the barely marked trail through the tropical jungle.

P.J. signaled for Harvard to wait, catching his eye.

You okay? he signaled back.

She pulled her lip microphone closer to her mouth. They

weren't supposed to speak via the radio headsets they wore unless it was absolutely necessary.

It was necessary.

"I'm slowing you down," she breathed. "And I'm making too much noise."

He turned off his microphone, gesturing for her to do the same. That way they could whisper without the three other teams overhearing.

"You can't expect to be able to keep up," he told her almost silently. "You haven't had the kind of training we have."

"Then why am I here?" she asked. "Why are any FInCOM agents here at all? We should be back on the *Irvin*. Our role should be to let the SEALs do their job without interference."

Harvard smiled. "I knew you were an overachiever. Two hours into the first of two training exercises, and you've already learned all you need to know."

"Two training exercises?"

He nodded. "This first one's almost guaranteed to go wrong. Not that we're going to try to throw it or anything. But it's difficult enough for Alpha Squad to pull off a mission like this when we're not weighed down with excess baggage—pardon the expression."

P.J. waved away his less than tactful words. She knew quite well how true they were. "And the second?"

"The second exercise is going to be SEALs only versus the Marines. It's intended to demonstrate what Alpha Squad can do if we're allowed to operate without interference, as you so aptly put it."

P.J. gazed at him. "So what you're telling me is that the SEALs never had any intention of making the Combined SEAL/FInCOM team work."

He met her eyes steadily. "It seemed kind of obvious right from the start that the CSF team was going to be nothing more than a source of intense frustration for both the SEALs *and* the finks."

She struggled to understand. "So what, exactly, have we been doing for all these weeks?"

"Proving that it doesn't work. We're hoping you'll be our link. We're hoping you'll go back to Kevin Laughton and the rest of the finks and make them understand that the only help the SEALs need from FInCOM is acknowledgment that we can best do our job on our own, without anyone getting in our way," he admitted. "So I guess what we've been doing is trying to win your trust and trying to educate you."

Lieutenant Hawken drifted into sight, a shadowy figure barely discernible from the foliage, his face painted with streaks of green and brown.

"So I was right about that poker game." P.J. nodded slowly, fighting the waves of disappointment and anger that threatened to drown her. Had her friendship with this man been prearranged, calculated? Was the bond between them truly little more than the result of a manipulation? She had to clear her throat before she could speak again. "I'm curious, though. Those times you put your tongue in my mouth—was that done to win my trust or to educate?"

Crash vanished into the trees.

"You know me better than to think that," Harvard said quietly, calmly.

Neither of them was wearing their protective goggles yet. They weren't close enough to the so-called terrorists' camp to be concerned about being struck by paint balls. The eastern sky was growing lighter with the coming sunrise, and P.J. could see Harvard's eyes. And in them she saw everything his words said, and more.

"We have two separate relationships," he told her. "We have this working relationship—" he gestured between them "—this mutual respect and sincere friendship that grew from a need on both our parts to get along."

He lifted his hand and lightly touched one finger to her lips. "But we also have *this* relationship." He smiled. "This one in which I find myself constantly wanting to put my tongue in your mouth—and other places, as well. And I assure you, my reasons for wanting that are purely selfish. They have nothing whatsoever to do with either SEAL Team Ten or FInCOM."

P.J. cleared her throat. "Maybe we can discuss this later—and then you can tell me exactly what kind of relationship you want between Alpha Squad and FInCOM. If I'm going to be your liaison, you're going to have to be up-front and tell me everything. And I mean *every*thing." She shifted the strap of her assault rifle on her shoulder. "But right now I think we've got an appointment to go get killed as part of a paint-ball slaughter to prove that the CSF team isn't going to work. Am I right?"

Harvard smiled, his eyes warm in the early-morning light. "We might be about to die, but you and me, we're two of a kind, and you better believe we're going to go down fighting."

CHAPTER THIRTEEN

"THEY'RE DEFINITELY NOT with the government," Wesley reported, his usual megaphone reduced to a sotto voce. "They're too well-dressed."

"Stay low." Blue McCoy's Southern drawl lost most of its molasses-slow quality as he responded to Wes from his position on the *Irvin*. "Stay out of sight until we know exactly who they are."

Harvard rubbed the back of his neck, trying to relieve some of the tension that had settled in his shoulders. This exercise had escalated into a full-blown snafu in the blink of an eye.

Wes reported that he and Bobby and Chuck Schneider were on a jungle road heading up the mountain when they'd heard the roar of an approaching truck. They'd gone into the crawl space beneath an abandoned building, purposely staying close to the road so they could check out whoever was driving by.

It turned out to be not just one truck but an entire military convoy. And this convoy wasn't just riding by. They'd stopped. Six Humvees and twenty-five transport trucks had pulled into the clearing. Soldiers dressed in ragged uniforms had begun to set up camp—directly around the building Bobby and Wes and Chuck were hiding in.

They were pinned in place at least until nightfall.

"No heroics." From the other side of the mountain, where his team was the closest to approaching the terrorist camp, Joe Cat added his own two cents to Blue's orders. "Do you copy, Skelly? Whoever they are, they've got real bullets in their weapons while you've only got paint balls."

"I hear you, Captain," Wes breathed. "We're making ourselves very, very invisible."

"Are the uniforms gray and green?" Crash asked.

Harvard looked at him. They were laying low, hidden in the thickness of the jungle, a number of clicks downwind of Joe Cat's team.

"Affirmative," Wes responded.

P.J. was watching Crash, too. "Do you know who they are?" she asked.

Lieutenant Hawken looked from P.J. to Harvard. Harvard didn't like the sudden edge in the man's crystal blue eyes. "Yes," Crash said. "They're the private army of a man known only as Kim. His nickname is the Korean, even though his mother is from the island. He's never moved his men this far north before."

Harvard swore under his breath. "He's one of the drug lords you were talking about, right?"

"Yes, he is."

From the USS *Irvin,* Blue McCoy spoke. "Captain I suggest we eighty-six this exercise now before we find ourselves in even deeper—"

"We're already in it up to our hips." Joe Cat's voice was tight with tension. "H., we're at the tree line near the Marines' training camp. How far are you from us?"

"Ten minutes away if you don't care who knows we're coming," Harvard responded. "Thirty if you do."

Joe swore.

"Captain, we're on our way." Harvard gestured for Hawken to take the point. As much as he wanted to lead the way, this island was Crash's territory. He could get them to Joe Cat more quickly.

"Joe, what's happening?" Blue demanded, his lazy accent all but gone. "Sit rep, please."

"We've got five, maybe six KIAs in the clearing outside

the main building," Joe Cat reported. "Four of 'em are wearing gray and green uniforms. At least one looks like one of our Marines."

KIA. Killed in action. Harvard could see P.J.'s shock reflected in her eyes as she gazed at him. His tension rose. If they'd stumbled into a war zone, he wanted her out of here. He wanted her on the *Irvin* and heading far away, as fast as the ship could move.

Unless...

"Captain, could it be nothing more than an elaborate setup?" Harvard's brain had slipped into pre-combat mode, moving at lightning speed, searching for an explanation, trying to make sense of the situation. And the first thing to do was to prove that this situation was indeed real. Once he did that, then he'd start figuring out how the hell he was going to get P.J. to safety. "I wouldn't put it past the Marines to try to freak us out with fake bodies, fake blood..."

"It's real, H." Joe Cat's voice left no room for doubt. "One of 'em crawled to the tree line before he died. He's not just pretending to be dead. This is a very real, very dead man. Whatever went down here probably happened during the night. The body's stonecold."

Blue's voice cut in. "Captain, I got Admiral Stonegate on the phone, breathing down my neck. I'm calling y'all back to the ship. Code eighty-six, boys and girls. Dead bodies—in particular dead Marines—aren't part of this training scenario. Come on in, and let's regroup and—"

"I've got movement and signs of life inside the main building," Joe Cat interrupted. "Lucky's moving closer to see if any of our missing jarheads are being held inside. We're gonna try to ID exactly who and how many are holding 'em."

"Probably not Kim's men," Crash volunteered. Over Harvard's headset, his voice sounded quiet and matter-of-fact. You couldn't tell that the man was moving at a near run up the mountain. "They wouldn't leave their own dead out at the mercy of the flies and vultures."

"If not Kim's men, then whose?" Harvard asked, watching P.J. work to keep up with Crash. He was well aware that he was disobeying Blue's direct order. And he was taking P.J. in the wrong direction. He should be leading her down this mountain, not up it. Not farther away from the ocean and the safety of the USS *Irvin*.

But until he knew for damn sure the captain and Lucky were safe, he couldn't retreat.

"The largest of the rival groups is run by John Sherman, an American expatriate and former Green Beret," Crash said.

"Captain, I know you want to locate the Marines," Blue's voice cut in. "I know you don't want to leave them stranded, but—"

"Lucky's signaling," Cat interrupted. "No sign of the Marines. Looks like there's a dozen tangos inside the structure and—"

Harvard heard what sounded like the beginning of an explosion. It was instantly muted, their ears protected by a gating device on one of the high-quality microphones. But whose microphone?

He heard Joe Cat swear, sharply, succinctly. "We've triggered a booby trap," the captain reported. "Greene's injured—and we've attracted a whole hell of a lot of attention."

Crash picked up the pace. They were running full speed now, but it still wasn't fast enough. The voices over Harvard's headset began to blur.

The sound of gunfire. Joe Cat shouting, trying to pull the injured fink to safety. P.J.'s breath coming in sobs as she fought to keep up, as they moved at a dead run through the jungle. Lucky's voice, tight with pain, reporting he'd been hit. Crash's quiet reminder that although they only had rifles that fired paint balls, they should aim for the enemies' eyes.

Joe Cat again—his captain, his friend—ordering Lucky to take Greene and head down the mountain while he stayed behind and held at least a dozen hostile soldiers at bay with a weapon that didn't fire real bullets.

Harvard added his voice to the chaos. "Joe, hang on—can you hang on? We're three minutes away!" But what was he saying? The captain had no real ammunition, and neither did they. They were charging to the rescue, an impotent, ridiculous cavalry, unable to defend themselves, let alone save anyone else.

But then Joe Cat was talking directly to him. His unmistakable New York accent cut through the noise, calm and clear, as if he weren't staring down his own death. "H., I'm counting on you and Crash to intercept Lucky and Greene and to get everyone back to the ship. Tell Ronnie I love her and that…I'm sorry. This was just supposed to be a training op."

"Joe, damn it, just hang on!"

But Harvard's voice was lost in the sound of gunfire, the sound of shouting, voices yelling in a language he didn't comprehend.

Then he heard the captain's voice, thick with pain but still defiant, instructing his attackers to attempt the anatomically impossible.

And then, as if someone had taken Joe Cat's headset and microphone and snapped it into two, there was silence.

Lucky's leg was broken.

P.J. was no nurse, but it was obvious the SEAL's leg was completely and thoroughly broken. He'd been hit by a bullet that had torn through the fleshy part of his thigh, and he'd stumbled. The fall had snapped his lower leg, right above the ankle. His face was white and drawn, but the tears in his eyes had nothing to do with his own pain.

He was certain that the Alpha Squad's captain was dead.

"I saw him go down, H.," he told Harvard, who was working methodically to patch up both Lucky and Greg Greene. Greg's hands and arms were severely burned from a blast that had managed to lift him up and throw him ten yards without tearing him open. It was a miracle the man was alive at all.

"I looked back," Lucky continued, "and I saw Cat take a direct shot to the chest. I'm telling you, there's no way he could've survived."

Harvard spoke into his lip mike. "What's the word on that ambulance? Farber, you still there?"

But it was Blue's voice that came through the static. "Senior Chief, I'm sorry, an ambulance is not coming. You're going to have to get Lucky and Greene down the mountain on your own."

Harvard came the closest to losing it that P.J. had seen since this mess had started. "Damn it, McCoy, what the hell are you still doing there? Get moving, Lieutenant! Get off that toy boat and get your butt onto this island. I need you *here* to get Cat out of there!"

Blue sounded as if he were talking through tightly clenched teeth. "The local government has declared a state of emergency. All U.S. troops and officials have been ordered off the island, ASAP. Daryl, I am unable to leave this ship. And I'm forced to issue an order telling you that you *must* comply with the government's request."

Harvard laughed, but it was deadly. There was no humor in it at all. "Like hell I will."

"It's an *order,* Senior Chief." Blue's voice sounded strained. "Admiral Stonegate is here. Would you like to hear it from him?"

"With all due respect, Admiral Stonegate can go to hell. I'm not leaving without the captain."

Harvard was serious. P.J. had never seen him *more* serious. He was going to go in after Joe Catalanotto, and he was going to die, as well. She put her hand on his arm. "Daryl, Lucky saw Joe get killed." Her voice shook.

She didn't want it to be true. She couldn't imagine the captain dead, all the vibrance and humor and light drained out of the man. But Lucky saw him fall.

"No, he didn't." Her touch was meant to comfort, but Harvard was the one who comforted her by placing his hand over hers and squeezing tightly. "He saw the captain get hit. Joe Cat is still alive. I heard him speak to the sol- diers who took him prisoner. I heard his voice before they cut his radio connection."

"You *wanted* to hear his voice."

"P.J., I *know* he's alive."

He was looking at her with so much fire in his eyes. He believed what he was saying, that much was clear. P.J. nodded. "Okay. Okay. What are we going to do about it?"

Harvard released her hand. "*You're* going back to the *Irvin* with Lucky and Greene. Crash will take you there."

She stared at him. "And what? You're going to go in after Joe all by yourself?"

"Yes."

"No." Blue's voice cut in. "Harvard, that's insanity. You need a team backing you up."

"Part of my team's injured. Part's pinned down by hostile forces, and part's pinned down just as securely by friendly forces. I don't have a lot to work with here, Lieutenant. Wes, you still got batteries? You still listening in?"

"Affirmative," Wesley whispered from his hiding place dead in the center of the rival army's camp.

"What are your chances of breaking free come night- fall?" Harvard asked him.

"Next to none. There're guards posted on all sides of this structure," Wes breathed. "Unless this entire army packs it in and moves out, there's no way we're getting out of here anytime soon."

P.J.'s heart was in her throat as she watched Harvard pace. She didn't know what the hell was going on, but she did know one thing for sure. There was no way she was going to walk away and leave him here. No way.

"Senior Chief, I have to tell you again to bring the wounded and get back to this ship," Blue said. "I have to tell you—we have no choice in this."

"What is this all about?" P.J. asked Blue. "What's happening? Why the state of emergency?"

"The missing Marines turned up at the U.S. Embassy about fifteen minutes ago," he told her. "Most were wounded. Two are still missing and presumed dead. They say they were ambushed late last night. They were taken prisoner, but they managed to evade their captors and make it down to the city.

"They're saying the men who attacked them are soldiers in John Sherman's private army. This is a drug war. If Joe is dead, he was killed as a result of a territorial dispute between two heroin dealers." His voice cracked, and he stopped for a moment, taking deep breaths before he went on.

"So we've got John Sherman up north, and this other army—the private forces of Sherman's rival, Kim—mobilizing. They're moving in Sherman's direction, as Bobby and Wes have seen, up close and personal. Both factions are armed to the teeth, and the government is staring down the throat of a full-fledged civil war. Their method of dealing with the situation is to kick all the Americans out of the country. So here we are. I'm stuck on this damn ship. Short of jumping over the side and swimming for shore, I cannot help you, H. I have to tell you—bring the rest of the team and come back in."

That was the third time Blue had said those words, *I have to tell you.* He was ordering them to come in because he had to. But he didn't want them to. He didn't want Harvard to return without the captain any more than Harvard did.

P.J. looked around, realizing suddenly that Crash was nowhere to be seen.

She turned off her lip mike and gestured for Harvard to do the same. He did, turning toward her, already guessing her question.

"He went to the encampment," he told her. "I asked him to go—to see if Joe really is alive."

P.J. held his gaze, feeling his pain, feeling her eyes fill with tears. "If Joe's dead," she said quietly, "we go back to the ship, okay?"

Harvard didn't nod. He didn't acknowledge her words in any way. He reached out and pushed an escaped strand of hair from her face.

"Please, Daryl," she said. "If he's dead, getting yourself killed won't bring him back."

"He's not dead." Crash materialized beside them, his microphone also turned off.

P.J. jumped, but Harvard was not surprised, as if he had some sixth sense that had told him the other SEAL had been approaching.

Harvard nodded at Hawken's news, as if he'd already known it. And he had, P.J. realized. He'd been adamant that Joe was still alive—and so the captain was. But for how long?

Crash turned on his microphone and pulled it to his mouth. "Captain Catalanotto's alive," he told Blue and the others on the ship without ceremony. "His injuries are extensive, though. From what I could see, he was hit at least twice, once in the leg and once in the upper chest or shoulder—I'm not certain which. There was a lot of blood. I wasn't close enough to see clearly. He was unable to walk—he was on a stretcher, and he was being transported north, via truck. My bet is he has been taken to Sherman's headquarters, about five kilometers up the mountain."

There was silence from the *Irvin,* and P.J. knew they'd temporarily turned off the radio. She could imagine Blue's heated discussion with the top brass and diplomats who cared more about the U.S.'s wobbly relationship with this little country than they did about a SEAL captain's life.

Harvard gestured to Crash to turn off his microphone.

"Tell me about Sherman's HQ," he demanded.

"It's a relatively modern structure," Hawken told him. "A former warehouse that was converted into a high-level security compound. I've been inside several times—but only because I was invited and let in through the front door. There are only a few places the captain could be inside the building. There're several hospital rooms—one in the northeast corner, ground floor, another more toward the front of the east side of the building." He met Harvard's eyes somberly. "They may well have denied him medical care and put him in one of the holding cells in the sub-basement."

"So how do I get in?" Harvard asked.

"Not easily," Crash told him. "John Sherman's a former Green Beret. He built this place to keep unwanted visitors out. There are no windows and only two doors—both heavily guarded. The only possibility might be access through an air duct system that vents on the west side of the building, up by the roof. I tried accessing the building that way, back about six years ago, and the ducts got really narrow about ten feet in. I was afraid I'd get stuck, so I pulled back. I don't know if getting inside that way is an option for you, Senior Chief. You've got forty or fifty pounds on me. Of course, it *was* six years ago. Sherman may have replaced the system since then."

"I bet *I* would fit."

Both men looked at P.J. as if they'd forgotten she was there.

"No," Harvard said. "Uh-uh. You're going back to the ship with Lucky and Greene."

She narrowed her eyes at him. "Why? I'm not wounded."

"That's right. And you're going to *stay* not wounded. There are real bullets in those weapons, P.J."

"I've faced real bullets before," she told him. "I've been a field agent for three years, Daryl. Come on. You know this."

"Crash needs you to help get Lucky and Greene to the ship."

She kept her voice calm. "Crash doesn't need me—*you* need me."

Harvard's face was taut with tension. "The only thing I need right now is to go into Sherman's headquarters and bring out my captain."

P.J. turned to face Crash. "Will I fit through the air ducts?"

He was silent, considering, measuring her with his odd blue eyes. "Yes," he finally said. "You will."

She turned to Harvard. "You need me."

"Maybe. But more than I need your help, I need to know you're safe." He turned away, silently telling her that this conversation was over.

But P.J. wouldn't let herself be dismissed. "Daryl, you don't have a lot of choices here. I know I can—"

"No," he said tightly. "I choose no. You're going back to the ship."

P.J. felt sick to her stomach. All those things he'd said to his sister, to his family, to her—they weren't really true. He didn't really believe she was his equal. He didn't really think she could hold her own. "I see." Her voice wobbled with anger and disappointment. "Excuse me. My fault.

Obviously, I've mistaken you for someone else—someone stronger. Someone smarter. Someone who actually walks their talk—"

Harvard imploded. His voice got softer, but it shook with intensity. "Damn it, I can't change the way I feel!" He reached for her, pulling her close, enveloping her tightly in his arms, uncaring of Lucky's and Greene's curious eyes. "You matter too much to me, P.J.," he whispered hoarsely. "I'm sorry, baby, I know you think I'm letting you down." He pulled away to look into her eyes, to touch her face. "I care too much."

P.J. could feel tears flooding her eyes. Oh, God, she couldn't cry. She never cried. She *refused* to cry. She fiercely blinked her tears back. This wasn't just about Harvard's inability to see her as an equal. This was more important than that. This was about his *survival*.

"I care, too," she told him, praying she could make him understand. "And if you try to do this alone, you're going to die."

"Yeah," he said roughly. "That's a possibility."

"No. It's more than a possibility. It's a certainty. Without me, you don't stand a chance of getting into that building undetected."

He was gazing at her as if he were memorizing her face for all eternity. "You don't know what a SEAL can do when he puts his mind to it."

"You've got to let me help you."

Blue's voice came on over their headsets. He sounded strangled. "There is no change in orders. Repeat, no change. Senior Chief, unless you are pinned down like Bob and Wes, and are unable to move, you *must* return to the ship. Do you copy what I'm saying?"

Harvard flipped on his microphone. "I read you loud and clear, Lieutenant." He turned it off again, still holding P.J.'s gaze. "You're going with Crash." He touched her cheek one last time before he pulled away from her. "It's time for you to get out of here."

"No," she said, her voice surprisingly calm. "I'm sorry, but I'm staying."

Harvard seemed to expand about six inches, and his eyes grew arctic cold. "This is not a matter of what you want or what you think is best. I'm giving you a direct order. If you disobey—"

P.J. laughed in his face. "You're a fine one to talk about disobeying direct orders. Look, if you can't handle this, maybe you should be the one who returns to the ship with Lucky and Greene. Maybe Crash is man enough to let me help him get Joe out of there."

"Yeah," Harvard said harshly. "Maybe that's my problem. Maybe I'm not man enough to want to watch you die."

His words washed her anger from her, and she took a deep breath. "I'll make a deal with you. I won't die if you don't."

He wouldn't look at her. "You know it doesn't work that way."

"Then we'll both do the best we can. We're two of a kind, remember? Your words." She moved toward him, touched his arm. "Please," she said softly. "I'm begging you to let me help. Trust me enough, respect me enough…"

The look on his face was terrible, and she knew this was the most difficult decision he'd ever made in his life.

P.J. spoke low and fast, aware he was listening, knowing that she would flat-out defy him if she had to, but wanting him to choose for her to stay.

"Trust me," she said again. "Trust *yourself.* You've stood up for me and supported me more times than I can count. You told me you would choose me to be on your team anytime. Well, it's time, brother. It's time for you to put your money where your mouth is. Choose me now. Choose me for something that truly matters." She took his hands, holding on to him tightly, trying to squeeze her words, her truth, into him. "I know it's dangerous—we both know that. But I've done dangerous before. It's part of my job to take risks. Look at me. You know me—maybe better than anyone in the entire world. You know my strengths—and my limitations. I may not be a SEAL, but I'm the best FInCOM agent there is, and I know—and you know—that I can fit through that air duct."

P.J. played her trump card mercilessly, praying it would be enough to make Harvard change his mind. "Joe Cat is *my* friend, too," she told him. "As far as I can see, I'm his only hope. Without me, you've got no way in. Take me with you, and maybe—maybe—together we can save his life."

Harvard was silent for several long moments. And then he pulled his lip mike close to his mouth and switched it on as he held P.J.'s gaze. "This is Senior Chief Becker. Lieutenant Hawken is proceeding down the mountain with Lieutenant O'Donlon and Agent Greene, as ordered. Unfortunately, Agent Richards and I have been pinned down and are unable to move. We'll report in with our status throughout the day, but at this moment, it looks as if we'll be unable to advance toward the *Irvin* until well after nightfall."

"I copy that, Senior Chief," Blue's voice said. "Be careful. Stay alive."

"Yeah." Harvard turned off his microphone, still holding P.J.'s gaze. "Why do I feel as if I've just lost my last toehold on my sanity?" He shouldered his weapon, turning his gaze toward Crash.

"If I can, I'll try to drop them into friendly territory," Hawken said, referring to Lucky and Greene, "then come back to help."

"Please do. It's hard to do our Mod Squad imitation without you." Harvard turned to P.J. "You ready?"

She nodded.

He nodded, too. "Well, that makes one of us."

"Thank you," she whispered.

"Hurry," he said, "before I change my mind."

CHAPTER FOURTEEN

"WHAT NOW?" P.J. asked as she and Harvard backed away from John Sherman's private headquarters.

"Now we find a place to lay low until nightfall," he said tersely, stopping to secure his binoculars in the pocket of his combat vest. "We'll take turns getting some sleep."

He hadn't said anything that wasn't terse since they'd split up from Hawken, five hours earlier.

P.J. knew Harvard was questioning his decision to let her help him. He was angry at himself, angry at her, angry at the entire situation.

They were going up against some seriously bad odds here. It was entirely possible that one or both of them could be dead before this time tomorrow.

P.J. didn't want to die. And she didn't want to plan around the possibility of her death. But she was damned if she was going to spend what could well be the last hours of her life with someone who was terse.

She gazed at Harvard. "I'm not sure how you're going to get any sleep with that great huge bug up your ass."

He finally, *finally* smiled for the first time in hours, but it was rueful and fleeting. "Yeah," he said. "I'm not sure, either." He looked away, unable to hold her gaze. "Look, P.J., I've got to tell you, I feel as if I'm hurtling down a mountain, totally out of control. Your being here scares the hell out of me, and I don't like it. Not one bit."

P.J. knew it hadn't been easy for him to tell her that. "Daryl, you know, I'm scared, too."

He glanced at her. "It's not too late for you to—"

"Don't say it," she warned him, narrowing her eyes. "Don't even think it. I'm scared, but I'm going to do what I need to do. The same way you are. You need my help getting into that place, and you know it."

They'd spent most of the past five hours lying in the underbrush, watching the comings and goings of the ragtag soldiers around John Sherman's private fortress.

And it was a fortress. It was a renovated warehouse surrounded by a clearing that was in constant danger of being devoured by the lushness of the jungle. Harvard had told P.J.—tersely—that the building dated from before the Vietnam War. It had been constructed by the French to store weapons and ammunition. Sherman had updated it, strengthening the concrete block structure and adding what appeared to be an extremely state-of-the-art security system.

Harvard and P.J. had studied the system, had watched the pattern of the guards and had kept track of the trucks full of soldiers coming and going. They'd examined the building from all angles and sides. Harvard had paid particular attention to the air duct near the roofline on the west side of the building, staring at it for close to thirty minutes through his compact binoculars.

"If I had two more SEALs—just two more—I wouldn't need to get in through the damn air duct," Harvard told her. "I'd use a grenade launcher and I'd blow a hole through the side of the building. With two more men, I could get Joe out that way."

"With two more men—and an arsenal of weapons," P.J. reminded him. "You haven't got a grenade launcher. You've got a rifle that fires paint balls."

"I can get the weapons we'd need," he told her, and she believed him. She wasn't sure how he'd do it—and she wasn't sure she wanted to know how. But the look in his eyes and the tone of his voice left little doubt in her mind that if he said he could get weapons, he could get weapons.

"In fact, I'm planning to confiscate some equipment as soon as it's dark. No way am I letting you go in there armed only with this toy gun." He turned away, reacting to the words he'd just spoken. "I may not let you go in there, anyway."

"Yes, you will," she said quietly.

He glanced at her again. "Maybe by nightfall Bob and Wes will break free."

P.J. didn't say anything. Harvard knew as well as she did that at last report, Wes had been close to certain the trapped SEALs wouldn't be able to move anytime soon. And he knew, too, that it was no good waiting for Crash to reappear.

They'd both listened over their radio headsets three hours earlier as Crash brought Lucky and Greene to safety. Anti-American sentiment in the city was high, and he'd had to bring the wounded men all the way down to the docks. Once there, he was trapped. The soldiers who were assisting in the American evacuation of the island were adamant about Crash returning to the *Irvin* with the other members of the CSF team.

Sure, Crash had tried to talk his way out of it. He'd tried to convince the soldiers to let him slip into the mountains, but they were young and frightened and extremely intent upon following their orders. Short of using excessive force, Crash had had no choice. At last report, he was with Blue McCoy on the USS *Irvin*.

And Harvard and P.J. were on their own.

There were no other SEALs to help Harvard rescue Joe Cat. There was only P.J.

She followed Harvard from Sherman's headquarters, trying to move even half as silently as he did through the jungle.

He seemed to know where he was going. But if there was an actual trail he was following, P.J. couldn't see it.

He slowed as they came to a clearing, turning to look

at her. "We're going to need to be extra careful crossing this field," he told her. "I want you to make absolutely sure that when you walk, you step in my footprints, do you understand?"

P.J. nodded.

Then she shook her head. No, she didn't really understand. Why?

But Harvard had already started into the clearing, and she followed, doing as he'd instructed, stepping in the indentations he made in the tall grass.

Was it because of snakes? Or was there something else—something even creepier, with even bigger teeth—hiding there? She shivered.

"If you really want me to do this, you've got to shorten your stride," P.J. told him. "Although it's probably not necessary because I can see—"

"Step *only* where I step," he barked at her.

"Whoa! Chill! I can pretty much see there're no snakes, so unless there's another reason we're playing follow the leader—"

"Snakes? Are you kidding? Jesus, P.J.! I thought you knew! We're walking through a field—a *mine*field."

P.J. froze. "Excuse me?"

"A minefield," Harvard said again, enunciating to make sure she understood. "P.J., this is a minefield. On the other side, across that stream, in those trees over there, there's a hut. It's kind of run-down because most folk know better than to stroll through this neighborhood to get there. Hawken told me about it—told me it was the safest place on this part of the island. He told me a way through this field, too—that's what we're doing right now."

Her eyes were huge as she stared at him, as she stared at the field that completely surrounded them. "We're taking a stroll through a *mine*field."

"I'm sorry. I thought you were listening when Crash told me about it." He tried to smile, tried to be reassuring. "It's no big deal—if you step exactly where I step. The good news is that once we get across we're not going to have to worry about locals running into us. Crash told me people around here avoid this entire area."

"On account of the minefield."

"That's right." Harvard went forward, careful to step precisely where Hawken had told him to.

"Has it occurred to you that this is insane? Who put these mines here? Why would they put *mines* here?"

"The French put the mines in more than thirty years ago." Harvard glanced back to see that she was following him carefully. "They did it because at the time there was a war going on."

"Shouldn't this field be cleared out—or at least fenced off? There wasn't even a sign warning people about the mines! What if children came up here and wandered into this field?"

"This was one of the projects the Marine FID team was working on," Harvard told her. "But there's probably a dozen fields like this all over the island. And hundreds more—maybe even thousands—all over Southeast Asia. It's a serious problem. People are killed or maimed all the time—casualties of a war that supposedly ended decades ago."

"How do you know where to step?" P.J. asked. "You *are* being careful aren't you?"

"I'm being *very* careful." His shirt was drenched with sweat. "Crash drew me a map of the field in the dirt. He told me the route to take."

"A map in the dirt," she repeated. "So, you're going on memory and a map drawn in the dirt."

"That's right."

She made a muffled, faintly choking sound—a cross between a laugh and a sob.

Harvard glanced at her again. Her face was drawn, her mouth tight, her eyes slightly glazed.

They were almost there. Almost to the edge of the field. Once they were in the stream, they'd be in the clear. He had to keep her distracted for a little bit longer.

"You okay?" he asked. "You're not going to faint on me or anything, are you?"

Her eyes flashed at that, instantly bringing life to her face. "No, I'm not going to faint. You know, you wouldn't have asked that if I were a man."

"Probably not."

"Probably— God, you admit it?"

Harvard stepped into the water, reaching back and lifting her into his arms.

"Put me down!"

He carried her across the shallow streambed and set her down on the other side. "All clear."

She stared at him, then she stared across the stream at the minefield. Then she rolled her eyes, because she knew exactly what he had done.

"The real truth is, I've seen plenty of big, strong guys faint," he informed her. "Gender doesn't seem to play a big part in whether someone's going to freeze up and stop breathing in a tense situation."

"I don't freeze up," she told him.

"Yeah, I'm learning that. You did good."

P.J. sat in the dirt. "We're going to have to do that again tonight, aren't we? Walk back through there? Only—God! This time we'll be in the dark."

"Don't think about that now. We've got to get some rest."

She smiled ruefully at him. "Yeah, I'm about ready for a nap. My pulse rate has finally dropped down to a near catatonic two hundred beats per minute."

Harvard couldn't help but laugh as he held out his hand to help her up. Damn, he was proud of her. This day had been wretchedly grueling—both physically and emotionally. Yet she was still able to make jokes. "You can take the first watch if you want."

"You're kidding. You trust me to stand watch?"

He looked at their hands. She hadn't pulled hers free from his, and he held on to it, linking their fingers together. "I trust you to do everything," he admitted. "My problem's not with you—it's with me. I trust you to pull off your Wonder Woman act without a hitch. I trust you to go into the building through that air duct, and I trust you to find Cat. I trust you to make all the right choices and all the right moves. But I've been in this business long enough to know that sometimes that's not enough. Sometimes you do everything right and you *still* get killed." He swore softly. "But you know, I even trust you to die with dignity, if it comes down to that."

He was silent, but she seemed to know he had more to say. She waited, watching him. "I just don't trust myself to be able to handle losing you. Not when I've just begun to find you. See, because I'm..." His voice was suddenly husky, and he cleared his throat. "Somehow I've managed to fall in love with you. And if you die...a part of me is going to die, too."

There it was. There *he* was. Up on the table, all prepped and ready for a little open heart surgery.

He hadn't meant to tell her. Under normal circumstances, he wouldn't have breathed a word. Under normal circumstances, he wouldn't have admitted it to himself, let alone to her.

But the circumstances were far from normal.

Harvard held his breath, waiting to see what she would say.

There were so many ways she could respond. She could turn away. She could pretend to misunderstand. She might make light of his words—make believe he was joking.

Instead, she softly touched his face. As he watched, tears

flooded her beautiful eyes, and for the first time since he'd met her, she didn't try to fight them.

"Now you know," she whispered, smiling so sweetly, so sadly, "why I couldn't go back with the others. Now you know why I wanted so badly to stay."

Harvard's heart was in his throat. He'd heard the expression before, but he'd never experienced it—not like this. He'd never known these feelings—not with Rachel, not ever.

It was twice the miracle, because although she hadn't told him she loved him, she'd made it more than clear that she felt something for him, too.

He bent to kiss her, and she rose onto her toes to meet him halfway. Her lips were soft and so sweet, he felt himself sway. He could taste the salt of her tears. Her *tears*. Tough, stoic P.J. was letting him see her cry.

He kissed her again, harder this time. But when he pulled her closer, the gear in his combat vest bumped into the gear in hers, and their two weapons clunked clumsily together. It served as a reminder that this was hardly the time and place for this.

Except there was nowhere else for them to go. And Harvard was well aware that this time they had, these next few hours, could well be the only time they'd ever have.

Unless they turned around and headed down the mountain. Then they'd have the entire rest of their lives, stretching on and on, endlessly into the future. He would have a limitless number of days and nights filled with this woman's beautiful smiles and passionate kisses.

He could see their love affair continue to grow. He could see him on his knees, asking her to be his wife. Hell, with enough time to get used to the idea, she might even say yes. He could see babies with P.J.'s eyes and his wicked grin. He could see them all living, happily ever after, in a little house with a garden that overlooked the ocean.

Harvard nearly picked her up and carried her across

that stream, through that minefield and toward the safety of the USS *Irvin*.

But he couldn't do it. He couldn't have that guaranteed happily ever after.

Because in order to have it, he'd have to leave Joe Cata-lanotto behind.

And no matter how much Harvard wanted the chance of a future with this woman, he simply couldn't leave his captain for dead.

Everything he was thinking and feeling must have been written on his face, because P.J. touched his cheek as she gazed into his eyes.

"Maybe we don't have forever," she said quietly. "Maybe neither one of us will live to see the sunrise. So, okay. We'll just have to jam the entire rest of our lives into the next six hours." She stood on her toes and kissed him. "Let's go find that hut of Crash's," she whispered. "Don't let me die without making love to you."

Harvard gazed at her, uncertain of what to say and how to say it. Yes. That was the first thing he wanted to say. He wanted to make love to her. As far as last requests went, he couldn't think of a single thing he'd want more. But her assumption was that they were going to die.

He might die tonight, but she wasn't going to. He had very little in his power and under his control, but he *could* control that. And he'd made up his mind. When he left tonight, he wasn't going to take her with him.

And she wouldn't follow him.

He'd made certain of that by bringing her here, to this cabin alongside this minefield. She'd be safe, and he'd radio Crash and Blue and make sure they knew precisely where she was. And after he got Joe out—*if* he got Joe out—he'd come back for her. If not, Blue would send a chopper to pick her up in a day or so, after the trouble began to die down.

She misread his silence. "I promise you," she told him,

wiping the last of her tears from her eyes. "I'll have no regrets tomorrow."

"But what if we live?" Harvard asked. "What if I pull this off and get Joe out and we're both still alive come tomorrow morning?"

"Yeah, right, I'm *really* going to regret *that*."

"That's not what I meant, and you know it, smart-ass."

"No regrets," she said again. "I promise." She tugged at his hand. "Come on, Daryl. The clock's running."

Harvard's heart was in his throat because he knew P.J. truly believed neither of them would survive this mission. She thought she had six hours left, but she was ready and willing to share those six hours—the entire rest of her life—with him.

He remembered what she'd told him, her most private, most secret childhood fantasy. When she was a little girl, she'd dreamed that someday she'd find her perfect man, and he'd love her enough to marry her before taking her to bed.

"Marry me." Harvard's words surprised himself nearly as much as they did her.

P.J. stared at him. "Excuse me?"

Still, in some crazy way, it made sense. He warmed quickly to the idea. "Just for tonight. Just in case I—we—don't make it. You told me you'd always hoped that your first lover would be your husband. So marry me. Right here. Right now."

"That was just a silly fantasy," she protested.

"There's no such thing as a *silly* fantasy. If I'm going to be your lover, let me be your husband first."

"But—"

"You can't argue that you don't have the time to support that kind of commitment, to make a marriage work. There's not much that can go sour in six hours."

"But it won't be legal."

She liked the idea. He could see it in her eyes. But the realistic side of her was embarrassed to admit it.

"Don't be so pragmatic," Harvard argued. "What is marriage, really, besides a promise? A vow given from one person to another. It'll be as legal as we want it to be."

P.J. was laughing in disbelief. "But—"

Harvard took her hand more firmly in his. "I, Daryl Becker, do solemnly…" She was still laughing. "Well, maybe not solemnly, but anyway, I swear to take you, P.J.—" He broke off. "You know, I don't even know what P.J. stands for."

"That's probably because I've never told you."

"So tell me."

P.J. closed her eyes. "Are you sure you're ready for this?"

"Uh-oh. Yeah. Absolutely."

She opened her eyes and looked at him. "Porsche Jane."

"Portia? That's not so strange. It's pretty. Like in the Shakespeare play?"

P.J. shook her head. "Nope. Porsche like in the really fast car."

Harvard laughed. "I'm not laughing at you," he said quickly. "It's just… It's so cool. I've never met anyone who was named after a car before. Porsche. It suits you."

"I guess it could have been worse. I could've been Maserati. Or even Chevrolet."

"I could see you as a Spitfire," he said. "Spitfire Jane Richards. Oh, yeah."

"Gee, thanks."

"Why Porsche? There's a story there, right?"

"Uh-huh. The nutshell version is that my mother was fourteen when I was born." P.J. crossed her arms. "So are we going to stand here talking for the next six hours, or what?"

Harvard smiled. "First I'm going to marry you. Then we'll get to the *or what*."

They were going to do this. They were going to go inside that run-down little hut that was guarded by a swamp on one side and a minefield on the other, and they were going to make love.

P.J. was trying so hard not to be nervous. Still, he knew she was scared. But he couldn't help himself—he had to kiss her.

As his mouth touched hers, there was an instant conflagration. His canteen collided with her first aid kit, but he didn't care. He kissed her harder, and she kissed him back just as ferociously. But then his binoculars slammed against her hunting knife, and he pulled back, laughing and wanting desperately to be free of all their gear—and all their clothes.

P.J. was breathless and giddy with laughter, too. "Well, my pulse rate is back up to a healthy three hundred."

Harvard let himself drown for a moment in her eyes. "Yeah. Mine, too." He cleared his throat. "Where was I? Oh, yeah. This marriage thing. I, Daryl Becker, take you, Porsche Jane Richards, to be my lawfully wedded wife. I promise to love you for the rest of my life—whether it's short or long."

P.J. stopped laughing. "You said only for tonight."

Harvard nodded. "I'm hoping that tonight will last a very long time." He squeezed her hand. "Your turn."

"This is silly."

"Yup. Do it anyway. Do it for me."

P.J. took a deep breath. "I, P. J. Richards, take you, Daryl Becker, as my husband for tonight—or for the rest of my life. Depending. And I promise…."

She promised what? Harvard was standing there, waiting for her to say something more, to say something deeply emotional. She wanted to tell him that she loved him, but she couldn't do it. The words stuck in her throat.

But he seemed to understand, because he didn't press her for more. Instead, he bowed his head.

"Dear God, we make these vows to each other here, in Your presence," Harvard said quietly. "There are no judges or pastors or notarized papers to give our words weight or importance. Just You, me and P.J. And really, what the three of us believe is all that truly matters, isn't it?"

He paused, and P.J. could hear the sound of insects in the grass, the stream gurgling over rocks, the rustle of leaves as a gentle breeze brought them a breath of cool ocean air.

Harvard looked up, met her gaze and smiled. "I think that since we haven't been struck down by lightning, we can pretty much assume we've been given an affirmative from the Man." He pulled her closer. "And I don't think I'm going to wait for Him to clear His throat and tell me it's okay to kiss the bride." He lowered his mouth to hers, but stopped a mere whisper from her lips. "You belong to me now, P.J. And I'm all yours. For as long as you want me."

P.J. stood in the jungle on the side of a mountain as Daryl Becker gently lifted her chin and covered her lips with his. She wasn't dressed in a white gown. He wasn't wearing a gleaming dress uniform. They were clad in camouflage gear. They were dirty and sweaty and tired.

None of this should have been romantic, but somehow, someway, it was. Harvard had made it magical.

And even though their vows couldn't possibly have stood up in a court of law, P.J. knew that everything he'd told her was true. She belonged to him. She had for quite some time now. She simply hadn't let herself admit it.

"Let's go inside," he whispered, tugging gently at her hand.

It was then she realized they'd been standing within ten yards of the hut the entire time.

It was covered almost completely by vines and plants.

With the thick growth of vegetation, it was camouflaged perfectly. She could have walked within six feet of it and gone right past, never realizing it was there.

Even the roof had sprouted plant life—long slender stalks with leaves on the end that grew upward in search of the sun.

"You said you wanted a house with a garden," Harvard said with a smile.

P.J. had to laugh. "This house *is* a garden."

The door was hanging on only one hinge, and it creaked as Harvard pushed it open with the barrel of his rifle.

P.J. held her weapon at the ready. Just because the house looked deserted, that didn't mean it was.

But it was empty. Inside was a single room with a hard-packed dirt floor. There were no plants growing—probably because they died from lack of sun.

It was dim inside, and cool.

Harvard set down his pack, then slipped the strap of his weapon over his shoulder. "I'll be right back." He turned to look at her before he stepped out the door. "I should've carried you over this threshold."

"Don't be prehistoric."

"I think it's supposed to bring luck," he told her. "Or guarantee fertility. Or something. I forget."

P.J. laughed as he went out the door. "In the neighborhoods *I* grew up in, those are two hugely different things."

She set her rifle against the wall, then slipped out of her lightweight pack. It was too quiet in there without Harvard. Too dark without his light.

But he was back within minutes, just after she'd taken off her heavy combat vest and put it beside her weapon and pack. He'd cut a whole armload of palm fronds and leaves, and he tossed them onto the floor. He took a tightly rolled, lightweight blanket from his pack and covered the cushion of leaves.

He'd made them a bed.

A wedding bed.

P.J. swallowed, and she heard the sound echo in the stillness.

Harvard was watching her as he unfastened the Velcro straps on his combat vest and unbuttoned the shirt underneath. His sleeves were rolled up high on his arms, past the bulge of his biceps, and P.J. found herself staring at his muscles. He had huge arms. They were about as big around as her thighs. Maybe even bigger. His shoulders strained against the seams of his shirt as he opened his canteen and took a drink, all the while watching her.

He was her husband.

Oh, she knew that legally what they'd done, what they'd said, wasn't real. But Harvard clearly had meant the words he'd spoken.

She got a solid rush of pleasure from that now. It was foolish—she knew it was. But she didn't care.

He held out his hand for her, and she went to him. Her husband.

Harvard caught his breath as P.J. slipped her hands inside the open front of his shirt. It was like her to be bold in an attempt to cover her uncertainty and fear. And she was afraid. He could see it in her eyes. But more powerful than her fear was her trust. She trusted him—if not completely, then at least certainly enough to be here with him now.

He felt giddy with the knowledge. And breathless from the responsibility. A little frightened at the thought of having to hurt her this first time. And totally turned on by her touch.

He slipped off his vest, turning away from her slightly to set it and the valuable equipment it held on the floor.

Her hands swept up his chest to his neck. She pushed his shirt up and off his shoulders. "You're so beautiful," she murmured, trailing her lips across his chest as she ran her palms down his arms. "You don't know how long I've been wanting to touch you this way."

"Hey, I think that's supposed to be my line." Harvard shook himself free from his shirt, letting it lie where it fell as he pulled her into his arms. Damn, she was so tiny, he could have wrapped his arms around her twice.

He felt the tiniest sliver of doubt. She was so small. And he…he wasn't. The sensation of her hands and mouth caressing him, kissing him, had completely aroused him. He couldn't remember the last time he'd been so turned on. He wanted her now. Hard and fast, right up against the cabin wall. He wanted to bury himself in her. He wanted to lose his mind in her fire.

But he couldn't do that. He had to take this slow. God help him, he didn't want to hurt her any more than he had to. He was going to have to take his time, be careful, be gentle, stay completely in control.

He kissed her slowly, forcing himself to set a pace that was laid-back and lazy. Because she certainly was going to be nervous and probably a little bit shy—

But then he realized with a shock that she'd already unbuttoned her shirt. He tried to help her pull it off, but he only got in the way as he touched the satiny smoothness of her arms, her back, her stomach. She was wearing a black sports bra. He wanted it off her, too, but he couldn't find the fastener. But then she began unbuckling her belt, and he was completely distracted.

She pulled away from him and sat on the blanket to untie her boot laces.

Harvard did the same, his blood pounding through his veins. His fingers fumbled as she kicked off her boots and socks, and then she was helping him—as if she were the old pro and he the clumsy novice.

She helped him get his boots off. Then, in one fluid motion, she quickly peeled off her pants and pulled her sports bra up and over her head.

So much for her being shy.

As she turned toward him, he wanted to stop her, to hold her at arm's length and just look at her. But his hands had other plans. He pulled her close and touched her, skimming his fingers along the softness of her skin, cupping the sweet fullness of her breasts in the palm of his hand.

She was the perfect mix of lithe athletic muscles and soft curves.

He kissed her, trying his damnedest not to rush. But she wasn't of the same mind. She opened her mouth to him, inviting him in, kissing him hungrily. She was an explosion of passion, a scorching embodiment of ecstasy, and he couldn't resist her. He groaned and kissed her harder, deeper, claiming her mouth with his tongue and her body with his hands. He rolled on the blanket, pulling her on top of him, letting her feel his hard desire against the softness of her belly, as he tried desperately to stay in control.

"I want to touch you," she whispered as she kissed his face, his neck, his chin. She pulled away slightly to look into his eyes. "May I touch you?"

"Oh, yeah." Harvard didn't hesitate. He took her hand and pressed her palm fully against him.

P.J. laughed giddily. "My God," she said. "And you intend to put that *where?*"

"Trust me," Harvard said. He drew in a breath as she grew bolder, as her fingers explored him more completely, encircling him, caressing him.

"Do I look like a woman who doesn't trust you?" she asked, smiling at him.

She was in his arms, wearing only her trust and a very small pair of black bikini panties. Yes, she trusted him. She just didn't trust him enough. If she had, she would have told him that she loved him, too. And she wouldn't have looked so frightened when he vowed to love her for the rest of his life.

It didn't matter. Harvard told himself again that it didn't

matter. Although he would have liked to hear it in words, P.J. was showing him exactly how she felt.

He touched the desire-tightened tip of her bare breast with one knuckle, then ran his finger down to the elastic edge of her panties. "You look like a woman who's not quite naked enough."

She shivered at his touch. "I'm more naked than you." Her hands went to his belt. "Mind if I try to even out the odds…and satisfy my raging curiosity at the same time?"

"I love your raging curiosity," Harvard said as she tugged down the zipper of his pants.

He hooked his thumbs in his briefs and pushed both them and his pants down his legs, and then—damn, it felt good!—she was touching him, skin against skin, her fingers curled around him.

Her eyes were about the size of dinner plates, and he leaned back on both elbows, letting her look and touch to her heart's content while he silently tried not to have a pleasure-induced stroke.

It was not like her to be quiet for so long, and she didn't disappoint him when she finally did speak. "Now I know," she told him, "what they mean when they talk about penis envy."

Harvard had to laugh. He pulled her to him for another scorching kiss, loving the sensation of her breasts soft against his chest, their legs intertwined, her hand still touching him, gently exploring, driving him damn near wild. And as much as he loved her touch, he loved this feeling of completeness, this sense of belonging and profound joy. Nothing had ever felt so right.

Or felt so wrong. The clock was ticking. All too soon this pleasure was going to end. He was going to have to lie to her, and then he was going to walk away—maybe never to see her again. That knowledge loomed over him, casting the bleakest of shadows.

Harvard pushed it away, far away. *Slow down.* He took a deep breath. He had to slow things down for more than one reason. He wanted this afternoon to last forever. And he didn't want to scare her.

But she kissed him again, and he lost all sense of reason. He took her breast into his mouth, tasting her, kissing and laving her with his tongue, and she arched against him in an explosion of pleasure so intense he nearly lost control.

He drew harder, and she moaned. It was a slow, sexy noise, and it implied that whatever she was feeling, it certainly wasn't fear.

He dipped his fingers beneath the front edge of her panties, and she stiffened, pulling away slightly. He slowed but didn't stop, lightly touching her most intimately as he gazed at her.

"Oh!" she breathed.

"Tell me if I'm going too fast for you," he murmured, searching her eyes.

"That feels so good," she whispered. She closed her eyes and relaxed against him.

"If you want, we can do it like this for a while," he told her.

She looked at him, surprised. "But…what about you? What about *your* pleasure?"

"This gives me pleasure. Holding you, touching you like this, watching you…" He took a moment to rid her of her panties. She was, without a doubt, the most beautiful woman he'd ever seen. "Believe me, we could do this all afternoon, and I'd do just fine in the pleasure department."

She cried out, and her grip on him tightened as his exploring fingers delved a little deeper. Her hips moved upward instinctively, pressing him inside her. She was slick and hot with desire, and he loved knowing that he'd done that to her.

She was his—and his alone. No other man had touched her this way, no other man before him. No other man had heard her moan with this passion. No other man would ever have this chance to be her first lover.

He kissed her possessively, suddenly dizzy from wanting and damn near aching with need, pressing the hard length of his arousal against the sweet softness of her thigh, still touching her, always touching her, harder now, but no less gently.

She returned his kisses fiercely, then pulled back to laugh at him. "You are such a liar," she accused him breathlessly. She imitated his voice. "We could do this all afternoon...."

"I'm not lying. It's true that I want you more than I've ever wanted anyone—I can't argue with that. But this is good, too. This is beyond good," he told her, taking a moment to draw one deliciously tempting nipple into his mouth. "I could do this for the rest of my life and die a happy man."

He gently grazed her with his teeth, and she gasped, her movement opening herself to him more completely. "Please," she said. "I want..." She was breathing raggedly as she looked at him.

"What?" he whispered, kissing her breasts, her collarbone, her throat. "Tell me, P.J. Tell me what you want."

"I want you to show me how we can fit together. I want to feel you inside of me."

He kissed her again, pushing himself off her. "I'll get a condom."

P.J. pushed herself onto her elbows. "You brought condoms on a training operation?"

Harvard laughed as he opened one of the Velcro pockets of his vest. "Yeah. You did, too. You should have three or four in your combat vest. To put over our rifle barrels in case of heavy rain, remember?"

She wasn't paying attention. She was watching him as he tore open the foil packet, her eyes heavy-lidded with desire. Her hair had come free from her ponytail, and it hung thickly around her shoulders. Her satin-smooth skin gleamed exquisitely in the dim light that filtered through the holes in the ancient ceiling.

Harvard took his time covering himself, wanting to memorize that picture of her lying there, naked and waiting for him. He wanted to be able to call it up at will. He wanted to be able to remember this little corner of heaven when he left tonight, heading for hell.

But then he could wait no longer.

She held out her arms for him, and he went to her. He crawled onto the blanket and he kissed her, his body cradled between her legs. He kissed her again and again—long, slow, deep kisses calculated to leave her breathless. They worked their magic on him, as well, and he came up for air, breathing hard and half-blind with need.

He reached between them, feeling her heat, knowing it was now or never. In order to give her pleasure, he first had to give her pain.

But maybe he could mask that pain with the heat of the fire he knew he could light within her.

He kissed her hard, launching a sensual attack against her, stroking her breasts, knowing she loved that sensation. He touched her mercilessly and kissed her relentlessly as he positioned himself against her, letting her feel his weight. Her hips lifted to meet him, and she rubbed herself against his length, damn near doing him in.

The wildfire he'd started was in him, as well, consuming him, burning him alive.

"Please," she breathed into his mouth between feverish kisses. "Daryl, please…"

Harvard shifted his hips and drove himself inside her.

She cried out, but it wasn't hurt that tinged her voice and echoed in the tiny hut. She clung to him tightly, her breath coming fast in his ear.

He could barely speak. He made his mouth form words. "Are you all right? Do you want to stop?"

She pulled back to look at him, her dark eyes wide with disbelief. "Stop? You want to *stop? Now?*"

He touched her face. "Just tell me you're okay."

"I'm okay." She laughed. "Understatement of the year."

Harvard moved. Gently. Experimentally. Holding her gaze, he filled her again, slowly this time.

"Oh, my," P.J. whispered. "Would you mind doing that again?"

He smiled and complied, watching her face.

When P.J. wanted to, she was a master at hiding her emotions. But as he made love to her, every sensation, every feeling she was experiencing was right there on her face for him to see. Their joining was as intimate emotionally as it was physically.

He moved faster, still watching her, feeling her move with him as she joined him in this timeless, ageless, instinctive dance.

"Kiss me," she murmured.

He loved looking in her eyes, but he would have done anything she asked, and he kissed her. And as she always did when she kissed him, she set him on fire.

And he did the same to her.

He felt her explode, shattering in his arms, and he spun crazily out of control. His own release ripped through him as she clung to him, as she matched his passion stroke for stroke. His heart pounded and his ears roared as he went into orbit. He couldn't speak, couldn't breathe.

He could only love her.

He rocked gently back to earth, slowly becoming aware that he was on top of her, pinning her down, crushing her. But as he began to move, she held on to him.

"Stay," she whispered. "Please?"

He held her close as he turned onto his back. "Is this okay?" She was on top of him, but he was still inside her.

P.J. nodded. She lifted her head and met his gaze. "Good fit."

Harvard had to laugh. "Yeah," he said. "A perfect fit."

She tucked her head under his chin, and he held her tightly, feeling her breath, watching the dappled light stream through the holes in the roof.

He couldn't remember the last time he'd felt such peace.

And then he did remember. It was years ago. Some holiday. Thanksgiving or Christmas. His sisters were still kids—he'd been little more than a child himself. He'd been away at college, or maybe it was during one of his first years in the Navy.

He'd been home, basking in the glow of being back, enjoying that sense of belonging after being gone for so long.

He felt that sense of completeness now—and it certainly wasn't because there was anything special about this little barely standing hut.

No, the specialness was lying in his arms.

Harvard held P.J. closer, knowing he'd finally found his home.

In less than six hours he was going to have to leave. It was entirely possible he was going to die. But Harvard knew that even if he lived, he'd never have this peace again. Because if he lived, P.J. was never going to forgive him.

CHAPTER FIFTEEN

BLUE McCoy paced the ready room of the USS *Irvin* like a caged panther.

Crash set the cardboard cups of coffee he carried in down on a table and silently pushed one of them toward the other man.

He went to the door and closed it in the face of the master-at-arms who'd been following him since he returned to the ship. It was obvious that everyone on board the *Irvin* expected him to try to get back to the island. McCoy was being watched just as closely. They'd both been warned that leaving the ship for any reason would be a court-martial-able offense.

"I can't stand this," McCoy said through clenched teeth. "He's alive. We should be able to go in after him *now*. You said yourself you don't think he's going to last more than a few days with the kind of injuries he's sustained."

It was possible Joe Catalanotto was already dead. McCoy knew that as well as Crash did. But neither of them spoke the words.

"Harvard's still there." Crash tried his best to be optimistic, even though experience told him reality more often than not turned out to be more like the worst-case scenario than the best. "You know as well as I do that the only thing pinning H. down is his inability to move during the daylight. He's planning to go in after the captain come nightfall."

"But Bob and Wes are really pinned down." Blue McCoy

sat at the table, his exhaustion evident, his Southern drawl pronounced. "Harvard's only one man."

Crash sat across from him. "He's got P.J. I think between the two of them, they can get Joe out." He took a sip of coffee. "What they may not be able to do is get Joe down the mountain and safely to this ship."

McCoy opened the tab on the plastic cover of his coffee, staring at it sightlessly for a moment before he looked at Crash. For all his fatigue, his eyes were clear, his gaze sharp.

"We need a helo. We need one standing by and ready to go in and pull them out of there the moment Harvard gives us the word." McCoy shook his head in disgust. "But I've already requested that, and the admiral's already turned me down." He swore softly. "They're not going to let an American helicopter in, not even for a medivac."

McCoy looked at Crash again, and there was murder in his eyes. "If the captain dies, there's going to be hell to pay."

Crash didn't doubt that one bit.

"You know, now I can add 'sacrificial virgin' to the vast list of employment opportunities that will never be open to me," P.J. mused.

As Harvard laughed, she felt his arms tighten around her. "Are there really that many on the list?"

She turned her head to look at him in the growing twilight, loving the feeling of his powerful, muscular body spooned next to hers, her back to his front. It still astonished her that a man so strong could be so tender. "Sure. Things like professional basketball player. Not only am I too short, but now I'm too old. And sperm donor is on the list for obvious reasons. So is the position of administrative assistant to a white supremacist. And then there's professional wrestler. That's never going to happen."

"Skyscraper window washer?" he suggested, amusement dancing in his eyes.

"Yup. High on the list. Along with rock climber and tightrope walker. Oh, yeah—and teen singing sensation. That went on the list the year I was an angel in a Christmas pageant. The singing part I could handle, but I *hated* the fact that everyone was looking at me. It's hard to be a sensation when you won't come out from behind the curtains."

His smile made his eyes warmer. "You get stage fright, huh? I never would've thought."

"Yeah, and I bet you don't get it. I bet come karaoke night at the officers' club you're the first one up on stage."

"I'm not an officer," he reminded her. "But yeah, you're right. I've definitely inherited my mother's acting gene."

"Your mother was an actress?"

"She still is," he told her. "Although these days, she's mostly doing community theater. She's really good. You'll have to see her some day."

Except it was all too likely they wouldn't have tomorrow, let alone some day. All they had was now, but the sun was sinking quickly, and *now* was nearly gone. Harvard must have realized what he'd said almost as soon as the words had left his lips, because his smile quickly faded. Still, he tried to force a smile, tried to ignore the reality of their nonexistent future, tried to restore the light mood.

He cupped his hand around her bare breast. "You might want to put *nun* on your list."

"Nun's been on the list for a while," she admitted, shivering at his touch, making an effort, too, to keep her voice light. "I say far too many bad words to ever have a shot at being a nun. And then, of course, there's all my impure thoughts."

"Ooh, I'd love to hear some of those impure thoughts. What are you thinking right now?" His smile was genuine, but she could still see the glimmer of a shadow in his eyes.

"Actually, I'm wondering why you're not an officer," she told him.

He made a face at her. "That's an impure thought?"

"No. But it was what I was thinking. You asked." P.J. turned to face him. "Why didn't you become an officer, Daryl? Joe told me you were approached often enough."

"The chiefs run the Navy," he told her. "Everyone thinks the officers do—including most of the officers—but it's really the chiefs who get things done."

"But you could've been a captain by now. You could've been the man leading Alpha Squad," she argued.

Harvard smiled as he ran one hand across her bare torso, from her breast to her hip and then back up, over and over, slowly, deliciously, hypnotically.

"I'm one of the men leading Alpha Squad," he told her. "Cat's a good captain. But he's a mustang—an enlisted man who made the switch to officer. He's had to fight like hell for every promotion. In some ways, that's good. He knows he's not randomly going to get bumped any higher into some job he's not suitable for. What he does best is right here, out in the real world."

"But you would be a mustang, too."

"I would be a mustang who'd attended Harvard University," he countered. "Every time I was approached by folks who wanted me to go to officer's training, I could see my future in their eyes. It involved spending a lot of time behind a desk. I don't know if the reason they wanted me so badly was to fill a quota, or what, but…"

"You don't really think that, do you?" she asked.

Harvard shrugged. "I don't know. Maybe. All my life, I watched my father struggle. He was one of the top—if not *the* top—English lit professors in the Northeast. But he wasn't known for that. He was 'that *black* English lit professor.' He was constantly being approached to join the staff of other colleges, but it wasn't because of his knowledge. It was because he would fulfill a quota. It was a constant source of frustration for him. I'm sure, particularly as a woman, you can relate."

"I can," she told him. "I don't know how many times I've been called in to join a task force and then told to take a seat at the table and look pretty. No one wanted my input. They wanted any news cameras that might be aimed in their direction to see that they had women on staff. Like, 'Look, y'all. We're so politically correct, we've got a *woman* working with us.'"

"That's why I didn't want to become an officer. Maybe I was just too leery, but I was afraid I'd lose my identity and become 'that black officer.' I was afraid I'd be a figurehead without any real power, safely stashed behind a desk for show." He shook his head. "I may not make as much money, and every now and then a smart-ass lieutenant who's nearly half my age comes along and tries to order me around, but other than that, I'm exactly where I want to be."

P.J. kissed him. His mouth was so sweet, so warm. She kissed him again, lingering this time, touching his lips with the tip of her tongue.

She could feel his mouth move into a smile. "I *know* you're thinking something impure now."

She was, indeed. "I'm thinking that if you only knew what I was thinking, you'd discover my awful secret."

He caught her lower lip between his teeth, tugging gently before he let go. "And what awful secret might that be?"

"The fact that no matter what I do, I can't seem to get enough of you."

His eyes turned an even warmer shade of whiskey brown as he bent to kiss her. "The feeling is definitely mutual."

She reached between them, searching for him—and

found him already aroused. Again. "You want to go four for four, my man?"

"Yes." He kissed her again, a sweet kiss. "And no. And this time, *no* wins. You're going to be sore enough as it is." His gaze flickered to the drying bloodstains on the blanket.

He'd been so gentle and tender after the first time they'd made love. He'd helped her get cleaned up, and he'd cleaned her blood off himself, as well. P.J. knew he hated the idea that he'd caused her any pain at all, and the blood proved he'd hurt her. Unintentionally. And necessarily, of course. But he *had* hurt her.

Still, he'd also made her feel impossibly good.

Harvard propped himself on one elbow and looked at her in the dwindling light. "Besides, my sweet Porsche Jane, it's time to think about heading out."

The fear P.J. had buried inside her exploded with a sudden rush. Their time was up. It was over. They had a job to do. A man's life to save. Their own lives to risk.

Harvard gently extracted himself from her arms and stood up. He gathered her clothes and handed them to her, and they both quietly got dressed.

Before they went to John Sherman's stronghold, Harvard was determined to find them some real weapons. He'd told her earlier he intended to do that alone.

P.J. broke the silence. "I want to go with you."

Harvard glanced up from tying his bootlaces. He'd propped opened the rickety door to the hut to let in the last of the fading evening light. His face was in the shadows, but P.J. knew that even if he'd been brightly illuminated, she wouldn't have been able to read his expression. It didn't seem possible that this was the man who'd spent the afternoon with her, naked and laughing in her arms.

"You know for a fact that I'll be able to do this faster—cleaner—without you." His voice was even, matter-of-fact.

Yeah, she did know that. It took him more than twice as long to move quietly through the jungle when she was with him. And *quietly* was a relative term. Her most painstakingly silent version of quiet was much noisier than his.

Without her, he could approach the fringes of the armed camp where Wes and Bobby were pinned down and he could appropriate real weapons that fired real, live ammunition.

Harvard straightened, pulling the edges of his shirt together.

P.J. watched his fingers fastening the buttons. He had such big hands, such broad fingers. It seemed impossible that he should be able to finesse those tiny buttons through their tiny buttonholes, but he did it nimbly—faster even than she could have.

Of course, she was far more interested in undressing the man than putting his clothes back on him.

"If something happens," he said, his voice velvety smooth like the rapidly falling darkness as he shrugged into his combat vest, "if I'm not back before sunup, get on the radio and tell Blue where you are." He took several tubes of camouflage paint from his pocket and began smearing black and green across his face and the top of his head. "Crash will know how to get here."

P.J. couldn't believe what she was hearing. "If you're not back before *sunup?*"

"Don't be going into that minefield on your own," he told her sternly, mutating into Senior Chief Becker. "Just stay right here. I'm leaving you what's left of my water and my power bars. It's not much, but it'll hold you for a few days. I don't expect it'll be too much longer before Blue can get a helicopter up here to extract you."

She pushed herself to her feet, realization making her stomach hurt. "You're not planning to come back, are you?"

"Don't be melodramatic. I'm just making provisions for

the worst-case scenario." He didn't look her in the eye as he fastened his vest.

P.J. took a deep breath, and when she spoke, her voice sounded remarkably calm. "So what time do you *really* expect to be back? Much earlier than sunrise, I assume."

He set his canteen and several foil-wrapped energy bars next to her vest, then looked straight at her and lied. She knew him well enough by now to know that he was lying. "I'll be back by ten if it's easy, midnight if it's not."

P.J. nodded, watching as Harvard checked his rifle. Even though the only ammunition he had was paint balls, it was the only weapon he had, and he was making sure it was in working order.

"You said you loved me," she said quietly. "Did you really mean it?"

He turned to look at her. "Do you really have to ask?"

"I have trust issues," she told him bluntly.

"Yes," he said without hesitation. "I love you."

"Even though I'm a FInCOM agent? A fink?"

He blinked and then laughed. "Yeah. Even though you're a fink."

"Even though you know that I get up and go to work every day, and sometimes that work means that people fire their weapons at me?"

He didn't try to hide his exasperation. "What does that have to do with whether or not I love you?"

"I have a very dangerous job. I risk my life quite often. Did you know that?"

"Of course I—"

"And yet, you claim you fell in love with me."

"I'm not just claiming it."

"Would you describe me as brave?" she asked.

"P.J., I don't understand what you're—"

"I know," she said. "I'm trying to make you understand. Just answer my questions. Would you describe me as someone who's brave?"

"Yes."

"Strong?"

"You know you are."

"*I* know exactly who and what I am," P.J. told him. "I'm trying to find out if *you* know."

"Yes, you're strong," he conceded. "You might not be able to bench press a lot of weight, but you can run damn near forever. And you have strength of character. Stamina. Willpower. Call it whatever you want, you've got it."

"Do you respect me for that?"

"Of course I do."

"And maybe even admire me a little?"

"P.J.—"

"Do you?" she persisted.

"You know it."

"As far as finks go, do you think I'm any good?"

He smiled.

"At my job," she clarified.

"You're the best," he said simply.

"I'm the best," she repeated. "At my *dangerous* job. I'm strong, and I'm brave, and you respect and admire me for that—maybe you even fell in love with me for those reasons."

"I fell in love with you because you're funny and smart and beautiful inside as well as out."

"But I'm also those other things, don't you think? If I weren't strong, if I didn't have the drive to be the best FInCOM agent I could possibly be, I probably wouldn't be the person I am right now, and you probably wouldn't have fallen in love with me. Do you agree?"

He was silent for a moment.

"Yeah," he finally said. "You're probably right."

"Then why," P.J. asked, "are you trying to change who I am? Why are you trying to turn me into some kind of romantic heroine who needs rescuing and protecting? Why are you trying to wrap me in gauze and keep me safe from harm when you know damn well one of the reasons you fell in love with me is that I don't need any gauze wrapping?"

Harvard was silent, and P.J. prayed her words were sinking in.

"Go and get the weapons you think we'll need," she told him. "And then come back so we can go about bringing Joe home. Together."

She couldn't read the look in his eyes.

She pulled him close and kissed him fiercely, hoping her kiss would reinforce her words, hoping he'd understand all she'd left unsaid.

He held her tightly, then he stepped toward the door.

"I'll be waiting for you," P.J. told him.

But he was already gone.

Across the room, Blue McCoy shot out of his seat as if someone had fired a rocket under his chair. He swore sharply. "That's it!"

Crash leaned forward. "What's it?"

"The solution to getting Joe out. I said it myself. They're not going to let an *American* helicopter fly into the island's airspace."

Crash laughed softly. "Of course. Let's go find a radio. I know who we can call. This could actually work."

Blue McCoy wasn't ready to smile yet. "Provided Harvard can get the job done on his end."

P.J. paced in the darkness.

She stopped only to flip up the cover of her waterproof watch and glance at the iridescent hands. As she watched, the minute hand jerked a little bit closer to midnight.

Harvard wasn't coming back.

She sank onto the cool dirt floor of the hut and sat leaning against the rough wooden wall, her rifle across her lap, trying to banish that thought.

It wasn't midnight yet.

And until it was after midnight, she was going to hang on tight to her foolhardy belief that Daryl Becker was going to return.

Any minute now he was going to walk in that door. He would kiss her and hand her a weapon that fired bullets made of lead rather than paint, and then they would go find Joe.

Any minute now.

The minute hand moved closer to twelve.

Any minute.

From a distance, she heard a sound, an explosion, and she sprang to her feet.

She crossed to the open doorway and looked out. But the hut was in a small valley, and she could see no farther in the otherworldly moonlight than the immediate jungle that surrounded her.

The explosion had been from beyond the minefield—of that much she was certain.

She heard more sounds. Distant gunfire. Single shots, and the unforgettable double bursts of automatic weapons.

P.J. listened hard, trying to gauge which direction the gunfire was coming from. John Sherman's home base was to the north. This noise was definitely coming from the south.

From the direction Harvard had headed to acquire his supply of weapons.

Cursing, P.J. switched on her radio, realizing she might be able to hear firsthand what the hell was going on. She'd turned the radio on now and then in the hours Harvard had been gone, but there was nothing to hear, and she'd kept turning it off to save batteries.

She could hear Wesley Skelly.

"Some kind of blast on the other side of the camp," he said sotto voce. "But the guards around this structure have not moved an inch. We are unable to use this diversion to escape. We remain pinned in place. Goddamn it."

P.J. held her breath, hoping, praying to hear Harvard's voice, as well.

She heard Blue McCoy telling Wes to stay cool, to stay hidden. Intel reports had come in informing them that Kim's army was rumored to be heading north. Maybe even in as few as three or four hours, before dawn.

P.J. made certain her mike was off before she cursed again. Dear Lord Jesus, the news kept getting worse. They would have to try to rescue Joe Catalanotto knowing that in a matter of hours Sherman's installation was going to be under attack from opposing forces.

That is, if Harvard weren't already lying somewhere, dead or dying.

And even if he weren't, she'd only been kidding herself all evening long. He wasn't going to come back. He couldn't handle letting her face the danger. He may well love her, but he didn't love her enough to accept her as she was, as an equal.

She was a fool for thinking she could convince him otherwise.

Then she heard another noise. Barely discernible. Almost nonexistent. Metal against metal.

Someone was coming.

P.J. faded into the hut, out of range of the silvery moonlight, and lifted the barrel of her rifle. Aim for the eyes, Crash had advised her. Paint balls could do considerable damage to someone not wearing protective goggles.

Then, as if she'd conjured him from the shadows, tall and magnificent and solidly real, Harvard appeared.

He'd come back.

He'd actually come back!

P.J. stepped farther into the darkness of the hut. The hot rush of emotion made her knees weak, and tears flooded her eyes. For the briefest, dizzying moment, she felt as if she were going to faint.

"P.J." He spoke softly from outside the door.

She took a deep breath, forcing back the dizzyness and the tears, forcing the muscles in her legs to hold her up. She set down her weapon. "Come in," she said. Her voice sounded only a tiny bit strained. "Don't worry, I won't shoot you."

"Yeah, I didn't want to surprise you and get a paint ball in some uncomfortable place." He stepped inside, pausing to set what looked like a small arsenal—weapons and ammunition—on the floor.

"Was that you? All that noise from the south?" she asked, amazed that she could stand there and ask him questions as if she had expected him to return, as if she didn't desperately want to throw her arms around him and never let go. "How did you get here so fast?"

He was organizing the weapons he'd stolen, putting the correct ammunition with the various guns. Altogether, there looked to be about six of them, ranging from compact handguns to several HK MP5 submachine guns. "I cut a long fuse. And I ran most of the way here."

P.J. realized his camouflaged face was slick with perspiration.

"I tried to create a diversion so Bob, Wes and Chuck could escape," he told her. He laughed, but without humor. "Didn't happen."

"Yeah," she said. "I heard." God, she wanted him to hold her. But he kept working, crouched close to the ground. He glanced at her in the darkness. She asked, "Are you sure you're all right?"

"I had hardly any trouble at all. The outer edges of the camp aren't even patrolled. The place should've had a sign saying Weapons R Us. I walked in and helped myself to what I wanted from several different tents. The irony is that the only real guards in the area are the ones standing by the structure where the CSF team is hiding." He straightened and held a small handgun—a Browning—and several clips of ammunition out to her. "Here. Sorry I couldn't get you a holster."

That was when she saw it—the streak of blood on his cheek. "You're bleeding."

He touched his face with the back of his hand and looked at the trace of blood that had been transferred to it. "It's just a scratch."

She worked to keep her voice calm. Conversational. "Are you going to tell me what happened? How you got scratched?"

He met her eyes briefly. "I wasn't as invisible as I'd hoped to be. I had to convince someone to take a nap rather than report that I was in the neighborhood. He wasn't too happy about that. In the struggle, he grabbed my lip mike and snapped it off—tried to take out my eye with it, too. That's what I get for being nice. If I'd stopped him with my knife right from the start, I wouldn't be out a vital piece of equipment right now."

"You can use my headset," P.J. told him.

"No. You're going to need it. I can still listen in, but I'm not going to be able to talk to you unless I can get this thing rewired." He laughed again, humorlessly. "This op just keeps getting more and more complicated, doesn't it?"

She nodded. "I take it you heard the news?"

"About Kim's sunrise attack? Oh, yeah. I heard."

"And still you came back," she said softly.

"Yeah," he said. "I lost my mind. I came back."

"I guess you really do love me," she whispered.

He didn't say anything. He just stood there looking at her. And P.J. realized, in the soft glow of the moonlight, that his eyes were suddenly brimming with tears.

She stepped toward him as he reached for her and then,

God, she was in his arms. He held her tightly, tucking her head under his chin.

"Thank you," she said. "Thank you for listening to what I told you."

"This is *definitely* the hardest thing I've ever done." His voice was choked. "But you were right. Everything you said was too damn *right*. I *was* trying to change who you are, because part of who you are scares the hell out of me. But if I'd wanted a lady who needed to be taken care of, someone who was happier sitting home watching TV instead of chasing bad guys across the globe, I would've found her and married her a long time ago." He drew in a deep breath. "I do love who you are. And right now, God help me, who you are is the FInCOM agent who's going to help me save the captain."

"I know we can pull this off," she told him, believing it for the first time. With this man by her side, she was certain she could do anything.

"I think we can, too." He pushed her hair from her face as he searched her eyes. "You're going to go in that air duct and—with stealth—you're going to locate the captain and then you're going to come out. You find him, we pinpoint his location and then we figure out the next step once you're safely out of there. Are we together on this?"

She nodded. "Absolutely, Senior Chief."

"Good." He kissed her. "Let's do this and go home."

P.J. had to smile. "This is going to sound weird, but I feel kind of sad leaving here—kind of like this place *is* our home."

Harvard shook his head. "No, it's not this place. It's this thing—" he gestured helplessly between the two of them "—this thing we share. And that's going to follow wherever we go."

"You mean love?"

He traced her lips with his thumb. "Yeah," he said. "I wasn't sure you were quite ready to call it that, but…yeah.

I know it's love. Gotta be. It's bigger than anything I've ever felt before."

"No, it's not," P.J. said softly. "It's smaller. Small enough to fill all the cracks in my heart. Small enough to sneak in when I wasn't looking. Small enough to get under my skin and into my blood. Like some kind of virus that's impossible to shake." She laughed softly at the look on his face. "Not that I'd ever want to shake it."

The tears were back in his beautiful eyes, and P.J. knew that as hard and as scary as it was to put what she was feeling into words, it was well worth it. She knew that he wanted so badly to hear the things she was saying.

"You know, I expected to live my entire life without knowing what love really is," she told him quietly. "But every time I look at you, every time you smile at me, I think, Oh! So *that's* love. That odd, wonderful, awful feeling that makes me both hot and cold, makes me want to laugh and cry. For the first time in my life, Daryl, I know what the fuss is all about.

"I was hoping you'd understand when I gave you my body today that my heart and soul were permanently attached. But since you like to talk—you do like your words—I know you'd want to hear it in plain English. I figured since we weren't going to get much of a chance to chat after we leave this place, I better say this now. I love you. *All* of you. Till death do us part, and probably long after that, too. I was too chicken to say that when we were…when I—"

"When you married me," Harvard said, kissing her so sweetly on the lips. "When we got back to the States, I was going to make you realize just how real those vows we made were. I was going to wear you down until you agreed to do an encore performance in front of the pastor of my parents' new church."

When we get back. Not *if.*

But marriage?

"Marriage takes so much time to make it work," P.J. said cautiously. "We both have jobs that take us all over the country—all over the world. We don't have time—"

Harvard handed her one of the submachine guns. "We don't have time *not* to spend every minute we can together. I think if I learned only one thing in these past few hours, it's that." He looped the straps of the other weapons over his shoulders. "So what do you say? Are you good to go?"

P.J. nodded. "Yes," she said. It didn't matter if he were talking about this mission or their future. As long as he was with her, she was definitely good to go.

CHAPTER SIXTEEN

"YOU HAVE AN HOUR, NINETY MINUTES TOPS," Harvard told P.J., "before the guards' shift changes."

P.J. had made the climb to the roof of Sherman's head-quarters with no complaining. And now she was going to have to dangle over the edge of the roof while she squeezed herself into an air vent in which Harvard couldn't possibly fit.

He'd taken several moments in the jungle to try to rewire his microphone. He got a connection, but it was poor, at best, coming and going, crackling and weak. It was held together by duct tape and a prayer, but it was better than nothing.

They'd also switched to a different radio channel from the one being monitored by the USS *Irvin*.

P.J. stripped off her pack and combat vest to make her-self as small as possible for her trip through the ventilation system. She tucked the handgun into her pants at the small of her back and carried the MP5 and a small flashlight.

She took a deep breath. "I'm ready," she said.

She was cool and calm. He was the one having the cold sweats.

"The clock's running," she reminded him.

"Yeah," he said. "Talk to me while you're in there."

"I will—if I can."

He couldn't ask for anything more. They'd been over this four hundred times. There wasn't much else he could say, except to say again, "If something goes wrong, and you do get caught, tell me where you are in the building.

Which floor you're on, which corner of the building you're closest to. Because I'll come and get you out, okay? I'll figure out a way." He removed the grille from the vent and lifted P.J. in his arms. "Don't look down."

"I won't. Oh, God."

She had to go into the vent headfirst. Weapon first.

"Be careful," he told her.

"I promise I will."

Bracing himself, Harvard took a deep breath, then lowered the woman he loved more than life itself over the edge of the roof.

It was hot as hell in there.

P.J. had imagined it would be cool. It was part of the air-conditioning system, after all. But she realized the duct she was in was the equivalent of a giant exhaust pipe. It was hot and smelled faintly of human waste.

It was incredibly close, too.

Small places didn't bother her, thank God. But Harvard would've hated it. He certainly would have done it if he had to, but he would have hated it the entire time.

Of course, the point was moot. He would never fit. She barely fit herself.

Her shirt caught on another of the metal seams, and she impatiently tugged it free. It caught again ten feet down the vent, and she wriggled out of it.

She checked it quickly, making sure it was sanitized—that there was nothing on it, no marks or writing that would link it to her or to anyone American. But it was only a green and brown camouflage shirt. High fashion for the well-dressed guerrilla in jungles everywhere.

P.J. left it behind and kept going.

She concentrated on moving soundlessly. Moving forward was taking her longer than she'd anticipated. She had to exert quite a bit of energy to remain silent in the boomy metal air duct. Unless she was very, very careful, her boots could make a racket, as could the MP5.

She pulled herself along on her elbows, weapon in front of her, praying this duct would lead her straight to Captain Joe Catalanotto.

As Harvard attached the grille to the air duct, he had to be careful. The mortar between the concrete blocks was crumbling. He didn't want a pile of fine white dust gathering on the ground to catch some alert guard's eye and tip him off to the activity on the roof.

Up close, it was clear the entire building was in a more pronounced state of decay than he'd thought.

Harvard felt a tug of satisfaction at that. No doubt the past few years' crackdown on the local drug trade had had an effect on John Sherman's bank accounts.

If they were lucky—if they were *really* lucky—he and P.J. would pull the captain out, and then these two warring drug lords would efficiently proceed to wipe each other out.

"Approaching a vent." P.J.'s voice came over his headset and he gave her his full attention.

"It's on the left side of the air duct," she continued almost soundlessly. "Much too small to use as an exit, even for me."

Harvard found himself praying again. Please, God, keep her safe. Please, God, don't let anyone hear her.

More minutes passed in silence.

"Wait a minute," he heard her say. "There's something, some kind of trapdoor above me."

Harvard held his breath. He had to strain to hear her voice, she was speaking so quietly.

"It opens into some kind of attic," she reported. "Or at least part of it is an attic. I'm going up to take a look."

For several moments, Harvard heard only her quiet breathing, then, finally, she spoke again.

"The building's actually divided into thirds. The two outer thirds have this atticlike loft I'm standing in. They're clearly being used for storage. The edges—the loft—overlooks the center of the building, which is open from the roof all the way down to the ground floor. There are emergency lights—dim yellow lights—by the main doors. From what I can see, it looks big enough to house half a dozen tanks." Her voice got even lower. "Right now it's being used as sleeping quarters for what's got to be five hundred men."

Five hundred...

"Here are my choices," she continued. "Either I take a set of stairs down and tiptoe across a room filled with sleeping soldiers—"

"No," Harvard said. "Do you copy, P.J.? I said, *no*."

"I copy. And that was my first reaction, too. But the only other way to the northeast section of the building—where Crash thought Joe might be held—is a series of catwalks up by the roof."

Harvard swore.

"Yeah, I copy that, too," she said.

"Come back," he said. "We'll figure out another way in."

"Can't hear you, Senior Chief," she told him. "Better fix that mike again. Your message is breaking up."

"You heard me and you damn well know it."

"I can do this, Daryl." Her voice rang with conviction. "I know I can. All I have to do is think of you, and it's like you're right here with me. Holding my hand, you know?"

He knew. He opened his mouth to speak, but then shut it. He took a deep breath before he spoke. "Just don't look down."

P.J. had to look down. She had to make sure none of the men sleeping below had awakened and spotted her.

There were no guards in the room, at least. That was a lucky break.

She moved silently and very, *very* slowly along the catwalk.

Of course, even taking that one lucky break into account, this was about as bad as it could be. The catwalk swayed slightly with every step she took. It was metal and ancient and didn't even give the illusion of being solid. The part she was walking on was like a grille. She could see through the strips of metal, past her feet, all the way down to the concrete floor.

Adrenaline surged through her, making her ears roar. What she needed most was a clear head and total silence to hear the slight movement that would indicate one of the five hundred men was rolling over, temporarily awake and staring at the ceiling.

Still, being up here was better than walking through a minefield, of that she was certain.

P.J. took another step.

She could feel Harvard's presence. She could sense him listening to her breathing. She could feel him with her, every step she took.

She clutched her weapon—the Browning he'd risked his life to get for her—and took another step forward. And another step. And another.

Crash leaned over Blue McCoy's shoulder.

"Harvard's not responding," Blue said grimly. "Either his radio's off or he's switched to another channel."

They both knew there was another possibility. He could be dead.

"I'll start looking for him." The look in Blue's eyes told Crash he would not consider that third possibility.

Crash keyed the thumb switch to his radio and spoke in rapid French. He turned to Blue. "Let's keep that original channel open, too."

"Already doing that."

* * *

Harvard sat on the roof, watching for an unexpected guard and listening to P.J.'s steady breathing as she walked across a flimsy catwalk two stories above five hundred sleeping enemy soldiers.

She was doing okay. He could tell from the way she was breathing that she was doing okay. He was the one who was totally tied in knots.

"I'm still here with you, baby," he murmured, hoping his microphone worked well enough for her to hear him.

She didn't answer. That didn't necessarily mean she couldn't hear him. After all, she was trying to be silent.

He tried to listen even harder, tried to hear the sound of her feet, but all he could hear was the desperate beating of his own heart.

Finally, she spoke.

"I'm across," she said almost silently, and Harvard drew in the first breath he'd taken in what seemed like hours.

There was more silence as one minute slipped into two, two into three. He tried to visualize her moving down metal stairs, slowly, silently, moving through corridors where there was no place to hide.

Damn, this was taking too long. P.J. had been inside for close to twenty-five minutes already. She only had five more minutes before she'd reach the halfway point as far as time went. She had only five minutes before she would have to turn around and come back—or risk certain discovery when the guards' shift changed and the men they'd temporarily put out of action were discovered.

"I've found the first of the hospital rooms," P.J. finally said. "The one in the northeast corner is dark and empty. Moving to the next area, toward the front and middle of the building."

He heard her draw in her breath quickly, and his heart

rate went off the chart. "Situation report!" he ordered. "P.J., what's happening?"

"The other room has a guard by the door. He's sitting in a chair—asleep," she breathed. "But the door's open. I'm going to go past him."

Harvard sat up straight. "Go inside and close and lock the door after you. Do whatever you can to keep them from getting in behind you, do you understand?"

P.J. pulled her lip mike closer to her mouth. "Harvard, you're breaking up. I heard you tell me to lock the door behind me, but I lost the rest. Come back."

Static.

Damn. What had he been trying to tell her? What good would locking herself into a room with the captain do? And she didn't even know if Joe was in that room.

She moved slowly, soundlessly toward the sleeping guard.

She could do this. She could be as invisible and silent as Harvard was—provided she was on a city street or inside a building.

The guard's slight snoring stopped, and she froze, mere feet away from the man. But then he snorted, and his heavy breathing resumed. She slipped through the door.

And found Captain Joe Catalanotto lying on the floor.

It was obvious he'd started out on a hospital bed. He'd been cuffed to the bed. The opened cuffs were still attached to the railing.

Somehow he'd managed to get himself free.

But he hadn't had the strength to make it more than a few steps before he'd collapsed, apparently silently enough not to alert the guard.

P.J. quietly closed the door, locking it as Harvard had instructed. It was dark without the dim glow from the emergency lights in the hallway.

She took her flashlight from her pocket and switched it

on, checking quickly around the room to make sure there was no other door, no other way in or out.

There wasn't.

This was definitely insane. She'd locked the door, but someone on the other side surely had a key.

Holding her breath, she knelt next to Joe and felt for a pulse.

Please, God…

His skin was cool and clammy, and her stomach lurched. Dear Lord Jesus, they'd come too late.

But wait—he *did* have a pulse. It was much too faint, far too slow, but the man was still alive.

"Daryl, I found him," P.J. whispered into her mike. "He's alive, but he won't be for long if we don't get him out of here now."

Static. Harvard's voice was there, but she couldn't make out what he was telling her. "…scribe…cation…"

Scribe? Cation?

Describe her location!

She did that quickly, telling him in detail how many meters away from the northeast corner room she and Joe were. She gave him an approximation of the room's dimensions, as well as a list of all the medical equipment, the counters and sinks, even the light fixtures on the ceiling.

She also told him, in detail, about Joe's condition as she quickly examined the captain's wounds. "He's got both an entrance and an exit wound in his upper right leg," she reported. "And he wasn't shot in the chest, thank God. He took a bullet in his left shoulder—no exit wound, it's still in there. As far as I can tell, there was only the vaguest effort made to stop his bleeding—as a result he's lost a lot of blood. His face looks like hell—his eyes are swollen and bruised, and his lip's split. It looks like the bastards gave him one hell of a beating. God only knows if he's got internal injuries from that. Daryl, we've got to get him to the sick bay on the *Irvin*. Now."

Static. "…backup…ready for me!"

God knows they needed backup, but she knew for damn sure it wasn't coming.

As far as getting ready for him went, get ready for him to do what?

"Please repeat," she said.

Static.

"I don't copy you, Senior Chief! Repeat!"

More static.

P.J. flashed her light around the room. The beam came to rest against the concrete blocks of the wall. She flashed her light around the room again. Only one wall was made of concrete blocks, the outer wall.

P.J. remembered Harvard telling her that all he'd need were two more SEALs and a grenade launcher and…

Back up. Harvard wasn't talking about backup. He was telling her to back up. To move back, away from the outer wall.

The captain was much too close to it. P.J. grabbed him under both arms and pulled.

Joe groaned. "Ronnie?" he rasped.

"No, I'm sorry, Joe, it's only me. P. J. Richards," she told him. "I know I'm hurting you, sweetie, but Harvard's coming, and we've got to move you out of his way."

"That's *Captain* Sweetie," he said faintly. "Gonna have to…help me. Don't seem to have muscles that work."

God, he was big. But somehow, between the two of them, they moved him into the corner farthest from the outside wall. P.J. quietly pulled the mattress from the hospital bed and set it in front of them—a better-than-nothing attempt to shield them from whatever was coming.

This was definitely insane.

Even if they made it out by blowing a hole through the wall, the noise was going to raise a few eyebrows. Wake up a few hundred sleeping soldiers.

And then what? Then they'd be screaming down the

mountain—provided Harvard could hotwire one of those trucks out front—with five hundred of Sherman's soldiers on their tail, and God knows how many of Kim's men advancing toward them.

If they were going to get out of here, there was only one way they could go without getting caught.

And that was straight up.

P.J. flipped to the main channel on her radio. "Blue, are you there?" *Please, God, please be there.*

"P.J.? Lord, where have you been!" The taciturn SEAL sounded nearly frantic.

"I'm with Joe right now. He's alive, but just barely."

Blue swore.

"You said you were the voice of God," P.J. told him, "and I hope you're right. We need you to make us a miracle, Lieutenant. We need a chopper, and we need it now."

"I copy that, P.J.," Blue's voice said. "We've got—"

He kept talking, but she didn't hear what he had to say, because, with a thundering crash, the wall in front of her collapsed.

She shielded Joe with her body as alarms went off and dust and light filled the air. But it wasn't light from a fire.

It was light from the headlights of a truck.

Harvard had driven one of Sherman's armored trucks right through the wall!

The man himself appeared through the flying dust like some kind of wonderful superhero.

"I've got Cat." He picked up the captain effortlessly as if he weighed nothing at all. "Drive or shoot?" he asked.

P.J. didn't hesitate as she scrambled into the truck. "Shoot." She did just that, aiming at the soldiers and guards who were coming to investigate the crash.

Harvard was behind the wheel in an instant, the captain slumped on the bench seat between them.

"I can shoot, too," Joe Cat gasped as Harvard spun the wheels, backing them up and out of the rubble.

"Yes, sir," P.J. said. "I don't doubt that you can. But right now, Captain, your job is to keep your head down."

She squeezed the trigger of an HK MP5, firing through a special slot in the side of the vehicle. All around them, soldiers scattered.

Harvard put the truck in gear. Tires screaming, they headed down the mountain.

"I had time to disable all but one other truck," Harvard announced. "And we got it right on our tail." He swore.

"We've also got an entire army advancing toward us," P.J. reminded him.

"I'm well aware of that," he said grimly. He was driving with two hands tight on the steering wheel as he negotiated the steep, curving mountain roads.

There was a jolt as the truck behind them rammed them. Clearly the driver knew the roads better than Harvard did.

Harvard punched the truck into overdrive and slammed the gas pedal to the floor. They shot forward. "Get this guy off my butt," he told P.J. "The windshield's bulletproof—don't aim for him. Shoot out his tire."

She held up her submachine gun. "This thing isn't exactly a big favorite among sharpshooters," she told him. "I'll be lucky if I can—"

"There's a rifle on the floor. Use it."

P.J. lifted her feet. Sure enough, there was a small arsenal stored there. She grabbed the rifle, checked that it was loaded and opened the window that looked out onto the open back of the truck.

It wasn't an easy shot—not with both trucks moving. She sighted the front left tire.

Before she could squeeze the trigger, a helicopter appeared, roaring above them, tracking them down the jungle road. There was a red cross on its underside, clearly visible even in the predawn, along with a painting of the French flag.

Blue McCoy had come through with that miracle.

P.J. took careful aim at the other truck and fired the rifle.

The truck jerked, skidded and careened off the road and into the trees.

"Nice shot," Harvard said matter-of-factly. "For a girl."

P.J. laughed as she pulled her lip microphone closer to her mouth. "This is FInCOM Agent P. J. Richards, hailing the French medivac chopper. Captain Catalanotto and Senior Chief Becker and I are traveling south, currently without immediate pursuit, in the armored vehicle you are tracking. The captain is in need of immediate medical attention. Let's find a place we both can stop so we can get him on board."

"This is Captain Jean-Luc Lague," a heavily accented voice informed her. "There is a clearing half a kilometer down the road."

"Good," P.J. said as she put her arms around Joe, cradling him against the jostling of the truck. His shoulder had started bleeding again, and she used a scrap of his shirt to lightly apply pressure to the wound. "We'll stop there. But you'll have to take us on board without landing, Captain Lague. There are minefields all over this island."

"I can hover alongside the road."

"Great," P.J. told him. She glanced over to find Harvard smiling at her. "I'm sorry," she said, suddenly self-conscious. She turned off her mike. "It's just...I figured I was the only one of us who had a microphone that worked, and..."

"You did great," Harvard said. "And you're right. My mike's not working, Joe's mike is gone. Who else was going to talk to Captain Lague?"

"But you're sitting there laughing at me."

"I'm just smiling. I'm really liking the fact that we're all still alive." His smile broadened. "I'm just sitting here absolutely loving you."

"Uh, H.?" Blue's voice cut in. "Your mike's working again."

Harvard laughed as he pulled up next to the open field. "Is there anyone out there who *doesn't* know that I'm crazy about this woman?"

"Admiral Stonegate probably didn't know," Blue drawled.

The chopper hovered, and Harvard lifted the captain in his arms. Several medics helped Joe into the helicopter, then Harvard gave P.J. a boost before he climbed in himself.

The door was shut, and the medics immediately started an IV on Joe. The chopper lifted and headed directly for the ocean and the USS *Irvin*.

The captain was fighting to stay awake as the medics cut his clothing away from his wounds. "H.!" he rasped.

Harvard reached out and took his friend's hand, holding on to it tightly. "I'm here, Joe."

"Tell Ronnie I'm sorry…"

"You're going to get a chance to do that yourself," Harvard told him. "You're going to be okay." As he looked at P.J., she wasn't at all surprised to see tears in his eyes. "We're going home."

EPILOGUE

THE ENTIRE REST OF THE United States was having a wretchedly awful heat wave, but San Diego remained a perfect seventy-five degrees.

P.J. glanced at Harvard as he slowed his truck to a stop at a traffic light. He turned and smiled at her, and the last of the tension from the plane flight floated away. God, she hated flying. But this trip was definitely going to be worth the anxiety she'd suffered. This was day one of a greatly needed two-week vacation.

And she was spending every single minute of those two weeks with Daryl Becker.

It had been close to three weeks since she'd seen him last, since they'd returned to the USS *Irvin* on board a French medical helicopter. Bobby and Wes had arrived at the ship several hours later, dragging Chuck Schneider along behind them.

They'd spent the next three days in debriefings—all except Joe Cat, Lucky and Greg Greene, who had been sent to a hospital in California.

P.J. had slept in Harvard's arms each of those nights. They'd been discreet, but the truth was, she really didn't care what people thought. Not anymore. She would have walked naked through the enlisted mess if that was the only way she could have been with him.

When the debriefings were over, Harvard had flown to Coronado, while she'd been summoned for a series of meetings in Kevin Laughton's office in Washington, D.C.

Kevin had been sympathetic about her need to take

some time off, but he'd talked her into writing up her reports on the failed Combined SEAL/FInCOM team project first. And that had taken much longer than she'd hoped.

But now she was free and clear for two weeks. Fourteen days. Three hundred and thirty-six hours.

Harvard had met her at the gate, kissed her senseless and whisked her immediately into his truck.

"How's Joe?" she asked.

"Great," he told her. "He's been home from the hospital for about a week. Lucky's doing really well, too."

"I'd like to visit them." She looked at him out of the corner of her eye. "But definitely not until after we get naked—and stay naked for about three days straight."

He laughed. "Damn, I missed you," he told her, drinking her in with his gaze.

She knew she was looking at him just as hungrily. He was wearing jeans and a T-shirt, and even dressed in civilian clothes, he was impossibly handsome.

"I missed you, too." Her voice was husky with desire. As he gazed into her eyes, she let him see the fire she felt for him.

"Hmm," he said. "Maybe we should go straight to my apartment."

"I thought you said there was something important you wanted to show me," she teased.

"Its importance just dropped a notch or two. But since we're already here…"

"We are?" P.J. looked out the window. They were on a quiet street in a residential neighborhood overlooking the ocean.

"I want you to check this out," Harvard said. He climbed out of the truck, and P.J. joined him.

It was only then that she noticed the For Sale sign on the lawn of the sweetest-looking little adobe house she'd ever seen in her entire life. It was completely surrounded by flower gardens. Not just one, but four or five of them.

"Come on," Harvard said. "The real-estate agent is waiting for us inside."

P.J. went through the house in a daze. It was bigger than she'd thought from the outside, with a fireplace in the living room, a kitchen that rivaled Harvard's mom's and three good-size bedrooms.

There was a deck off the dining room, and as she stepped outside, she realized the house overlooked the ocean.

Harvard leaned on the rail, gazing at the changing colors of the sea.

"I've already qualified for a mortgage, so if you like it, we should make an offer today," he told her. "It's not going to be on the market too much longer."

P.J. couldn't speak. Her heart was in the way, in her throat.

He misinterpreted her silence.

"I like it," he said. "But if you don't, that's okay. Or maybe I'm moving too fast—I have the tendency to do that, and—" He broke off, swearing. "I *am* moving too fast. We haven't even talked about getting married—not since we were out in the real world. For all I know, you weren't really serious and…"

P.J. finally found her voice. "I was dead serious."

Harvard smiled. "Yeah?" he said. "Well, that's good, because I was, too, you know."

P.J. looked pointedly around. "Obviously."

He pulled her closer. "Look, whether it's this house we share or some other—or none whatsoever, hell, we could live in hotels for the rest of our lives—that's not important. What's important is that we're together as often as we can be." He looked around and shrugged helplessly. "I don't know what I was thinking. Your office is in D.C. Why would you want a house in San Diego?"

"I might want one in San Diego if I'm going to work in San Diego. I found out there's an opening in the San Diego field office."

"Really?"

P.J. laughed at his expression. "Yeah. And don't worry—I'll still be able to work as Kevin Laughton's official SEAL liaison and adviser." She turned to look at the house. "So you really love this place, huh? You think we could make it into a real home?"

He wrapped his arms around her. "I really love *you,* and like I said, it honestly doesn't matter to me where we live. Whenever I'm with you, I feel as if I've come home."

P.J. looked at the house, at the ocean, at the flowers growing everywhere in the little yard, at the man who was both warrior and poet who stood before her.

Her lover.

Her husband.

Her life.

"This'll do just about perfectly." She smiled at him. "Welcome home."

* * * * *

HAWKEN'S HEART

✳ ✳ ✳ ✳

For Tom Magness
(1960–1980)
I never had the chance to tell you that
I'm glad I didn't miss the dance.

ACKNOWLEDGMENTS

Huge thanks to my swimming buddy, Eric Ruben,
for suggesting I write a book with a navy SEAL hero.

Thanks also to Team Ten list
(http://groups.yahoo.com/group/teamten/)
for their enthusiastic support!

Thanks to the real teams of SEALs and to all the
courageous men and women in the U.S. military,
who sacrifice so much to keep America the land
of the free and the home of the brave.

Last but not least, a heartfelt thank-you to the wives,
husbands, children and families of these real-life
military heroes and heroines. Your sacrifice is
deeply appreciated.

Any mistakes I've made or liberties I've taken in
writing this book are completely my own.

PROLOGUE

CRASH HAWKEN SHAVED in the men's room.

He'd been keeping vigil at the hospital in Washington, D.C., for two days running, and his heavy stubble, along with his long hair and the bandage on his arm, made him look even more dangerous than he usually did.

He'd left only to change the shirt he'd been wearing—the one that had been stained with Admiral Jake Robinson's blood—and to access a computer file that Jake had sent him electronically, mere hours before he had been gunned down in his own home.

Gunned down in his own home... Even though Crash had been there, even though he'd taken part in the firefight, even though he'd been wounded himself, it still seemed so unbelievable.

Crash had thought that last year's dismal holiday season had been about as bad as it could get.

He'd been wrong.

He was going to have to call Nell, tell her Jake had been wounded. She'd want to know. She deserved to know. And Crash could use a reason to hear her voice again. Maybe even see her. With a rush of despair, he realized something he'd been hiding from himself for months—he wanted to see her. God, he wanted so badly to see Nell's smile.

The men's room door opened as Crash rinsed the disposable razor he'd picked up in the hospital commissary. He glanced into the mirror, and directly into Tom Foster's scowling face.

What were the odds that the Federal Intelligence Commission commander had only come in to take a leak?

Slim to none.

Crash nodded at the man.

"What I don't understand," Foster said, as if the conversation they'd started two nights ago had never been interrupted, "is how you could be the last man standing in a room with five-and-a-half dead men, and not know what happened."

Crash put the plastic protective cap on over the razor's blade. "I didn't see who fired the first shot," he said evenly. "All I saw was Jake getting hit. After that, I know exactly what happened." He turned to face Foster. "I took out the shooters who were trying to finish Jake off."

Shooters. Not men. They'd lost their identities and become nothing more than targets when they'd opened fire on Jake Robinson. And like targets in a shooting range, Crash had efficiently and methodically taken them out.

"Who would want to assassinate the admiral?"

Crash shook his head and gave the same answer he'd given Tom two days earlier. "I don't know."

It wasn't a lie. He *didn't* know. Not for sure. But he had a file full of information that was going to help him find the man who had orchestrated this assassination attempt. Jake had fought both pain and rapidly fading consciousness to make sure he had understood there was a connection between this attempt on his life and that top secret, encoded file Crash had received that very same morning.

"Come on, Lieutenant. Surely you can at least make a *guess.*"

"I'm sorry, sir, I've never found it useful to speculate in situations like this."

"Three of the men you brought into Admiral Robinson's house were operating under false names and identifications. Were you aware of that?"

Crash met the man's angry gaze steadily. "I feel

sick about that, sir. I made the mistake of trusting my captain."

"Oh, so now it's your *captain's* fault."

Crash fought a burst of his own anger. Getting mad wouldn't do anyone any good. He knew that from the countless times he'd been in battle. Emotion not only made his hands shake, but it altered his perceptions, as well. In a battle situation, emotion could get him killed. And Foster was clearly here to do battle. Crash had to detach. Separate. Distance himself.

He made himself feel nothing. "I didn't say that." His voice was calm and quiet.

"Whoever shot Robinson wouldn't have gotten past his security fence without your help. You brought them in, Hawken. You're responsible for this."

Crash held himself very still. "I'm aware of that." They—whoever they were—had used him to get inside Jake's home. Whoever had set this up had known of his personal connection to the admiral.

He'd barely been three hours stateside, three hours off the Air Force transport he'd taken back to D.C. when Captain Lovett had called him into his office, asking if he'd be interested in taking part in a special team providing backup security at Admiral Robinson's request.

Crash had believed this team's job was to protect the admiral, when in fact there'd been a different, covert goal. Assassination.

He should have known something was wrong. He should have stopped it before it even started.

He *was* responsible.

"Excuse me, sir." He had to check on Jake's condition. He had to sit in the waiting area and hope to hear continuous reports of his longtime mentor's improvement, starting with news of the admiral finally being moved out of ICU. He had to use the time to mentally sort through all the information Jake had passed to him in that file. And then he had to go out and hunt down the man who had used him to get to Jake.

But Tom Foster blocked the door. "I have a few more questions, if you don't mind, Lieutenant. You've worked with SEAL Team Twelve for how long?"

"On and off for close to eight years," Crash replied.

"And during those eight years, you occasionally worked closely with Admiral Robinson on assignments that were not standard SEAL missions, did you not?"

Crash didn't react, didn't blink, didn't move, carefully hiding his surprise. How had Foster gotten *that* information? Crash could count the number of people who knew he'd been working with Jake Robinson on one hand. "I'm afraid I can't say."

"You don't have to say. We know you worked with Robinson as part of the so-called Gray Group."

Crash chose his words carefully. "I don't see how that has any real relevance to your investigation, sir."

"This is information FInCOM has received from naval intelligence," Foster told him. "You're not giving away anything we don't already know."

"FInCOM takes part in its share of covert operations," Crash said, trying to sound reasonable. "You'll understand that whether I am or am not a part of the Gray Group is not something I'm able to talk freely about."

Reasonable wasn't on the list of adjectives Tom Foster was working with today. His voice rose and he took a threatening stop forward. "An *admiral* has been shot. This is *not* the time to conceal *any* information *what*soever."

Crash held his ground. "I'm sorry, sir. I've already given you and the other investigators all the information I'm able to provide. The names of the deceased, as I knew them. An account of my conversation with Captain Lovett that afternoon. An account of the events that led to one of the men in the team opening fire upon the admiral—"

"What exactly is your reason for concealing information, Lieutenant?" Foster's neck was turning purple.

"I'm concealing nothing." Except for the shocking information Jake had sent him in a top secret, high-level security-clearance file.

If Crash wanted to get to the bottom of this—and he *did*—it wouldn't help to go public with all that Jake had told him. Besides, Crash had to treat the information in that file with exactly the same care and secrecy as he treated every other file Jake had ever sent him. And that meant that even if he wanted to, he couldn't talk about it with anyone—except his Commander-in-Chief, the President of the United States.

"We know that Jake Robinson sent you some kind of information file on the morning of the shooting," Foster informed him tightly. "I will need you to turn that file over to me as soon as possible."

Crash met the man's gaze steadily. "I'm sorry, sir. You know as well as I do that even if I *did* have access to this alleged file from Admiral Robinson, I wouldn't be able to reveal its contents to you. The status of all of the work I did for the admiral was 'need to know.' My orders were to report back to Jake and to Jake only."

"I *order* you to hand over that file, Lieutenant."

"I'm sorry, Commander Foster. Even if I had such a file, I'm afraid you don't have the clearance rating necessary to make such a demand." He stepped dangerously close to the shorter man and lowered his voice. "If you'll excuse me, I'm going to see how Jake's doing."

Foster stepped aside, pushing open the door with one hand. "Your concern for Robinson is heartwarming. At least, it would be if we didn't have indisputable evidence that proves *you* were the man who fired those first shots into Admiral Robinson's chest."

Crash heard the words Foster said, but they didn't make sense. The crowd of men standing outside the bathroom door didn't make sense, either. There were uniformed cops, both local and state police, as well as dark-suited FInCOM agents, and several officers from the shore patrol.

They were obviously waiting for someone.

Him.

Crash looked at Foster, the meaning of his words becoming clear. "You think *I'm*—"

"We don't *think* it, we *know* it." Foster smiled tightly. "Ballistic reports are in."

"Are you Lt. William R. Hawken, sir?" The shore-patrol officer who stepped forward was tall and young and humorlessly earnest.

"Yes," Crash replied. "I'm Hawken."

"By the way, the bullet taken from your arm was fired from Captain Lovett's weapon," Foster told him.

Crash felt sick, but he didn't let his reaction show. His captain had tried to kill him. His captain had been a part of the conspiracy.

"Lt. William R. Hawken, sir," the shore-patrol officer droned, "you are under arrest."

Crash stood very, very still.

"The ballistic report also shows that your weapon fired the bullets that were found in four of the five other dead men, as well as those removed from the admiral," Foster told him tightly. "Does that information by any chance clear up your foggy memory of who fired the first shots?"

"You have the right to remain silent," the shore-patrol officer chanted. "Anything you say can and will be used against you in a court of law. You have the right to an attorney—"

This was impossible. Bullets from *his* weapon…? That wasn't the way it had happened. He looked into the blandly serious eyes of the young officer. "What exactly am I being charged with?"

The young officer cleared his throat. "Sir. You have

been charged with conspiracy, treason and the murder of a United States Navy Admiral."

Murder?

Crash's entire world tilted.

"Admiral Robinson's wounds proved fatal one hour ago," Tom Foster announced. "The admiral is *dead*."

Crash closed his eyes. Jake was *dead*.

Disassociate. Detach. Separate.

The shore-patrol officer slipped handcuffs onto Crash's wrists, but Crash didn't feel a thing.

"Aren't you going to say *any*thing to defend yourself?" Foster asked.

Crash didn't answer. *Couldn't* answer. Jake was dead.

He was completely numb as they led him from the hospital, out to a waiting car. There were news cameras everywhere, aimed at him. Crash didn't even try to hide his face.

He was helped into the car, someone pushing down his head to keep him from hitting it on the frame. Jake was dead. Jake was dead, and Crash should have been able to prevent it. He should have been faster. He should have been smarter. He should have paid attention to the feeling he'd had that something wasn't right.

Crash stared out through the rain-speckled window of the car as the driver pulled out into the wet December night. He tried to get his brain to work, tried to start picking apart the information Jake had sent him in that file— the information that was recorded just as completely and precisely in his head.

Crash was no longer simply going to find the man responsible for shooting and killing Jake Robinson. He was going to find him, hunt him down and destroy him.

He had no doubt he'd succeed—or die trying.

Dear, sweet Mary. And he'd thought *last* Christmas had been the absolute pits.

CHAPTER ONE

One year earlier

IT WAS ONLY TWO DAYS after Thanksgiving, but the city
streets were already decked with wreaths and bows and
Christmas lights.

The cheery colors and festive sparkle seemed to mock
Nell Burns as she drove through the city. She'd come into
Washington, D.C. that morning to do a number of errands.
Get a new supply of watercolor paper and paint for Daisy.
Stop at the health food store and get more of that nasty
seaweed stuff. Pick up the admiral's dress uniform from
the dry cleaners near the Pentagon. It had been a week
since Jake had been in town, and it looked as if it would
be a while before he returned.

Nell had saved the hardest, most unpleasant task for
last. But now there was no avoiding it.

She double-checked the address she'd scribbled on a
Post-it note, slowing as she drove past the high-rise building that bore the same number.

There was a parking spot open, right on the street, and
she slipped into it, turning off her engine and pulling up
the brake.

But instead of getting out of her car, Nell sat there.

What on earth was she going to say?

It was bad enough that in just a few minutes she was
going to be knocking on William Hawken's door. In the
two years since she'd started working as Daisy Owen's

personal assistant, she'd met the enigmatic Navy SEAL that her boss thought of as a surrogate son exactly four times.

And each time he'd taken her breath away.

It wasn't so much that he was handsome....

Actually, it was *exactly* that he was handsome. He was incredibly, darkly, mysteriously, broodingly, *gorgeously* handsome. He had the kind of cheekbones that epic poems were written about and a nose that advertised an aristocratic ancestry. And his eyes... Steely blue and heart-stoppingly intense, the force of his gaze was nearly palpable. When he'd looked at her, she'd felt as if he could see right through her, as if he could read her mind.

His lips reminded her of those old gothic romances she'd read when she was younger. He had decidedly cruel lips. Upon seeing them, she'd suddenly realized that rather odd descriptive phrase made perfect sense. His lips were gracefully shaped, but thin and tight, particularly since his default expression was not a smile.

In fact, Nell couldn't remember ever having seen William Hawken smile.

His friends, or at least the members of his SEAL team—she wasn't sure if a man that broodingly quiet actually *had* any friends—called him "Crash."

Daisy had told her that Billy Hawken had been given that nickname when he was training to become a SEAL. His partner in training had jokingly started calling him Crash because of Hawken's ability to move silently at all times. In the same manner in which a very, very large man might be nicknamed "Mouse" or "Flea," Billy Hawken had ever after been known as Crash.

There was no way, *no* way, Nell would ever consider becoming involved with a man—no matter *how* disgustingly handsome and intriguing—whose work associates called him "Crash."

There was also no way she would ever consider

becoming involved with a Navy SEAL. From what Nell understood, SEAL was synonymous with *superman*. The acronym itself stood for Sea, Air and Land, and SEALs were trained to operate with skill and efficiency in all three environments. Direct descendants from the UDTs or Underwater Demolition Teams of World War II, SEALs were experts in everything from gathering information to blowing things up.

They were Special Forces warriors who used unconventional methods and worked in small seven- or eight-man teams. Admiral Jake Robinson had been a SEAL in Vietnam. The stories he'd told were enough to convince Nell that becoming involved with a man like Crash would be sheer insanity.

Of course, she was failing to consider one important point as she made these sweeping statements. The man in question had barely even said four words to her. No wait— he'd said *five* words the first time they'd met. "Pleased to meet you, Nell." He had a quiet, richly resonant voice that matched his watchful demeanor damn near perfectly. When he'd said her name, she'd come closer to melting into a pathetic pool of quivering protoplasm at his feet than she'd ever done in her life.

The second time they'd met, *that* was when he'd said four words. "Nice seeing you again." The other times, he'd merely nodded.

In other words, it wasn't as if he was breaking down her door, trying to get a date.

And he certainly wasn't doing anything as ridiculous as not only counting the number of times they'd met, but adding up the total number of words she'd ever said to *him*.

With any luck, he wouldn't even be home.

But then, of course, she'd have to come back.

Daisy and her longtime, live-in lover, Jake Robinson,

had invited Crash out to the farm for dinner several times over the past few weeks. But each time he'd cancelled.

Nell had made this trip into the city to tell him that he *must* come. Although he wasn't their child by blood, Crash was the closest thing to a son both Daisy and Jake had ever had. And from what Daisy had told her, Nell knew that Crash considered them his family, too. From the time he was ten, he'd spent every summer and winter break from boarding school with the slightly eccentric pair. From the time his own mother had died, Daisy had opened her home and her heart to him.

But now Daisy had been diagnosed with an inoperable cancer, and she was in the very late stages of the disease. She didn't want Crash to hear the news over the phone, and Jake was refusing to leave her side.

That had left Nell volunteering to handle the odious task.

Damn, what *was* she going to say?

"HI, BILLY, UM, BILL, how are you? It's Nell Burns…remember me?"

Crash stared at the woman standing out in the hallway, aware that he was wearing only a towel. He held the knot together with one hand while he pushed his wet hair up and out of his eyes with the other.

Nell laughed nervously, her eyes skimming his near-naked body before returning to his face. "No, you probably don't know who I am, especially out of context this way. I work for—"

"My cousin, Daisy," he said. "Of course I know who you are."

"Daisy's your cousin?" She was so genuinely surprised, she forgot to be nervous for a moment. "I didn't realize you were actually related. I just though she was…I mean, that you were…"

The nervousness was back, and she waved her hands gracefully, in a gesture equivalent to a shrug.

"A stray she and Jake just happened to pick up?" he finished for her.

She tried to pretend that she wasn't fazed, but with her fair coloring, Crash couldn't miss the fact that she was blushing. Come to think of it, she'd started blushing the minute she'd realized he was standing there in only a towel.

A grown woman who still could blush. It was remarkable, really. And it was reason number five thousand and one on his list of reasons why he should stay far away from her.

She was too nice.

The very first time they'd met, the very first time Crash had looked into her eyes, his pulse had kicked into high gear. There was no doubt about it, it was a purely physical reaction. Jake had introduced him to Nell at some party Daisy had thrown. The instant he'd walked in, Crash had noticed Nell's blond hair and her trim, slender figure, somehow enhanced by a fairly conservative little black dress. But up close, as he'd said hello, he'd gotten caught in those liquid blue eyes. The next thing he knew, he was fantasizing about taking her by the hand, pulling her with him up the stairs, into one of the spare bedrooms, pinning her against the door and just…

The alarming part was that Crash knew the physical attraction he felt was extremely mutual. Nell had given him a look that he'd seen before, in other women's eyes.

It was a look that said she wanted to play with fire. Or at least she *thought* she did. But there was *no way* he was going to seduce this girl that Jake and Daisy had spoken so highly of. She was too nice.

He couldn't see more than a trace of that same look in her eyes now, though. She was incredibly nervous—and upset, he realized suddenly. She was standing there, looking as if she was fighting hard to keep from bursting into tears.

"I was hoping you'd have a few minutes to spare, to sit down and talk," she told him. For someone so slight of build, she had a deceptively low, husky voice. It was unbelievably sexy. "Maybe go out and get a cup of coffee or...?"

"I'm not exactly dressed for getting coffee."

"I could go." She motioned over her shoulder toward the bank of beat-up elevators. "I can wait for you downstairs. Outside. While you get dressed."

"This isn't a very good neighborhood," he said. "It'd be better if you came inside to wait."

Crash opened the door wider and stepped back to let her in. She hesitated for several long seconds, and he crossed the idea that she was here to seduce him off his list of possible reasons why she'd come.

He wasn't sure whether to feel disappointed or relieved.

She finally stepped inside, slipping off her yellow, flannel-lined slicker, hanging it by the hood on the doorknob. She was wearing jeans and a long-sleeved T-shirt with a low, scooped collar that accentuated her honey-blond chin-length hair and her long, elegant neck. Her features were delicate—tiny nose, perfectly shaped lips—with the exception of her jawline, which was strong and stubbornly square.

She wasn't conventionally beautiful, but as far as Crash was concerned, the intelligence and the sheer life in her eyes pushed her clear off the scope.

As he watched, she looked around his living room, taking in his garish purple-and-green-plaid sofa and the two matching easy chairs. She tried to hide her surprise.

"Rented furniture," he informed her.

She was startled at first, but then she laughed. She

was outrageously pretty when she laughed. "You read my mind."

"I didn't want you thinking I was a purple-and-green-plaid furniture type by choice."

There was a glimmer of amusement in Crash's eyes, and his mouth quirked into what was almost a smile as Nell gazed at him. God, was it possible that William Hawken actually had a sense of humor?

"Let me get something on," he said as he vanished silently down a hallway toward the back of the apartment.

"Take your time," she called after him.

The less time he took, the sooner she'd have to tell him the reason she'd come. And she'd just as soon put that off indefinitely.

Nell paced toward the picture window, once again fighting the urge to cry. All of the furniture in the room was rented, she could see that now. Even the TV had a sticker bearing the name of a rental company. It seemed such a depressing way to live—subject to other people's tastes. She looked out at the overcast sky and sighed. There wasn't much about today, or about the entire past week and a half, that hadn't been depressing. As she watched, the clouds opened and it started to rain.

"Do you really want to go out in that?"

Crash's voice came from just over her shoulder and Nell jumped.

He'd put on a pair of army pants—fatigues, she thought they were called, except instead of being green, these were black—and a black T-shirt. With his dark hair and slightly sallow complexion, he seemed to have stepped out of a black-and-white film. Even his eyes seemed more pale gray than blue.

"If you want, I could make us some coffee," he continued. "I have beans."

"You *do?*"

The amused gleam was back in his eyes. "Yeah, I know.

You think, rented furniture—he probably drinks instant. But no. If I have a choice, I make it fresh. It's a habit I picked up from Jake."

"Actually, I didn't really want any coffee," Nell told him. His eyes were too disconcertingly intense, so she focused on the plaid couch instead. Her stomach was churning, and she felt as if she might be sick. "Maybe we could just, you know, sit down for a minute and…talk?"

"Okay," Crash said. "Let's sit down."

Nell perched on the very edge of the couch as he took the matching chair positioned opposite the window.

She could imagine how dreadfully awful it would be if some near stranger came to *her* apartment to tell her that *her* mother had only a few months left to live.

Nell's eyes filled with tears that she couldn't hold back any longer. One escaped, and she wiped it away, but not before Crash had noticed.

"Hey." He moved around the glass-topped coffee table to sit beside her on the couch. "Are you okay?"

It was like a dam breaking. Once the tears started, she couldn't make them stop.

Silently, she shook her head. She *wasn't* okay. Now that she was here, now that she sitting in his living room, she absolutely couldn't do this. She couldn't tell him. How could she say such an awful thing? She covered her face with her hands.

"Nell, are you in some kind of trouble?"

She didn't answer. She couldn't answer.

"Did someone hurt you?" he asked.

He touched her, then. Tentatively at first, but then more firmly, putting his arm around her shoulders, pulling her close.

"Whatever this is about, I can help," he said quietly. She could feel his fingers in her hair, gently stroking. "This is going to be okay—I promise."

There was such confidence in his voice. He didn't have

a clue that as soon as she opened her mouth, as soon as she told him why she'd come, it *wasn't* going to be okay. Daisy was going to die, and nothing ever was going to be okay again.

"I'm sorry," she whispered. "I'm so sorry."

"It's okay," he said softly.

He was so warm and his arm felt so solid around her. He smelled like soap and shampoo, fresh and innocently clean, like a child.

This was absolutely absurd. She was *not* a weeper. In fact, she'd held herself together completely over the past week. There had been no time to fall apart. She'd been far too busy scheduling all those second opinions and additional tests, and cancelling an entire three-week Southwestern book-signing tour. Cancelling—not postponing. God, that had been hard. Nell had spent hours on the phone with Dexter Lancaster, Jake and Daisy's lawyer, dealing with the legal ramifications of the cancelled tour. Nothing about that had been easy.

The truth was, Daisy was more than just Nell's employer. Daisy was her friend. She was barely forty-five years old. She should have another solid forty years of life ahead of her. It was so damned unfair.

Nell took a deep breath. "I have some bad news to tell you."

Crash became very still. He stopped running his fingers through her hair. It was entirely possible that he stopped breathing.

But then he spoke. "Is someone dead? Jake or Daisy?"

Nell closed her eyes. "This is the hardest thing I've ever had to do."

He pushed her up, away from him, lifting her chin so that she had to look directly into his eyes. He had eyes that some people might have found scary—eyes that could seem too burningly intense, eyes that were almost inhumanly pale. As he looked at her searchingly, she felt nearly seared, but at the same time, she could see beneath to his all-too-human vulnerability.

"Just say it," he said. "Just tell me. Come on, Nell. Point-blank."

She opened her mouth and it all came spilling out. "Daisy's been diagnosed with an inoperable brain tumor. It's malignant, it's metastasized. The doctors have given her two months, absolute tops. It's more likely that it will be less. Weeks. Maybe even days."

She'd thought he'd become still before, but that was nothing compared to the absolute silence that seemed to surround him now. She could read nothing on his face, nothing in his eyes, nothing. It was as if he'd temporarily vacated his body.

"I'm so sorry," she whispered, reaching out to touch his face.

Her words, or maybe her touch, seemed to bring him back from wherever it was that he'd gone.

"I missed Thanksgiving dinner," he said, talking more to himself than to her. "I got back into town that morning, and there was a message from Jake on my machine asking me to come out to the farm, but I hadn't slept in four days, so I crashed instead. I figured there was always next year." Tears welled suddenly in his eyes and pain twisted his face. "Oh, my God. Oh, God, how's Jake taking this? He can't be taking this well…."

Crash stood up abruptly, nearly dumping her onto the floor.

"Excuse me," he said. "I have to…I need to…" He turned to look at her. "Are they sure?"

Nell nodded, biting her lip. "They're sure."

It was amazing. He took a deep breath and ran his hands down his face, and just like that he was back in control. "Are you going out to the farm right now?"

Nell wiped her own eyes. "Yeah."

"Maybe I better take my own car, in case I need to get back to the base later on. Are you okay to drive?"

"Yeah. Are *you?*"

Crash didn't answer her question. "I'll need to pack a few things and make a quick phone call, but then I'll be right behind you."

Nell stood up. "Why don't you take your time, plan to come out a few hours before dinner? That'll give you a chance to—"

Again, he ignored her. "I know how hard this must've been for you." He opened the door to the hallway, holding her jacket out for her. "Thank you for coming here."

He was standing there, so distant, so unapproachable and so achingly alone. Nell couldn't stand it. She put her jacket down and reached for him, pulling him close in a hug. He was so stiff and unyielding, but she closed her eyes, refusing to be intimidated. He needed this. Hell, *she* needed this. "It's okay if you cry," she whispered.

His voice was hoarse. "Crying won't change anything. Crying won't keep Daisy alive."

"You don't cry for her," Nell told him. "You cry for *you.* So that when you see her, you'll be able to smile."

"I don't smile enough. She's always on my case because I don't smile enough." His arms suddenly tightened around her, nearly taking her breath away.

Nell held him just as tightly, wishing that he was crying, knowing that he wasn't. Those tears she'd seen in his eyes, the pain that had been etched across his face had been a slip, a fluke. She knew without a doubt that he normally kept such emotions under careful control.

She would have held him all afternoon if he'd let her, but he stepped back far too soon, his face expressionless, stiff and unapproachable once again.

"I'll see you back there," he said, not quite meeting her eyes.

Nell nodded, slipping into her raincoat. He closed the

door quietly behind her, and she took the elevator down to the lobby. As she stepped out into the grayness of the early afternoon, the rain turned to sleet.

Winter was coming, but for the first time Nell could remember, she was in no real hurry to rush the days to spring.

CHAPTER TWO

"WHAT YOU WANT TO DO," Daisy was saying, "is not so much draw an exact picture of the puppy—what a camera lens might see—but rather to draw what *you* see, what you *feel*."

Nell looked over Jake's shoulder and giggled. "Jake feels an aardvark."

"That's not an aardvark, that's a *dog*." Jake looked plaintively at Daisy. "I thought I did okay, don't you think, babe?"

Daisy kissed the top of his head. "It's a beautiful, *won*derful…aardvark."

As Crash watched from the doorway of Daisy's studio, Jake grabbed her and pulled her onto his lap, tickling her. The puppy started barking, adding canine chaos to Daisy's shouts of laughter.

Nothing had changed.

Three days had passed since Nell had told Crash about Daisy's illness and he'd gone out to the farm, dreading facing both Daisy and Jake. They'd both cried when they saw him, and he'd asked a million questions, trying to find what they might have missed, trying to turn it all into one giant mistake.

How could Daisy be dying? She looked almost exactly the same as she ever had. Despite being given a virtual death sentence by her doctors, Daisy was still Daisy—colorful, outspoken, passionately enthusiastic.

Crash could pretend that the dark circles under her eyes

were from the fact that she'd been up all night again, painting, caught in one of her creative spurts. He could find
an excuse for her sudden, sharp drop in weight—it was
simply the result of her finally finding a diet that she stuck
to, finally finding a way to shed those twenty pounds that
she always complained were permanently attached to her
hips and thighs.

But he couldn't ignore the rows of prescription medi-
cines that had appeared on the kitchen counter. Painkillers. They were mostly painkillers that Crash knew Daisy
resisted taking.

Daisy had told Crash that he and Jake and Nell would
all have to learn to grieve on their own time. She herself
had no time to spare for sad faces and teary eyes. She
approached each day as if it were a gift, as if each sunset
were a masterpiece, each moment of shared laughter a
treasure.

It would only be a matter of time, though, before the
tumor affected her ability to walk and move, to paint and
even to speak.

But now, as Crash watched, Daisy was the same as
always.

Jake kissed her lightly, sweetly on the lips. "I'm going to
take my aardvark into my office and return Dex's call."

Dexter Lancaster was one of the few people who actually knew of Daisy's illness. Dex had served in Vietnam
when Jake had, but not as part of the SEAL units. The
lawyer had been with the Army, in some kind of support-
services role.

"I'll see you later, babe, all right?" Jake added.

Daisy nodded, sliding off his lap and straightening his
wayward dark curls, her fingers lingering at the gray at his
temples.

Jake was the kind of man who just kept getting better
looking as he got older. He'd been incandescently, gleam-
ingly handsome in his twenties and rakishly handsome in

his thirties and forties. Now, in his fifties, time had given his face laugh lines and a craggy maturity that illustrated his intense strength of character. With deep blue eyes that could both sparkle with warmth and laughter or penetrate steel in anger, with his upfront, in-your-face, honestly sincere approach and his outrageous sense of humor, Crash knew that Jake could have had any woman, *any* woman he wanted.

But Jake had wanted Daisy Owen.

Crash had seen photos of Daisy that Jake had taken back when they'd first met—back when he was a young Navy SEAL on his way to Vietnam, and she was a teenager dressed in cotton gauze she'd tie-dyed herself, selling her drawings and crafts on the streets of San Diego.

With her dark hair cascading down her back in a wild mass of curls, her hazel eyes and her bewitching smile, it was easy to see how she'd caught Jake's eye. She was beautiful, but her beauty was far more than skin-deep.

And at a time when the people of the counterculture were spitting on the boots of men in uniform, at a time when free love meant that strangers could become the most intimate of lovers, then part never to meet again, Daisy gave Jake neither disdain nor a one-night stand. The first few times they'd met, they'd walked the city streets endlessly, sharing cups of hot chocolate at the all-night coffeehouses, talking until dawn.

When Daisy finally did invite Jake into her tiny apartment, he stayed for two weeks. And when he came back from Vietnam, he moved in for good.

During their time together, at least during all the summer vacations and winter breaks Crash had spent with the two of them, he had only heard Daisy and Jake argue about one thing.

Jake had just turned thirty-five, and he'd wanted Daisy to marry him. In his opinion, they'd lived together, unwed, for long enough. But Daisy's views on marriage were unswerving. It was their love that bound them together, she said, not some foolish piece of paper.

They'd fought bitterly, and Jake had walked out—for about a minute and a half. It was, in Crash's opinion, quite possibly the only battle Jake had ever lost.

Crash watched them now as Jake kissed Daisy again, longer this time, lingeringly. Over by the window, Nell's head was bent over her sketch pad, her wheat-colored hair hiding her face, giving them privacy.

But as Jake stood, Nell glanced up. "Is it my turn or yours to make lunch, Admiral?"

"Yours. But if you want I can—"

"No way am I giving up my turn," Nell told him. "You get a chance to make those squirrelly seaweed barf-burgers every other day. It's *my* day, and *I'm* making grilled cheese with Velveeta and bacon."

"What?" Jake sounded as if she'd said "arsenic" instead of bacon.

"Vegetarian bacon," Daisy told him, laughter in her voice. "It's not real."

"Thank God," Jake clutched his chest. "I was about to have a high-cholesterol-induced heart attack just from the thought."

Crash took a deep breath, and went into the room.

"Hey," Jake greeted him on his way out the door. "You just missed the morning art lesson, kid. Check this out. What do you think?"

Crash had to smile. Calling the object Jake had drawn an aardvark was too generous. It looked more like a concrete highway divider with a nose and ears. "I think you should leave the artwork to Daisy from now on."

"Tactfully put." Jake blew Daisy a kiss, then disappeared.

"Billy, are you here for the day or for longer?" Daisy asked as Crash gave her a quick hug. She was definitely much too skinny.

Focus on the positive. Stay in the moment. Don't project into the future—there would be time enough for that when it arrived. Crash cleared his throat. "I had the last of my debriefings this morning. My schedule's free and clear until the New Year, at least." Scooping the puppy into his arms, he glanced at Nell, changing the subject, not wanting to talk about the reasons why he'd arranged an entire month of leave. "Is this guy yours?"

Nell was smiling at him, approval warming her eyes as she put away her sketch pad and pencils and stood up.

"This *guy* is a girl, and she's only here on loan from Esther, the cleaning lady, unfortunately." Nell reached out and scratched the puppy's ears. She moved closer—close enough that he could smell the fresh scent of her shampoo, and beneath it, the subtle fragrance of her own personal and very feminine perfume. "Jake was afraid that you were going to be sent on another assignment right away."

"I was asked, but I turned it down," Crash told her. "It's been over a year since I've taken any leave. My captain had no problem with that." Especially considering the circumstances.

Nell gave the puppy a final pat and her fingers accidentally brushed his hand. "I better go get lunch started. You're joining us, right?"

"If you don't mind."

Nell just smiled as she left the room.

The puppy struggled in Crash's arms, and when he put her onto the floor, she scampered after Nell. He looked up to find Daisy watching him, a knowing smile on her face.

"'If you don't mind,'" she said, imitating him. "You're either disgustingly coy or totally dense."

"Since I don't know what you're talking about—"

"Totally dense wins. Nell. I'm talking about *Nell*." Daisy kicked off her shoes and pulled her legs up so that she was sitting tailor-style. "She's giving you all the right body-language signals. You know, the ones that say she wants you to jump her bones."

Crash laughed as he sat down on the window seat. "Daisy."

She leaned forward. "Go for it. She spends far too much time with her head in a book. It'll be good for her. It'll be good for you, too."

Crash looked at her. "You're actually serious."

"How old are you now?"

"Thirty-three."

She grinned. "I'd say it's definitely time for you to lose your virginity."

He couldn't help but smile. "You're very funny."

"It's not entirely a joke. For all *I* know, you *haven't* been with a woman. You've never brought anyone home. You've never mentioned so much as a name."

"That's because I happen to value my privacy—as well as respecting the privacy of the woman I'm seeing."

"I know you're not seeing anyone right now," Daisy said. "How could you be? You were away for four months, you got back for two days, and then you were gone again for another week. Unless you have a girlfriend in Malaysia or Hong Kong, or wherever it is you're sent…"

"No," Crash said, "I don't."

"So what do you do? Stay celibate? Or *pay* for sex?"

That question made Crash laugh out loud. "I've never paid for sex in my life. I can't believe you're asking me about this." Daisy had always been outrageous and shockingly direct, but she'd always steered clear from the subject of his sex life in the past. Some subjects were too personal—or at least they had been, before.

"I'm no longer worried about shocking anyone," she told him. "I've decided that if I want to know the answer to a question, dammit, I'm going to ask it. Besides, I love you, and I love Nell. I think it would be really cool if the two of you got together."

Crash sighed. "Daisy, Nell's great. I like her and I…
think she's smart and pretty and…very nice." He couldn't
help but remember how perfectly she had fit in his arms,
how soft her hair had felt beneath his fingers, how good
she'd smelled. "Too nice."

"No, she's not. She's sharp and funny and tough and
she's got this real edge to her that—"

"Tough?"

Daisy lifted her chin defensively. "She can be, yeah.
Billy, if you'll just take some time and get to know her, I
know you'll fall in love with her."

"Look, I'm sorry, but I don't do 'in love.'" Crash wanted
to stand up and pace, but there was no room. Besides, he
knew without a doubt that Daisy would read some deep
meaning into his inability to sit still. "The truth is, I don't
even do long-term. I couldn't even if I wanted to—and I
don't want to. You know that I'm never around for more
than a few weeks at a time. And because I'm aware of those
realities, I don't ever give anyone false hope by bringing
them here to meet you."

"All those *don'ts* are so negative. What *do* you do?"
Daisy asked. "One-night stands? You know, that's dangerous these days."

Crash looked out the window. The sky was overcast
again. December in Virginia was wet and dreary and ut-
terly depressing.

"What I do is, I walk into a bar," he told her, "and I
look around, see who's looking back at me. If there are
any sparks, I approach. I ask if I can buy her a drink. If she
says yes, I ask her to take a walk on the beach. And then,
away from the noise of the bar, I ask her about her life,
about her job, her family, her last scumbag of a boyfriend—
whatever—and I listen really carefully to what she tells
me because not many people bother to listen, and I know
I'll win big points if I do. And by the time we've walked

a quarter mile, I've listened so well, she's ready to make it with me."

Daisy was silent, just watching him. Her expression was sad, as if what he was telling her wasn't what she'd hoped to hear. Still, there was no judgment and no disapproval in her eyes.

"Instead, I take her home and I kiss her good-night," Crash continued, "and I ask her if I can see her again— take her to dinner the next night, take her someplace nice. She always says yes, so the next night we go out and I treat her really well. And then I tell her over dessert, right up front, that I want to sleep with her but I'm not going to be around for long. I lay it out right there, right on the table. I'm a SEAL, and I could be called away at any time. I tell her I'm not looking for anything that's going to last. I've got a week, maybe two, and I want to spend that time with her. And she always appreciates my honesty so much that she takes me home. For the next week or however long it is until I get called out on some op, she cooks for me, and she does my laundry, and she keeps me very warm and very, very happy at night. And when I leave, she lets me go, because she knew it was coming. And I walk away—no guilt, no regrets."

"Didn't you learn *any*thing from me at all? All those summers we spent together…"

Crash looked up. Daisy's eyes were still so sad. "I learned to be honest," he told her. "You taught me that."

"But what you do seems so…cold and calculated."

He nodded. "It's calculated. I don't pretend it's not. But I'm honest about it—to myself and to the woman I'm with."

"Haven't you ever met anyone that you *burn* for?" she asked. "Someone you just want to lie down in front of and surrender to? Someone you absolutely live and die for?"

Crash shook his head. "No," he said. "I'm not looking

for that, and I don't expect to find it, either. I think most people go through life without that kind of experience."

"That is so sad." There were tears in her eyes as she looked up at him. "It's crazy, too. I'm the one who's dying, but right now I feel so much luckier than you."

NELL WAS MOVING AT a dead run as she rounded the corner by the stairs and plowed smack into Crash.

Somehow he managed to catch her and keep them both from landing on the ground in a tangled pile of arms and legs.

"Sorry." Nell felt herself blushing as he made sure she was steadily on her feet again.

"Is everything all right?" he asked, finally letting go of her arms. "Is Daisy…?"

"She's fine," Nell said. "But she said *yes*."

He didn't bother to ask. He just waited for her to explain. He was dressed all in black again today, but because the chill of winter was in the air, he wore a turtleneck instead of his usual T-shirt.

Most men managed to look good in a simple black turtleneck. William Hawken looked incredible.

It hugged his shoulders and arms, accentuating his streamlined muscles. It was funny, Nell had always thought of him as somewhat thin—more lean and wiry than muscular—because most of the time he wore clothes that were just a little too large. His T-shirts were never tight and he always wore his pants just a little low on his hips and slightly loose.

But the truth was, he was built as solid as a rock.

Nell felt herself flush again as she realized she was standing there, staring at the man. "You look really good today," she admitted. "I like that shirt."

"Thank you," he said. If she'd surprised him, he didn't show it. But then again, he didn't show much of anything. With the exception of that one time in his apartment, he played all of his emotional cards extremely close to his chest.

"I'm going to need your help," Nell started toward the second-floor office she'd shared with Daisy. "What do you know about swing bands and health-food caterers? Or how about where I can find a florist specializing in poinsettias and holly?"

"Any florist should be able to handle a Christmas-style arrangement," Crash said, keeping pace. "Health-food caterers—I'm not the one to ask about that. As for swing bands, I've always preferred Benny Goodman."

"Benny Goodman's great, but unfortunately he's dead." Nell turned on the office lights and sat down at the desk with the computer, using the mouse and the keyboard to sign on to the Internet. "I need to find someone good who's alive, *and* ready to be booked for the evening before Christmas eve." She looked back at Crash. "Any idea where we can get a half dozen twelve-foot Christmas trees with root balls attached—delivered? And then there's lights and decorations… But we can't hire a decorator, because they do that 'monochromatic garbage'—that's a direct quote— all silver or all red, and that's not any good. We need *real* ornaments, all different colors and sizes."

Crash sat down on the other side of the desk. "Are we having a Christmas party?"

Nell laughed. And then, to her horror, her eyes filled with tears. She blinked them back, but she knew he saw them, because for a fraction of a second, a very peculiar mix of trepidation and an answering flash of pain crossed his face.

"I'm not going to cry," she told him, fiercely willing herself to do just that. "I'm just…" She forced a smile. "I feel so bad for Jake, you know? In a way, Daisy's got it easier, because Jake's the one who's going to have to go on living. And sometimes, when Daisy's not around, I see him, and he has this look in his eyes that just breaks my heart."

Nell sank down, resting her head on top of her desk.

Crash knew she was fighting tears again, and she didn't want him to see. Nell's loyalty impressed him. He understood loyalty. It was the one strong emotion he could relate to—and could allow himself to feel.

"You don't have to be here," he said.

She lifted her head and looked at him through a curtain of rumpled hair, her expression aghast. "Yes, I most certainly do. Daisy needs me now more than ever."

"This wasn't what you were hired to do."

"I was hired as her personal assistant."

"You were hired to take care of all the business aspects of Daisy's career," Crash pointed out, "so that she would have more time to paint."

"A good personal assistant does whatever's needed," Nell argued. "If the dishes need washing, I'll do the dishes. Or I'll clean the fish tank, or—"

"Most people would've given their notice weeks ago. Instead of that, you moved in."

"Yeah, well, the idea of Daisy having to go into a hospice was unacceptable." Nell swept her hair out of her face as she reached for a tissue and briskly blew her nose. "And she hated the thought of hiring some stranger to provide round-the-clock personal care. But she didn't want to dump all that responsibility on Jake, so…" She shrugged.

"So you volunteered."

"I haven't had any medical training, so when the time comes that she needs a nurse, someone's still going to have to come in, but at least she'll know I'll be there, too." Nell tossed the crumpled tissue across the room, sinking it expertly into the wastebasket. "It's no big deal." She took a deep breath and pretended to look at the computer screen.

"That's not true and you know it."

She looked up at him, gazing directly into his eyes. "Are you going to help me, Hawken, or what?"

Crash had to smile. He liked her direct approach. He liked *her*. He was definitely going to help with whatever it was that she was doing, but first he had to make something clear to her.

"I know we're all trying to be as upbeat as Daisy is," he said quietly, "but that gets hard sometimes. I don't want you to have to worry about what I'll say or do if you need to cry. You don't need *that* weighing you down, too. We're living with a lot of emotional upheaval here. There's nothing normal about this, and we can't expect each other to behave normally. So, let's make a deal, okay? You can cry whenever you want, but you can't hold it against me if I stand up and walk away when you do, because…everything that you're feeling…I'm fighting it, too."

Nell just sat there, looking at him. Her eyes were rimmed with red, she wore no makeup, and she looked as if she'd slept about as much as he had in the past few days—which wasn't much at all.

Maybe they'd both sleep better if they shared a bed.

Crash gently pushed that thought away. He knew it would be true, but he also knew that the absolute, *absolute* last thing Nell needed in her life right now was to become intimately entangled with him.

She was the kind of woman he avoided like the plague when he walked into a bar. He'd recognized her on sight that first time they'd met. She was too sweet, too smart, too innocently full of life and hope and promise.

She was the kind of woman who wouldn't believe him when he said he wasn't looking for long-term or permanent. She was the kind of woman who would think that she could change him.

She was the kind of woman who would cry great big, silent tears as he packed his bag—the kind of woman who would beg him to come back.

No, under completely normal conditions, Crash wouldn't allow himself to get close to Nell. And right now she was a bubbling caldron of high-octane emotions. He knew—not with any sense of ego, but from that same flatly factual voice of experience—that it wouldn't take very much for her to fancy herself in love with him. He knew because he was experiencing the very same highs and lows himself.

But, like he'd told Daisy, he didn't do "in love" and he knew himself well enough to recognize that the rush of emotions he was feeling wasn't real. It couldn't possibly be real. And giving in to this powerful physical temptation would be the worst thing he could do to this woman, no matter how badly he longed for something—for *someone*— to hold on to. No matter how badly he longed for the distraction of sexual release.

He liked Nell too much to use her that way. And knowing what he knew about her, he *would* be using her.

Crash forced himself to take a step back, to separate a little bit more from his emotions. He'd file his red-hot attraction for Nell in that mental holding area he'd created, right next to all the anger and grief and pain he felt over Daisy's impending death. All he needed was just a little more distance, a little more detachment.

But Nell finally moved, holding out her hand to him, stretching her arm across her desk. "I'll accept your deal," she said. "I want to state for the record, though, that I don't usually cry at the drop of a hat."

He took her hand. It was so much smaller than his, her fingers slender and cool. Her grip was firm, and that, along with the crooked smile she gave him, almost made him toss his resolve out the window.

He nearly asked her, point-blank, if she wanted to try to release some tension with him tonight. Daisy had purposely put them in bedrooms next to each other. It wouldn't be difficult for him to slip into her room and...

Nell was looking at him, her eyes wide, as if she knew

what he was thinking. But then he realized that he was still holding her hand. Quickly, he let it go.

Detach.

He cleared his throat. This entire conversation had started with evergreen trees, swing bands and poinsettias. "So, are Jake and Daisy throwing a Christmas party?"

Nell lifted an eyebrow. "Do you really think they'd do something *that* mundane or predictable—or easy to plan? No, this is not your average Christmas party. I was just up in the studio while Daisy was painting," she told him, "and Jake came in and asked her what she wanted to do tonight. He thought maybe she'd want to go to a movie. And she said that lately they only did what *she* wanted to do, and that wasn't fair. She thought that tonight they should do something that *Jake* wanted. And they got into this discussion about Daisy's list—the list of all the things she wants to do before…you know."

Crash nodded. He knew.

"So Daisy said she thought it would be fair if Jake made a similar list, and he said that he didn't need to. He said there was only one thing on *his* wish list—a wish that she would get well and live with him for another twenty years. And if he couldn't have that, then his only other wish would be for her to marry him."

Crash felt a lump forming in his throat. After all this time, Jake still wanted Daisy to marry him.

"So she said yes," Nell continued softly.

He tried to clear it, but it wouldn't go away. "Just like that?"

Nell nodded. "Yeah. She's finally giving in."

Poor Jake. He'd wanted forever, but all he was getting was a cheap illusion.

Crash felt helplessness and rage churning inside of him, fighting to break free and sweep him away like a tidal wave. It wasn't fair. He had to look away from the gentle blue of Nell's eyes, or, dammit, *he* was going to start to cry.

And once he started, he'd never be able to stop.

"Maybe," Nell said quietly, "maybe knowing that Daisy loved him enough to give in and marry him will help. Maybe someday Jake will find some comfort in that."

Crash shook his head, still unable to meet her gaze. He stood up, knowing that if he just walked away, she would understand. But she'd also asked for his help. He sat back down, willing himself to detach even more, to stop *feeling* so damn much. He took a deep breath and let it slowly out. And when he spoke, his voice was even. "So now we're planning a wedding."

"Yup. Daisy said yes, and then turned to me and asked if I could take care of the details—in exactly three weeks. Of course, I said yes, too." She laughed, and it came out sounding just on the verge of hysterical, just a little bit giddy. "Please, *please* say that you'll help me."

"I'll help you."

She briefly closed her eyes. "Thank God."

"But I don't have a lot of experience with weddings."

"Neither do I."

"In fact, I tend to avoid weddings like the plague," he admitted.

"All of my college friends who are married either eloped or got married on the other coast," Nell said. "I've never even *been* to a real wedding. The closest I've ever gotten was watching the TV broadcast of Princess Diana's wedding to Prince Charles when I was little."

"That probably had just a *little* bit more flash and fanfare than Daisy and Jake are going to want."

Nell laughed and then stopped short. He'd just made a joke. That *had* been a joke, hadn't it?

He wasn't smiling, but there definitely was a glint of something in his eyes. Amusement. Or was it tears?

Crash turned his head and examined the toe of his

boot. With his lids lowered, Nell couldn't see his eyes, and when he looked up again, he was carefully devoid of all expression.

"We should probably make a list of all the essential supplies for a wedding," he suggested.

"We've got the bride and the groom. They're pretty essential, and we can already cross them off the list."

"But they'll need clothes."

"A wedding gown—something funky that'll make Daisy feel as if she's still thumbing her nose at convention." Nell started an Internet search. "There must be some kind of wedding checklist somewhere that we can use—so we don't forget something important."

"Like wedding rings."

"Or—God!—someone to perform the ceremony." She looked up, pushing the phone and the yellow pages toward him. "Trees," she said. "A half a dozen twelve-foot Christmas trees. Live."

"Delivered ASAP," he said. "You can already cross it off your list." He reached for the phone, but she didn't let it go, and he looked up at her.

"Thanks," she said quietly. They both knew she was talking about more than just his help with this project.

Crash nodded. "You can cross that off your list, too."

"A PRENUPTIAL AGREEMENT?" Nell's voice was loaded with disbelief.

Crash paused in the kitchen doorway, looking in to find her sitting at the table across from Dexter Lancaster, Jake and Daisy's lawyer.

She'd made them both tea, and she sat with her hands wrapped around her cup, as if she were cold.

Lancaster was a big man. He had at least five inches and seventy pounds on Crash, but most of those pounds were the result of too many doughnuts and Danishes in the morning and too many servings of blueberry cheesecake at night. Age and a sweet tooth had conspired to take the sharp edges off Lancaster's WASP-y good looks and as a result, somewhat ironically, he was probably more handsome at age forty-nine than he'd been at thirty.

He was a friendly-looking bear of a man, with warm blue eyes that actually twinkled behind round, wire-framed glasses. His hair was sandy-blond and still thick and untouched by gray.

He sighed as he answered Nell. "Yeah, I know, it sounds crazy, but in a way, it'll clarify exactly which parts of Daisy's estate she wishes to leave to persons other than Jake. If it's in both the prenup *and* the will, it'll speed the process along after she's…" He shook his head, taking off his glasses and wiping his eyes with both hands. "Sorry."

Nell took a deep breath. "Don't be. It's coming, you know. Daisy faces it. She talked about it matter-of-factly. We should be able to do that, too." She made a sound that was half laughter, half sob. "Easier said than done, though, huh?"

Dex Lancaster set his glasses down and reached across the table to cover her hand with his. "You know, your being here is a godsend to both of them."

The exact same thought had crossed Crash's mind at least three times a day. But he'd never said it aloud. He'd figured that Nell surely knew.

She smiled at Lancaster. "Thanks."

The lawyer smiled back at her, still holding her hand.

The man liked her. He *more* than liked her.

Dexter Lancaster had a thing for Nell. The man was twenty years her senior, at *least,* but Crash knew from his subtle body language and from the way he was looking at her that he found her undeniably attractive.

Lancaster was no fool. And judging from the fact that his law firm had one of the best reputations in the country, he also was not an underachiever. Any second now, he was going to ask Nell out to dinner.

"I was wondering…" Lancaster started.

Crash coughed and stepped into the room.

Nell slipped her hand out from beneath Lancaster's as she turned to look up at him. "You're back," she said, giving him a smile. It was a bigger smile than the one she'd given Dex Lancaster. "Did you have any problem getting the rings?"

Crash took the two jeweler's boxes from the inside pocket of his jacket and set them on the table in front of her. "None whatsoever."

"You know Dex, don't you?" she asked.

"We've met a few times," Crash said.

The lawyer stood up as he held out his hand, and the two men shook.

But their handshake wasn't a greeting. It was a not-so-subtle sizing up. It was more than obvious, from the once-over Lancaster was giving him, that he was trying to figure out what claim—if any—Crash had already staked out.

Crash met the older man's gaze steadily. And after the handshake was done, he moved slightly to stand closer to Nell, putting one hand on the back of her chair in a gesture that was clearly possessive.

What the hell was he doing?

He didn't want this girl.

He'd resolved to stay away from her, to keep his distance, both physically and emotionally.

But as much as he didn't want her, he didn't want to see her taken for a ride, either.

Crash didn't trust lawyers any further than he could throw them, and Dexter Lancaster was no exception to his rule, despite the fact that his eyes twinkled like Santa Claus's.

Lancaster checked his watch. "I have to get going." He twinkled at Nell. "I'm sure I'll talk to you soon." He nodded at Crash as he slipped on his overcoat. "Nice seeing you again."

Like hell it was. "Take care," Crash lied in return.

"What was *that* all about?" Nell turned to ask as the door closed behind Dexter Lancaster.

Crash opened the refrigerator and pretended to be engrossed by its contents. "Just a little Army/Navy rivalry."

Nell laughed. "You're kidding. All that tension just because you're in the Navy and he was in the Army?"

Crash took a can of soda out and shut the refrigerator door. "Crazy, huh?" he said as he escaped into the other room.

CHAPTER THREE

NELL GLANCED UP FROM her computer to see Crash standing in her office. She jumped, nearly knocking over her cup of tea, catching it with both hands, just in time.

"God!" she said. "Don't *do* that! You're always sneaking up on me. Make some noise when you come in, will you? Try stomping your feet, okay?"

"I thought I'd made noise when I opened the door. I'm sorry. I didn't mean to scare you."

She took a deep breath, letting it slowly out. "No, *I'm* sorry. I've been...feeling sideways all day. There must be a full moon or something." She frowned at the half-written letter on her computer screen. "Of course, now I've got so much adrenaline raging through my system, I'm not going to be able to concentrate."

"Next time, I'll knock."

Nell looked up at Crash in exasperation. "I don't want you to *knock*. You've been working as hard as I have—this is your office, too. Just...clear your throat or play the bagpipes or whistle, or *some*thing." She turned back to the letter.

Crash cleared his throat. "I've been ordered to tell you that after two days of rain, the sky's finally clear, and the sun's due to set in less than fifteen minutes," he said.

Sunset. Nell glanced at her watch, swearing silently. Was it really that time already?

"I'm waiting for a fax from the caterer, and Dex Lancaster's supposed to call me right back to tell me if Friday is okay to come out and discuss some changes Daisy wants to make to her will, but I guess he can leave a message on the machine," she told him, thinking aloud. "I'm almost done with this letter, but I'll hurry. I'll be there. I promise."

Crash stepped closer. "I've been ordered to make sure you arrive on time, not five minutes after the sun has gone down, like last Monday. Daisy said to tell you that the rest of the week's forecast calls for total cloud coverage. In fact, the prediction is for snow—maybe as much as two or three inches. This could be the last sunset we see for a while."

The last sunset. Every sunset they saw was one of Daisy's very last sunsets.

Every clear day for the past two weeks, Daisy had brought Nell's work to a screeching halt as they'd all met in the studio to watch the setting sun. But now there was less than a week before the wedding, and the list of things that needed to be done was *still* as long as her arm. On top of that, the sun was setting earlier and earlier as midwinter approached, cutting her workday shorter and shorter.

It was also reminding her that the passage of time was bringing them closer and closer to the end of Daisy's life.

Nell looked at her watch again, then up into the steely blue of Crash's eyes.

To her surprise, there was amusement gleaming there.

"I've been ordered not to fail," he told her, giving her an actual smile, "which means I'm going to have to pick you up and carry you downstairs to the studio if you don't get out of that chair right now."

Yeah, sure he was. Nell turned back to the computer. "Just let me save this file. And wait—here comes that fax from the caterer now. I just have to— Hey!"

Crash picked her up, just as he'd said he would, throwing her over his shoulder in a fireman's hold as he carried her out of the door.

"Okay, Hawken, very funny. Put me down." Nell's nose

bumped his back and her arms dangled uncomfortably. She wasn't sure where to put her hands.

He seemed to have no problem figuring out where to put *his* hands. He held her legs firmly with one arm, and anchored her in place by resting his other hand squarely on the seat of her jeans. Yet despite that, his touch seemed impersonal—further proof that the man was not even remotely interested in her.

And after two weeks of living in the same house, sleeping in a room one door down the hall from his, and working together twenty-four hours a day, seven days a week, on this wedding that had somehow grown from a small affair with forty guests into a three-hundred-person, Godzilla-size event, Nell probably didn't need any further proof.

William Hawken *wasn't* interested.

Nell had given him all the full-speed-ahead signs—body language, lingering eye contact, subtle verbal hints. She'd done damn near everything but show up naked in his room at night.

But he'd kept at least three feet of air between them at all times. If he was sitting on the couch and she sat down next to him, he soon stood up on the pretense of getting something from the kitchen. He was always polite, always asking if he could get her a soda or a cup of tea, but when he came back, he was careful to sit on the opposite side of the room.

He never let her get too close emotionally, either. While she had babbled on about her family and growing up in Ohio, he had never, not even once, told her anything about himself.

No, he was definitely not interested.

Except whenever she turned around, whenever he thought she wasn't looking, he was there, looking at her. He moved so soundlessly, he just seemed to appear out of thin air. And he was always watching.

It was enough to keep alive that little seed of hope. Maybe he *was* interested, but he was shy.

Shy? Yeah, right. William Hawken might've been quiet, but he didn't have a shy bone in his body. Try again.

Maybe he was in love with someone else, someone far away, someone he couldn't be with while he was here at the farm. In that case, the careful distance that he kept between them made him a gentleman.

Or maybe he simply wasn't interested, but he didn't have anything better to look at, so he stared at her.

And maybe *she* should stop obsessing and get on with her life. So what if the most handsome, attractive, fascinating man she'd ever met only wanted to be friends? So what if every time she was with him, she liked him more and more? So what? She'd be friends with him. No big deal.

Nell closed her eyes, miserably wishing that he were carrying her to his room. Instead, he took her all the way down the stairs and into Daisy's art studio.

Jake had set up the beach chairs in front of the window that faced west. Daisy was already reclining, hands lazily up behind her head as Jake gently worked the cork free from a bottle of wine.

The last sunset. Crash's words rang in Nell's ear. One of these evenings, Daisy was going to watch her last sunset. Nell hated that idea. She *hated* it. Anger and frustration boiled in her chest, making it hard to breathe.

"Better lock the door before you put her down," Daisy told Crash. "She might run away."

"Just throw her down fast and sit on her," Jake recommended.

But Crash didn't throw her down. He placed her, gently, on one of the chairs.

"Watch her," Daisy warned. "She'll try to squeeze in just one more call."

Nell looked at the other woman in exasperation. "I'm

here. I'm not going anywhere, okay? But I'm not going to drink any wine. I still have too much work to—"

Jake put a wineglass in her hand. "How can you make a toast if you don't have any wine?"

Daisy sat up to take a glass from Jake, who took the chair next to her. She leaned forward slightly to look across him to Nell. "I have an idea. Let's just let this wedding happen. No more preparations. We've got the dress, the rings, the band's set to come and nearly all the guest have been called. What else could we possibly need?"

"Food would be nice."

"Who eats at weddings, anyway?" Daisy said. Her cat-green eyes narrowed as she looked at Nell. "You look exhausted. I think you need a day off. Tomorrow Jake and I are going skiing over in West Virginia. Why don't you come along?"

Skiing? Nell snorted. "No thanks."

"You'd *love* it," Daisy persisted. "The view from the ski lift is incredible, and the adrenaline rush from the ride down the mountain is out of this world."

"It's really not my style." She preferred curling up in front of a roaring fire with a good book over an adrenaline rush. She smiled tightly at Crash. "See, I'm one of those people who ride the Antique Cars in the amusement park instead of the roller coaster."

He nodded, pouring soda into the delicate wineglass Jake had left out for him. "You like being in control. There's nothing wrong with that." He sat down next to her. "But skiing's different from riding a roller coaster. When you ski, you've still got control."

"Not when *I* ski," Daisy said with a throaty chuckle.

Crash glanced at her, his mouth quirking up into one of his near smiles. "If you had bothered to learn how to do it instead of just strapping the skis on for the first time at the top of a mountain—"

"How could I waste my time on the bunny slope when

that great huge mountain was sitting there, waiting for me?" Daisy retorted. "Billy, talk Nell into coming with us."

Crash's eyes met Nell's, and she wondered if he could tell just from looking how brittle she felt today. She'd been tense and out of sorts just a few minutes ago, but now she felt as if she were going to snap.

Crash on the other hand, looked exactly as he always did. Slightly remote, in careful control. That was how he did it, Nell realized suddenly. He stayed in control by distancing himself from the situation and the people involved.

He'd cut himself off from all his emotions. Sure, he probably didn't feel as if his rage and grief were going to come hurtling out of him in some terrible projectile vomit of emotion. But on the other hand, he didn't laugh much, either. Oh, occasionally something she or Daisy said would catch him off guard, and he'd chuckle. But she'd never seen him laugh until tears came.

He'd protected himself from the pain, but he'd cut himself off from the joy, as well.

And that was another desperate tragedy. Daisy, so full of life, was dying while Crash willingly chose to go through life emotionally half-dead.

Nell was clinging to the very edge of the cliff that was her control, and the sheer tragedy of that thought made her fingernails start slipping.

Crash leaned slightly toward her. "I can teach you to ski, if you want," he said quietly. "I'd take it as slowly as you like—you'd be in control, I promise." He lowered his voice even further. "Are you all right?"

Nell shook her head quickly, jerkily, like a pitcher shaking off a catcher's hand signal. "I can't go skiing. I have *way* too much to do." She turned toward Daisy, unable to meet the other woman's eyes. "I'm sorry."

Daisy didn't say it in front of Jake and Crash, but Nell could see what she was thinking—it was clearly written on her face. She thought Nell was missing out. She thought Nell was letting her life pass her by.

But life was about making choices, dammit, and Nell was choosing to stay home, to stay warm instead of strapping slabs of wood onto her feet and risking broken arms and legs by sliding at an alarming speed down an icy slope covered with artificial snow. The only thing Nell was missing was fear, discomfort and the chance for a trip to the hospital.

She sat back in her chair, feeling as if the sudden silence in the room was the fault of her bitchiness. Her chest got even tighter and the suffocating feeling she was fighting threatened to overwhelm her. She looked at Crash. He was watching the sky begin to change colors as he sipped soda from his wineglass.

What did it look like to him? Did he look at the beautiful pink and reddish-orange colors with as much detachment as he did everything else? Did he see the fragile lace of the high clouds only as a meteorological formation, only as cirrus clouds? And instead of the brilliant colors, did he see only the dust in the atmosphere, bending and distorting the sun's light?

"How come you're not required to drink wine?" Her words came out sounding belligerent, nearly rude. But if he noticed, he didn't take offense.

"I don't drink alcohol," he told her evenly, "unless I absolutely have to."

That didn't make sense. Nothing about her life right now made any sense at all. "Why would you *have* to?"

"Sometimes, in other countries, when I meet with… certain people, it would be considered an insult not to drink with them."

That was it. Nell boiled over. She stood up and set down her glass, sloshing the untouched contents on the tablecloth. "Could you possibly be *any* more vague when you talk about yourself? I mean, don't bother adding a single detail, please. It's not as if I give a damn."

Nell was furious, but Crash knew that her anger wasn't aimed at him. He'd just been caught in her emotional cross fire.

For the past two weeks, she had been in as carefully tight control as he was. But for some reason—and it didn't really matter what had triggered it—she'd reached her limit tonight.

She was staring at him now, her face ashen and her eyes wide and filled with tears, as if she'd realized just how terribly un-Nell-like she'd just sounded.

Crash got to his feet slowly, afraid if he moved too quickly she'd run for the door.

But she didn't run. Instead, she forced a tight smile. "Well, I sure am the life of the party tonight, huh?" She glanced at the others, still trying hard to smile. "I'm sorry, Daisy. I think I have to go."

"Yeah, I have to go, too," Crash said, hoping that if he sounded matter-of-fact, Nell might let him walk with her. The stress she'd been under for the past few weeks had been hellishly intense. She didn't deserve to be alone, and he, God help him, was the only candidate available to make sure that she wasn't. He took her arm and gently pulled her with him toward the door.

She didn't say a word until they reached the stairs that led to the second floor of the rambling modern farmhouse. But then, with the full glory of the pink sky framed by the picture window in the living room, she spoke. "I ruined a really good sunset for them, didn't I?"

Crash wished that she would cry. He would know what to do if she cried. He'd put his arm around her and hold her until she didn't need him to hold her anymore.

But he didn't know what to do about the bottomless sorrow that brimmed like the tears in her eyes—brimmed, but wasn't released.

"There'll be other sunsets," he finally said.

"How many will Daisy get to see?" She turned to him, looking directly into his eyes as if he might actually know the answer to that question. "Probably not a hundred. Probably not even fifty. Twenty, do you think? Twenty's not very many."

"Nell, I don't—"

She turned and started quickly up the stairs. "I have to do better than this. This cannot happen again. I'm here to help her, not to be *more* of a burden."

He followed, taking the steps two at a time to catch up to her. "You're human," he said. "Give yourself a break."

She stopped, her hand on the knob of the door that led to her room. "I'm sorry I said…what I said." Her voice shook. "I didn't mean to take it out on you."

He wanted to touch her, and knew that she wanted him to touch her, too. But he couldn't do it. He couldn't take that risk. Not without the excuse of her tears. And she still wasn't crying. "I'm sorry I…frustrate you."

It was a loaded statement—one that was true on a multitude of levels. But she didn't look up. She didn't acknowledge it at all, in *any* way.

"I think I have to go to sleep now," she whispered. "I'm *so* tired."

"If you want, I'll…" What? What could he possibly do? "I'll sit with you for a while."

At first he wasn't sure she heard him. She was silent for a long time. But then she shook her head. "No. Thanks, but…"

"I'll be right next door, in my room, if you need me," he told her.

Nell turned and looked up at him, then. "You know, Hawken, I'm glad we're friends."

She looked exhausted, and Crash was hit with a wave of the same fatigue. It was a nearly overwhelmingly powerful feeling, accompanied by an equally powerful sense of irrationality. It was all he could do to keep himself from reaching out and cupping the softness of her face, and lowering his lips to hers.

Instead, he stepped back, away from her. Detach. Separate. Distance.

And Nell slipped into her room, shutting the door tightly behind her.

AT TWO IN THE AFTERNOON, the trees were delivered.

As the huge truck rolled into the driveway, Nell pulled her brown-leather bomber jacket on over her sweater and, wrapping her scarf around her neck, went out to meet it.

She stopped short before she reached the gravel of the drive.

Crash was standing next to one of the trucks.

What was he doing there?

He was wearing one of his disgustingly delicious-looking black turtlenecks, talking to the driver and gesturing back toward the barn.

It was starting to snow, just light flurries, but the delicate flakes glistened and sparkled in his dark hair and on his shirt.

What *was* he doing there?

The driver climbed back into the cab of the truck, and Crash turned as Nell came toward him.

"I thought you went skiing." She had to raise her voice to be heard over the sound of the revving engine and the gasping release of the air brakes.

"No," he said, watching as the truck pulled around the house, in the direction he had pointed. "I decided to stay here."

He started following the truck, but Nell stood still, glancing back at the house. "You should get a jacket." She was suddenly ridiculously nervous. After last night, he must think her an idiot. Or a fool. Or an idiotic fool. Or…

"I'm fine." He turned to face her, but he didn't stop walking. "I want to make sure the barn is unlocked."

Nell finally followed. "It is. I was out there earlier. I picked up the decorations in town this morning."

"I figured that's where you went. You left before I could offer to help."

Nell couldn't stand dancing around the subject of the night before one instant longer. "You didn't go skiing today because you thought I might still need a babysitter," she said, looking him straight in the eye.

He smiled slightly. "Substitute *friend* for *baby-sitter,* and you'd be right."

Friend. There was that word again. Nell had used it herself last night. *I'm glad we're friends.* If only she could convince herself that friendship was enough. That was not an easy thing to do when the very sight of this man made her heart beat harder, when the fabric of his turtleneck hugged the hard muscles of his shoulders and chest, clinging where she ached to run her hands and her mouth and...

And there was no doubt about it. She had it bad for a Navy SEAL who called himself Crash. She had it bad for a man who had cleanly divorced himself from all his emotions.

"I want to apologize," she started to say, but he cut her off.

"You don't need to."

"But I *want* to."

"All right. Apology accepted. Daisy called while you were out," he said, changing the subject deftly. They walked around the now idling truck toward the outbuilding that Jake and Daisy jokingly called the barn.

But with its polished wood floors, one wall of windows that overlooked the mountains and another of mirrors that reflected the panoramic view, this "barn" wasn't used to hold animals. Equipped with heating and central air-conditioning, with a full kitchen attached to the ballroom-size main room, it was no ordinary stable. Even the rough, exposed beams somehow managed to look elegant. The previous owners had used the place as a dance studio and exercise room.

Crash swung open the main doors. "Daisy said she and Jake were getting a room at a ski lodge, and that they wouldn't be back until tomorrow afternoon, probably on the late side."

She and Crash would be alone in the house tonight. Nell turned away, afraid he would read her thoughts in her eyes. Not that it mattered particularly. He probably already knew what she was thinking—he had to be aware of what she wanted. She'd been far less than subtle over the past few weeks. But he didn't want the same thing.

Friends, she reminded herself. Crash wanted them to be friends. Being friends was safe, and God forbid he should ever allow anything to shake him up emotionally.

Crash stepped to the side of the room, gently pulling Nell with him as three workmen carried one of the evergreen trees into the building.

She moved out of his grasp, but not because she didn't want him to touch her. On the contrary. She liked the sensation of his hand on her arm too much. But she was afraid if she stood there like that, so close to him, it wouldn't be long before she sank back so that she was leaning against him.

But friends didn't do that.

Friends kept their distance.

And there was no need to embarrass herself in front of this man two days in a row.

CHAPTER FOUR

CRASH HELD THE STEPLADDER while Nell positioned the angel on the top of one of the trees.

She'd brought a portable CD player into the barn, and Bing Crosby sang "White Christmas" over remarkably natural-sounding speakers. Nell sang along, right in Bing's octave, her voice a low, throaty alto.

She looked out the window as she came down the ladder. The snow was still falling. "I can't remember the last time it snowed for Christmas. Certainly not since I've lived in Virginia. And last year, I visited my parents in Florida. I was on the beach on Christmas Eve. The sand was white, but it just wasn't the same."

Crash was silent as he carried the stepladder to the last tree, as Nell removed the plastic wrapping from the final angel.

"You didn't make it out here to the farm last Christmas, did you?"

"No."

Nell glanced at him and he knew what she was looking for. She'd tossed him the conversational ball, and wanted him to run with it. She wanted him to tell her where *he'd* spent last Christmas.

He cleared his throat. "Last December, I was on a covert military op that is still so top secret, I can't even tell you which hemisphere of the globe I was in."

"Really?" Her eyes were wide. And very blue. Ocean blue. But not the stormy blue of the Atlantic, or even the turquoise of the Caribbean. Nell's eyes were the pure blue of the South China Sea. In fact, there was a beach there that— He cut his thought off abruptly. What was he doing? Allowing himself to submerge in the depths of this woman's eyes? That was insanity.

He turned away, making sure the stepladder was close enough to the tree. "Most of what I do, I can't talk about. Not to anyone."

"God, that must be really tough—considering the way you love to run off at the mouth."

She'd caught him off guard, and he laughed. "Yeah, well… What can I say?"

"Exactly." Nell paused on the rung of the ladder that brought them eye to eye. "Actually, I shouldn't be making jokes. It's probably really hard for you, isn't it?"

Malaysia. The beach was in Malaysia, and the ocean had been an impossibly perfect shade of blue. He'd sat there in the sand for hours, drinking it in, watching the sunlight dance across the water.

"It's my job," he said quietly.

Unlike in Malaysia, Crash forced himself to look away.

He could feel her gazing at him for several long moments before continuing on up the stepladder. She set the angel on the top branch of the tree, carefully adjusting its halo. "I know that part of what Jake does has to do with these…covert ops you're sent on. Although…they were called something else, weren't they? *Black* ops?"

Crash waited several beats before speaking. "How do you know about that?"

Something in his voice must have been different, because she glanced down at him. "Uh-oh. I wasn't supposed to know, was I? Now you're going to have to kill me, right?"

He didn't laugh at her joke. "Technically, your having access to that information is a breach of security. I need to know what you saw or heard, to make sure it doesn't happen again."

She slowly came back down the ladder. "You're serious."

"There are only five—now six—people in the world who know I work covert ops for Admiral Robinson," Crash told her. "One of them is the President of the United States. And now one of them is *you*."

Nell sat down on the second to last rung of the stepladder. "Oh, my God, you *are* going to have to kill me." She looked up at him. "Or vote me into office."

He nearly laughed at that one. But in truth there was nothing funny about this. "Nell, if you knew how serious…" Crash shook his head.

"But that's just it," she said imploringly. "I *don't* know. How can I know when you won't even finish your sentences? I know close to nothing about you. I'm friends with you almost entirely on faith—on vague gut instincts and the fact that Daisy and Jake think that the sun rises and sets with you. Do you know that in the past two weeks, you've told me *nothing* about yourself? We talk about books, and you tell me you're currently reading Grisham's latest, but you never say if you like it. You wouldn't even tell me your favorite color! I mean, what kind of friendship is *that?*"

The problem she had with him was nothing compared to the problem he currently had with her. He pinned her into place with his eyes. "Nell, this is extremely important. I need to know how you found out I was working with Jake. Have you mentioned this to anyone else? *Any*one at all?"

She shook her head, holding his gaze steadily. "No."

"Are you sure?"

"I'm positive," she said. "Look, I overheard Jake and Daisy talking. I didn't mean to, but they were being loud. They were…exchanging heated words. It wasn't quite an argument, but it was the closest to it that I've ever heard. Daisy accused Jake of sending you out on a black op. Those are the exact words she said. A black op. I remember because it sounded so spooky and dangerous. Anyway, Daisy wanted to know where you were. It was back when all that trouble was happening in the Middle East, and she was worried about you. She wanted Jake to stop using you for those dangerous covert missions—again, that's pretty much a direct quote—and he told her there was no one he trusted as much as you to get the job done. Besides, he said, you could take care of yourself."

Crash was silent.

"They both love you an awful lot," Nell told him.

He couldn't help himself. He started to pace. "You had a security check run on you before you started working for Daisy," he said, thinking aloud.

"No, I don't think so."

He shot her a look. "You probably didn't know about it, but you definitely have a FInCOM file with a copy at the NAVINTEL office. Think about it—you're working for Admiral Robinson's significant other. Believe me, you were checked out before you even met her." He took a deep breath. "I'm going to talk to Jake, and what's probably going to happen is we'll run a deeper, more invasive check." He stopped pacing and gazed down at her. "You'll be asked to make a complete list of people that you know. A *complete* list. Family, friends, lovers. Even casual acquaintances, so that—"

Nell laughed in disbelief. "My God, have you caught a whiff of the irony here? It positively reeks. I've been complaining because you never talk about yourself, but now *I've* got to give you a list of my lovers." She shook her head. "What's wrong with this picture?"

"You won't have to give those lists to me. You'll be contacted directly by FInCOM."

"But you'll probably see it." She stood up. "You've probably already seen my current file, haven't you?"

Crash closed the stepladder, carefully hooking the two sides together. "Should I put this back?"

"Leave it out. We'll probably be using it again before the party."

He set it against the wall by the kitchen. "How about we get a pizza delivered for dinner?"

"You're purposely not answering me." Nell slipped on her jacket and fastened her scarf around her neck. "You do that all the time—don't think I haven't noticed. You change the subject to avoid answering my questions. I *hate* that, you know."

Crash might have sighed.

Or maybe Nell only imagined it. God, he gave *so* little away. She crossed her arms.

"Aren't you hungry?" he asked. "I'm hungry."

"I'm waiting," she said. "I believe the question was, you've already seen my current FInCOM file, *haven't you?*"

He turned off the overhead lights. In the dimness, the six trees they'd decorated looked spectacular. The colorful lights glistened and the ornaments gleamed.

"I'm not looking at the trees. I'm refusing to be distracted." She put her hands up around her eyes, like a horse's blinders. "I'm going to stand here until you answer my question."

Crash almost smiled, and for once she knew exactly what he was thinking. How could she even *dream* of winning this kind of contest of wills with him?

The answer to that was simple. She couldn't win. There was absolutely nothing she could do to force him to answer her question.

So she answered for him.

"Yes," she said. "You've seen it. I *know* you've seen my file. If you hadn't, you would have said so already. So what's the big deal, right? It's probably full of all kinds of boring details. Grew up in Ohio, just outside of Cleveland, oldest of three kids, attended NYU, graduated with a liberal-arts degree and without a clue. Stumbled into a personal assistant job for a Broadway-musical director who owned a chain of convenience stores on the side, went to work for Daisy Owens several years later. Any of this sound familiar?"

He didn't say a word. She hadn't really expected him to. "My personal life's been just as dull. In the past six years, I've dated three different men, all nice, respectable professionals with solid futures. Two proposed marriage. I think they thought they'd be getting some kind of bonus deal—a wife who worked as a personal assistant. I was like some kind of yuppie fantasy woman. Buy me some Victoria's Secret underwear, and I'd be perfect. I turned them both down. The one who *didn't* want me instantly became the one I wanted, and I pursued him—only to find out he was as boring as the rest of 'em. My mother is convinced I'm a victim of the fairy tales I read as a little girl. She thinks I suffer from 'Someday My Prince Will Come' syndrome, and I think she's probably right, although I'm not sure *that's* in my file."

Crash finally spoke. "Probably not in so many words. But all FInCOM files include psychological evaluations. Your reasons for remaining unmarried would have been touched on."

Nell snorted. "God, I can just see the fink-shrinks sitting around psychoanalyzing me. 'Subject is a complete chicken. Sits around reading books on her days off. Never does anything even remotely interesting, like skiing. Subject is a total loser who is afraid of her own shadow.'" Without looking at him she turned and walked out the door.

And then stopped short. It was still snowing. The sky was already dark, and the falling snow swirled around her face, reflecting the light from the lamps that lit the walkway to the house.

Nell looked up at the millions of flakes falling dizzily down from the sky. She could hear the softest, slightest hiss as the snow hit the frozen ground.

"It's beautiful," she whispered, if there was one thing she'd learned from these past few hellish weeks, it was to stop and take note of the sheer beauty of the world around her.

"It's been a while since I've seen snow."

She turned to see Crash standing behind her. He'd actually made a somewhat personal comment without her dragging it out of him. And he didn't stop there.

"Being cautious doesn't mean you're a loser," he said.

Nell looked out at the field that went halfway up the hill back behind the barn before ending at a stone wall on the edge of the woods. It was covered with snow, so pristine and inviting.

"I used to like to do all sorts of things that scare me now," she admitted. "When I was little, the sight of that hillside would've sent me running for my sled." She turned to face him. "But now even the thought of doing something like skiing makes me break out into a cold sweat. When did I learn to be so afraid?"

"Not everyone was born to like the sensation of wind in their face."

"Yeah, but that's where it gets really stupid. There's a part of me that *wants* that. A part of me is really ticked that I didn't go skiing with Daisy and Jake. There's a part of me that has these incredible fantasies…."

One of his eyebrows went up an almost imperceptible fraction of an inch, and Nell hastened to explain.

"Fantasies like riding a motorcycle. I've always secretly yearned for an enormous Harley. I've always wanted to come roaring up to some important meeting on a huge bike, with those long, black leather fringes coming out of the ends of the hand grips, wearing one of those helmets with the kind of visor you can't see through. I have this really vivid picture of myself taking off the helmet and shaking out my hair and unstrapping my briefcase from the back and…" She shook her head. "Instead, I drive a compact car and I can't even get up enough nerve to go skiing—and you're standing out here without a jacket on," she interrupted herself. "We should go inside the house and order that pizza."

"Large, extra cheese with sausage, peppers and onions," Crash told her. "Unless you don't like sausage, peppers or onions, and then you get to pick what's on it. Go call from the barn while I get my jacket, then meet me out by the garage."

The garage? "You want to go pick it up?"

"No, have it delivered."

"But—"

Crash was already gone, disappearing into the shadows as easily as he appeared.

"Why by the garage?" she called in the direction he'd vanished.

He didn't answer. She hadn't really expected him to.

NELL STOPPED SHORT when she saw Crash holding the Flexible Flyer sled that he'd dug out of the garage.

"Oh, no," she said with a laugh. "No, no…"

The snow still fell with a whispering hiss around them. It was the perfect evening for sledding.

"The snow's supposed to turn to rain before midnight," Crash told her. "It'll probably all melt off by tomorrow."

"In other words, now or never, huh?"

Crash didn't answer. He just looked at her. The bright red scarf she was wearing accentuated the paleness of her face, and flakes of snow clung to her thick, honey-colored hair. On anyone else the combination of pale skin and not quite blond, not quite brown hair might have been drab, but her eyes were so blue and warm, and her smile was so perfect….

Crash found her impossibly beautiful, and he knew that his attempt to take her sledding was nothing but an excuse to get close to her. He wanted to put his arms around this woman and he was resorting to subterfuge to do it.

"The pizza will be here in about thirty minutes," she told him. "We don't really have time to—"

"We have enough time to make at least a couple of runs down the hill."

She gestured up behind the barn. "*That* hill?"

"Come on." Crash held out his hand. He was wearing gloves and she had on mittens. It wasn't as if he would really be touching her.

But when she took his hand, Crash knew he was dead wrong. It didn't matter. Touching her was touching her. But he couldn't stop now. He didn't *want* to stop. He pulled her up the hill, dragging the sled behind them.

It was slippery, but they finally reached the top.

Away from the lights of the house, the snow was even more beautiful as it fell effortlessly from the sky. And the snow that covered the ground seemed to glow in the darkness, reflecting what little light there was.

It was just dark enough. In this kind of shadow, Crash didn't have to worry about Nell seeing every little thought—every little desire—that flickered in his eyes.

"I'm not sure I can do this." Nell sounded breathless, her voice huskier than usual. "I'm not sure I remember *how* to do this."

"Sit on the sled and steer with your feet."

She sat gingerly down on the Flexible Flyer, but then looked up at him. "Aren't you coming, too?"

There was room for him—but just barely. They'd have to squeeze tightly together, with Nell positioned between his legs. Crash forced himself not to move toward her. "Do you want me to?"

"No way am I doing this without you." She inched forward a little. "Get your butt on this thing, Hawken."

"It helps if you start out by aiming the front of the sled *down* the hill."

Nell didn't move. "I thought we might take a more leisurely, zigzag path to the bottom."

Crash had to smile.

"All right, all right," she grumbled, swinging the front of the sled around. "If *you're* smiling at me, I must look pretty damn ridiculous. Get on the sled, Mona Lisa, and hold on tight. We're taking this sucker express, all the way to the barn."

Nell closed her eyes as Crash lowered himself onto the sled behind her. He had to press himself tightly against her back—there was no way they could both sit on this thing without nearly gluing themselves together. His legs were much longer than hers, and with her boots on the outer part of the steering bar, he didn't have anywhere to put his feet.

She turned slightly to find that his face was inches from hers and she froze, trapped by his eyes. It might have been her imagination, or it might only have been a trick of the darkness, but he seemed almost vulnerable, almost uncertain. He smelled impossibly good, like coffee and peppermint. Her gaze dropped to the tight line of his gracefully shaped mouth. What would he do if she kissed him?

She didn't have the nerve. "Maybe you should steer."

"No. This is your ride. You're in control."

In control. God, if he only knew. She was shaking, but she wasn't sure if it was because she was afraid of falling off and breaking her leg or because he was sitting so close. She could feel his warmth against every inch of her back and she was nearly dying from the anticipation of feeling his arms around her. Because that was the only reason she was doing this. She wanted to feel his arms around her.

"Let me put my legs under yours," he continued.

Nell lifted her legs obediently and he set his boots against the metal bumper. She lowered her legs, resting her thighs on top of his, stretching around the outside for the steering bar. But it was no longer within reach.

"Move forward," he ordered.

She didn't want to move forward. She liked the sensation of his body against hers too much to want to move away from him. But when she hesitated, he pushed them both up closer to the front of the sled. Her feet reached the bar, and he was *still* pressed tightly against her.

He looped his arms around her, holding her securely. It was heaven. Nell closed her eyes.

"Ready?"

"God, no! What am *I* supposed to hold on to?" Her voice was breathy, betraying her. She couldn't reach the side rail—his legs were in the way.

"Hold on to me."

Nell touched his legs, tentatively sliding her hands down underneath his thighs. He was all muscle, all solid, perfectly male. She wondered if he could feel her heart hammering through all her layers of clothing.

"Ready?" he asked again. She could feel his breath against her neck, just underneath her ear.

Nell held tighter and closed her eyes. "Yeah."

"You're in control." His voice was just a whisper. "Get us started by rocking forward a little…"

She opened her eyes. "Can't you just give us a push?"

"I could, but then you'd only have survived the ride. You wouldn't have *taken* it if you know what I mean. Come on. All you have to do is rock us forward."

Nell looked down the hill. The barn seemed to far away, and the hill suddenly seemed dreadfully steep. She was having trouble breathing. "I'm not sure I can."

"Take your time. I can wait—at least until the pizza-delivery man comes."

"If we sit here much longer, we'll be covered with snow."

"Are you cold?" he asked. His breath warmed her ear and his arms tightened slightly around her.

Cold? Nell couldn't remember her name, let alone a complicated concept like *cold*. "Maybe we can take this in steps," she said. "You know. Just sit here on the sled for a while. I mean, I made it all the way up the hill, and I actually got *on* the sled. That's a solid start. I should be really proud of myself. And then maybe by the next time it snows, I'll be ready to—"

"This is Virginia," he reminded her. "This may be all the snow we get this year. Come on, Nell. Just rock us forward."

Nell stared down the hill. She couldn't do it. She started to get up, but he held her in place.

"Blue," he said quietly. "My favorite color is blue. The color of the South China Sea. And I didn't really like the latest Grisham book as much as I liked his other stuff."

Nell turned her head and stared at him.

"And you're right, I've seen your FInCOM file," he continued. "I helped gather the information that's in it."

She knew what he was doing. She knew *exactly* what he was doing. He was showing her that he, too, could take little risks. Maybe he wasn't afraid to sled down a hill, but talking about himself was an entirely different story. She knew he never, *ever* willingly volunteered any information about himself.

True, he wasn't telling her anything terribly personal, but Nell knew that saying anything at all had to have been incredibly difficult for him.

At least as difficult as riding a Flexible Flyer down a relatively gentle hill. If she fell off, she wouldn't break her leg. She'd only bruise her bottom and her pride. This was no big deal.

She rocked the sled forward.

"I knew you could do it," Crash said softly into her ear as the sled teetered and then went over the edge of the hill.

It went slowly at first, nearly groaning under their weight, but then it began to pick up speed.

Nell screamed. The runners of the sled swished as the ground sped past, as the falling snow seemed to scatter and swirl around them.

Faster and faster they went, until it seemed as if they were almost flying. Nell clung to Crash's legs as they hit a bump and for a moment they *did* leave the ground, and when they landed, the sled wasn't quite underneath them.

She felt rather than heard the giddy laughter that left her throat as they skidded off the sled and slid for a moment on the slippery hillside without it, a tangle of arms and legs, Crash still holding her tightly.

She was still laughing as they slowed to a stop, and she realized that Crash was laughing, too. "You screamed all the way down the hill," he said.

"No, I didn't! God, did I really?" She was half on top of Crash, half sprawled in the snow, and she lay back, relaxing against him as she caught her breath, gazing up at the falling snowflakes.

"You sure did. Are you okay?" he asked.

"Yeah." In fact, she couldn't remember having been better. His arms were still around her and one of his legs was thrown casually across hers. Yes, she was very much okay. "That almost was…fun."

"You want to go again?"

Incredulous, Nell turned her head to look at him.

He smiled at her expression.

He was an outrageously good-looking man in repose, but when he smiled, just a little smile like that one, he was off the charts.

He got to his feet, holding out his hand for her.

She must have been insane or hypnotized because she reached for him, letting him pull her to her feet.

He released her and ran, skidding in the snow, to collect the sled, then came back up the hill, catching her by the hand again and pulling her along with him.

This time he didn't ask. This time he got behind her, holding her around the waist with an easy familiarity.

Nell couldn't believe she was doing this again.

"This time try to steer around that bump," he said, his breath warm against her ear.

Nell nodded.

"You're in control," he said.

"Oh, God," she said, and rocked the sled forward.

CHAPTER FIVE

"I REMEMBER WHEN I WAS A KID," Crash said softly, "Jake showed me how to make angels in the snow."

They were lying closer to the bottom of the hill this time, looking up at the snow streaking down toward them. It looked amazing from that perspective. The sensation was kind of like being in the middle of a living computer screen saver or a *Star Wars* style outer-space jump to light speed.

This time they'd skidded off the sled in different directions. This time they weren't touching, and Crash tried rather desperately not to miss Nell's softness and warmth.

Nell pushed herself up on one elbow. "Jake? Not Daisy?"

"No, it was Jake. It was Daisy's birthday, and Jake and I made snow angels all over the yard and…" He glanced over to find her watching him, her eyes wide.

"From what Daisy's said, I've gathered that you spent some of your summer and winter vacations from boarding school with her and Jake," she said softly.

Crash hesitated.

But this was Nell he was talking to. Nell, who'd trusted *him* enough to take not one or two but five separate trips down this hill on his old sled. His friend Nell. If they were lovers he wouldn't dare tell her anything, but they were *not* going to become lovers.

"I spent all of my vacations with them," he admitted.

"Starting when I was ten—the year my mother died. I was scheduled to go directly from school to summer camp. I didn't even go home in between. My father was away on business and—" He broke off, realizing how pathetic he sounded.

"You must've been miserable," she said softly. "I can't imagine having been sent away to boarding school when I was only ten. And you went when you were what? *Eight?*"

Crash shook his head. "It wasn't that bad."

"I think it must've been awful."

"My mother was dying—it was a lot for my father to deal with. Imagine if Jake and Daisy had an eight-year-old."

Nell snorted. "You can bet your ass Jake Robinson wouldn't send *his* kid away to boarding school. You were deprived of your mother two years before you absolutely had to be. And your poor mother…"

"My mother was so loaded on painkillers, the few times I was allowed to see her, she didn't even know me and…I don't want to talk about this." He shook his head, swearing softly. "I don't even want to *think* about it, but…"

"But it's happening all over again, with Daisy," Nell said quietly. "God, this must be twice as hard for you. I know *I* feel as if I'm stretched to the absolute end of my emotional rope as it is. What are we going to do when the tumor affects her brain to the point that she can't walk?"

Crash closed his eyes. He knew what he *wanted* to do. He wanted to run, to pack up his things and go. It would only take one phone call, and an hour later he'd be called in on a special assignment, his leave revoked. Twenty-four hours after that, he'd be on the other side of the world. But running away wouldn't really help him. And it wouldn't help Daisy, either. If there'd ever been a time that she needed him—that *Jake* needed him—it was now.

And God knew Daisy and Jake had been there for him. They'd *always* been there for him.

Nell was still watching him, her eyes filled with compassion. "I'm sorry," she whispered. "I shouldn't have brought that up."

"It's something we're both going to have to deal with."

Tears brimmed in her eyes. "I'm terrified that I'm not going to be strong enough."

"I know. I'm afraid that—" Crash broke off.

"What?" She moved closer, almost close enough to touch him. "Talk to me. I know you're not talking to Jake or Daisy about any of this. You've got to talk to *some*one."

Crash looked toward the house, squinting slightly, his mouth tighter than Nell had ever seen it. When he spoke, his voice was so low, she had to lean closer to hear him. "I'm afraid that when the time comes, when the pain gets too intense, when she can't walk anymore, she's going to ask me to help her die." When he glanced up at her, he didn't bother to hide the anguish in his eyes. "I know she'd never ask Jake to do that."

Nell drew in a shaky breath. "Oh, God."

"Yeah," he said.

Nell couldn't stand it any longer. She put her arms around him, knowing full well that he would probably push her away. But he didn't. Instead, he pulled her close. He held her tightly as, around them, the snow began to thicken and turn to freezing rain.

"I remember the day she came to get me from summer camp like it was yesterday," he said softly, his face buried in her hair, his breath warm against her neck. "I'd only been there two days when I got a message from the head counselor that Daisy was coming to see me." He lifted his face, resting his cheek against the top of her head. "She hit the place like a hurricane. I swear she came up the path to the camp office like Joan of Arc marching into battle. She was wearing a long skirt that just kind of flowed around her when she walked and about twenty bangles on her arm and a big beaded necklace. Her hair was down—it was long back then, it went down past her waist, and she was carrying her sandals. Her feet were bare and I remember there was bright red polish on her toenails."

He was talking about the year he was ten, Nell realized. The year his mother had died and his father had sent him directly to summer camp from boarding school.

"I was waiting for her on the porch of the office, and she stopped and gave me a big hug and she asked me if I liked it there. I didn't, but I told her what my father had told me—that there was no place else for me to go. I didn't really know her that well—she was my mother's cousin and they hadn't been particularly close. But she stood there, and she asked me if I would like to spend the summer out in California with her and Jake. I didn't know what to say and she told me that I didn't have to go with her if I didn't want to, but—" he cleared his throat "—that she and Jake very much wanted me to come stay with them."

Nell could hear his heart beating as he was silent for a moment.

"I guess I didn't really believe her, because I didn't go to my cabin to pack when she went into the office. I stayed on the porch, and I heard her talking to the administrator. Without my father's permission, he refused to let me leave. Daisy called my father—he was in Paris—right from the camp office, but she couldn't get through. He was in negotiations. He wasn't taking any calls until after the weekend. No one would interrupt him. He was...pretty formidable.

"So Daisy came back outside and she gave me another hug and told me she'd be back tomorrow at dinnertime. She said, 'When I get here, be packed and ready to go.'"

He was quiet again for a moment. "I remember feeling disappointed when she left without me. It was a strange feeling because I'd gone so long without any expectations at all. And that night I actually packed my stuff. I felt really stupid doing it, because I really couldn't believe she was going to come back. But something made me do it. I guess—even though most of it had been shaken out of me by then—I still had some hope left. I wanted her to come back so much I could barely breathe."

It was raining harder now, but Nell was afraid to move, almost afraid to breathe herself for fear she would break the quiet intimacy and he would stop talking.

But he was silent for so long, she finally lifted her head and looked at him. "Was she able to get in touch with your father?"

"She couldn't get anyone to interrupt his meetings, so she flew to Paris." Crash laughed ruefully, his mouth curving up into a half smile. "She just walked in on him with a letter for him to sign, giving her permission to take me out of the camp. I remember doing the math, adding up the hours, and realizing that she must have been traveling continuously from the time she left the camp to make it to Paris and back in a single day.

"It was so amazing to me," he continued quietly. "The fact that someone actually *wanted* me that badly. And Daisy really did. Both she and Jake actually wanted me around. I think about all the time Jake spent with me, that summer in particular, and it *still* amazes me. They really wanted me. I wasn't in the way."

Nell couldn't keep the tears that were filling her eyes from overflowing and mixing with the rain that was falling.

Crash gently touched her cheek with one knuckle. "Hey, I didn't mean to make you cry."

She pulled away from him slightly, using her hands to wipe her face. "I'm not crying," she insisted. "I never cry. I'm not a crier, I swear it. I just…I'm so glad you told me."

"I would do anything for Daisy and Jake," Crash said

simply. "Anything." He paused. "Watching Daisy die is hard enough, though. If I have to help her to…" He shook his head. "It's raining—and our pizza's here."

It was. The delivery truck was pulling into the driveway.

Nell stood up and followed Crash the rest of the way down the hill. She put the Flexible Flyer back inside the garage as he paid for the pizza.

Unfortunately, her appetite was completely gone.

"TODAY WE'RE DOING *what?*"

"Learning to tap-dance," Daisy said, taking a sip of her orange juice.

Nell glanced up. The look on Crash's face was nearly as good as the look on Jake's.

"I don't think SEALs are allowed to tap-dance," Crash said.

Daisy set down her glass. "The instructor should be here in about an hour. I told her to meet us in the barn."

"She's kidding," Jake said. He looked at Daisy. "You *are* kidding?"

She just smiled.

Nell drained the last of her coffee and set the mug on the breakfast table with a thump. "I already know how to tap-dance," she announced. "And since I have four million phone calls to make, I'm going to excuse myself from this morning's activity."

Crash actually laughed out loud. "Oh, not a chance," he said.

"You know how to tap-dance?" Daisy was intrigued. "How come you never told me that?"

"Oh, come on, Daisy, she's bluffing," Crash said. "Look at her."

"I never mentioned it because it's not something that usually comes up in normal conversation," Nell said. "I don't go around introducing myself to people and saying,

'Hi, I'm Nell Burns—oh, by the way, I know how to tap-dance.'"

"I don't buy it." Crash shook his head. "No way. She's just trying to get out of this."

He was teasing. There was a light in his eyes that told Nell he was teasing. Ever since the evening they went sledding, the evening he'd actually *talked* about himself, their relationship had continued to grow. But only in one direction. They only continued to be friends.

It was driving her nuts.

"You just think because you're helping FInCOM do an advanced security check, you know everything there is to know about me," Nell countered. "I'm glad you don't believe me. This proves that I'm still capable of having secrets. God knows everyone needs at least *one* little secret— even if it's only that they know how to tap-dance."

The truth was, Nell had more than one secret. And one of those secrets she was keeping was enormous. She was falling for Crash. With every moment that passed, she was falling harder for this man who was determined to be no more than her friend.

She glanced at Daisy, who was watching her with a smile. Strike that. The way Nell felt about Crash was apparently quite obvious to *some* people in the room.

"I believe you," Jake told her. "But there's only one way you're going to convince Lieutenant Skeptic here. You're going to have to tap-dance for him."

"That's right." Crash gestured toward the spacious kitchen floor. "Come on, Burns. Knock yourself out."

"Right *here?* In the kitchen?"

"Sure." He leaned back in his chair, waiting.

Nell shook her head. "I…don't have tap shoes."

"I bought us each a pair," Daisy said helpfully. "They're out in the barn."

Nell stared. "You bought four pairs of—"

Crash stood up. "Let's go."

"Now?"

He started for the door. "Jake was right. The only way I'll let you get out of the required beginners' class is if you walk your talk, so to speak."

Nell rolled her eyes at Daisy, then followed Crash out to the barn. She shivered as he unlocked the door.

He glanced at her. "Where's your jacket?"

"You didn't take yours."

"I usually don't need one."

"You usually work in the jungles of Southeast Asia where the average December temperature is a steamy eighty degrees."

"You aren't supposed to know that." He held the door open for her and then closed it behind them. "It's cold in here, too. I'll turn up the heat."

"Don't. It's not good for the trees to be really warm until they absolutely *have* to be," Nell explained. "If we keep 'em inside at seventy-two degrees for a week, and then put them outside when it's in the twenties…it blows their minds."

"They're trees," Crash pointed out dryly. "They don't have minds."

"That's not what my mother thinks. She talks to all her plants. And I think it works. My parents' entire house is like a botany experiment gone wild."

"I hate to break it to you, Burns, but that says more for the power of CO_2 than anything else."

"Yeah, yeah," Nell said. "Be that way." The morning was gray and she turned on the overhead lights.

Four shoe boxes were neatly stacked underneath one of the Christmas trees that she and Crash had decorated.

Tap shoes. Two pairs of men's shoes, and two pairs of women's. They were all black leather, and the women's had a sturdy two-inch heel.

Somehow Daisy had known Nell's exact shoe size. She sat on the floor and pulled off her boots. "It's been a while," she said, looking up at Crash as she strapped on the shoes. "I learned to tap back when I was in high school. I was a theater-major wannabe—you know, in the chorus of all the school musicals, never good enough to get a lead role. I was an okay dancer, but not talented enough to get into a performing-arts program at any college. At least not any college *I* wanted to go to."

She stood up. Trust Daisy to spend the money on quality shoes that fit comfortably.

Nell caught sight of herself in the wall of mirrors. Dressed in jeans and a turtleneck, she felt odd in fancy black heels. She felt odder still about Crash, leaning against the wall, arms crossed, waiting to watch her dance. She knew he wouldn't laugh at her—at least not out loud.

She glanced over her shoulder at him. "You know, I really shouldn't have to do this," she said. "We're friends. You should believe me. You should take on faith what I've told you is true."

He nodded. "Okay. I believe you. Dance."

"No, what you should say is that you believe me, and because you believe me you don't have to see me dance."

"But I want to see you dance."

"All right, but I'm warning you. It's been years, and even back when I was taking lessons I wasn't very good."

Crash turned toward the windows. "What's that?"

"What?"

He straightened up, pushing himself off the wall. "A siren."

"I don't hear…" She heard it then. In the distance, moving closer.

Nell went toward the door, but Crash was even faster. He pulled it open and went outside at a run. Her tap shoes clattered on the macadam as she followed. Somehow the kitchen door had gotten locked, and they raced around to the front of the house, arriving just as an ambulance bounced over the speed bump and up into the main part of the driveway.

God, what had happened? It hadn't been more than fifteen minutes since they'd left Daisy and Jake in the kitchen.

"Jake!" Crash burst into the house.

"In the studio," the admiral bellowed back.

Nell held the door for the paramedics. "Down the hall on the left," she instructed them, standing back to let them go first. They were moving fast and she raced after them.

Please, God... Nell stopped in the studio doorway as the three paramedics crowded around Daisy.

She was on the floor, as if she'd fallen, with Jake beside her, and Crash crouched beside him. Nell hung back, suddenly aware that she was not a member of the family.

"She blacked out," Jake was telling the paramedics. "It's happened before, but not like this. This time I couldn't rouse her." His voice broke. "At first I thought..."

"I'm okay," Nell heard Daisy murmur. "I'm all right, baby. I'm still here."

Nell shivered, holding on to herself tightly. She knew what Jake had thought. Jake had thought that Daisy had slipped into a coma. Or worse.

The paramedics were deep in discussion with both Jake and Daisy. They wanted to take Daisy to the hospital, to run some tests.

"Nell."

She looked up to find Crash gazing at her. He'd straightened up and now held out his hand to her—a silent invitation to come stand beside him.

She took both his invitation and his hand, lacing their fingers tightly together.

"Your hand is cold," he whispered.

"I think my heart stopped beating for a minute."

"She's okay, you know," he told her.

"For now." She felt her eyes fill with tears.

Crash nodded. "Now is all we've got. It stinks, but it's better than the alternative, which is *not* to have now."

Nell closed her eyes, willing her tears away.

To her surprise, he touched her, gently pulling a strand of her hair free from where it had caught on her eyelashes, pushing it back, dragging his fingers lightly through her hair. "But remember that line of thinking doesn't apply to every situation," he said quietly. "Sometimes taking advantage of now doesn't do anyone any good."

He was talking about…them? Was it possible…? Nell looked up at him, but he'd let go of her hand, all of his attention on Jake, who was pushing himself to his feet.

As she watched, Jake backed away to let the paramedics put Daisy on a stretcher.

"She didn't agree to go in for tests, did she?" Crash asked incredulously.

Jake gave him a you've-got-to-be-kidding look. "No chance. She's only letting them help her into the bedroom. She's still feeling kind of dizzy." He forced himself to smile as Daisy was carried past. "I'll be in in a sec, babe," he told her before turning back to Nell. "I know this is asking a lot, but… What are the chances of moving the wedding up a few days?"

Nell glanced from Jake to Crash then back. "How many days?"

"As many as possible. To tomorrow, if you can swing it."

Tomorrow. Oh, God.

"I'm afraid…" Jake cleared his throat and started again. "I'm afraid we're running out of time."

She would have to call the pastor, see if he could change his schedule. And the caterer was going to have a cow. It wasn't a weekend, so the band might be open to switching the dates. But—the guests! She'd have to call them individually. That meant close to two hundred phone calls. But first she'd have to *find* all those phone numbers and…

Crash touched her shoulder. When she looked up at him, he nodded, as if he could read her mind. "I'll help."

Nell took a deep breath and turned back to Jake. "Consider it done."

CHAPTER SIX

AS FAR AS WEDDINGS WENT, this one had been perfect.

Or rather, it *would* have been perfect, had the bride not been dying.

Crash closed his eyes. He didn't want to go there. All day long, he'd avoided that dark place.

The barn sparkled and glistened with the decorations he'd helped Nell hang. It rang with laughter and music. It glowed with warmth and light.

The band was great, the food was first-rate, the guests were bemused by the bride and groom's sudden change of plans—because none of them knew the truth.

And amidst all the sparkle and joy, Crash could almost pretend that he was just as ignorant.

The champagne he'd had hadn't hurt much, either.

The crowd was really thinning out as it approached eleven o'clock. Crash watched Nell from across the room as she spun around the dance floor in the arms of a man he'd met just that evening. He blanked on the name. Tall, dark and distinguished-looking, whoever he was had just been elected to the U.S. Senate. Mike something. From California. Garvin. That was it. Senator *Mark* Garvin.

Garvin said something to Nell and she laughed.

Crash was certain that Garvin—along with the other 299 wedding guests—couldn't tell that Nell hadn't had more than two hours of sleep in the past forty-eight. The only reason he knew that she hadn't slept much was because in the past two days he hadn't had time to catch more than a short combat nap himself.

Of course, *he* was used to going without sleep. He was trained to be able to stay alert and functioning under severe conditions.

Nell was running on adrenaline and sheer grit.

"She's great, isn't she?"

Crash looked up to see Dexter Lancaster standing beside him, following his gaze. He was talking about Nell.

"Yeah," Crash agreed. "She's great."

"I figured you out, you know." Lancaster took a sip of his drink. "I've danced with Nell four times tonight. Garvin over there has danced with her twice. A collection of other gentlemen have taken her around the floor this evening, as well. But you, my friend, have not danced with her at all."

"I don't dance."

Lancaster smiled and his blue eyes twinkled warmly. "She doesn't have a clue that you're hung up on her, does she?"

Crash met the man's gaze steadily. "She's my friend," he said quietly. "I happen to know that she's emotionally vulnerable right now. She doesn't need me—or anyone else—taking advantage of her."

The lawyer nodded, setting his empty glass down on a nearby table. "Fair enough. I'll wait to call her until spring or early summer."

Crash gritted his teeth and forced himself to nod. By spring or early summer, unless there was some kind of miracle and Daisy went into remission, he'd be on the other side of the world. "Fair enough."

"Say good-night to her for me," Lancaster said.

Across the room Mark Garvin gallantly kissed the back of Nell's hand before releasing her. What was it about Nell that attracted older men like flies to honey? Garvin was

Jake's age—maybe even older. He was a walking ad for Grecian Formula.

Nell seemed unaffected by the blazing-white flash of Garvin's perfectly capped teeth as she turned and approached a group of women who were putting on their coats.

She looked incredible.

She was wearing a long gown, befitting the black tie formality of the evening wedding. It was long-sleeved, with something Crash had heard Daisy describe as a sweetheart neckline that dipped elegantly down between her breasts. It was a rich shade of emerald, which—Daisy claimed—was Nell's duty to wear as maid of honor, because it accentuated the bride's green eyes.

The gown was made of some kind of stretchy velvet material that clung to Nell's slender figure, and drew Crash's attention—along with Garvin's and Lancaster's apparently—away from the bride's eyes.

As Crash watched, Nell laughed at something one of the women said. And as she laughed, she looked up and directly over at him.

He was in trouble. He knew that everything he'd tried for so long to hide from her was written clearly on his face. He knew everything he was feeling, all of his longing and desire, was burning in his eyes. But he couldn't look away.

Nell's smile slowly faded as she stared across the room at him, trapped by his gaze, just as he was by hers. He could see the hint of a blush rising in her cheeks.

Any second now, she would look away. Crash knew it. Any second, she'd turn and…

She didn't turn. She walked toward him. She came right across the dance floor.

Yes, he was in trouble here. He *knew* he was in *big* trouble. But he still couldn't bring himself to look away.

"I owe you a dance."

Bad idea. If he took her in his arms, if he touched the soft velvet of her dress, felt it warmed by the heat of her body beneath…

"I know it's not the same as tap-dancing," Nell said, "but for now it'll have to do."

She took his hand and led him onto the dance floor. And just like that, he was holding her. He wasn't sure exactly what she'd done, but he knew it wasn't entirely her doing that had put her in his embrace. He'd surely done something stupid, like hold open his arms.

And now that she was there, now that they were dancing, his instinct was confirmed. This was a *very* bad idea. He'd had way too much to drink to be doing this. "I'm not a very good dancer."

"You're doing fine." The fingers of her right hand were looped gently around his thumb, and her left hand was resting comfortably on his shoulder. He was holding her loosely, his hand against the small of her back, against the warm softness of her dress. Her legs brushed against his as they moved slowly in time to the music. She smelled deliciously sweet. Her face was tilted up, her mouth close enough to kiss. "How are you holding up?" she asked, looking up into his eyes.

He was dying. "I'm hanging in," he said.

She nodded. "I noticed you broke your no-drinking-unless-you-have-to rule tonight."

Crash gazed down into the calming blue of her eyes. "No, I didn't. Tonight I had to."

"'Til death do us part,'" Nell said quietly. "That was what really got to me."

"Yeah." Crash nodded. He desperately didn't want to talk about that. "Do you think if I kissed you tonight, we could both pretend it never happened tomorrow?"

Her eyes widened.

"I didn't really mean that," he said quickly. "I was only

trying to change the subject to an allegedly less emotional topic. It was a bad attempt at an even worse joke."

She wasn't laughing. "You know, Hawken—"

"I don't want to go there, Nell. I shouldn't have said that. Look, I don't know what I'm doing here, dancing with you like this. I'm a lousy dancer, anyway." He forced himself to let go of her, to step back, away. Distance. Separation. Space. Please, God, don't let him kiss her....

He turned to walk away. It was the best possible thing he could do for her. He knew that. He believed it with all of his heart. But she put her hand on his arm, and he hesitated.

He who hesitates is lost....

He turned and looked into her eyes, and indeed, he was lost.

"This whole night's been like some kind of fairy tale," Nell whispered. "Like some kind of fantasy. If I close my eyes, I can pretend that Daisy's going to be all right. Give me a break, will you, and let me have my dance with Prince Charming. My world's going to turn back into a rotten pumpkin soon enough."

"You've got it wrong," he said harshly. "I'm no prince."

"I never said you were. Not really. This is just a fantasy, remember? I just want to hold someone close—and pretend."

Somehow she was back in his arms again, and he was holding her even closer this time. He could feel the entire length of her, pressed against the entire length of him. Her hand was no longer on his shoulder but instead was wrapped around his neck, her fingers entwined in the hair at the nape of his neck. It felt impossibly good.

He was no longer dying. He *had* died—and gone to heaven.

"You know what's really stupid?" she whispered.

He was. He was impossibly stupid and certifiably insane. He should've walked away. He should do it now. He should just turn and walk out of the barn and stand for several long minutes in the bracing cold. And then he should walk into the house, up the stairs and into his bedroom, and lock himself in until his sanity returned with the rising sun.

Instead he bent his head to brush his cheek and nose against the fragrant softness of Nell's hair. Instead, he let his fingers explore the velvet-covered warmth of her back. Please, God, he absolutely *couldn't* let himself kiss her. Not even once. He knew one taste would never be enough.

"It's really stupid, but even after all these weeks, I never know what to call you," she murmured.

He could feel her breath, warm against his skin, her lips a whisper away from his throat. Her words didn't seem to make any sense.

Not that *any* of this made any sense at all.

"I don't know what you mean." His voice was hoarse. She felt so good pressed against him, her breasts full against his chest, the softness of her stomach, the taut-ness of her thighs…

She lifted her head to look up at him. "I don't know what name to use when I talk to you," she explained. "Crash seems to…well, strange."

He was hypnotized by her eyes, drugged by the scent of her perfume, held in thrall by the beautiful curves of her lips.

"I mean, what am I supposed to say? 'Hi, Crash. How are you, Crash?' It sounds like I'm talking to one of the X-Men. 'Excuse me, Crash, would you and your buddy Cyclops mind carrying this tray into Daisy's office?'" She shook her head. "On the other hand, I find it nearly impos-sible to call you Billy, the way Jake and Daisy do. Calling you Billy is kind of like calling a Bengal tiger *Fluffy*. I guess there's always Bill, but you don't seem very much like a Bill." She narrowed her eyes, still gazing up at him. "Maybe William…"

Crash *still* didn't walk away. "No, thanks. My father always called me William."

"Ew. Forget *that*."

"I guess you could always call me 'The SEAL Operative Formerly Known as Billy.'"

She laughed. "And I suppose I'd have to call you 'The SEAL Operative' for short."

"It works for me."

Nell's eyes sparkled. "God, if that's my choice, I'm going to have to rethink this 'Crash' thing. Maybe after a decade or two, I'll get used to it."

Crash didn't kiss her. For one instant, he thought he'd totally lost control and was going to do it. He'd even lowered his head, but somehow he'd stopped himself. He felt sweat bead on his upper lip, felt a trickle slide down past his ear. For someone who had a reputation of always keeping cool, he was losing his, fast.

Nell didn't seem to notice. "What's the latest word on my security check?"

"So far, so good. After this is over, you'll be able to get a job working at FInCOM Headquarters, if you want." As soon as he said the words, he realized how awful they sounded. "I meant, after the security check is over," he amended. "I didn't mean…"

But the sparkle had already left her eyes. "I know," she said quietly. "I'm just…I'm not letting myself think that far into the future. I know it's coming, but…" She shook her head. "Damn. And we were doing so well."

The song had ended. Crash gently stepped away from her and led her off the dance floor. "I'm sorry."

"It's not your fault. I'm just…so tired." Nell laughed softly. "God, am I tired."

He put his hands in his pockets to keep himself from reaching for her again. "Is there anything else you need to do tonight? I could handle it for you."

"No, I'm mostly done. Jake slipped the band God knows

how much extra to play another hour, even though most of the guests have gone home. The caterer packed up hours ago. The only thing I have to remember is to turn the heat down in the barn so the trees don't bake all night long."

"I can take care of that," Crash told her. "Why don't you go to bed? Come on, I'll walk you back to the house."

She didn't protest, and he knew she was more exhausted than she'd admitted.

Jake and Daisy were still on the dance floor, wrapped in each other's arms, oblivious to anyone else. Crash opened the door, holding it for Nell, then followed her out into the crisp coldness of the December night.

She didn't have a jacket and he quickly slipped off his tuxedo coat and put it around her shoulders.

"Thanks."

Even as tired as she was, her smile made his stomach do flips. He had to get her inside, and then he had to get himself away from her. He'd walk her to the kitchen, no farther. He'd unlock the door, and he'd close it behind her.

But the stars were brilliant, Orion's belt glittering like jewels against the black-velvet backdrop of the night sky. Nell was looking up at them, standing completely still, not hurrying toward the kitchen door. "It's beautiful, isn't it?"

What could he possibly say? "Yeah."

"Now might be a really great time for you to kiss me." She glanced at him, and in the darkness, her eyes seemed colorless and unearthly. "Just as a tonight kind of thing, like you said, you know? The grand finale to the perfect fantasy evening."

Crash's lips were dry, and he moistened them. "I'm not sure that's such a good idea." Christ, what was he saying? He wasn't *sure?* He was certain that kissing her was a very, very *bad* idea.

Nell looked back up at the sky. "Yeah, I thought you

might think that. It's all right. It's been a nice fantasy anyway."

God, he wanted to kiss her. And he also wanted her to go inside so he wouldn't be faced with such an incredibly hellish temptation.

She took a deep breath and let it out in a rush as she turned again to look at him. "Tell me, 'The SEAL Operative Formerly Known as Billy,' do you believe in God?"

Her blunt question caught him even more off guard than her talk about kissing, but fortunately her somewhat unorthodox delivery gave him time to recover. "You're not really going to call me that, are you?"

She smiled.

His stomach flipped again.

"Do you?" she asked.

"Are you?" he countered.

"Yes. But if you want, I'll call you Billy for short. But you better believe I'll be thinking the whole thing." Another smile.

This time his entire heart did a somersault. Crash nodded. "Yes."

"Yes, you want me to call you Billy for short, or yes, you believe in God?"

"Yes for Billy, and… Yes, I believe in something that could probably be called God." He smiled ruefully. "I've never admitted that to anyone before. Of course, no one's ever dared to ask me that question. I think they've all assumed I'm soulless—considering the kind of work I sometimes do."

"What kind of work do you sometimes do?"

Crash shook his head. "I couldn't tell you even if I wanted to, but believe me, I don't want to—and you don't want to know."

"But I *do*."

He stood there for a moment, just looking at her.

"I really, *really* do," she said.

"There are certain…covert ops," he said slowly, carefully choosing his words, "in which a team might target—and eliminate—known confessed terrorists. The key word there is *confessed*. The kind of scumbags who take out an entire 747 of innocent civilians, then take credit—boast about it."

Nell's eyes were wide. *"Eliminate…?"*

He held her gaze steadily. "Still want me to kiss you?"

"Are you telling me that *Jake* asks you to—"

Crash shook his head. "No, I'm telling you nothing. I've already said way too much. Come on. It's cold out here. Let's get you inside before you catch the flu."

She stepped directly in front of him. "Yes," she said. "I still want you to kiss me."

Crash had to pull up short to keep from knocking her over. "No, you don't. I promise you, you don't."

She just laughed. And she went up on her toes, and she brushed her lips across his, and Crash's world went into slow motion.

One heartbeat.

He couldn't move. He knew that the smart thing to do would be to go for the kitchen door. He knew he should get it unlocked, push this woman inside, then lock it tightly again, with him on the outside.

Instead he stood there, holding his breath, waiting to see if she'd do it again.

Two heartbeats. Three. Four.

And then she did kiss him once more, slowly this time. She stared into his eyes as she stood on her toes again, her gaze finally flickering down to his mouth and back, before she touched her lips to his again—her lips, and the very tip of her tongue. She tasted him, softly, lightly, and the last of his control shattered.

He pulled her close and kissed her, *really* kissed her, lowering his head and claiming her lips, sweeping his tongue deeply inside of her sweet mouth, his heart pounding crazily.

Crash felt her fingers in his hair as she kissed him back just as fiercely, just as hungrily. She pressed herself against him even as he tried to pull her closer and he knew without a doubt that she wanted far more than a kiss. All he had to do was ask, and he knew he could spend the night in her bed.

She was a sure thing. He could sate himself, with Nell as a willing participant. He could bury himself inside her. He could lose himself completely in her sweetness.

And tomorrow, she would wake him up with a kiss, her hair tangled charmingly around her pretty face, her eyes sleepy and smiling and...

And the light and laughter would fade from her eyes as he quietly tried to explain why he couldn't become a permanent fixture there in her bed. Not couldn't—*didn't want to.* He didn't really want her. He'd just wanted *someone,* and she'd been there, willing and ready and...

And he knew he couldn't do that to Nell.

Crash found the strength to push her gently away. She was breathing hard, her breasts rising and falling rapidly beneath her dress, her eyelids heavy with passion. Dear God, what was he doing? What was he giving up?

"I'm sorry," he said. He'd been saying that far too often lately.

Realization dawned in her eyes. Realization and shocked embarrassment. "Oh, God, *I'm* sorry," she countered. "I didn't mean to attack you."

"You didn't," he said quickly. "That was me. That was my fault."

Nell stepped even farther back, away from him. "It was just, um, part of tonight's fantasy, right?"

She was searching his eyes, and Crash knew that she was more than half hoping he'd deny her words. But instead, he nodded. "Yeah," he said. "That's all it was. We're both tired, and…that's all it was."

Nell hugged his jacket more tightly around her, as if she'd suddenly felt the cold. "I better get inside."

Crash went up the stairs and unlocked the kitchen door, holding it open. She slipped out of his jacket, handing it back to him.

"Good night," he said.

To his surprise, she reached out and touched the side of his face. "Too bad," she said softly.

And then she was gone.

Crash locked the door behind her. "Yeah," he said. "Too bad."

OUT IN THE BARN, the band was finally packing up. But as Crash watched from the shadows beyond the doorway, Jake and Daisy still danced to music only they could hear.

Admiral and Mrs. Jacob Robinson.

The evening had been one of laughter and celebration. Jake had accepted the congratulations of friends and colleagues. He'd smiled through the toasts that wished the two of them long life and decades more of happiness. He'd laughed as friends had joked, trying to guess exactly how he'd finally convinced this longtime lover to willingly accept the chains of matrimony.

Jake had finally gotten what he'd always wanted, but Crash knew he would trade it all for a miracle cure.

As Crash watched them dance, Jake wiped his eyes, careful to keep Daisy from seeing that he was crying.

Jake was crying.

All evening long, Crash had fought to keep the constant awareness of Daisy's mortality at bay.

But now death's shadow was back.

Crash waited until the band had left, until Jake and Daisy slowly made their way out to the house.

He turned down the heat and locked the barn door, then went to his room.

Nell's door was closed, and as he passed it, it stayed tightly shut.

He was glad for that. Glad she was asleep, glad she hadn't been waiting for him. He didn't think he would have had the strength to turn her down again.

He hesitated outside his own bedroom door, looking back down the hall toward Nell's room.

Yes, he was glad. But he was also achingly disappointed.

CHAPTER SEVEN

NELL SAT NUMBLY ON HER BED, next to her suitcase. She was aware that she was going to have to stand up and walk over to her dresser if she wanted to transfer her socks and underwear from the drawer into that suitcase.

It couldn't have happened so quickly, it didn't seem possible. But yet it had.

Two days after the wedding, Daisy had had another of her fainting spells. It had taken even longer for her to be roused, and when she was conscious, she'd found that she could no longer walk unassisted.

The doctor had come out to the house, leaving behind a final, chilling prognosis—the end was near.

Yet Daisy and Jake had continued to celebrate their newlywed status. They'd sipped champagne while watching the sunset from Daisy's studio. Jake had carried Daisy wherever she wished to go, and when he grieved, he did it out of her sight.

And then, three days after Christmas, Daisy and Jake went to sleep in their master-bedroom suite, and only Jake had awakened.

Just like that, in the blink of an eye, in the beat of a heart, Daisy was gone.

The evening before, they'd all been together in the kitchen. Nell had been making a cup of tea, and Jake, with Daisy in his arms, had stopped in to say good-night. Crash had come in from outside, wearing running clothes and a reflective vest. Even though Nell had offered to make him some tea as well, he'd gone upstairs shortly after Daisy and Jake. Ever since the night of the wedding, he'd been careful not to spend any time alone with her.

But he'd come into her room the next morning, to wake her up and tell her that Daisy had died, peacefully, painlessly, in her sleep.

That day and the next had passed in a blur.

Jake grieved openly, as did Nell. But if Crash had cried at all, he'd done it in the privacy of his own room.

The wake had been filled with many of the same people who'd come to the wedding barely a week before. Senators. Congressmen. Naval Officers.

Washington's elite.

Four different people had given Nell their card, knowing that she had not only lost a friend but was suddenly out of work. It was a gesture of kindness and goodwill, Nell tried to tell herself. But still, she couldn't shake the image of herself in the middle of a feeding frenzy. Good personal assistants were hard to find, and here she was, suddenly available.

Senator Mark Garvin had talked for ten minutes about how his fiancée was seeking a personal assistant. With their wedding only a few months away, she was hard-pressed to keep her social schedule organized. Nell had stood there uncomfortable until Dex Lancaster had come to her rescue and pulled her away.

Still, despite that, the wake had been lovely. As at the wedding, laugher resounded as everyone told of their own special memories of Daisy Owen Robinson.

The funeral, too, had been a joyous celebration of a life well lived. Daisy definitely would have approved.

But through it all, Crash had been silent. He'd listened, but he hadn't responded. He didn't tell a story of his own, he didn't laugh, he didn't cry.

Several times, Nell had been tempted to approach

him and take his pulse, just to verify that he was, indeed, alive.

He'd distanced himself so completely from all of the grief and turmoil around him. She didn't doubt for a minute that he'd distanced himself from everything he was feeling inside, as well.

That was bad. That was really bad. Did he honestly expect to keep everything he was feeling locked within him forever?

Nell stood up, took her socks from the drawer and tossed them into her suitcase. Just as quickly as Daisy had died, other changes were happening, too. She was leaving in the morning. Her job here was finished.

As much as she wanted to stay, she couldn't help but hope that once he was alone with Jake, Crash would be able to come to terms with his grief.

Her favorite pair of socks had rolled out of the suitcase, and as Nell picked them up off the floor, she noticed the heels were starting to wear through. The sight made her cry. For someone who never, *ever* used to cry, nearly everything made her burst into tears these days.

She lay back on her bed, holding the rolled-up ball of socks to her chest, staring at the familiar cracks in the ceiling, letting her tears run down into her ears.

She'd loved it here at the farm. She'd loved working here, and she'd loved living here. She'd loved Daisy and Jake, and she loved…

Nell sat up, wiping her face with the back of her hand. No. She definitely didn't love Crash Hawken. Even *she* wouldn't do something as foolish as fall in love with a man like him.

She put the socks in her suitcase and went back to the dresser for her underwear.

Sure, she loved Crash, but only in a non-romantic way— only the way she'd loved Daisy, the way she loved Jake. They were friends.

Yeah, right. She sat down on her bed again. Who was she trying to kid? She wanted to be friends with Crash about as much as she wanted to sign on to be personal assistant to oily California Senator Mark Garvin's pampered debutante fiancée. In a single word—*not*.

What she *wanted* was to be Crash Hawken's lover. She wanted him to kiss her again, the way he'd kissed her on the night of the wedding. She wanted to feel his hands against her back, pulling her close.

She wanted to tear off her clothes and share with him the hottest, most powerful sexual experience of her entire life.

But those feeling weren't necessarily based on love. They were the result of attraction. Lust. Desire.

There was a knock on her door, and Nell nearly fell of her bed. Heart pounding, she went to open it.

But it was Jake, not Crash. He looked exhausted, his eyes rimmed with red. "I just wanted to let you know that I'm going to be sleeping downstairs again tonight."

Nell had to clear her disappointment out of her throat before she could speak. "Okay." Had she honestly thought that it might be Crash knocking on her door? What was she thinking? In the entire month that they'd slept under the same roof, with the sole exception of the night of Jake and Daisy's wedding, Crash had never made a move on her. He'd never done anything at all that even *remotely* suggested that he was interested in anything but her friendship. So why on earth had she thought he would knock on her door now?

"What time are you leaving tomorrow?" Jake asked.

She was going home to Ohio for a week or two. "First thing in the morning. Before seven. I want to try to miss the rush-hour traffic."

He reached into his jacket pocket and drew out an envelope. "I better give this to you now, then. I want to sleep as long as I can in the morning." His mouth twisted into an approximation of a smile. "Like, until April." He handed her the envelope. "Severance pay. Or a bonus. Call it whatever you like. Just take it."

Nell tried to give it back. "I don't want this, Jake. It's bad enough that Daisy left me all that money in her will."

Somehow Jake managed a more natural smile. "Yeah, well, she *really* wanted to give you Crash. She was sorry that didn't work out."

Nell felt herself blush. "It didn't *not* work out," she said. "It just… There was nothing there. No spark."

Jake snorted. "You really don't think Daisy and I didn't notice the two of you staring when you didn't think the other was looking? Yeah, right, there were no sparks— there were nuclear-powered *fireworks*."

She shook her head. "I don't know what you think you saw." She lowered her voice. "I did everything but throw myself at him. I'm telling you, he's not interested in me that way."

"What he *is* is scared to death of you." Jake pulled her in close for a quick hug. "You know I'll never be able to thank you enough for all you did, but right now I have to go lie down and become unconscious. Or least attempt it."

"Admiral, are you sure you want to be alone? I could get Billy, and we could all have something to eat and—"

"I've got to get used to it, you know? Being alone."

"Maybe tonight's not the night to start."

"I just want to sleep. The doctor gave me something mild to help me relax. I'm not proud—if I need to, I'll take it." Jake gave her a gentle noogie on the top of her head. "Just give me a call when you get to your mom and dad's so that I know you made it to Ohio safely."

"I will," Nell promised. "Good night, sir." She was still holding the envelope he'd given her. "And thank you."

Jake was already gone.

She turned and looked at Crash's door.

It was tightly shut, the way it always was when he was inside his bedroom.

What he is is scared to death of you.

What if Jake was right? What if the attraction Nell felt for Crash really was mutual?

If she didn't do *something* now, if she didn't walk over to that tightly shut door and knock on it, if she didn't get up the courage to look Crash in the eye and tell him exactly how she felt, she could very well lose the opportunity of a lifetime—a chance to start a very real relationship with a man who excited her on every level. Emotionally, physically, intellectually, spiritually—there was no doubt about it, William Hawken turned her on.

When she woke up in the morning, he'd probably already be downstairs, coming back inside from his morning run. She would load up her car, then shake his hand and that would be it. She would drive away, and probably never see him again.

She stood a chance at making a royal fool of herself, but if she wasn't going to see him ever again, what did that matter?

As she stood there, gazing at Crash's closed door, she could almost hear Daisy whispering in her ear, "Go for it."

Nell tossed the envelope Jake had given her into her suitcase and, straightening her shoulders, she went back into the hall, heading for Crash's room.

CRASH SAT IN THE DARK, fighting his anger.

He'd sat through the funeral as if he were watching it from a distance. It didn't seem possible that Daisy was dead. Part of him kept looking around for her, waiting for her to show up, listening for her familiar laughter, watching for her brilliant smile.

He didn't know how Jake could possibly stand it. But for the past two days, Jake had accepted condolences with a graciousness and quiet dignity that Crash couldn't imagine pulling off.

The anger Crash felt was something he could manage. He was good at controlling his anger. He was practiced in distancing himself from it. But the grief and the pain he was feeling—they were threatening to overpower him.

He'd found he could stomp down the grief, controlling it with his stronger feelings of anger. But after two solid days, the anger was getting harder and harder to control.

And so he sat in the dark with his hands shaking and his teeth clenched, and he silently let himself rage.

Nell was leaving in the morning. The thought made him even angrier, the feeling washing over him in great, thick waves.

He heard a sound in the hallway. It was Jake, knocking on Nell's door. He heard the door open, heard the two of them talking. He could hear the murmur of voices, but he couldn't make out the words. Still, he managed to get the gist. Jake and Nell were saying their goodbyes. Then he heard Jake walk away.

Crash closed his eyes, listening even harder, but he didn't hear Nell's door close. A board creaked in the hall, and his eyes opened. She was standing right outside of his room.

Dear, sweet Mary, how was he supposed to fight the temptation that Nell brought as well as all his grief and pain?

He closed his eyes, again, willing her to walk away. Walk away.

She didn't. She knocked on his door.

Crash didn't move. Maybe if he didn't answer, she would just go away. Maybe…

She knocked again.

And then she opened the door a crack, peering in, looking in the direction of his bed. "Billy? Are you asleep?"

He didn't answer, and she stepped farther into the room.

"Hawken...?" The light from the hallway fell onto the bed, and he saw when she realized it was empty. "Crash, are you even in here?"

He spoke then. "Yes."

Nell jumped, startled by his voice coming from the other side of the room.

"It's dark in here," she said, searching for him in the shadows. "May I turn on the light?"

"No."

She flinched at the flatness of his reply. "I'm sorry. Are you... Are you all right?"

"Yes."

"Then why are you sitting in the dark?"

He didn't answer.

"This all must seem like some terrible kind of déjà vu to you," she said quietly.

"Have you come to psychoanalyze me, or did you have something else in mind?"

It was too dark to see her clearly, even with the light from the hall, but he could picture the slight flush rising in her cheeks.

"I came because I'm leaving in the morning and I wanted to...say goodbye."

"Goodbye."

She flinched again, but instead of turning and walking out of the room the way he hoped she would, she moved toward him.

He was sitting on the floor with his back against the wall, and she sat down right next to him. "You're not alone in what you're feeling," she said. "There was nothing any of us could do to keep her from dying."

"So you *are* here to psychoanalyze. Do me a favor and keep it to yourself."

He couldn't see her eyes, but he could tell from the silhouette of her profile that she was not unaffected by the harshness of his words.

"Actually," she started. Her voice wobbled and she stopped and cleared her throat. When she spoke again, her voice was very, very small. "Actually, I'm here because *I* didn't want to be alone tonight."

Something clenched in Crash's chest. It was the same something that tightened his throat and made tears heat his eyes. It made his bitter anger start to fade, leaving behind a hurt and anguish that was too powerful to keep inside. There was no way he could detach and move far enough away from the pain he was feeling. It was too strong.

"I'm so sorry," he whispered. "What I said was rude and uncalled-for."

Crash tried to get mad at himself. He'd been a son of a bitch from the moment she walked in, a jerk, a complete ass, a total bastard. He tried to get good and angry—because that anger was the only thing that was going to keep him from breaking down and crying like a baby.

Nell moved in the darkness beside him, and he knew she was wiping her eyes on the sleeve of her shirt. "That's okay," she said. "I'd rather have you mad at me than have to watch you do your zombie impression."

"Maybe you should go," Crash said desperately. "Because I'm not feeling very steady here, and—"

She interrupted, turning in the darkness to face him. "I came to your room because I wanted to tell you something before I left." She reached out, touching him on the arm. "I wanted to—"

"Nell, I'm not sure I can—"

"Make sure that you knew that—"

"—handle sitting here like this with you." He'd meant to shake her hand off, but somehow he'd reached for her instead, gripping her tightly by the elbow.

"I've wanted to be your lover since the first time we met," she whispered.

Oh, Lord.

All of the intense feelings—the wanting, the guilt, the

desire, the relentless pain—of the past few days, the past few *weeks,* spun together inside of him, in a great, huge tornado of emotion.

"I just wanted you to know that before I left," she said again, "in case you maybe felt something similar and, even though we've only got one night—"

Crash kissed her. He had to kiss her, or everything inside of him, this churning maelstrom of despair and heartache and guilt and grief would erupt from him, tearing him apart, leaving him open and exposed.

He kissed her—and he didn't have to cry. He pulled her close—and he didn't need to break things, he didn't lash out in anger, he didn't fall apart with grief.

She nearly exploded in his arms, clinging to him as desperately as he clung to her, matching the fury of his kisses, the ferociousness of his embrace.

He pulled her onto his lap so that her legs straddled him, her heat pressed tightly against him.

Sweet God, he'd wanted her for so long.

This was wrong. He knew it was wrong, but he no longer cared. He needed this. He *needed* her—just as she needed him tonight.

And Lord, how she needed him.

Her fingers were running through his hair, her hands skimming down his back as if she couldn't get enough of touching him. She kissed him as if she wanted to inhale him. She pressed herself against him as if she would die if he didn't fill her.

Nothing else existed. For right now, for this time, there was no past, no future—only this moment. Only the two of them.

As they still kissed, he touched her just as greedily, slipping one hand between them to cup the sweet fullness of her breast. She made a low, unbearably sexy noise deep in the back of her throat, then pulled her lips away from his, just long enough to grab the hem of her shirt and pull it quickly over her head.

And then she kissed him again, as if the few seconds they'd been apart had been an eternity.

Her skin was so smooth, so perfect beneath his hands. She reached between to unfasten the front clasp of her bra. The sensation was nearly unbearable then and, as she tugged at his own shirt, he knew that feeling her naked against him would drive him mindlessly past the point of no return.

"Is this really what you want?" he breathed, pushing her hair back from her face, trying to see her eyes in the dimness.

"Oh, yes." She kissed the palm of his hand, catching his thumb between her teeth, touching him with her tongue, damn near sending him through the roof.

When she pulled at his shirt again, this time he helped her, yanking it off.

And then she was touching him, her hands skimming his shoulders as she kissed his throat, his neck, her delicate lips driving him mad.

He pulled her close, crushing his mouth to hers, crushing the softness of her breasts to the hard muscles of his chest.

Skin against skin.

Crash wanted to take his time. He wanted to pull back and look at her, to taste her, to fill his hands with her, but he couldn't slow down without that emotional tornado inside of him breaking free and wreaking havoc.

But there was no way in hell he was going to take her here on the floor.

He swept his hands to the soft curve of her rear end and stood, pulling himself to his feet with Nell still in his arms.

Two long strides brought him close enough to kick the door closed. Two more took them both to his bed.

He put her down and pulled away to rid himself of his boots, and when he turned back, he found she'd opened the curtains on the window over the bed.

Pale winter moonlight filtered in, giving Nell's beautiful skin a silvery glow.

Crash reached for her, and she met him halfway, kissing him and pulling him back with her onto the bed. He felt her hands at the waistband of his pants even as he unfastened the top button of her jeans.

"Please tell me you've got a condom," she breathed as she helped him pull her jeans down the long, smooth length of her legs.

"I've got a condom."

"Where?"

"Bathroom."

She slid off the bed as he wrestled with his own pants, but even so, he still managed to beat her into the attached bath. He always kept protection in his toilet kit on the counter next to the sink, and he searched for a foil-wrapped square without even turning on the light.

She pressed herself against him, her breasts soft against his back, reaching around him to slide both hands down past the waistband of his shorts. As he found what he was looking for, she did, too. Her fingers closed around him and it was all he could do to keep from groaning aloud.

Never in his wildest dreams had he imagined sweet Nell Burns would be so bold.

He could have had this for an entire month. He could have…

She took the foil packet from his hands, tore it open, and began to guide the condom onto him.

But she took too long, touched him too lightly, and he pulled away, breathing hard, quickly finishing the task himself as she dragged his shorts down his legs. When he turned to face her, he saw that she'd taken off her own panties as well.

She was beautiful, standing there naked in the moon-light, all silvery-smooth skin and shining hair, like some kind of goddess, some kind of faerie queen.

Crash reached for her, and she was there, filling his arms, kissing him hungrily. He reached between them, touching her intimately, finding her more than ready for him.

She turned them around, backing herself up against the sink counter. He knew by now that she was far from shy when it came to sex, but when she lifted herself up onto the counter, opening herself to his exploring fingers, pressing him more deeply inside of her, he thought his heart would stop.

But then he stopped thinking as she wrapped her legs around his waist and pulled him toward her. She kissed him hard, and with one explosive thrust, he was inside her.

Crash heard himself cry out, his voice mixing with hers.

It was too good, too incredible. He could feel her fingernails sharply against his back as she gripped him, as her legs tightened around him. She wanted him hard and fast and he wasn't about to deny her anything.

She moved beneath him, meeting each of his thrusts with a wild abandon, a savage passion that left him breathless. And he knew that this was more than mere sex for her, too. This was a way for them both to take comfort. This was a way to reaffirm that they were both still very much alive. It wasn't so much about pleasure as it was about trying to drive away the pain.

He'd always been a considerate lover, always taking his time, giving slow, leisurely pleasure to the woman he was with, making certain that she was satisfied several times over before he allowed himself his own release. He'd always been in careful control.

But tonight, his control had gone out the window with his good judgment. Tonight, he was on fire.

He lifted her off the counter, still kissing her, still moving inside her. He carried her toward the bed, stopping to press her back against the bathroom wall, the closet door, the bedroom wall, stopping to drive himself inside her as deeply as he possibly could.

She strained against him, her head thrown back and her breath catching in her throat as he roughly took first one, then the other of her breasts into his mouth, drawing hard on her deliciously taut nipples.

It was there, against the wall that separated his room from hers, that he felt her climax. It was there, as she cried out, as she shook and shattered around him, that he lost all that remained of his shredded control. He exploded, his release like a fiery rocket scorching his very soul.

And then it was over, but yet it wasn't. Nell still gripped him, still clung to him as if he were her only salvation. And he was still buried deeply inside of her.

Crash stood, his forehead resting on the wall above her shoulder, more than just physically spent. He was emotionally exhausted.

One minute slid into two, two into three and Nell didn't move either, didn't shift, didn't stir, didn't do more than hold him and breathe.

He kept his eyes closed, afraid to open them, afraid to *think*.

Dear God, what had he done?

He'd used her. She'd come to him for comfort, offering her own sweet comfort in return, and he'd done little more than use her to vent his anger and frustration and grief.

He lifted his head and somehow the Jell-O that had once been his legs made it over to the bed. He sank down, pulling himself free from Nell. He immediately missed the intimacy of that connection, but who was he kidding? They couldn't stay joined that way for the rest of their lives. He leaned back on the mattress, pulling her down with him, so that her back nestled against his chest, so that he wouldn't have to meet her gaze.

She lifted her head only slightly—not far enough to look into his eyes. "May I sleep in here with you tonight?"

She sounded so uncertain, so afraid of what he might say. Something in his chest tightened. "Yeah," he said. "Sure."

"Thank you," she whispered, shivering slightly.

He shifted them both so he could cover them with the sheet and blanket. He pulled her closer, wrapping her tightly in his arms, wishing he could make her instantly warm, wishing for a lot of things that he knew he couldn't have.

He wished that he could keep her safe from the rest of the world. But how could he? He hadn't even been able to keep her safe from himself.

CHAPTER EIGHT

CRASH SAT UP IN BED. "What time is it?"

One second, he'd been sound asleep, and the next his eyes were wide open, as if he'd been awake and alert for hours.

"It's nearly six." Nell resisted the urge to dive back under the sheet and blanket and cover herself. Instead, she sat on the edge of the bed with her back toward him, briefly closing her eyes, feeling her face heat with a blush.

Her jeans were here on the floor. Her shirt and bra were across the room. Her underpants...in the bathroom, she remembered suddenly, with a dizzying surge of extremely vivid memory.

She slipped into her jeans, forsaking her underpants. There was no way she was going to walk naked all the way across this room with Crash watching. Yes, he'd seen her naked last night, but that had been last night. This was the morning. This was very different. She was leaving for Ohio today, and if he shed any tears at her departure, they were surely only going to be tears of relief.

Nell knew with a certainty that could have gotten her hired by one of those psychic hotlines, that what had happened between herself and William Hawken last night had been a fluke. It had been a result of the high emotions of the past few days, of Daisy's death and the wake and funeral that had quickly followed.

It had been an incredible sexual experience, but Nell knew that a single episode of great sex didn't equal a romantic relationship. When it came down to it, nothing had changed between them. They were still only friends— except now they were friends who had shared incredibly great sex.

She stood up, fastening the button on her jeans, knowing that she couldn't keep her back to him as she went across the room in search of her shirt and bra. She was just going to have to be matter-of-fact about it. That's all. She had breasts, he didn't—big deal.

But Crash caught her arm before she could take a step, his fingers warm against her bare skin. "Nell, are you all right?"

She didn't turn to face him, wishing that he would prove her wrong. Right now, he could do it—he could prove her entirely, absolutely wrong. He could slide his hand down her arm in a caress. He could pull her gently to him, move aside her hair and kiss her neck. He could run those incredible hands across her breasts, down her stomach, and unfasten the waistband of her pants. He could pull her back into the warmth of his bed and make love to her slowly in the gray morning light.

But he didn't.

"I'm…" Nell hesitated. If she said *fine,* she would sound tense and tight, as if she *weren't* fine. His hand dropped from her arm, and her last foolish hopes died. She crossed the room and picked up her shirt.

It was inside out, of course, and she turned away from him as she adjusted it. She slipped it over her head and only then could she turn and look at him.

Bed head. He had bed head, his dark hair charmingly rumpled, sticking out in all different directions. He looked about twelve years old—except for the fact that even the simple act of sitting up in bed had made many of his powerful-looking muscles flex. God, he was sexy, even with bed head.

Nell used all her limited acting skills to sound normal.

"I'm...still pretty amazed by what happened here last night."

"Yeah," he said. His pale blue eyes were unreadable. "I am, too. I feel as if I owe you an apology—"

"Don't," she said, moving quickly toward him. "Don't you *dare* apologize for what happened last night. It was something we both needed. It was really *right*—don't turn it into something wrong."

Crash nodded. "All right. I just..." He glanced away, closing his eyes briefly before he looked back at her. "I've been so careful to stay away from you all this time," he said, "because I didn't want to hurt you this way."

Nell slowly sat down at the foot of the bed. "Believe me, last night didn't hurt at all."

He didn't smile at her poor attempt at a joke. "You know as well as I do," he said quietly, "that it wouldn't work, right? A relationship between us..." He shook his head. "You don't really know me. You know this...kind of PG-rated, goody-two-shoes, Disney cartoon version of me."

Nell wanted to protest, but he wasn't done talking and she held her tongue, afraid if she interrupted, he would stop.

"But if you really knew me, if you knew who I really am, what I do...you wouldn't like me very much."

She couldn't hold it in any longer. "How can you just make that kind of decision *for* me?"

"Maybe I'm wrong. Maybe you have some kind of sick thing for cold-blooded killers—"

"You are *not* cold-blooded!"

"But I *am* a killer."

"You're a soldier," she argued. "There's a difference."

"Okay," he said levelly. "Maybe you could get past that. But being involved with a SEAL who specializes in black ops is not something I'd wish on my worst enemy." His usually quiet voice rang with conviction. "I certainly wouldn't wish it on you."

"Again, you're just going to decide that for me?"

He threw off the covers, totally unembarrassed by his nakedness. He found his pants, but they were the ones he'd worn to the funeral. Dress pants. He tossed them over a chair and pulled a pair of army fatigues from the closet.

Nell closed her eyes at a sudden vivid image from last night. His hands around her waist, his mouth locked on hers, his *body...*

"Here's the deal with black ops," he said, zipping his fly and fastening the button at his waist. "I disappear—literally—sometimes for months at a time. You would never know where I was, or for how long I'd be gone."

He ran his fingers back through his hair in a failed attempt to tame it, the muscles in his chest and arms standing out in sharp relief. "If I were KIA—killed in action—you might never be told," he continued. "I just wouldn't come back. Ever. You'd never find out about the mission I was on. There'd be no paper trail, no way to know how or why I'd died. It would be as if I'd never existed." He shook his head. "You don't need that kind of garbage in your life."

"But—"

"It wouldn't work." He gazed at her steadily. "Last night was...nice, but you've got to believe me, Nell. It just wouldn't work."

Nice.

Nell turned away. *Nice?* Last night had been wonderful, amazing, fantastic. It hadn't been *nice.*

"I'm sorry," he said softly.

She looked out the window. She looked at the rug. She looked at a painting that hung on the wall. It was one of Daisy's—a beach scene from her watercolor phase.

Only then did she look up at him. "I'm sorry, too. I'm

sorry you think it wouldn't work," she finally said. "You know, I knew most of what you were going to say before you even said it. And I was going to pretend to agree with you. You know, 'Yeah, you're right, it would never work, different personalities, different worlds, different lives, whatever.' But to hell with my pride. Because the truth is, I *don't* agree with you. I think it *would* work. *We* would work. I think we'd be great together. Last night could be just the beginning and I'm…saddened that you think otherwise."

Crash didn't say anything. He didn't even look at her.

Nell bolstered the very last of her rapidly fading courage and tossed the final shred of her pride out the door. "Can't we at least *try?*" Her voice broke slightly—her final humiliation.

Crash didn't speak, and again she found the courage to go on.

"Can't we see what happens? Take it one day at a time?"

He looked up at her, but his eyes were so distant, it was as if he wasn't quite all there.

"I'm sorry," he said again. "I'm not looking for any kind of a relationship at all right now. I was wrong to give in to this attraction between us. I wanted the comfort and the instant gratification, and the real truth is, I used you, Nell. That's all last night was. You came along, and I took what you offered. There's nothing for us to try. There's nothing more to happen."

Nell stood up, trying desperately to hide her hurt. "Well," she said. "I guess that clears *that* up."

"It's my fault, and I *am* sorry."

She cleared her throat as she moved toward the door. "No," she said. "I knew last night…I mean, it was clear that's what it was. Comfort, I mean. It was that way for me, too, sort of, at first anyway, and…I was just hoping… Billy, it's *not* your fault."

She opened the door and stepped into the hall. Crash hadn't moved. She wasn't even sure if he'd blinked.

"Happy New Year," she said quietly, and shut the door behind her.

CHAPTER NINE

A year later

SOMEONE OPENED FIRE.

Someone opened fire, and the world went into slow motion.

Crash saw Jake pushed back by the force of the gunshots, arms spread, face caught in a terrible grimace as an explosion of bright red blood bloomed on the front of his shirt.

Crash heard his own voice shouting, saw Chief Pierson fall as well, and felt the slap as a bullet hit his arm. His years of training kicked in and he reacted, rolling down onto the office floor, taking cover and returning fire.

He shut part of his brain down as he always did in a firefight. He couldn't afford to think in terms of human beings when he was spraying lead around a room. He couldn't afford to feel anything at all.

He analyzed dispassionately as he evaded and struck back. Jake had pulled out the compact handgun he always wore under his left arm, and even though the glimpse Crash had had of the other man's chest wound made him little more than a still-breathing dead man, the admiral somehow found the strength to pull himself to cover, and to fight back.

There could be as few as one and as many as three possible shooters.

Crash noted emotionlessly that his captain, Mike Lovett,

and Chief Steve Pierson, a SEAL known as the Possum, were undeniably dead as he efficiently took down one of the shooters.

Not a man. A shooter. The enemy.

At least two other weapons still hiccuped and stuttered.

He could hear the rush of blood in his ears as he tipped what had once been Daisy's favorite table on its side and used it as a shield to work his way around to an angle where he could try to take out another of the shooters.

Not men. Shooters.

In the same way, Mike and the Poss weren't his teammates anymore. They were KIAs. Killed in action. Casualties.

Crash could do nothing for them now. But Jake wasn't dead yet. And if Crash could eliminate the last of the shooters, just maybe Jake could be saved….

Crash wanted Jake to live. He wanted that with a ferocious burst of emotion that he immediately pushed away. Detach. He had to detach more completely. Emotion made his hands shake and skewed his perception. Emotion could get him killed.

He separated himself cleanly from the man who wanted to rage and grieve over the deaths of his teammates. He set himself apart from the man who was near frantic from wanting to rush to Jake's side, to stanch the older man's wounds, to force him to fight to stay alive.

Crash felt clarity kick in as he looked at himself from the outside. He felt his senses sharpen, felt time slow even further. He knew the last of the shooters was circling the room, looking for a chance to finish off Jake, and then take Crash out, as well.

One heartbeat.

He could hear the sound of the admiral's FInCOM security team, shouting as they pounded on the outside of the locked office door.

Two heartbeats.

He could hear the almost inaudible scuff as the shooter moved into position. There was only one left now, and he was going for the admiral first. Crash knew that without a doubt.

Three heartbeats.

He could hear Jake struggling for breath. Crash knew, also dispassionately, that Jake's wounds had made at least one lung collapse. If he didn't get medical help soon, the man was definitely going o die.

Four heartbeats.

Another scuff, and Crash was able to pinpoint precisely where the shooter was.

He jumped and fired in one smooth motion.

And the last shooter was no longer a threat.

"Billy?" Jake's voice was breathy and weak.

With a pop and a skip as jarring as a needle sliding across a phonograph record, the world once again moved at real time.

"I'm still here." Crash was instantly at his old friend's side.

"What the hell happened...?"

Jake's shirtfront was drenched with blood. "That's just what I was going to ask you," Crash replied as he gently tore the shirt to reveal the wound. Dear, sweet Mary, with an injury like this, it was a miracle Jake had clung to life as long as he had.

"Someone...wants me...dead."

"Apparently." Crash had been trained as a medic—all SEALs were—but first aid wasn't going to cut it here. His voice shook despite his determination to maintain his usual deadpan calm. "Sir, I need to get you help."

Jake clutched Crash's shirt, his eyes glazed with pain. "You need...to *listen*. Just sent you...file...incriminating evidence...last year's snafu in Southeast Asia...six months ago... You were...there. Remember?"

"Yes," Crash said. "I remember." A civil war had started in a tiny island nation when two rival drug lords had pitted their armies against each other. "Two of our marines were killed—Jake, please, we can talk about this on the way to the hospital."

But Jake wouldn't let him go. "The military action…was instigated by an American…a U.S. navy commander."

"*What?* Who?"

The door burst open and Jake's security team swarmed inside the room.

"I need an ambulance *now!*" the security chief bellowed after just one look at the admiral.

"Don't know…who," Jake gasped. "Some…kind of… cover-up. Kid, I'm counting…on you…"

"Jake, don't die!" Crash was pushed back, out of the way, as a team of paramedics surrounded the admiral.

Please, God, let him make it.

"For God's sake, what happened?"

Crash turned to find Commander Tom Foster, Jake's security chief, standing behind him. He took a deep breath and let it out in a rush of air. When he spoke, his voice was calm again. "I don't know."

"How the hell could you not know what happened?"

He didn't let himself react, didn't let himself get angry. The man was understandably shaken and upset. Crash could relate. Now that the shooting was over, his own hands were shaking and he was dizzy. He hunkered down, sliding his back against the wall of Jake's private office as he lowered his rear end all the way to the floor.

He realized then that his arm was bleeding pretty profusely, and had been since the battle had started. He'd lost quite a bit of blood. He set down his weapon and applied pressure with his other hand. For the first time since he was hit, he noticed the searing pain. He looked up. "I didn't see who fired the first shots," he said evenly.

He turned to watch as the paramedics carried Jake from the room. *Please, let him make it.*

The security chief swore. "Who would want to kill Admiral Robinson?"

Crash shook his head. He didn't know *that* either. But he sure as hell was going to find out.

DEX LANCASTER kissed her good-night.

Nell knew from his eyes, and from the gentle heat of his lips, that he was hoping that she would ask him to come inside.

It wasn't that outrageous a hope. They'd had dinner seven or eight times now, and she honestly liked him.

He lowered his head to kiss her again, but she turned her head and his mouth only brushed her cheek.

She liked him, but she wasn't ready for this.

She forced a smile as she unlocked the door. "Thanks again for dinner."

He nodded, resignation and amusement in his blue eyes. "I'll call you." He started down the steps, his long overcoat fanning out behind him like an elegant cape, but then he stopped, turning back to look up at her. "You know, I'm not in any real big hurry either, so take as long as you need. I've decided that I'm not going to let you scare me off." With a quick salute, he was gone.

Nell smiled ruefully as she locked her door behind her, turning on the light in the entryway of her house. The single women in her exercise class would have been lining up for a chance to invite a man like Dexter Lancaster into their homes.

What was wrong with her, anyway?

She had just about everything she'd ever wanted. A house of her own. A great job. A handsome, intelligent, warmhearted man who wanted to spend time with her.

Thanks to the money Daisy Owen had bequeathed her, she'd bought her own house, free and clear—a drafty old

Victorian monster with prehistoric plumbing and ancient wiring that still ran on a fuse box. Nell was fixing the place up, little by little.

And she'd found a new job that she really loved, working part-time for the legendary screen actress, Amie Cardoza. Amie had had most of her successes on film in the seventies and eighties, but as she approached and then passed middle age, the better roles had disappeared, and she'd turned to the stage. She'd started an equity theater in the heart of Washington, D.C., her hometown. She'd really needed a personal assistant—the theater company was still struggling and Amie was becoming politically active, as well.

Dex had introduced Nell to Amie, and Nell had liked the famous actress instantly. She was outspoken and funny and passionate—much like Daisy in many ways. With the life of her theater hanging by a thread, Amie couldn't afford to pay as much as Daisy had, but Nell didn't mind. She'd used the remainder of the money from Daisy to make investments that were already making her a profit. With that, and her house fully paid for, Nell was more than happy to be able to work for someone she admired and respected at a little bit less than the going rate.

She'd only been with Amie for the past four months, but her days had settled into a comfortable routine. On Monday mornings, she'd work at the actress's home, dealing with her day-to-day household affairs. On Tuesday and Wednesday afternoons, they'd meet at the theater. Thursdays and Fridays depended on what additional projects Amie had going. And there was always *something* additional going.

Dex often dropped in. He was a member of an organization called Volunteer Lawyers for the Arts, and he did pro bono work for the theater. Although he was older than the men Nell had dated in the past, she liked him. And when he'd asked her out to dinner several months ago, she couldn't think of a single reason why she shouldn't go.

It had been almost a year since her last romantic entanglement. Or rather, her last *non*-romantic entanglement. She'd tangled, so to speak, with Crash Hawken, a man she should have accepted as a friend. Instead, she'd pushed for more, and she'd lost that friendship.

Crash had never called her. He'd never even dropped her a postcard in response to the letters she'd written. When she'd spoken to Jake and asked, he'd told her the SEAL had been spending a great deal of time out of the country. Jake had also told her very clearly that if she were waiting for Crash to come back, she shouldn't hold her breath.

Well, she wasn't holding her breath. But sometimes, when her guard was down, she still dreamed about the man.

And even now, the nearly year-old memory of his kisses was stronger and more powerful than the two-minute-old memory of Dex's lips.

Nell briefly closed her eyes, willing that particular memory away. She refused to waste her time consciously letting her thoughts stray in that direction. It was bad enough when she did it *sub*consciously.

She hung her coat in the front closet and went into the kitchen to fix herself a cup of tea.

The next time Dex asked her out to dinner, she'd invite him in. She had been wrong. It *was* time. It was definitely time to exorcise some old ghosts.

The phone rang, and she glanced at the clock on the microwave. It was eleven. It had to be Amie with something urgent she'd forgotten about—something that needed to be done first thing in the morning.

"Hello?"

"Thank God you're home!" It *was* Amie. "Turn on the TV right now!"

Nell reached for the power button on the little black-and-white set that sat on her kitchen counter. "What channel? Is there something on the news about the theater?"

"Cable channel four. It's not the theater. Nell, my God, it's something about that man you used to work for—that Admiral Robinson?"

"There's…a commercial playing on channel four."

"They showed one of those previews," Amie imitated a TV announcer's voice. "'Coming up at eleven.' They said something about an *assassination!*"

"What?" The commercial ended. "Wait, wait, it's on!"

The credits rolled endlessly and finally a news anchor gazed seriously into the camera. "Tonight's top story— Navy spokesmen have released confirmation that a gun battle raged three nights ago at the home of U.S. Navy Admiral Jacob Robinson, injuring the admiral and killing several others. Early reports indicate that four or five people are dead. All are believed to be members of the admiral's security team. Let's go to Holly Mathers, downtown."

Nell couldn't breathe. *A gun battle.* At the farm?

The picture changed to a chilled-looking young woman, standing outside a brightly lit building. "Thanks, Chuck. I'm here outside of the Northside Hospital. A number of additional statements have just been released, the first and most tragic of which is that Jake Robinson has *not* survived. I repeat, the fifty-one-year-old U.S. Navy admiral was declared dead from gunshot wounds to the chest, here at Northside just one hour ago."

"Oh, my God." Nell reached blindly behind her for a chair, but couldn't find one, and sank down onto the kitchen floor instead. Jake was dead. How could Jake be *dead?*

"Navy spokesmen have stated that the suspected assassin is in custody, also here at Northside Hospital," the reporter continued, "where it's speculated that he was being treated for minor wounds. They have not yet released the name of this man, nor the names of the men—apparently a team of Navy SEALs—who gave their lives attempting to protect Robinson."

Navy SEALs. Nell went hot and then cold. Please dear God, don't let Crash be dead, too.

She wasn't aware she had spoken aloud until Amie's voice asked. "Crash? Who's Crash?"

Nell was still holding the phone, the line open. "Amie, I'm sorry. I have to go. This is…terrible. I've got to go and…"

What? What could she do?

"I'm so sorry, sweetie. I know how much you liked Jake. Do you want me to come out there?"

"No, Amie, I have to…" Call someone. She had to call someone and find out if Crash was one of the men who had died today at the farm.

"I won't expect to see you for the next few days. Take as much time as you need, all right?"

Nell didn't answer. She couldn't. She just pressed the power button on the cordless phone.

She tried to think. Tried to remember the names of Jake's high-powered friends—people she'd called both to tell about the change in wedding plans, and then about Daisy's death. There were several other admirals that Jake knew quite well. And what was the name of that FInCOM security commander. Tom something. He'd come out to the farm a few times to double-check the security fence….

On the television, the reporter was talking with the anchor, discussing Jake's career in Vietnam, his long-term relationship with popular artist Daisy Owen, their marriage and her relatively recent death.

The reporter touched her earpiece. "I'm sorry," she said, interrupting the anchor in midsentence. "We've just received word that the alleged assassin, the man believed to be responsible for Admiral Jake Robinson's murder and the murders of at least five members of his security team, is being brought out of the hospital, being transferred to FInCOM Headquarters to await arraignment."

The camera jiggled sickeningly as the cameraman rushed to get into position. The hospital doors opened, and a crowd of police and other uniformed men came out.

Nell got to her knees, still holding the telephone as she moved closer to the TV set, wanting a glimpse of the face of the man who had killed her friend.

That man was in the center of the crowd, his long, dark hair parted in the middle and hanging slackly down to his shoulders. The picture was still wobbling, though, and Nell could see little more than the pale blur of his face.

"Admiral Stonegate!" the reporter called to one of the men in the crowd. "Admiral Stonegate, sir! Can you identify this man for our viewers?"

The camera zoomed in on the murder suspect, and the cordless phone dropped out of Nell's hands and clattered on the kitchen floor.

It was Crash. The man being led to the police cars was Crash Hawken.

His hair was long and stringy—parted in the middle and hanging around his face in a style that was far from flattering. But Nell would have known that face anywhere. Those cheekbones, that elegant nose, the too-grim mouth. His pale eyes were nearly vacant, though. He seemed unaware of the explosion of questions and cameras focusing on him.

The relief that flooded through Nell was so sharp and overpowering, she nearly doubled over.

Crash was alive.

Thank God he was alive.

"I've been authorized to release the following statement. The man in our custody is former Navy Lieutenant William R. Hawken," a raspy male voice said.

On the screen, Crash was pushed into the backseat of a car. The camera focused for a moment on his hands, cuffed at the wrist behind his back, before once again settling, through the rain-streaked window of the car, on his seemingly soulless eyes.

"The charges include conspiracy, treason and first-degree murder," the male voice continued. As the car pulled away, the camera moved to focus on the reporter, who was one of a crowd surrounding a short, white-haired navy admiral. "With the evidence we have, it's an open-and-shut case. There's no question in my mind of Hawken's guilt. I was a close friend of Jake Robinson's and I intend, personally, to push for the death penalty in this case."

The *death* penalty.

Nell stared at the TV as the words being spoken finally broke through her relief that Crash was alive.

Crash was being arrested. His hands had been cuffed. He'd been charged with conspiracy, the man had said. And treason. And *murder*.

It didn't make sense. How could anyone who claimed to be a friend of Jake's possibly believe that Crash could have killed him? Anyone who knew them both would have to know how ridiculous that was.

Crash could no more have killed Jake than she could have gone to the window, opened it, and flown twice around the outside of her house before coming back inside. It was ridiculous. Impossible. Totally absurd.

Nell pushed herself up off the kitchen floor and went into the little room she'd made into her home office. She turned on the light and her computer. Somewhere, in some forgotten file deep in the bowels of her hard disk, she must still have the names and phone numbers of the people she'd invited to Jake and Daisy's wedding. *Someone* would be able to help her prove that Crash was innocent.

She wiped her face and went to work.

CRASH HAD TO SHUFFLE when he walked. Even for the short trip from his cell to the visiting room, he had to be handcuffed and chained like a common criminal. His hands and feet were considered to be deadly weapons because of his martial-arts skills. He couldn't raise his hands to push his hair out of his face without a guard pointing a rifle in his direction.

He couldn't imagine who had come to see him—who, that is, had the pull and the clout and the sheer determination to request and be granted a chance to talk one-on-one to a man charged with conspiracy, treason and murder.

It sure wasn't any of the members of his SEAL Team. His *former* SEAL Team. He'd been stripped of his commission and rank upon his arrival here at the federal prison. He'd been stripped of everything but his name, and he was almost certain that they would've have taken that as well, if they could have.

But no, there was no one in his former SEAL Team who would want to sit down and talk to him right now. They all thought he'd killed Captain Lovett and the Possum— Chief Steven Pierson—in the gun battle at Jake Robinson's house.

And why shouldn't they believe that? The ballistics report showed that Crash's bullets had been found in both of the SEALs' bodies—despite the fact Crash had been standing right next to the Possum when the man was hit.

It was quite possible that the only reason Crash was still alive today was because the chief had fallen in front of him when he'd gone down, also taking the bullets that had been meant for Crash.

No, Crash's mysterious visitor wasn't a member of SEAL Team Twelve. But it *was* possible he was a member of SEAL Team Ten's elite Alpha Squad. Crash had worked with Alpha Squad this past summer, helping to train an experimental joint FInCOM/SEAL counterterrorist team.

Crash had worked with Alpha Squad on the same operation in Southeast Asia that Jake had believed was the cause of this entire hellish tragedy. It had been that very op that

Jake had been investigating right before his death—and
had detailed in the encoded file he had sent Crash. Crash
couldn't deny that that particular operation had gone about
as wrong as it possibly could. Jake had believed that the
snafu had not been accidental, and that the mistakes made
were now being covered up.

And Jake never could abide a cover-up.

But was a cover-up of a botched op enough reason to
kill an admiral?

Crash had had little else to think about day and night
during the past week.

But right now, he had a visitor and he turned his thoughts
toward wondering who was sitting on the other side of the
wired glass window in the visitors' room.

It might be his swim buddy, Cowboy Jones—the man
with whom he'd gone through the punishingly harsh SEAL
training. Cowboy wouldn't condemn him. At least not
before talking to him. And then there was Blue McCoy.
Last summer Crash had come to know and trust Alpha
Squad's taciturn executive officer.

He liked to think that Blue would want to hear Crash's
version of the story first, too.

Still, it was odd to imagine that someone he had met
only six months earlier would take the time to question
him about what had happened, when his own teammates,
men he'd worked with for years, had clearly already judged
and found him guilty as charged.

Crash waited while one of the guards unlocked the door.
It swung open and...

It wasn't Cowboy and it definitely wasn't Blue
McCoy.

Out of all the people in all the world, Nell Burns was
the *last* person Crash had expected to see sitting in that
chair on the other side of that protective glass.

Yet there she was, her hands tightly clasped on the table
in front of her.

She looked almost exactly the same as she had the last time he'd seen her—the morning she'd walked out of his room after they'd spent the night together.

It had been nearly a year, but he could still remember that night as if it had been yesterday.

Her hair was cut in the same chin-length style. Only her clothes were different—a severely tailored business suit with shoulder pads in the jacket, and a stiff white shirt that did its best to hide the soft curves of her breasts.

But she didn't have to wear sexy, revealing clothes. It didn't matter what she wore—boxy suit or burlap sack. The image of her perfect body was forever branded in his memory.

God, he was pathetic. After all this time, he still wanted Nell more than he'd ever wanted any woman.

The guard pulled out his chair and Crash sat, refusing to acknowledge just how much he'd missed her, refusing to let himself care that the glass divider kept him from breathing in her sweet perfume, refusing to care that she had to see him like this, chained up like some kind of animal.

But he *did* care. God, how he cared.

Separate. Detach. He had to start thinking like the kind of man he was—a man with no future. A man on a final mission.

Crash had a single goal now—to hunt down and destroy the man responsible for Jake Robinson's death. He had lost far more than his commanding officer when he'd been unable to save Jake's life. He'd lost a friend who'd been like a father to him. And he'd lost everything else that was important to him as well—the trust of his teammates, his rank, his commission, his status as a SEAL. Without those things he was nothing. A nonentity.

He was as good as dead.

But it was that very fact that gave him the upper hand against the unknown man who was behind his fall from grace. Because with everything that mattered to him gone,

Crash had nothing more to lose. He was going to succeed at his mission if it was the last thing he ever did. He was determined to succeed, even at the price of his own worthless life.

As Crash sat and gazed at Nell through the protective glass, he was struck by the irony of the situation. He'd worked hard to make sure that Nell wasn't his to have—or his to lose. Yet here he was, having lost everything else in his life, except, it appeared, her trust.

Yeah, the irony was incredible. His one ally, the only person who believed he didn't kill Jake Robinson, was a woman who by all rights should want nothing more to do with him.

And he knew Nell didn't believe that he'd killed Jake. Even after a year apart, he could still read her like a first-grade primer.

See Nell.

See Nell refuse to run.

See Nell's loyalty blazing in her eyes.

Crash sat in the chair and waited for her to speak.

She leaned forward slightly. "I'm so sorry about Jake."

It was exactly what he'd expected her to say. He nodded. "Yeah. Me, too." His voice came out sounding harsh and raspy, and he cleared his throat.

"I tried to go to his funeral, but apparently he'd requested it be private and…they didn't let you go either, did they?"

Crash shook his head no.

"I'm sorry," she whispered.

He nodded again.

"I would've come sooner," she told him, "but it took me nearly a week to talk my way in here."

A *week*. His chest felt tight at the thought of her going to bat for him day after day for an entire week. He wasn't sure what to say to that, so he didn't say anything.

Her gaze slipped to the bandage he still had on his arm. "Are you all right?"

When he didn't answer, she sat back, closing her eyes briefly. "I'm sorry. Stupid question. Of course you're not all right." She leaned forward again. "What can I do to help?"

Her eyes were so intensely blue. For a moment he was back in Malaysia, gazing out at the South China Sea.

"Nothing," he said quietly. "There's nothing you can do."

She shifted in her seat, clearly frustrated. "There must be *something*. Are you happy with your lawyer? It's important to have a good defense lawyer that you trust."

"My lawyer's fine."

"This is your life that's at stake, Billy."

"My lawyer's fine," he said again.

"Fine's not good enough. Look, I know a really good criminal defense lawyer. You remember Dex…"

"Nell, I don't need another lawyer, particularly not—" He cut himself off short. Particularly not Dexter Lancaster. Crash knew he had no right to be jealous, especially not now. An entire year had passed since he'd willingly given up his right to be jealous. But there was no way he was going to sit down with Dexter Lancaster and plan a defense he wasn't even going to need. He'd spend the entire time torturing himself, wondering if Dex was planning to leave their meeting and head over to Nell's house and…

Don't go there, don't go there, don't go there….

God, he was on the verge of losing it. All he needed was Nell finding out that he'd been keeping track of her this past year, that he knew she was seeing Lancaster socially. All she needed to know was that he'd made an effort to find out if she was okay—made a gargantuan effort, since he'd had to do it from some godforsaken corner of the world.

And then she would read some deep meaning into it. She would think he'd kept track of her because he'd cared.

And he would have to explain that it was only responsibility that had driven him to check up on her, and once again, she would be hurt.

What he needed to do was make her leave. He'd done it before, he could do it again.

"What *really* happened at the farm last week?"

That was one question he could answer honestly. "I don't know. Someone started shooting. I wasn't ready for it, and…" He shook his head.

Nell cleared her throat. "I was told that the ballistics reports prove that you killed Jake and most of the other men. That's pretty damning evidence."

It was damning evidence, indeed. It proved to Crash that this "Commander" that Jake had spoken about, this man Jake himself had believed was responsible for setting up the assassination, was someone with lots of clout in Washington. He was a powerful man with powerful connections. He *had* to be, in order to have had the results of those ballistics tests falsified. And those test results *had* been falsified.

Crash was being framed, and he was going to find out just who was framing him. He knew when he found that out, he'd also find the man responsible for Jake's death.

It was possible whoever had framed him was watching him, even now. They surely would be aware Nell had come to see him. It was important for her own safety that she not make a habit of this.

Nell leaned even closer to the protective glass. "Billy, I can't believe that you killed him, but…isn't it possible that in the chaos, your bullets accidentally hit Jake?"

"Yeah, right. That must've been what happened," he lied. He stood up. The last thing he needed was her brainstorming alternatives and coming up with the theory that he'd been framed. If she *did* come up with that, and if she was vocal about it, she'd be putting herself in danger. "I've got to go."

She stared at him as if he'd lost his mind. "Where?"

He moved very close to the microphone that allowed her to hear him on the other side of the glass. He spoke very softly, very quickly. "Nell, I don't want or need your help. I want you to stand up and walk out of here. And I don't want you to come back. Do you understand what I'm saying?"

She shook her head. "I still think of you as my friend. I can't just—"

"Go away," he said harshly, enunciating each word very clearly. *"Go away."*

He turned and shuffled toward the guards at the door, aware that she hadn't moved, aware that she was watching him, hating his chains, hating himself.

One guard unlocked the door as the other held his rifle at the ready.

Crash went out the door and didn't look back.

CHAPTER TEN

PEOPLE HAD TURNED OUT in droves to see the freak show.

Crash's chains clanked as he was led into the courtroom for his hearing. He tried not to look up at all the faces looking down at him from the gallery.

Tried and failed.

The surviving members of his SEAL Team—his *former* SEAL Team—were sitting in the back, arms crossed, venom in their eyes.

They thought he was responsible for Captain Lovett and the Possum's death. They believed the ballistics report. Why shouldn't they? Everyone else did.

Except Nell Burns. God, she was sitting there, as well. Crash felt a rush of hot and then cold at the thought that she hadn't stayed away. What was wrong with her? What did he have to say or do to make her stay away from him for good?

Crash didn't want to waste any time at all worrying about Nell running around, proclaiming his innocence, stirring things up and catching the attention of a man who'd killed an admiral to keep his identity hidden.

He would rather picture Nell safe at home. Sweet Mary, he'd rather picture Nell having breakfast in bed with Dexter Lancaster than have to worry about her becoming another target for a man with no scruples.

He purposely didn't meet her eyes, even though he made it clear that he saw her. He purposely, coldly, turned his back on her, praying that she would leave.

But as he turned, he saw another familiar face in the crowd.

Lt. Commander Blue McCoy of Alpha Squad was sitting in the front row of the side balcony.

Crash hadn't expected Blue McCoy to come to gape at him, to sit there mentally spitting at him, ready to cheer when the court expressed its desire to impose the death sentence.

He'd liked working with Blue. He'd trusted the quiet man almost immediately. And he'd thought that Blue had trusted him, as well.

He tried not to look in Blue's direction, either, but a flash of movement caught his eye.

He turned and Blue did it again. Moving quickly, almost invisibly, he hand-signaled Crash. *Are you okay?*

There were no accusations in Blue's eyes—no hatred, no animosity. Only concern.

Crash turned to face the judge without responding. He couldn't respond. What could he possibly say?

He closed his hand around the bent piece of metal he had concealed in his palm, feeling its rough edges scrape against his skin. He couldn't wait to be free of these chains. He couldn't wait to see the sky again.

He couldn't wait to find the man who had killed Jake, and send the bastard straight to hell.

It was only a matter of minutes now.

He sat through the procedure, barely hearing the droning of the lawyers' voices. He could feel his former SEAL Team members' hot eyes on his back. He could feel Blue watching him, as well.

And if he closed his eyes and breathed really deeply, he could pretend that he could smell Nell's sweet perfume.

As THE TWO GUARDS escorted Crash from the courtroom, Nell willed him to turn his head and acknowledge that she was there.

She didn't expect him to smile, or even to nod. All she wanted was for him to look into her eyes.

She'd dressed in a bright red turtleneck so that she would stand out among all the drab winter coats and business suits. She *knew* he'd seen her. He'd looked straight at her when he came in—he just hadn't met her gaze.

But he went out the door without so much as a glance in her direction, his actions echoing the words he'd said three days ago. *Go away.*

But Nell couldn't do that.

She wasn't going to do that.

She stood up, squeezing past the knees of the people still in their seats, people who'd settled in to wait for Crash's bail hearing—which had quickly been set for later in the afternoon.

That was going to be over before it even started. Crash's lawyer was going to request bail—after all, his client had pleaded not guilty.

But then the judge was going to take a look at Crash sitting there, chained up like some monster because his hands and feet were considered deadly weapons. The judge was going to realize that as a former SEAL, Crash could disappear, leaving the country with ease, never to be seen again. And the judge was going to deny bail.

Nell hiked her bag higher up on her shoulder and, carrying her leather bomber jacket over one arm, went out into the hallway.

Crash's lawyer, Captain Phil Franklin, a tall black man in a heavily decorated Navy uniform, was around some-where, and she was determined to talk to him.

She went out of the courtroom and into the hallway, spotting the captain stepping into an elevator.

There were too many people waiting to go up or down, so Nell could only watch to see which direction the elevator was heading.

Down. Directly down four flights, all the way to the

basement. There was a coffee shop down there. With any luck, she'd find the Navy lawyer there.

Nell opened the door to the stairwell. As she stepped inside, she was nearly knocked over by a man coming down from the floor above. He was taking two and three steps at once and wasn't able to stop himself in time.

He recognized her at the same instant she recognized him. Nell knew because he froze.

And she looked up into Crash's light blue eyes. He was alone—no guards, and his chains were gone.

She knew instantly what had happened. He'd broken free. She thrust her jacket at him. "Take this," she said. "My car keys are in the pocket."

He didn't move.

"Go!" she said. "Take it and *go!*"

"I can't," he said, finally moving. He backed one step away from her, and then two. "I'm not going to let you go to jail for helping me."

"I'll tell them you grabbed my jacket and ran."

The corner of his mouth twitched. "Right. Like they'd believe that, considering our history."

"How will they know? I never told anyone about that night."

Something flickered in his eyes. "I was referring to our friendship," he said quietly. "The fact that we lived in the same house for an entire month."

Nell felt her cheeks heat with a blush. "Of course."

Crash shook his head. "You've got to stay away from me. You've got to walk out of this courthouse and go home and not look back. Don't think about me, don't talk about me to anyone. Pretend that you never knew me. Forget I ever existed."

She closed her eyes. "Just *go,* all right? Get out of here, dammit, before they catch you."

Nell didn't hear him leave, but when she opened her eyes, he was gone.

FOUR HOURS. It had been nearly four hours, and no one was allowed to enter or exit the federal courthouse.

An alarm had sounded not more than thirty seconds after Crash had vanished in the stairwell, and within five minutes, the entire building had been locked up tight as the police searched for the fugitive.

It didn't seem possible that he hadn't been caught, but Crash was indisputably gone. It was as if he'd simply turned to smoke and drifted away.

Crash's lawyer had been questioned extensively by FInCOM agents, but now Captain Phil Franklin sat alone in the coffee shop, reading a newspaper.

Nell slipped into the seat across from him. "Excuse me, sir. My name is Nell Burns, and I'm a friend of your missing client's."

Franklin looked at her over the top of his paper, his dark browns eyes expressionless. "A friend?"

"Yes. A *friend*. I know for a fact that he didn't kill Admiral Robinson."

Franklin put his paper down. "You know for a fact, hmm? Were you there, Miss… I'm sorry, what did you say your name was?"

"Nell Burns."

"Were you there, Miss Burns?" he asked again.

Nell shook her head. "No, but I was there last year. I was Daisy Owens's—Daisy *Robinson's*—personal assistant right up until the day she died. I lived in the same house with Jake and Daisy—and William Hawken—for four weeks. There's no way Billy could have conspired to kill Jake. I'm sorry, sir, but the man I came to know loved Jake. He would've died himself before harming the admiral."

Franklin took a sip of his coffee, studying her with his disconcertingly dark eyes. "The prosecution has witnesses who overheard Admiral Robinson and Lieutenant Hawken arguing this past January," he finally said, "before Hawken left the country for an extensive length of time. Apparently my client…your friend, Billy, and the victim had a rather heated disagreement."

"I just don't see how that could have been," she countered. "Those witnesses had to have been mistaken. In the entire time I lived with Crash—I mean, we didn't *live* together," she corrected herself quickly. "What I meant to say was that during the time that we lived under one roof…" She was blushing now, but she staunchly kept going. "I never heard Lieutenant Hawken raise his voice. Not even once."

"The witnesses claim the two men were arguing over a woman."

"What?" Nell snorted, her embarrassment overridden by her disbelief. "That's impossible. The only woman in both of their lives was Daisy, and she died a few days after Christmas." She leaned forward. "Captain, I want to take the stand—be a character witness, isn't that what it's called?"

"That's what it's called. But when the defendant does something like jump his guards, pick the locks on his chains with the equivalent of a paper clip…" Franklin shook his head. "The man ran away, Miss Burns. If they ever catch him, if we ever *do* go to trial, I'm not sure a character witness is going to do your Billy-boy much good. Because when a man runs, he looks pretty damn guilty in the eyes of a judge and jury."

"He's not running away." There was no doubt about that in Nell's mind. "He went to find the person who's really responsible for Jake's death."

Franklin gazed at her. "Do you know where he is?"

"No. But I don't think they're going to find him until he comes back on his own. And you better believe that when he *does* come back, he's going to have the admiral's *real* killer in tow."

"It is possible that he'll try to contact you?"

Nell wished that he would. She shook her head. "No. He's been pretty adamant about me staying out of this."

Franklin's eyebrows lifted. "And this is what you call staying out of it."

She didn't answer that.

He was silent for several long moments. "To be honest with you, Miss Burns, in the conversations I've had with Lieutenant Hawken, I didn't get a real strong sense that he cared a whole lot about this hearing. He seemed very… distant and…odd, I guess would be the best word for it. When I asked, he told me he didn't conspire to kill Admiral Robinson. But the evidence those ballistic reports provides is damning. And I can't help but wonder if perhaps this man didn't suffer some kind of breakdown, or—"

"No," Nell said.

"…post-traumatic stress syndrome, or—"

"No," she said more loudly.

"It's just that he was positively strange."

"That's just his way. When things get hard to deal with, he shuts himself down. He loved Jake," she said again, "and these past few weeks must've been hell for him. To lose a man he loved like a father, and then be accused of killing that man?" Nell held his gaze steadily. "Look, Captain, I've been thinking. Whoever *did* kill Jake knew about his relationship with Billy. They used him to get the assassins into Jake's house. That's the only reason Billy—Crash— was there that night."

Franklin didn't hide his skepticism. "And the ballistic reports are totally wrong…?"

"Yes," Nell agreed. "They're wrong. I think someone made a mistake in the lab. I think the tests should be run again. In fact, as Crash's lawyer, you should *demand* that the guns be tested again."

The captain just looked at her. Then he sighed. "You really don't think Hawken did this, do you?"

"I don't just think it, I *know* it," she said. "Billy did *not* kill Jake."

Franklin sighed again. And then he pulled a notepad and a pen from his inside jacket pocket. He took a business card with his name and phone number on it and slid it across the table toward her. "That's my number," he said "You better give me yours. Address, too. And spell your last name for me while you're at it."

"Thank you." Nell felt almost weak with relief as she pocketed his card and gave him all the information he needed.

"Don't thank me yet," he said. "I'll talk to the judge about the possibility of getting those weapons retested. It's a long shot. There's no guarantee the court will foot the bill for that kind of redundant expense."

"I'll pay," she told him. "Tell the judge that I'll pay to have the ballistic tests redone. I don't care what it costs, I'll take care of it."

Captain Franklin closed his pad and slipped it back into his pocket. As he got to his feet, he held out his hand for Nell to shake.

"Thank you, Captain," she said again.

He didn't release her hand right away. "Miss Burns, God forbid I should ever get into the kind of trouble Lieutenant Hawken is in right now, but if I do, I sincerely hope I'd have someone who believed in me the way you believe in him." He smiled. "I can't believe I'm saying this, but he's a lucky man to have a friend like you."

"Please call the judge, Captain," Nell said. "The sooner the better."

NELL COULDN'T SLEEP.

It was 2:00 a.m. before she finished writing a grant proposal seeking funds for the theater, but even after she e-mailed a copy of the draft to Amie, she still was far too restless to sleep.

Crash was out there somewhere. For the first night in weeks, Nell didn't know exactly where he was.

She prowled around the kitchen once, opening the refrigerator door but, of course, finding nothing exciting inside. She then pulled on her sneakers and leather jacket. Dunkin' Donuts was calling. Five blocks away, there was a very exciting honey-dipped donut with her name on it.

Nell turned out the light and locked the door, ready to walk, but the air was so sharply cold, she hurried to her car instead. There had been a real cold spell like this last December, too, she remembered. It had even snowed. Crash had forced her to go sledding and...

And he hadn't kissed her. Yeah, that had been just another of the many, *many* nights that he *hadn't* kissed her.

She pulled out from the curb, gunning the engine, hoping her car would warm up soon so she could turn on the heat.

That lawyer, Captain Franklin, had been really impressed by her loyalty to Crash. But the truth was, she was an idiot. She was a certified fool.

There was nothing, *nothing* that bound the two of them together, except for her own, misguided wishful thinking.

Nearly a year ago, she'd had sex with the man. That's all it had been. Sex. Period, the end. All the intensity and seemingly high emotions of the moment had nothing to do with his feelings for her. All the emotion of that night had been about Daisy's death. When Crash had kissed her so fiercely, when he'd driven himself hard inside her, it wasn't because he wanted to join himself emotionally with Nell. No, what they'd done had been purely physical. He'd been using sex as a release for his pain and anger. He'd been taking temporary comfort in surrounding himself with her warm body. She could have been any warm body, any nameless, faceless woman. Her identity truly hadn't mattered.

The stupid thing was, Nell had been more hurt by the fact that Crash had ended their friendship than by his honest admission that the sex had been nothing more than sex.

She'd written him letters. She'd been brutally honest, too, telling him that she hoped that what had happened between them wouldn't affect their friendship. She'd asked him to call her when he was in town.

He hadn't called.

And he hadn't written.

And if this mess hadn't happened, Nell knew that she never would have so much as *seen* Crash Hawken again.

As she approached, she saw that the orange-lettered Dunkin' Donuts signs was dark. The all-night shop was inexplicably closed, and Nell said all of the absolutely worst bad words that she knew. She even said some of them twice. And then she kept driving. Somewhere in the District of Columbia there was a donut shop that was open right now, and dammit, she was going to find it.

Nell took a right turn, suddenly aware that she was driving the still-familiar route from the city to the Robinson farm.

She knew for a fact that there were no donut shops between here and there, but she kept going, pulled in that direction.

The interstate was empty except for a few truckers.

She kept the radio off during the twenty-minute drive, waiting for the hum of the tires to lull her into a state of fatigue.

It didn't happen. When she pulled off at the exit for the farm, she was as wide-awake as ever.

It was more than six months since she'd come out here to pick up a painting of Daisy's that Jake had wanted her to have for the new house. It had been summer then, but now the trees were bare, their branches reaching up toward the sky like skinny arms with clawed hands, tormented by the cold wind.

God, she hated winter. Why on earth had she bought a house here in D.C., rather than down in Florida? What had she been thinking?

She hadn't *really* been thinking that sooner or later Crash would come back and knock on her door. She hadn't actually believed that he'd just appear in her bedroom one night, although for a while, she'd gotten a lot of mileage out of *that* fantasy.

No, he'd made it more than clear that he didn't want her. And she wasn't the type to face that kind of rejection more than once.

But despite the fact that he clearly felt otherwise, she was still his friend. She had been his friend before that one night they'd slept together. And she could be a grown-up about the whole thing, and still be his friend.

But not if he didn't want to be hers.

Slowing to a stop as she finally approached the gates of the farm, her eyes filled with tears.

The Robinsons' farm had always buzzed with life. Even in the dead of night, there had been an intensity about the place—the lights were always on, there was a sense of someone being home.

But now the place was deserted. The dark windows of the house looked mournfully empty. Sagging yellow police tape flapped pathetically in the wind.

And there already was a For Sale sign on the gate.

Her first reaction was outrage. Jake had been dead less than two weeks, and already someone was selling off his beloved farm.

But then reality crept in.

The farm meant nothing to Jake now. Whichever of his distant relatives who'd inherited the place obviously realized that holding on to the property wouldn't do anyone any good. It wouldn't bring Jake back from wherever he'd gone—that was for sure.

Wherever he'd gone...

Wherever he was, she hoped he'd found Daisy again.

When Nell closed her eyes, she could picture Jake dancing with Daisy. The image was so clear, so real. In her mind's eye, they were both alive, vibrant and laughing.

It was bitterly ironic. Even as ghosts Jake and Daisy were more alive than either Nell or Crash.

The two who had survived were the ones who wouldn't let themselves live. They were quite a pair—one who willingly deadened himself by stepping back from his emotions, and one who was too afraid to live life to its fullest.

Except Nell wasn't afraid anymore.

She'd stopped being afraid on the night she'd found out Jake had died, but Crash was still alive. He was still alive, and dammit, she was going to be his friend, whether he liked it or not.

He was still alive, and she was going to fight for him. She was going to do whatever she had to in order to tell the entire world that he was an innocent man, that he'd been falsely accused.

In fact, she was going to go home and first thing in the morning, she was going to call every single reporter and news contact that she had in her media file. She was going to hold a press conference.

And she was going to make *damn* sure those ballistic tests were redone.

Hell, she was even feeling brave enough to ski down Mount Washington with a banner proclaiming Crash's innocence if that would help.

Nell turned her car around and headed for home.

IT WAS 4:00 A.M., but there was a traffic jam on Nell's street.

There was a traffic jam totally blocking the road, caused by four different fire trucks and three TV-news vans.

And they were blocking the road because Nell's house was on fire.

Her *house* was on *fire*.

She didn't bother to park. She just turned off the engine right there in the middle of the road and got out of her car.

She could feel the heat of the blaze from where she was standing. She could see flames licking out every single window.

"You better move that car!" one of the firemen shouted to her.

"I can't," she said dazedly. "My garage is on fire."

"Are you the owner?"

She nodded. She was the owner—but what she owned was going to be little more than a charred pile of ashes before this was over.

"Hey, Ted, we found the lady who lives here!"

Another, shorter man approached. His hat identified him as the fire chief. "Is there anyone else inside?" he asked.

Nell shook her head, staring at the flames. "No."

"Thank God." He raised his voice. "There's no one inside. Everyone get out of there, pronto!"

"How could this have happened?"

"It's probably an electrical fire," the chief told her. "It probably started small, but an old place like this'll go up like a tinderbox, especially this time of year. We'll have a better idea of how it started after it's out and we can go in and look around. Whatever the case, you're lucky you weren't home, or we'd probably be pulling your body out of there right now."

She was lucky.

She was *incredibly* lucky. Nell couldn't remember the

last time she'd not only been awake this late, but had left the house, as well. She was *damned* lucky.

She tried very hard to feel lucky as she stood in the early-morning darkness and watched everything she owned but her car and the clothes on her back go up in smoke. There were things that were burning right now that couldn't be replaced. Photographs. She'd had a really great photo of her and Crash and Jake that Daisy had taken. All of her books and CDs, the dishes her grandmother had given her, Daisy's irreplaceable watercolor painting. It was all gone. She'd been out of the house for only two hours, and just like that, nearly everything she'd cherished was gone.

Tears filled her eyes, and she fought them. She *was* lucky, dammit. She could have died.

IT WAS DAWN BEFORE the fire was down to a smolder, midmorning before the insurance forms were filled out and the paperwork was filed.

Nell drove to the Ritz-Carlton—one of the fanciest hotels in town—and checked herself into a very expensive room. She deserved it.

She was exhausted, but she took the time to call Captain Franklin's office, leaving the hotel phone number with the lawyer's administrative staff, with a message asking him to call if he heard any news of Crash's whereabouts.

Tired to the bone, Nell peeled off her clothes, climbed into bed and fell almost instantly into a deep, dreamless sleep.

CHAPTER ELEVEN

THE CURTAINS WERE HANGING open an inch or two, and Crash quietly slid them all the way closed.

They were effective in shutting out the last streaks of light in the late-afternoon sky. He moved silently through the now complete darkness of the room, toward the bathroom that was next to the door.

He closed the bathroom door all but an inch, and turned on the bathroom light.

It was dim, but no longer pitch-black. He went back into the other room. Yeah, it was bright enough for him to be able to see Nell's face as she slept.

She was curled up in the middle of the hotel room's king-size bed. The blankets covered all but her face and the very top of her head. She slept fiercely, eyes tightly shut.

Crash stood for a moment, just watching her, wishing he didn't have to disturb her, wishing for things he couldn't have. But there was no time now to let her sleep, and there'd never been time for the other things he wanted.

"Nell," he said quietly.

She didn't move.

He nudged the bed with his leg. "Nell, I'm sorry, but you've got to wake up."

Nothing.

He sat down on the bed, leaning over to gently shake her shoulder. "Nell."

Her eyes opened and widened in fear.

   Crash knew at that moment that he'd made a mistake. With the bathroom light shining dimly behind him, she couldn't see his face. All she could see was a big, dark figure looming menacingly over her.

   She took a deep breath to scream, and he quickly put his hand over her mouth. "Nell, shhh! It's me. Crash. *Billy.*"

   She sat up, shaking herself free from his hand, all but launching herself into his arms. "Billy! God! You scared me to death! Thank God you're all right!" She pulled back to look at him in the darkness. "*Are* you all right?"

   She smelled so good. Crash wanted nothing more than to bury his face in her hair and just sit on that bed with his arms around her. But that wasn't why he'd come.

   And after that one initial hug, Nell seemed as eager as he was to put distance between them.

   She let go of him quickly when he released her, wrapping her arms around her knees as he stood up. "I can't believe you came here. How did you find me?"

   Her low, husky voice was so familiar, so warm. God, how he'd missed her. He had to keep distance between them, or he was going to be tempted to do something that he'd later regret.

   Again.

   Crash turned on the desk lamp. "It wasn't that hard."

   "My house burned down last night. I went out for a donut, and when I came back, my house was on fire."

   "I know." When he'd seen the picture in the newspaper and realized it was Nell's house that had burned, his heart had stopped beating. And when he'd read that no one had been killed or injured, he'd gotten dizzy with relief.

   And even though he'd had plenty of other things to do in his quest to find the man responsible for Jake's death, Crash had spent the entire afternoon tracking Nell down. There was no way, no *way* he was going to let her die, too.

   She ran one hand back through her hair as if she was

suddenly conscious of the fact that it was rumpled from sleep. And she pulled the blanket up a little higher around her neck.

Crash saw that her jeans and shirt were in a pile on the floor. Under those covers she was wearing only her underwear. Or less. He had to turn away from her. He couldn't let his thoughts move in that direction.

"I can't believe you came to me for help," she said quietly.

He couldn't keep himself from turning back to look at her. Was that really what she thought? That he'd come here because he wanted or needed her help?

"I spoke to your lawyer about having the ballistic tests repeated," Nell told him.

She looked far too good in the soft, romantic light, sitting there, possibly naked beneath the covers of an Olympic-event-size bed. Crash turned on another lamp, and then another, trying to make the room as glaringly bright as possible. "So that's what it was."

She squinted slightly in the brightness. "That's what *what* was?"

"That's why they tried to kill you."

She stared at him. "Excuse me?"

He couldn't keep himself from pacing. "You don't really think that fire was an accident, do you?"

"According to the experts in the fire department, it was an electrical malfunction. The wiring was ancient, there was a power surge and—"

"Nell, someone tried to kill you. That's why I'm here. To make sure that when they try again, they don't succeed."

She was so completely blown away she almost dropped the blanket. "Billy! God! Who would want to kill *me?*"

"Probably the same person who killed Jake and framed me," Crash told her. "Did you tell anyone you were coming to this hotel?"

Nell shook her head. "No. Wait. Yes. I called your

lawyer and left this phone number in case he needed to get in touch with me."

He swore softly and Nell realized how infrequently she'd heard him use that kind of language. Even words like *damn* or *hell*—they just weren't part of his normal working vocabulary.

He picked up her clothes and put them next to her on the bed. "I'll go into the bathroom while you get dressed. And then we have to get out of here. Fast."

Nell quickly pulled on her shirt and slipped into her jeans before he'd even closed the bathroom door. "Billy, wait! You honestly think that whoever killed Jake is somehow privileged to your Navy lawyer's phone messages? Doesn't that sound just a *little* paranoid...?"

He pulled open the bathroom door and looked at her. He was dressed entirely in black. Black fatigues, black boots, black turtleneck, black winter jacket. Underneath the jacket he was wearing what looked to be some kind of equipment vest—also black. His preference for wearing black had nothing to do with fashion, she realized. He was dressed to blend with the shadows of the night.

"Here's what we know about the man we're after," Crash told her. "We believe him to be a U.S. Navy commander with a lot of connections. Whether he's that or not, we *do* know for certain that... *We.* God, listen to me." His voice shook. "I'm talking as if Jake is still alive."

He swiftly turned away from her, and for a minute Nell was certain that he was going to put his fist through the bathroom door. Instead he stopped himself, and slowly, carefully laid the palm of his hand against the wood instead. He took a deep breath, and when he spoke again, his voice was steady.

"*I* know for sure that this son of a bitch has got something to hide, something he was afraid Jake was about to uncover. And that something—whatever it is—is *so* important to him, he'd risk his eternal soul to keep it secret.

He had Jake killed, and set me up to take the fall. Whoever he is, he's powerful enough to falsify the results of those ballistic tests and believe me, that couldn't have been easy to do." Crash turned to face her. "Since he's already killed once, I wouldn't put it past him to decide that it'd be easier to kill you than to do whatever he'd had to do to fake those test results all over again. So, yes, it sounds paranoid, but I can't assume that someone that powerful *won't* have access to the information coming into and out of Captain Franklin's law office."

His hair was pulled back into a ponytail, and the severe style emphasized his high cheekbones, making his face look starkly handsome. And his eyes... The burning intensity of those eyes had haunted her dreams.

"Come on, Nell," he said softly as her silence stretched on. "Don't quit believing in me now."

As crazy as his theory was, it was clear that *he* believed it.

"You didn't come here to ask me to help you," Nell realized. "You came because you think *I* need *your* help."

He didn't answer. He didn't have to answer.

"What if I said I didn't want your help?" she asked.

It was obvious from the look on his face that he knew where she was going. She was revisiting the words he'd said to her. "This is different."

"No, it's not. We both think the other needs saving." Nell crossed her arms. "You want to save me? You better be ready to let me help save you."

"Maybe we can argue about this in the car."

She nodded, feeling lighter in spirit than she had in a long time. He may not have written. He may not have called. But he'd put in an appearance when he thought her life was in danger. Despite everything he'd said and done, he cared—he was still her friend.

Friend, she repeated to herself firmly. He'd jumped back as if her touch had burned him. It was clear that he had no intention of letting their relationship move past the friendship stage ever again. And that was good because she felt that way, too. She had absolutely no intention of making the same mistake twice.

"I'll put on my boots, and we can go." She turned back to look at him. "Do we have a destination in mind?"

"I'll tell you in the car."

A loud knock sounded on the hotel-room door, and Nell jumped. She hadn't seen Crash move, but suddenly he had a gun in his hand. He motioned for her to be silent, and to back away from the door.

Whoever was out there knocked again. "Room service. I have complimentary hors d'oeuvres and a bottle of Chablis for Ms. Burns."

Crash moved back toward her and spoke almost silently into her ear.

"Tell him to leave it outside the door. Tell him you're just about to take a shower. Then get under the bed, do you understand?"

She nodded, unable to pull her eyes away from his gun. It was enormous and deadly looking. This was the closest she'd ever come to that kind of weapon. And it was amazing in more than one way—despite the fact that Crash was the subject of the biggest manhunt of the decade, he'd somehow managed to arm himself.

He was holding her arm, and he gave her a quick squeeze before he released her. He moved quickly around the room, turning off all the lights that he'd turned on earlier.

Nell cleared her throat, raising her voice so that the person on the other side of the door could hear her. "I'm sorry, you caught me at a bad time. I'm just about to step into the shower. Can you leave it outside the door?"

"Will do," the voice cheerfully replied. "Have a good evening."

Crash motioned for her to move. As she slid underneath

the bed, she saw him go into the bathroom and heard the sound of the shower going on.

It all seemed kind of silly. The person who'd knocked on the door was probably a room-service waiter, just as he'd said.

She lifted the dust ruffle and saw Crash come back out of the bathroom. *He* sure didn't seem to think it was at all silly. He stood in the shadows, out of sight of the door, his gun held at the ready. Holding the gun that way, with his mouth set in equally grim resolve, he looked incredibly dangerous.

Crash had told her once that she didn't really know him, that he had only let her see a small, very whitewashed part of him.

Nell had a feeling that if she was wrong and there really was someone outside her door who wanted to hurt her, in the next few minutes she was going to get a good look at the other side of Crash. She was going to see the Navy SEAL in action.

And then she saw the door to her room open. The sound of the bolt being drawn back was drowned out by the noise from the shower. The bathroom door was ajar, and in the light that came through it, she saw a man come into the room.

He wasn't carrying a plate of cheese or a bottle of wine. Instead, he held a gun like Crash's.

Nell's heart was pounding. Crash had been right. This man *had* come here to kill her.

The intruder gently closed the door behind him, careful not to make any noise.

He was smaller than Crash, more wiry than Crash, and he had less hair on the top of his head than Crash.

But his gun looked just as deadly.

As Nell watched, he pushed open the bathroom door.

That was when Crash moved. One moment he was in the shadows, and the next he was almost on top of the man, his gun pressed against the back of his head. Even his voice sounded different—harsher, rougher. "Drop it."

The man froze but only for a second.

Crash knew when the man didn't instantly drop his weapon that this guy was not going to go down easily. The gunman's hesitation only lasted a fraction of a second, but it was enough for Crash to anticipate his next move.

He was, rightly, calling Crash's bluff. It didn't take the brain of a rocket scientist to figure out that, at this point, this gunman was the only potential link Crash had to the mysterious commander. The only real reason Crash had to shoot this man was to protect Nell.

The gunman, on the other hand, had no reason whatsoever not to shoot Crash.

But Crash was a nanosecond ahead of him. He hit the man hard on the side of the head with the barrel of his weapon, even as he disarmed him with a well-placed kick.

The man's handgun hit the door frame and bounced back, skittering across the rug and into the center of the room.

The blow to the head that Crash had delivered would have taken damn near anyone else in the world down, and down hard, but this guy wasn't about to call it a day.

Pain exploded as the gunman smashed his fist back into Crash's face and elbowed him hard in the ribs. The man tucked his chin against his chest, bending over in an attempt to throw the SEAL over his shoulder. But pain or no pain, Crash anticipated that move, too, and instead, the gunman hit the floor.

But he went down willingly, diving out into the room, going for his weapon.

The gun wasn't there.

Crash silently blessed Nell as he leapt on top of the man. The bastard fought as if he was possessed by the devil, but Crash would have taken on Satan himself in order to keep

Nell safe. He hit the man again and again until finally, *finally* he delivered a knockout punch and the son of a bitch sagged.

Searching the gunman quickly, Crash came up with a smaller automatic and a large combat knife. Both weapons had been securely holstered and—luckily for him—totally unreachable during the fight.

He looked up to see Nell peeking out from underneath the bed.

"Are you all right?" she asked, her eyes wide. "Oh, God, you're bleeding."

His cheek had been cut by the fancy ring the gunman wore on his pinky finger. Crash used the back of his hand to blot it. "I'm fine," he said. A little scrape like that didn't matter. Nor was the bruise he was going to get along his ribs even worth mentioning.

He'd hurt when he laughed for the next few days.

But since he couldn't remember the last time he'd laughed, he didn't think that would be much of a problem.

Crash pulled the man's wallet from the back pocket of his pants. There was a driver's license inside, along with several suspiciously new-looking credit cards. There were no papers, no receipts, no photos of child or wife, no little scraps of life.

"Who is he?"

"He's currently going by the name Sheldon Sarkowski," he told her. "But that's not his real name."

"It's not?" She began inching out from her hiding place, gingerly pushing Sheldon's handgun in front of her.

"Nope. He's a pro. He probably doesn't even remember his real name anymore." Crash took the weapon, pulled out the clip and stored both pieces in his vest, along with the other weapons he'd taken from the gunman.

"What are we going to do with him?"

"We're going to tie him up and take him with us. I have a question or two to ask him when he wakes up."

Nell had climbed to her feet, but then backed up so that she was sitting on the edge of the bed. She was so pale, she looked almost gray.

"Are *you* all right?" he asked. "We've got to get out of here right now before this guy's backup comes to see what's taking him so long. Are you going to be able to walk?"

"Yeah, I'm just...getting used to the idea that someone named Sheldon came in here to kill me."

Crash stood up. "I'm not going to let anyone hurt you, Nell. I swear, I'll keep you safe if it's the last thing I do."

Nell gazed up at him. "I believe you," she told him.

CHAPTER TWELVE

"WHAT EXACTLY ARE WE GOING to do with the guy in the trunk?" Nell laughed in disbelief as she turned slightly in her seat to face Crash. "I can't believe I just said that. I can't believe we've actually *got* a guy in the trunk. Isn't that very uncomfortable for him?"

Crash glanced at her. "That's his tough luck. He should've thought of that before he broke into your hotel room to kill you."

"Good point." Nell was silent for a moment, staring out the windshield at the stars. She looked over at Crash again. "So where *are* we going?"

"To California."

"By *car?*"

He glanced at her again. "They'll be looking for me at all the airports."

"Of course. I'm sorry. I..." Nell shook her head. "How long is it going to take us to get there?"

"Depends on how many times we stop to sleep. We've got to stop at least once so that I can question Sarkowski."

At *least* once. He wasn't kidding. They were going to drive all the way from the District of Columbia to California and they were quite possibly going to stop to sleep only once.

The car was luxurious. It was compact, but the seats were covered with soft leather that would be comfortable for sleeping.

The backseat was big enough for her to curl up on.

Currently, it was covered by several gym bags, a suitcase and what looked to be a laptop computer case.

"Where did you get all this stuff?" she asked. "This car?"

"The car belongs to a Navy officer who's doing a six-month tour on an aircraft carrier. I liberated it from storage. Same with the gear."

Liberated was just a fancy word for stole.

"I have every intention of returning everything," he told her, as if he knew what she was thinking. "Except maybe the bullets and some of the explosives."

Explosives? Bullets? Nell changed the subject.

"So what's in California?" she asked. "And where in California are we going? It's a pretty big state."

He gave her another glance before turning his attention back to the road. He turned on the radio to a classic rock station, adjusting the controls so that the signal only went to the speakers in the back. "In case Sarkowski wakes up," he explained. "I don't want him to be bored."

What he *really* didn't want was for the man who was tied up in the trunk to regain consciousness and overhear their conversation.

Nell waited for him to answer her question, but one mile rolled by and then two, and he still didn't speak.

"Oh, please," she said, exasperated. "We're not going to play this game again, are we? I ask you a question and you don't answer it. Can't you do something different for a change? Like tell me the truth about what's going on?"

It was starting to rain, and Crash put on the windshield wipers. He glanced at her again, but he didn't say a word.

"Because if we're going to play that old, dull game," Nell continued, "you'd better get off at the next exit. In fact, if you don't tell me everything, and I mean *everything*, starting from what happened at Jake's house, you can just pull over and let me out right now."

"I'm sorry," Crash said quietly. "I wasn't purposely not answering you. I was just thinking that…" He hesitated.

"Your apology will go a whole lot further if you actually finish that sentence."

"I was thinking that as a SEAL, I can't talk about any of this." He glanced at her again. His eyes looked almost silver in the darkness, his face shadowed and mysterious. "But I'm not a SEAL anymore."

Crash had been stripped of his commission, his pride, his very soul. There was a very strong chance that he was going to lose his life as well, finding and taking down the mysterious commander.

The truth was, he was prepared to die, if necessary. Most of what he'd already lost was more valuable to him than his life.

But if he *was* going to die, he wanted someone to know the whole story. He wanted someone to know what had *really* happened.

And he knew he could trust Nell.

"You already know that I do—did—special assignments for Jake," he said.

"Yeah." Nell nodded. "But I'm not really sure what that entailed."

"Jake would send me a coded file, usually electronically. These files were specially programmed so they couldn't be copied, and they were designed to self-delete after a very short time, so there'd be no information trail."

Crash could feel her watching him. She was all but holding her breath, waiting for him to continue. With the exception of that one time he'd told her the story of how Daisy had pulled him out of summer camp, he knew she'd never heard him string together so many sentences.

"The file would contain information about a situation that needed checking into, or correcting or…some other type of…revision, shall we say," he continued. "It would include a mission objective as well as recommended courses

of action. Sometimes the objective was simply to gather
more information. Sometimes it was more…complicated.
But when I was out in the real world, working the op, my
team and I—and Jake usually only assigned two or three
other SEALs to work with me—we were on our own.

"Anyway, Jake sent me an encoded file on the morning
he was shot. I had just flown into D.C. from California that
same day. I was coming home after spending nearly six
straight months out of the country. Usually the first thing
I do when I get stateside is take a few days of leave—get a
haircut and go out to the farm to see Jake and Daisy." He
caught himself and shook his head. "Just Jake, now. But
when I arrived at the base, Captain Lovett called me into
his office and told me that he was organizing a special
team. He said he'd received orders to go out to the farm
and provide additional security. He said the admiral had
been receiving death threats. And he asked if I wanted to
be part of this special security team."

"Of course you said yes."

Crash nodded. "I tried calling the farm as soon as I
left Lovett's office, but I couldn't get through. And then I
didn't have time to do much more than organize my gear
before I had to meet Lovett and the other members of the
team."

It had been lightly raining that night, too.

He glanced at Nell and cleared his throat. "When I got
to the chopper—our means of transport out to the farm—
there were three men there I'd never seen before. I was
tired. I hadn't slept in a full forty-eight hours, so I passed
my suspicions off as fatigue-induced paranoia. Lovett knew
these men, and he seemed to know them well. I figured
everything was kosher." He paused. "I figured wrong.

"When we got to the farm, Jake seemed really surprised
to see us, like no one had told him a SEAL Team would be
coming out," Crash continued. "That should have clinched
it for me. I should have known then that something was

off." He clenched his teeth. "But I didn't, and Jake died. But before he died, he told me about the file he'd sent." He turned to glance at Nell. "He believed that he was shot in an attempt to cover up the information he'd sent me in that file—that to keep his investigation from going any further, someone had set up this hit."

Nell nodded slowly. "And you think he was right, don't you?"

"Yeah." The rain was turning slushy and thick against the windshield. The night was getting cold, but it was nice and warm inside the car.

Too warm.

He glanced at Nell again. The way she was sitting, turned slightly toward him, her knee was only an inch and a half away from his thigh. Because of the car's compact design, she was sitting close enough to touch. She was close enough so that even if he'd wanted to, he couldn't have avoided breathing in her sweet perfume. He looked at the odometer. They'd only traveled forty-seven miles. Two thousand six hundred and fifty-three to go.

Crash stared at the road, trying to clear his mind, to desensitize himself to the scent of her perfume and the sound of her voice. He tried to focus on the feel of the leather-covered steering wheel beneath his hands, but all he could think about was the soft down that grew at the nape of her neck, and the silky smoothness of her bare back. Her skin was impossibly soft, like a baby's.

He'd let himself touch her, that night she'd spent in his room. After she'd fallen asleep, he'd allowed himself the luxury of running his fingers across her shoulders, down her back and along her arm until he, too, had fallen into a deep sleep.

He forced the image away. This was *not* the time to be thinking of Nell that way—at the beginning of a 2700-mile journey, at the start of a mission that in all likelihood was not going to end well.

"Can you tell me what was in the file Jake sent you?" she asked softly.

Crash kept his eyes on the road. "No, but I'm going to tell you anyway."

"You…are." Nell couldn't believe what she was hearing. He was going to tell her top secret, classified information.

"The mission objective was investigation. Jake believed there was a cover-up going on—that someone had screwed up bad during a SEAL training operation that took place six months ago.

"See, there's a small island nation in Southeast Asia," Crash told her, "that for the past forty years has been one of the major ports for illegal drug trafficking. When the United States began actively trying to cut off drug dealers closer to their source, we worked to establish an alliance with this island's government.

"Right up until recently," he continued, "we'd managed to build a foundation for a relationship that would be good for both countries."

Nell leaned back against the headrest, watching Crash as he drove. He was a good driver, always checking the mirrors, holding the wheel with both hands. She felt safe sitting next to him, despite the fact that he was number one on FInCOM's most-wanted, armed-and-dangerous list.

"But then, about six months ago, I was part of a team that intended to use this island as a training site. I'd hooked up with some SEALs from Team Ten's elite Alpha Squad, and we took four FInCOM agents to this island on a training mission to show them how we can kick ass in a potential terrorists-with-hostage situation. We were going to execute a rescue op, going up against some jarheads on the island, who were going to play the part of the tangos."

"Whoa," Nell said. "Back up a sec. You lost me. *Jarheads* and *tangos?*"

"I'm sorry. Jarheads are marines—the nickname comes

from their haircut. And tango's radio talk for the letter *T*, which is short for terrorists."

"Got it. Go on," she ordered him.

"When we inserted onto the island, we found ourselves jammed in the middle of one of the biggest training op snafus I've ever dealt with. See, as we approached the site where the simulated rescue mission was to take place, we found two KIAs." He interpreted before she could even ask. "We found the bodies of two of our marine friends—killed in action."

"My God." Nell sat up, transfixed by his story. "What happened?"

He glanced at her. "Apparently a firefight had broken out between the two major drug lords on the island between the time we left our ship and the time we hit the training site."

"Firefight. You mean, a gun battle between the two gangs, right?"

"Yeah," Crash told her, "but I wouldn't call them *gangs*. Both the drug lords had private armies with state-of-the-art technology. We're talking thousands of men and name-brand firepower. These armies were more powerful than the government's own armed forces. What started that day was more like a full-scale civil war." He glanced at her. "The average yearly income of the men who owned these armies was higher than the entire GNP of this country. One of 'em was an American expatriate named John Sherman—a former Green Beret, which really pissed off the jarheads. The other was a local man named Kim, nicknamed 'the Korean,' because his father was from there.

"Sherman and Kim had been careful not to go into each other's territory for years, and more than once, they'd helped each other out. But on that day, whatever agreement Sherman and Kim had between them disintegrated. And when they clashed, lots of innocent people were caught in the cross fire."

He took a deep breath. "It wasn't easy, but we finally got all of Alpha Squad and the surviving marines off the island. But the fighting went on for days after that. When the smoke cleared, the body count was in the tens of thousands, and property damage was in the millions. The only good thing that came of it was that both Sherman and Kim were killed, too."

He was silent for a minute, and the sound of the windshield wipers beat a rhythm that wasn't in sync with the Christmas pop song playing on the radio. "Rockin' Around the Christmas Tree."

"I don't get it," Nell finally said. "You said there was some kind of cover-up. What was there to cover up?"

"The file Jake sent me contained a copy of a secret deposition taken from Kim's widow," Crash told her. "She claimed to have overheard a conversation in which an American Naval commander supposedly approached Kim and told him that the Americans would look the other way when he did business, on the condition that Kim use his army to destroy John Sherman and his troops. There's no single officer in the entire U.S. Navy—admirals included—who has authority to make this kind of bogus deal, but apparently Kim didn't know that. The deal was done and the Korean began planning a surprise attack on Sherman's stronghold.

"But news of the so-called agreement and the impending attacked was leaked—for all we know, Kim's wife sold him out—and Sherman struck first. It was during this initial attack that our marines were targeted, too, and two of them were killed."

Crash glanced at Nell. Her face was only dimly illuminated by the greenish dashboard light, but he could see that she was hanging on to his every word, her eyes wide.

It was clear that she trusted him. She believed every word that fell from his lips. Even now, after the way he'd abused her friendship—all those letters he never answered, all those times he'd kept himself from calling—she had total faith in him. Something inside him tightened and twisted, and he knew with a sickening certainty that he'd let far more than he'd ever dreamed possible walk out of his room when Nell had left that morning, nearly an entire year ago.

And now it was too late.

He held the steering wheel tightly, telling himself that he'd been right to let her go. He'd been home all of five weeks in the past twelve months. Of course, he'd volunteered for every overseas assignment he could get his hands on. If he'd wanted to, he could have spent most of that time in the States.

But still, what he felt, what he wanted, shouldn't really matter.

The truth was exactly the same now as it had been a year ago. Nell deserved better than he could give her. Of course, in Crash's opinion, she deserved better than Dexter Lancaster, too, but even the lawyer won points simply for being available.

"Hey," Nell said. "Are you going to tell me the rest of this story, or do I have to figure out where to drop the quarter in to get you talking again?"

Crash glanced at her. "Sorry. I was—"

"Thinking," she finished for him. "I know. Trying to figure out how to track down this commander, right?"

"Something like that."

"Are you sure it's not just a rumor? You know, things go bad, and everybody tries to figure out who's to blame."

"In the aftermath, there were tons of rumors," he admitted. "There were people who believed that the U.S. *did* make a deal with Kim. There were people who believed that rumors of the agreement between Kim and the United States were falsely planted *by* the U.S. to cause Kim and Sherman to wipe each other out. But none of that was true. I'm very familiar with the policies used in dealing with this island, and I know we stood to gain far more by playing by the rules.

"If this commander really *did* make a deal with Kim, and I believe he did, he's responsible for starting a war. Thousands of innocent civilians were killed. Not to mention the fact that our alliance with this country has totally crumbled—all of their trust in us is gone. All the work we'd done to maintain goodwill and cooperation in stopping the drug traffic closer to its source was for nothing. The entire program's been set back a good twenty years."

"But if you don't know who the commander is," Nell said. "How are you going to find him? There must be *thousands* of commanders in the U.S. Navy. Kim's wife didn't know his name? Not even his first name? A nickname?"

Crash shook his head. "No."

"Can she describe him?" Nell asked. "Maybe make some kind of police composite sketch?"

He glanced at her again. "She's disappeared."

"And Jake really seemed to think she was telling the truth, huh?" Nell asked.

"He told me," Crash said. He had to stop and clear his throat. "After he was shot, he was still conscious for a while, and he told me that whoever this commander was, he had to be behind the shooting. I believe that, too. This son of a bitch killed Jake and framed me. And now he's trying to kill you, too."

Nell was silent, her eyes narrowed slightly as she stared out at the mixture of sleet and snow falling on the windshield. "What was his motive?" she finally asked. "This commander. What did he stand to gain by starting this civil war between Kim and what's-his-name?"

"John Sherman," Crash supplied the name. "I've been running that same question through my mind ever since I read the file. It's entirely possible that things went as wrong for the commander as they went for the rest of us. And in that case, his intent probably *wasn't* to start a civil war." He glanced at her. "I have a theory."

"Spill."

He looked at her again. Yes, that was kind of what it felt like. After so many years of silence, everything inside of him was in danger of spilling out.

"My theory is that the commander's motive was exactly what he'd told Kim. He wanted John Sherman dead. My theory is that this commander didn't give a damn about the drugs or the armies. My theory is that it was personal."

"Personal?"

"A man like Sherman's got to have lots of enemies. Over in Vietnam, his unit specialized in liberating large shipments of drugs and confiscating stashes of weapons. He spent quite a few years taking half of everything he liberated for himself—and turning around and selling it back to the highest bidder. It didn't matter that he was selling it to the enemy. Word got out that he was doing this, but before he was arrested he went AWOL."

"And you think, what? This commander was getting back at him for having gotten away?"

"I think it's possible that our commander served with Sherman in 'Nam. In fact, I've gained Internet access to some Navy personnel files, and I've hit on a list of three names—two commanders and one recently promoted rear admiral. They all served in Vietnam at the same time as Sherman. And they're all still on the active-duty list. I sent them vaguely threatening e-mail messages—you know, 'I know who you are. I know what you did.' But so far none of them have responded. I didn't really expect them to—it was kind of a long shot." He shook his head.

"Think about all the people we called last year, about Daisy and Jake's wedding," Nell said. "It seemed like every other man was Colonel This or Captain That. The guy you're looking for could have been retired for years and still be addressed as 'Commander.'"

"I know. And the list of *retired* Navy commanders who served in 'Nam when Sherman did is probably ten pages long." He looked over at Nell and smiled grimly. "If I want to find this bastard—and I do—my best bet is to try to shake some information loose from our friend who's napping in the trunk. But first I'm going to get you to a safe place."

"Excuse me?" She was giving him her best are-you-kidding? look, brows elevated and eyes opened wide. "I thought we'd decided that help was a two-way street—that I'd let you help me, on the condition that you let me help *you.*"

"There's nothing you can do to help me."

"Want to bet? I have an idea how I can help you get that information you need from our dear friend Sheldon. Without me, it'll be much harder. I may not be enough of an actress to win an Oscar, but I'm good enough to pull *this* off. We just need to stop at a convenience store and—"

"Nell, I don't want your help." Despite everything that Crash had told her, there was still so much that he hadn't said—so much that hadn't spilled out. He hadn't told her how sitting so close to her in this car was slowly driving him crazy from wanting to touch her. He hadn't told her about the sheer terror he'd felt when he picked up that newspaper and saw the picture of Nell's house engulfed in flames. He wasn't going to tell her about the way he'd stood in that hotel room and watched her as she'd slept, feeling a possessiveness he knew he had no right to feel, feeling an ache of longing and desire and need that he recognized as being something he had to push far, far away.

Separate, distance, disengage.

No, he didn't want any help from Nell.

"Maybe you don't want my help," she said quietly. "Maybe you don't even need it. But this guy in the trunk came to kill *me.* I'm involved in this, Billy, as much as you are. At least hear me out."

CHAPTER THIRTEEN

NELL WAS TOO NERVOUS to eat. She tossed her half-eaten slice of pizza back into the box and watched as Crash unzipped one of the gym bags he'd brought in from the car.

"Here's what we're going to do," he said in his deceptively soft voice, as he reached inside and pulled out a cylindrical tube that he screwed onto the barrel of his *Dirty Harry*-size handgun. "I'm going to ask you some questions, you're going to answer them and no one's going to get hurt."

Sheldon Sarkowski's left eye was swollen shut and his lip was puffy and still bleeding slightly. He'd still been out cold when Crash had stopped along a deserted stretch of road and pulled him from the trunk and into the back seat. Sheldon's hands had been cuffed and his feet tied, but Crash had covered both rope and handcuffs with a blanket as he'd then carried the smaller man into the cheap motel room they'd rented for the night.

There were only two or three other cars in the entire parking lot—none of them within shouting distance of their drafty room.

And that was good—in case there was going to be shouting. And Nell suspected that there *was* going to be some shouting. Not that Crash would be doing it. She'd never heard him raise his voice to anything louder than mezzo piano.

Crash had managed to rouse Sheldon once inside the room. An ice bucket full of cold water in the face had done the trick. The man now sat, sputtering and belligerent, tied very securely to a chair.

The gunman clearly wasn't in a position of power, yet he still managed to laugh derisively at both Crash and the gun. "I'll tell you right now, I'm not saying anything. So what are you going to do, kill me?"

Crash sat down on the bed, directly across from him, his gun held loosely on his lap. "Damn, Sheldon," he said. "Looks like you called my bluff."

Nell spun to face him turning away from the window where she'd been furtively peeking out at the parking lot. "Don't tell him that!"

"But he's right," Crash said mildly. "Killing him doesn't do anyone any good."

Nell took a deep breath, aware that her first line had been terribly overacted, and that she was in danger of breaking into giddy laughter. She went back to peeking out the window, praying that this would work.

"I don't have a lot of options here," Crash was saying. He sounded kind of like Clint Eastwood—his voice was soft, almost whispery but with an underlying intensity that screamed of danger. "I guess I could shoot you in the knee, but that's so messy. And it's unnecessary. Because all I really want is to be put on the commander's payroll."

Nell turned around again. "Hey—"

Crash held up one hand, and she obediently fell silent.

"Here's my deal, Sheldon," he said. "I've been set up. I didn't kill Admiral Robinson, but somehow those ballistic reports were fixed to say that I did. I haven't figured out yet how the commander managed that, but I will. And I haven't quite figured out the commander's connection to John Sherman, but I'll figure that out, too. Sooner or later, I'm going to know the whole nasty story—all the sordid little details."

He paused and then said, still in that same quiet voice, "What I'm thinking right now is that my silence is worth *some*thing. See, I think both you and the commander know as well as I do that even if I were to prove myself innocent, even if I were acquitted for the charges that have been brought up against me, I'm never going to shake the damage that's been done to my name and my career. In fact, I know for a fact that my career with the SEALs is over. No one's going to want me on their team.

"And since I'm no longer gainfully employed by my Uncle Sam," Crash continued, "I'm finding myself in a situation where I need a new source of income. I figure if the commander wants all the dirt I've already uncovered, and all the dirt I'm *going* to uncover about him to stay neatly under the rug, then he's going to have to pay. Two hundred and fifty thousand in small, unmarked bills."

Crash stopped talking. Nell gave him several beats of silence just to make sure he really was done. Then she spoke. "I can't believe what I'm hearing."

She really *was* a lousy actor. First she'd sounded too outraged, too over-the-top, and now she sounded too matter-of-fact. She wanted this guy to believe that she was intensely angry with Crash, not that she was bipolar.

Anger, anger. How did people look and act when they were angry?

More specifically, how did they look and act when they were angry with *Crash?*

Nell had quite a bit of personal experience to draw on in *that* department.

Over the past year, she'd spent a good amount of time angry as hell at herself, and angry at him, as well.

Why hadn't he at least scribbled a two-line postcard, acknowledging her existence? "Dear Nell, got your letters, no longer interested in being your friend. Crash. P.S. Thanks for the sex. It was nice."

Nice. He'd actually used that horribly insipid word to describe what they'd done that incredible, amazing, one-hundred-million-times-better-than-nice night.

Nell had been too emotionally overwhelmed to react at the time. But she'd had plenty of time to smolder in outrage since then.

She invoked those feelings now, and shot a lethal look in Crash's direction. "I *can not* believe what you just said." Her voice had just the slightest hint of an angry quiver. Nice. Nice. He thought making love to her had been *nice*. "You're actually planning to sell out to these scumbags?"

"I don't see too many choices here." Crash made himself sound wound tight with tension. "So just shut the hell up and keep watch."

Shut the hell up? The words were so un-Crash-like, Nell took a step backwards in surprise before she caught herself.

"No, I won't shut up," she shot back at him. "Maybe you don't have a choice, but—"

He stood up. "Don't push me." The expression on his face was positively menacing. His eyes looked washed out and nearly white—and flatly, soullessly empty.

Nell faltered, unable to remember what she was supposed to say next, frozen by the coldness of his gaze. It was as if nothing was there, as if nothing was inside him. She'd seen him look this way before—at Daisy's wake and funeral. She remembered thinking then that he may have been able to walk and talk, but his heart was barely beating.

Had it been an act back then, too, or was he really able to shut down so completely upon command?

He turned back to Sheldon. "You give up the commander's name, and seventy-five thousand of that money is—"

"What about Jake Robinson?" That was what she was supposed to say.

"Excuse us for a minute, Sheldon." Crash took her arm, and pulled her roughly toward the bathroom.

He didn't turn on the bathroom light because there was a fan attached, and he didn't want it to drown out their whispered words. Part of the plan was for Sheldon to be able to hear what they were saying.

"I thought you wanted to stay alive," he hissed through clenched teeth.

The tiny bathroom was barely large enough for both of them. Even though she had pulled her arm free from his grasp, they were still forced to stand uncomfortably close. She rubbed the place where his fingers had dug into her arm.

"I'm sorry about that," Crash said almost soundlessly. "I had to make it look real. Did I hurt you?" Concern warmed his eyes, bringing him back to life.

He cared. Something surged in her chest, in her stomach, and just like that, her anger faded. Because just like that, she understood why he hadn't returned her letters.

As much as she professed to want only to be friends, deep inside she wanted more.

She'd given *that* truth away on the morning she'd begged him to give their relationship a try.

He'd known that, and he'd also known that if he'd written to her, or if he'd called, his letters and phone calls would have kept alive the tiny seed of hope buried deep inside of her—the seed of hope that still fluttered to life at something so trivial as a flare of concern in his eyes.

God, she was pathetic.

She was pathetic, and he smelled so good, so familiar. She wanted to wrap her arms around him and bury her face in his shirt. It wouldn't have taken much—just a step forward an inch or two.

Instead, she jammed her hands into the front pockets of her jeans and shook her head, no. "I thought you wanted to get back at the bastard who killed Jake Robinson!" she whispered loudly enough for the man in the other room to overhear.

"Yeah, well, I changed my mind," he told her. "I decided I'd rather take the money and run. Disappear in Hong Kong."

"Hong Kong? Who said anything about going to *Hong Kong?*" Nell lowered her voice. "Do you think he's buying this?"

Crash shook his head. He didn't know. All he knew for certain was that it had been too damn long since he'd kissed this woman. She was really getting into this game they were playing. Her cheeks were flushed and her eyes were bright, making her impossibly attractive. He tried to put more space between them, but his back was already against the wall—there was nowhere else to go.

"No *way* am I letting you drag me to Hong Kong!" she continued. "You *promised* me—"

He cut her off. "I promised you nothing. What—do you think just because we got it on that suddenly you own me?"

Nell took a step back and bumped into the side of the tub. Crash caught her even as she reached for him, and for one brief moment, she was in his arms again. But he forced himself to release her, forced himself to step back.

What was wrong with him? True, bringing up the issue of sex would make their arguing more realistic, but it was definitely dangerous ground. And the words he'd spoken couldn't have been farther from the truth. They'd got it on, indeed, but then she'd let him go. Even the letters she'd written to him had been carefully worded. There was no question—she didn't have any expectations or demands.

Some of the sparkle had left her eyes as she looked up at him. "Oh, was *that* what you'd call what we did?" she said in a rough stage whisper loud enough for Sheldon to hear. "Getting it on? I think it's got to last longer than two-and-a-half minutes to be called anything other than 'getting off.' As in *you* getting off and me faking it so that you won't feel bad."

She was making it up. Crash knew that everything she was saying was based on some fictional joining. But still, he couldn't help but wonder.

The night they'd spent together *had* been over pretty quickly. He hadn't even managed to carry her all the way to the bed. But the way she had seemed to shatter in his arms—that couldn't have been faked, could it?

Something, some of his doubt, must have flickered in his eyes because Nell reached out to touch the side of his face. "How could you forget how incredibly perfect it was?" she asked almost inaudibly.

She lightly touched his lips with one finger, her eyes filled with heat from her memories of that night. But then her gaze met his and she pulled her hand away as if she had been burned. "Sorry. I know I shouldn't have…sorry."

"Just do what I say and keep your mouth shut," Crash harshly ordered her for Sheldon's benefit. "Don't make me wish I'd let Sarkowski shoot you."

He abruptly turned and went out of the room, afraid if he didn't leave he'd end up doing something incredibly stupid, like kiss her. Or admit that he *hadn't* forgotten. He'd tried to forget, God knows he had. But his memories of the night they'd spent together were ones he knew he'd take to his grave.

She stayed in the bathroom as he sat down again across from Sheldon.

"Women are always trouble," the gunman told him.

"It's nothing I can't handle," Crash replied tersely.

Nell slunk out of the bathroom then, her body language much like a dog with its tail between its legs. Despite everything she'd said to the contrary, she *was* good at acting. Unless her kicked-puppy look was the result of him rejecting her again. It was on a much smaller scale this time, but his lack of response to her nearly silent words was a rejection of sorts.

Nell reached the other side of the room and, just as

446HAWKEN'S HEART

they'd planned, she bolted for the door, throwing it open
and running out into the darkness of the night.

Sheldon snorted. "Yeah, right, man, you can really
handle her."

Crash checked to see that the gunman was still securely
tied to the chair and then he went after Nell, slamming
the door behind him. He didn't have far to go—she was
waiting for him right outside the door.

"You should gag me," she whispered quietly. "Because
if this was real, you better believe that I would scream. And
if you just covered my mouth with your hand, I'd have to
bite you."

"I don't have anything to gag you with." Of course,
if this was real, if he were desperate, he'd use one of his
socks. He didn't think she'd go for that, though.

Nell pulled the tail of her shirt out from her jeans. "Tear
off a piece of this."

Crash took out his knife to cut through the seam. And
then, as the fabric tore with a rending sound, Nell met his
eyes.

He knew she was thinking the exact same thing that
he was—that this was actually kind of kinky. With the
undercurrent of sexual tension that seemed to follow them
around, the idea of him tearing her shirt to gag her, with
the intention of dragging her back into the motel room and
tying her up...

She gave him a smile that was half embarrassed and
half filled with excited energy as he put his knife away.
Damned if she wasn't getting into this.

"You got the juice?" he asked. She'd poured some of it
into a plastic baggie back in the car.

"I put it under the bed that's farthest from the door.
Remember, when you knock me onto the ground, let me
crawl under the bed to get it. Give me a minute to stick it
under my shirt."

"How?" Crash asked. "I'm going to tie your hands

behind your back. I thought you were going to have it on you now."

"Are you kidding? And have it open too early?" His news slowed her down, but it didn't stop her. "Well, you're just going to have to do it. When you grab me to pull me out from under the bed, stick it up under my shirt."

"I can't believe we're doing this. If this actually works, I'm going to be amazed."

Nell smiled at him. "Prepare to be amazed," she said. "Come on. Let's make this look real." She took off, running out into the parking lot.

Crash sighed, and went after her. He caught her in less than four steps and grabbed her around the waist, swinging her up and into his arms. She was harder to hold on to than he'd thought, though—she was fighting him.

"Nell, take it easy! I don't want to hurt you," he hissed.

She took a deep breath and opened her mouth, and he knew without a single doubt that she was going to scream. Talk about taking role-playing a *little* too seriously. He wadded up the fabric from her shirt and put it in her mouth, trying really hard to be careful. She bit his fingers and he swore.

He all but kicked the motel room door open and *did* kick it closed behind them, swearing again as one of her legs came dangerously close to making him sing soprano for a week. He flung her onto the bed, flipping her onto her stomach, and holding her hands behind her back.

He had to sit on her as he tied her wrists together, resting nearly his full weight upon her after she tried to kick him again. Dammit, she was actually *trying* to kick him in the balls.

He cursed as he tied her, choosing words he couldn't remember using in years, and she was trying to get free, kicking and wriggling beneath him like a wild woman.

Her torn-off shirt rode up, exposing the pale smoothness

of her back and making him feel like a total degenerate. How could this possibly turn him on?

But this was just a game. He wasn't trying to hurt her—in fact, he was trying to do the opposite. He was tying her up using knots that she'd be able to slip out of. He was taking care that the roughness of the rope didn't abrade the soft skin of her wrists.

It was the sight and feel of Nell beneath him on a bed, his body pressed against hers, that was making him heat up. It wasn't the ropes or the struggle—that wasn't real. But Nell was real. Dear God, she was incredibly real.

He grabbed another rope from his bag and tied her feet, also with slipknots, aware that Sheldon Sarkowski was watching, disgust in his eyes.

He lifted Nell up, depositing her on the floor as gently as he could while making it look to Sarkowski as if he'd damn near thrown her there.

As she said she would, she immediately began wriggling, rolling all the way under the bed. She was smart—she didn't leave a leg or a foot sticking out for him to grab. He had to lift up the dust ruffle and crawl halfway under himself just to pull her out.

There, just where she said it was, was a thin plastic baggie, closed with a twist-tie like a little balloon, filled both with air and tomato juice, ready to be popped. Of all the absurd ideas he'd ever tried, this one had to take the cake.

Nell had rolled onto her back, and he grabbed the baggie, careful not to pop it, and thrust it up, underneath her shirt. He hooked part of the loose plastic around the front clasp of her bra, trying to ignore the sensation of his fingers brushing against her smooth, warm skin. God, why was he doing this?

Because there was a .001 percent chance that it would work. As ridiculous as it was, it could work. People often saw what they expected to see, and as long as Sarkowski didn't have *too* acute a sense of smell, he wouldn't see tomato juice spilling out onto Nell's shirt, he'd see blood.

Crash hauled Nell out from under the bed, making it look as if he'd hit her hard enough across the face to make her lie still, dazed from the blow.

He stood up then, straightening his combat vest and quickly running his fingers through his hair, putting himself back into order. He drew his weapon from his holster, and sat down across from Sarkowski as if none of that had happened.

"I want the commander's name," Crash said, "and I want it now. My patience is gone."

"Sorry, pal." Sarkowski shook his head. "The best I can do for you is to pass along your message about the two hundred and fifty thousand. But you're not dealing from a position of strength here. Unless you can guarantee the girl's silence as well as your own, my employer isn't going to consider paying that price."

"I can guarantee the girl's silence."

The gunman laughed derisively. "Yeah, right."

Crash didn't blink. He didn't move a muscle in his face. He simply turned and discharged his weapon, aiming directly at Nell's chest.

She rolled back, as if from the force of the bullet, and then feel forward. She struggled briefly against the ropes that held her and then was still.

Crash took a deep breath, but all he could smell was the pizza—its box left open on the top of the TV set.

He watched Sarkowski's face as a red stain slowly appeared from beneath Nell's body. The gunman had lifted his heavy eyelids higher than usual, and when he turned to look at Crash, there was wariness in his eyes.

Crash set his weapon in his lap, the barrel pointed casually in the other man's direction. "I want to know the commander's name," he said again. "Now."

Sarkowski was searching his eyes for any sign of

remorse, any hint of emotion, and Crash purposely kept his face devoid of expression, his eyes flat and cold and filled with absolutely nothing. From the gunman's perspective, he had no heart, no soul—and absolutely no problem with doubling the current body count.

"Kill me and you've got nothing," Sarkowski blustered. "You'll never know who I work for then."

But he spoke a little too quickly, his anxiety giving a little too much of an edge to his voice.

"That would only be a temporary problem," Crash pointed out. "I'd just have to wait for the commander to send someone else after me. Chances are *that* guy will talk. And if not him, then maybe the next. It doesn't matter to me. Time's one thing I've got plenty of." He lifted his weapon with the same kind of blasé casualness that he'd pointed it at Nell and aimed directly at Sarkowski's forehead.

"Wait," Sarkowski said. "I think we can make some kind of a deal."

Jackpot.

Nell didn't move. Crash couldn't even tell that she was breathing, but he knew that she was smiling.

CHAPTER FOURTEEN

THE MOTEL WINDOW WAS DARK as Crash pulled back into the parking lot.

A string of blinking Christmas lights had slipped from the edge of the roof, drooping pathetically across the front of the motel. The artificial tree visible through the lobby window listed to the left, its branches sagging under the weight of garish decorations.

Christmas was a grim undertaking here at this fleabag motel in the middle of nowhere. The festive trappings had all been brought out, but there was nothing merry about them. There was no hope, just resignation. Another season of bills that couldn't be paid and dreams that couldn't come true.

Somehow it all seemed appropriate.

Crash was exhausted. It had taken him longer than he'd hoped to find another motel in which to deposit Sheldon Sarkowski.

He'd planned to take Sarkowski out to the state park and leave him locked in the men's room, but the two men had made a deal of sorts. Sheldon had been bought by the promise of a cut of the blackmail money and the hope that if he gave up his employer's name, Crash wouldn't kill him.

The deal was bogus, of course. Crash had no intention of taking any money from the commander who had engineered Jake Robinson's death. His goal was still—and had always been—justice.

But Sheldon thought they were a team now. And team members didn't lock other team members in a freezing-cold men's room. Instead, Crash had taken the highway, going nearly twenty miles back in the direction they'd come before finding another appropriately ancient motel. And once inside, he'd handcuffed Sheldon to the radiator in the bathroom. He'd even apologized before tapping him on the side of the head with the butt of his handgun.

His apology was accepted. Sheldon would have done the very same thing to him. They were supposed to be teammates now, but unlike members of a SEAL Team, they didn't fully trust each other.

And Sheldon Sarkowski—or whoever he *really* was— was the last person Crash ever would have trusted. The man liked his work way too much. Just from the short conversations they'd had, Crash knew Sheldon enjoyed pulling the trigger and delivering death. He'd volunteered to get rid of Nell's body and Crash got the sense that the offer was made not so much to help Crash, but for the pleasure doing so would give Sheldon.

The thought of Sheldon touching Nell was enough to make Crash's skin crawl.

He fought a wave of fatigue as he unlocked the door to the first motel room. He didn't have time to be tired. It was probably true that Sarkowski wouldn't be found by the maid until morning, but he wasn't about to take any chances. He'd wake up Nell and they were going to get back on the road.

She would be shocked to find out that she'd danced with the man responsible for this entire fiasco at Jake and Daisy's wedding. Senator—and retired U.S. Navy Commander—Mark Garvin was the man they were after.

There were no lights on at all in the room. Nell had no doubt showered and climbed into bed by now. God help him, he was going to have to stare down temptation and pull her out of bed rather than climb in with her, the way he so desperately wanted to and—

Nell hadn't moved. In the darkness, Crash could see her, still lying on the floor where he'd left her.

Dear Lord, the bullet he'd fired at her *had* been a blank, hadn't it? He'd double-checked and triple-checked it. But God knew he was exhausted. And when men were exhausted, they made mistakes.

He slapped the light switch on the wall and the dim light only verified what he already knew. Nell was lying on the floor, hands still tied behind her back, eyes closed, almost exactly the way he'd left her.

Crash's chest was tight with fear, and his throat was clogged with the closest thing to panic he'd ever felt in his life as he crossed toward her.

"Nell!" She still didn't move.

He knelt next to her and pulled her into his arms, tearing at her clothes, praying that the sticky redness was indeed the result of the tomato juice they'd picked up at the convenience store, praying that he wasn't going to find some awful, mortal wound beneath the stained fabric.

Buttons flew everywhere as he ripped her shirt open. He swept his hands across the smoothness of her skin and looked down in her eyes, which were now opened very, very wide.

She was all right. The blood wasn't blood after all, the bullet he'd fired *had* been a blank. Relief made him so dizzy he nearly lost his balance.

But he wasn't too dizzy to realize that his hand was still on her chest, his fingers against her delicate collarbone, his wrist between her lace-covered breasts.

She was in his arms, her face inches from his, her shirt torn and stained, her hands and feet still tied.

Nell cleared her throat. "Well, this is quite the little fantasy come true."

Crash moved his hand, but then didn't quite know where

to put it. "Are you all right? When I saw you still lying here, I thought…"

"I couldn't get free."

"I purposely used slipknots to tie you."

"I tried," she admitted, "but they just seemed to get tighter."

"You're not supposed to pull at them." He helped her up into a sitting position and swiftly used his knife to cut her hands free. "You're suppose to finesse them. Pulling just tightens them."

"So much for my lifelong dream of becoming an escape artist."

Crash's ribs hurt as he cut her feet free, and he realized that she had made him laugh. He wanted to pull her back into his arms, but she had turned away from him, as if suddenly self-conscious that her torn shirt was hanging open, all its buttons neatly removed.

She rubbed her wrists. "Damn—that tomato juice stings!"

"It's acidic. Come here."

Nell let him help her up and lead her to the set of double sinks right outside the bathroom door. He turned on the water and she held her wrists under the flow as he turned on the light.

"I'm sorry about this." His hands were so gentle as he lifted her hands to look at her rope burns.

She looked up at him. "It worked, didn't it?"

"Yeah."

"Then it's worth it."

His gaze flickered down to the open front of her shirt. "You better take a shower. I'll find you something clean to wear."

He was still touching her, still holding her hands. Nell knew that it was now or never—and she couldn't bear for it to be never. Not without trying one more time.

She reached out and touched the edge of the front pocket

of his pants. In his haste to make sure she was all right, he'd knelt in the puddle of tomato juice. "You look like you could use a shower yourself," she said softly. "And I could use a little company."

Crash didn't move. For a minute, she wasn't even sure if he was still breathing. But the sudden rush of heat in his eyes left her little doubt. The sexual tension she'd felt building over the past few days was *not* a figment of her imagination. He felt it, too. He *suffered* from it, too. Thank God.

"That was your big cue," she prompted him. "That was where you were supposed to kiss me and pull me with you into the shower."

"Why are you here?" he asked hoarsely. "What do you want? Why did you even come to the jail?"

Nell knew she should break the spell by saying something funny, something flip. But in a flash of clarity, she realized that she used humor to maintain a distance—much in the same way that Crash separated from his emotions. So she didn't make a joke. She told him the truth.

"I want to help you prove your innocence. You once told me that I didn't really know you, but you were wrong." She held his gaze, daring him to look away, to step away, to pull away from her. "I *do* know you, Billy. My heart knows you. Even though your heart doesn't seem to want to recognize me."

He touched the side of her face, and she closed her eyes, pressing her cheek into his palm, daring to hope that he felt even a fraction of what she did.

"So that's why you're here," he whispered. "To try to save me."

"I'm here because you need me." Nell opened her eyes and let slip another dangerous truth. "And because I need you."

He was looking at her, and she could see everything

he was feeling mirrored in his eyes. For once, he wasn't trying to hide from her. Or from himself.

"I want you," she told him softly. "All these months, and I still haven't stopped wanting you. I dream about your kisses." She smiled crookedly. "I've been sleeping a lot lately."

Crash kissed her then.

It was so different from that night after Daisy's funeral, where one minute he was looking at her and the next he was inhaling her. It was different, because this was a kiss that she actually saw coming.

She saw it in his eyes first, in the way his gaze dropped to her mouth for just a fraction of a second. And she saw it in the way his pupils seemed to expand, just a little. Then he leaned toward her, slowly, as his hand tilted her chin up. And then his mouth met hers, softly, sweetly.

He tasted like tomato juice.

He deepened the kiss, pulling her gently toward him, and Nell felt herself melt, felt her pulse kick into double time, felt her heart damn near burst out of her chest. This was what she'd been waiting for. This was why she had never invited Dex Lancaster inside after a dinner date.

She'd tried to deny it so many different times. It wasn't pure attraction and simple sex. It wasn't friendship, either. It wasn't anything she'd ever felt before.

She loved his man. Completely. Absolutely. Forever.

"Nell." He was breathing hard as he pulled back slightly to look at her. "I want you, too, but…" He took a breath and let it out quickly. "We shouldn't do this. Bottom line— nothing's changed between us." He laughed. "Truth is, it's gotten even more impossible. I can't give you—"

She stopped his words with a kiss. "Honesty's all I need. I know exactly what you can't give me and I'm not asking for that. All I want is another night with you." She knew he didn't love her, but she told herself she didn't need him to love her. And she didn't need false promises of forever, either. She just wanted this moment. She kissed him again. "I can't think of anything I want more than to spend tonight in your arms."

She watched his eyes, holding her breath, praying he wouldn't turn away, knowing that she was risking so much by telling him this.

He touched her face again, the edges of his mouth twisting up into what could almost be called a smile. "You're looking at me like you don't have a clue what I'm going to do next," he said perceptively. He softly traced her lower lip with his thumb. "You don't *really* think I'm strong enough to hear you say all that, then walk away, do you?"

Nell's breath caught in her throat. "I think you're the most remarkable man I've ever met, and you're right. I *never* have a clue what you're going to do next."

"Tonight I'm going to be selfish," he said quietly.

He kissed her slowly, completely. It was a kiss that promised her all of the passion of their first joining and even more. She clung to him, breathless and dizzy and giddy with desire, barely aware as he pulled her with him into the tiny bathroom.

They'd stood right here just hours ago.

Nothing had changed, Crash had said. But everything had changed. Two hours ago she'd had her hands in her pockets to keep from touching him. Now those same hands were unfastening the buckle of his belt, even as his hands helped her out of her own clothes.

She was covered with tomato juice and he stepped into the tub, pulling her with him, and turned on the water, rinsing her clean.

He washed her so slowly, so carefully, stopping to give her deliciously long, exquisitely sweet kisses that made her weak-kneed with desire. She could feel his arousal, hot and hard against her, and she opened herself to him, winding one leg around him in an attempt to pull him even closer.

He'd taken a foil-wrapped condom from his vest and tossed it into the soap-holder as they'd stepped into the shower. He opened it now, covering himself.

She kissed him again and he groaned, pulling her up, lifting her, pressing her back against the cool tile wall as he filled her.

It was heaven. The water raining down from the shower seemed to caress her sensitized body as he kissed her, touched her, claimed her so completely.

She was moments from release when he pulled back, breaking their kiss to gaze down at her. His gaze was hot, his breathing ragged. "I want to make love to you in a bed," he told her. "I want to look at you and touch you and taste every inch of you. I want to take my time and be absolutely certain that you're satisfied."

She pushed herself more deeply on top of him. "I'm satisfied," she told him. She was already more satisfied than she'd thought she'd be ever again. "Although the bed thing sounds really nice. Maybe we can do that later."

"We don't have time. We have to leave," he told her.

Nell opened her eyes. *"Now?"*

"Soon." He kissed her. "I'm sorry. I should have told you right when I came in."

She tightened and released her legs around him, setting a rhythm that he soon obligingly matched. "You were too busy tearing off my shirt."

"I was." He held her gaze as he drove himself deeply inside of her again and again and again.

His beautiful eyes were half-closed and he was smiling very, very slightly—for him it was the equivalent of an all-out grin. He knew damn well what he was doing to her. He knew damn well that she was seconds away from total sensual meltdown.

But she could feel his heart pounding and she could read the heat in his eyes. She knew that when she exploded, she would take him with her. He was that close, too.

"Can we pretend tonight doesn't end when the sun comes up?" he asked softly. "I want to drive as far from here as possible before we stop again and…Nell, I need to make love to you in a bed."

He *needed* her. Dear God, he was actually admitting that he needed her.

"I would like that, too." She laughed. "Understatement of the year."

Hope filled her. The tiny seed that she'd tried to crush for so long burst to life inside her. He needed her. He didn't want tonight to end. She never dreamed he'd ever confess to either of those things.

At that moment, anything was possible. At that moment, she didn't need wings to fly.

She left the ground in an explosion of sensation and emotion that was deliriously intense. She felt herself cry out, heard an echo of her voice shouting his name. She felt him kiss her, possessing her mouth as completely as he possessed her body, felt him shake from his own cataclysmic release.

It was wonderful.

And it was even more wonderful knowing this time that she was going to get a chance—soon—to make love to him like this again.

NELL SLEPT IN THE FRONT SEAT of the car, her head resting in Crash's lap.

She'd folded up her jacket to use as padding over the lump from the parking brake. She was wearing one of his shirts and a pair of his pants, the cuffs rolled up about six times and the waistband cinched with a belt.

Her golden hair gleamed in the dim light of dawn. He ran his fingers through its baby-fine softness, loving the sensation.

She slept so ferociously, her eyes tightly shut and her fists clenched.

What on earth had he done?

Crash felt sick to his stomach. It could have been from fatigue, but he suspected it was, instead, a result of that look he'd seen in Nell's eyes while they were making love.

He'd made a mistake and admitted that he wanted more—more than quick, emotionless sex in the shower.

He'd opened his mouth, and now she was no doubt dreaming of their wedding.

He glanced down at her again and had to smile. She looked so fragile and tiny, nearly lost in his too-large clothes. And yet even in sleep she looked like she was ready at any given moment to hold her own in a boxing match.

No, she wasn't dreaming of their wedding. She was probably dreaming about getting her hands on Senator Mark Garvin and tearing him limb from limb.

He was the one who was dreaming about their wedding.

God help him, he was in love with this woman.

Crash wasn't sure exactly when he'd realized it. Maybe it was when he walked into that motel room and thought for one god-awful moment that he'd actually shot and killed her. Or maybe it didn't sink in until she looked him in the eye and bared her soul, telling him that she needed him, that she wanted him, that she ached for him. Or maybe it was when they made love in the shower, and she held his gaze while he moved inside her. Maybe it was the realization that mere sex had never felt remotely like what he was feeling at that moment.

Or maybe it was when he hadn't been able to keep his fool mouth shut. Maybe it was when he'd told her that he wanted more, and she just lit up from within, her eyes shining with hope. His initial reaction hadn't been instant regret. No, he was double the pathetic fool. He'd actually been glad. That light in her eyes had made him feel happy.

That was when he knew he loved her. When he'd found himself happy at the thought that maybe she loved him, too.

The really stupid thing was that he'd been in love with her for years. *Years*. Probably since the very first time they'd met. Certainly during the previous year, while they'd lived together in Jake and Daisy's house, their beds separated only by one thin wall.

He'd loved her, but he'd refused to acknowledge it, refused to believe that she would want the kind of life she'd have with him.

She was the real reason he'd spent most of last year out of the country.

Somehow he knew that if he'd seen her again, if he'd so much as run into her on the street, he wouldn't have been able to keep away from her. Somehow he knew that he had no control at all when it came to Nell.

The sky lightened behind him as he drove relentlessly west.

The morning sky was pewter-gray and dull, promising rain or maybe even more sleet or snow.

His future was just as bleak. As hard as he tried, Crash couldn't see any kind of happy ending for him and Nell.

What he *could* see was heartbreakingly tragic.

Unless he was able to hunt down and destroy Commander Garvin, USN Retired, the woman he loved was a target. Unless Crash could win, Nell would die.

But Crash *would* win.

His career might be over. His name and his reputation were definitely ruined. He was wanted by ever law-enforcement agency in the country, and probably some that were outside of the country, as well. He had no kind of life left and what he did have, he didn't deserve—not after the way he'd let Jake die.

First Daisy, then Jake. There was no way in *hell* he was going to let Nell die, too.

He was willing to give up everything he had left to save her—and all he had left was his life.

NELL AWOKE TO FIND HERSELF alone in the bed.

They'd stopped shortly after crossing the border into New Mexico, and she had fallen asleep with Crash's arms around her.

But first, they'd made the most incredible love.

Crash had delivered everything he'd promised and then some. He'd made love to her so thoroughly, so sweetly, Nell had almost let herself believe that he loved her.

Almost.

Now he was sitting, half-naked, in front of a powerful-looking laptop computer that he'd hooked up to the room's phone system. His hair stood up, as if he'd frequently run his fingers through it, and the screen lit his bare chest with a golden glow.

He pushed his chair back with a sigh and stood up, stretching his long legs and twisting a kink from his back. He turned as if he felt her watching, and froze. "I'm sorry, did I wake you?"

Nell shook her head, suddenly uncertain, suddenly wondering if their night together had officially come to an end. "Have you slept at all?"

"Not yet." He looked exhausted. His eyes were rimmed with red and he reached up to rub the back of his neck with one hand. "I've been trying to find the connection between Garvin and Sherman. But I need to sleep. I'm starting to go in circles."

He sat down on the second of the two double beds in the room, and Nell thought for a second that he was sending her a message. Their night *was* over. He was going to sleep alone. But when he looked at her, she realized that he was feeling as uncertain as she was.

"You look like you could use a back rub," she said softly.

He met her eyes. "What I really want is to make love to you again."

Nell's mouth was suddenly dry. She tried to moisten her lips, tried to smile. "The odds of that actually happening will increase enormously if you sit on this bed instead of over there on that one."

He smiled tiredly at that. "Yeah. I just didn't want to…" He shook his head, running his hand down his face. "I don't want to take advantage of you."

"Come here. Please?"

He stood up, crossing the short distance between the two beds. Nell sat forward, pulling him down so that he was sitting, facing slightly away from her. The covers fell away from her as she knelt behind him, gently massaging the tight muscles in his shoulders and neck.

He closed his eyes. "God, that's good."

"Did you find anything about Garvin at all?"

"He was definitely in 'Nam in '71 and '72—the same time as John Sherman served with the Green Berets."

Nell gently pushed him down, so that he was lying on the bed, on his stomach, arms up underneath his head. She straddled his back to get real leverage as she tried to loosen the muscles in his shoulders.

"I hacked my way into Garvin's tax records. He inherited a substantial sum of money in 1972—money his first wife used to buy a house while he was still in Vietnam. I searched the tax records of the elderly relative he claims the inheritance came from, but there's no record of income from the interest for a sum of money that large. Unless the old guy kept a quarter of a million dollars under his mattress."

"So what are we going to do?"

"I sent him a coded message that should be easy enough for him to break. I told him I had proof that his so-called inheritance was really the money he'd made dealing in the black market with John Sherman."

"But you don't have proof."

"He doesn't know that. I need to talk to him, face-to-face, record the conversation, and hope that he slips and says something that incriminates him."

Nell paused. "Face-to-face? This is a man who wants to kill you."

"That makes two of us."

"Billy—"

"I could just go after him. Take him out. An eye for an eye. A commander for an admiral. It wouldn't be the first time I've played the part of the avenging angel."

Nell took a deep breath. "But—"

"But if I do it that way, no one will know what he did. He killed Jake, he killed all those people in that war he started, and I want the world to know it. God, you're beautiful."

Nell turned her head, following his gaze, and realized that he was watching her in the wall mirror opposite the bed. The only light in the room was from his computer screen, but it was enough to give her breasts and her stomach and the curve of her rear end an exotic cast.

She looked like some wild, hedonistic version of herself. A naked love slave ministering to the needs of her master. All he had to do was turn over, and he could watch as she kept caressing him, kissing her way down his chest, down to his stomach, down...

She met the fire of his gaze in the mirror, feeling her cheeks heat with a blush. It wasn't the first time she'd believed him capable of reading her mind.

He didn't look tired any longer.

He turned, rolling beneath her so that he could look up at her, so that the hardness of his arousal pressed against her.

"This is the closest I figure I'll ever actually get to heaven," he said softly.

Nell leaned forward to kiss him and he held her close,

telling her again, although not in so many words, just how much that he needed her.

She kissed his neck, his throat, his chest, trailing her mouth across his incredible body as she reached between them to unfasten his pants.

She turned to look, and, just as she'd imagined, found him watching her in the mirror. She smiled at him.

And then she took him to heaven.

CHAPTER FIFTEEN

"I'M *NOT* GOING."

"Nell—"

"But you don't even have a plan to…" Nell broke off, gazing at him wide-eyed from the other side of the car. "Oh, my God," she said softly. "You *do* have a plan to get the evidence you need against Garvin, don't you? And you weren't even going to tell me."

It would have been easier if she'd shouted at him.

He tried to explain. "There are some things that are better if you don't know."

She turned to look out the window. "The things I don't know—particularly about you—could fill a book."

"I'm sorry."

She looked back at him. "You say that a lot."

"I mean it a lot."

"So this is it," she said. "You're just going to drop me off here in Coronado, at the house of somebody named Cowboy. And I'm just supposed to hide until you either come back or you don't."

The southern-California streets were filled with lengthening shadows and heavy traffic as the sun began to set. Crash had never been to the house that his swim buddy Cowboy shared with his young wife and infant son. But he had the address and he'd checked the map back when they'd last stopped for gas. He knew exactly where he was going.

"Silence," she said quietly. "With you, silence tends to

imply an affirmative." She turned toward him then, reaching for him. "Billy, please don't shut me out now."

He let her take his hand, lacing their fingers together. "I know you want to help me, but the best way you can help me right now is to let me make sure that you're someplace safe." He braked to a stop at a traffic light and turned to look at her. "I need to know that you're okay, so that I can do what I have to do without being distracted—without worrying whether or not you're in danger."

"Please." Nell's husky voice broke very slightly. "Please tell me what it is that you're going to do."

Crash lost himself for a moment in the perfect blue of Nell's eyes. The car behind him honked—the light had turned green and he hadn't even noticed. He looked back at the road as he drove, wishing he had an eternity to fall into the ocean of her eyes and knowing that he only had hours left. Minutes. "A guy I know, a SEAL instructor, has a cabin in the mountains, not far from here. I know he's not going to be using it—the latest class of candidates are going through Hell Week. This guy's disabled and he does almost all of his teaching in a classroom, but he's still going to be busy this week."

"So you're going to use his cabin to wait for Garvin to contact you?"

He glanced at her again. "Actually, I got a response from Garvin this morning. Via e-mail. He's accepted my deal."

"My God. Isn't that the proof that you need? I mean, if he's letting himself be blackmailed…"

Crash smiled. "Unfortunately he didn't send me back a message that said. 'Yes, I'll pay you a quarter of a million dollars to make sure that you keep silent about the fact that I not only killed Jake Robinson but also started a war in Southeast Asia.' No, I've got to go face-to-face with Garvin, try to get something he says down on tape. I need something concrete."

"Face-to...? But he's going to try to kill you! There's no way he's going to *pay* you all that money to be quiet when killing you guarantees your silence."

Crash signaled to make a left turn onto the street where Cowboy lived. "I'll be ready for him. I have enough C-4 in my bag to take out the entire mountain if I have to."

"C-4?"

"Explosives."

"Oh, God."

There was a break in the oncoming traffic and Crash made the left turn into the residential neighborhood. He swore sharply as he saw the cars idling farther down the street. "Nell, kiss me, then laugh, make it big, like we're on our way to a party. No worries."

She didn't hesitate. She slipped her arms around his neck, turning his head, forcing him to watch the road with only one eye as she kissed him full on the mouth. She tasted like coffee with sugar, like slow, delicious early-morning lovemaking, like paradise on earth. When she finally pulled back, she threw back her head and laughed—just as he'd asked. "Who's watching us?" she asked, nuzzling his neck again.

He had to clear his throat before he could speak. That was such a good performance, she'd nearly fooled *him*. "I'm not sure exactly, but there's at least one car that's got to be FInCOM, one I *know* is NIS, and one other a little farther down the road, a little harder to pick out, that I'd bet my life savings belongs to whoever's working for Garvin."

She kissed him again, even longer this time. "Where did they come from? Are they following us?"

"No." He glanced in the rearview mirror. None of the cars had moved. "They're all doing surveillance outside of Cowboy's house—waiting for me to show up." He swore again. "They found the one man I know I can still trust. I should've known they'd figure that out."

"Is there some other way you can contact your friend? By phone or at work?"

Crash shook his head. "If they're watching Cowboy's house this closely, they've surely put a tap on his phone. And they'll follow him to work. Besides, my goal was to bring you into his house, not just talk to him. But there's no way that's going to happen now."

"So what happens now?"

"We go to Plan B."

"Funny, I didn't know about Plan A until minutes ago, and now we're already onto Plan B. What's Plan B?"

He checked the rearview mirror again before he glanced at her. "I'll let you know when I figure it out."

As Nell got an apple from the car and went back across the clearing toward the cabin, she could feel Crash's eyes on her.

She knew what he was thinking. He was wondering what on earth he was going to do with her.

It didn't matter how many times she protested. It didn't matter how brilliantly she argued with him. He was convinced that he needed to find some kind of haven for her, while he went one-on-one with a man they both *knew* had killed before to keep his secrets safe.

She sat down next to him on the cabin's front steps. "What's that?" He'd taken several blocks of gray, putty-colored modeling clay and several spools of wire from one of his gym bags. The clay was soft, so he was easily able to tear it into smaller chunks.

He looked up at her. "It's C-4."

She nearly choked on her apple. "*That's* an explosive? Don't you need to be really careful with it?"

He gave her one of his rare smiles. "No. It's stable. I could hit it with a hammer if I wanted to. It's no big deal."

She tossed what was left of her apple into the woods. "I

remember watching Western movies where the bank robbers all sweated bullets when they got out the nitroglycerine."

"We've progressed a long way since those days."

"That depends on your definition of progress." Nell looked around. "It's nice here. So peaceful and quiet. So naturally, you've decided to blow it up."

Crash put down the chunk of C-4 he was working with and kissed her. Of all the things she'd expected him to say or do, a kiss wasn't one of them. It wasn't just a quick kiss, either. It was a very well-planned kiss, as if he'd been thinking about doing it for a good long while.

It was more than just an I-want-your-body kiss. It was filled with a flood of emotions, most too complicated to name, and the rest too risky to acknowledge. He couldn't quite meet her eyes when he pulled away. Instead, he held her close for several long moments, lightly running his fingers through her hair.

"I've been thinking," he finally said.

Nell held her breath, praying that he'd finally come to the realization that what tied them together was uncontrollable and inevitable. He loved her. She *knew* he loved her. He wouldn't have been able to kiss her that way if he didn't.

"At sundown we're heading back into town. There's a SEAL I know, the executive officer of Alpha Squad. His name's McCoy. He was at the hearing, and he signaled me, you know, with hand signals—asked if I was all right. He wasn't like the guys from Team Twelve, ready to help strap me in for the lethal injection without even hearing my side of the story." Crash took a deep breath. "So I'm going to tell Blue McCoy my side of the story and ask him to take care of you. I know that he might feel obligated to turn me in, but I won't give him that opportunity. And I also know if I ask him, he'll make damn sure that you stay safe."

Nell fought her disappointment, keeping her face pressed against his shoulder, breathing in his warm, familiar scent.

Those weren't the words she'd wanted to hear. In fact, they were words she *hadn't* wanted to hear. "Can't we stay here until the morning? Spend one more night together?"

His arms tightened around her. "God, I wish we could." He spoke so quietly, she almost didn't hear him. "But I've already sent Garvin an encoded message, giving him these coordinates. He's up at his home in Carmel right now. By the time he breaks the code—and I know he won't be able to do that in less than six hours—by the time he gets down here, even if he takes a private plane, it'll be dawn."

She straightened up. "Don't you think he's going to take those coordinates and send an army of Sheldon Sarkowskis here to kill you?"

"My message was very clear. If he doesn't make an in-person appearance, I'll evade whoever he *does* send. I'll disappear—until I conjure myself up some night in one of the dark corners of his bedroom. And then—I told him—I'll show him how a covert-assassination op is done right. No one will ever know it was me—except for him. I'll make sure *he* knows."

Nell shivered. "But you're only bluffing, right? I mean, you wouldn't really just kill him…would you?"

He released her and went back to his work with the C-4 explosives. Silence. A silent affirmative. Dear God, what was he planning to do?

"I know you believe Garvin killed Jake, but Billy, God! What if you're wrong? You'd be killing an innocent man!"

"I'm not wrong. Garvin's credit-card records show him paying for a plane ticket to Hong Kong three days before the fighting started between Sherman and Kim. There's no record of him leaving Hong Kong during that time, but there wouldn't be. He would've paid cash and made sure that any side trips he took wouldn't show up on his passport."

"That's all circumstantial evidence."

He gave her a long look. "Maybe. But when you put them together with a few more facts I dug up, such as that the Hong Kong trip was a week before his wedding to Senator McBride's daughter... He didn't try to claim the trip as a business expense on his tax return, and I find it hard to believe he took a three-day vacation in the middle of the week, five days before his wedding to the daughter of the man who would secure him the Vice Presidential nomination in two years' time."

"Yeah, okay, that looks bad, but it's not *proof*—"

"I've also found out that Dexter Lancaster has been Mark Garvin's tennis partner for fifteen years."

Nell sat back. "What?"

Crash nodded. "I figure Garvin was being blackmailed by John Sherman for a while—probably since he won the senate seat last November. Certainly by the time he attended Jake and Daisy's wedding. My bet is that six months later, after everything hit the fan, Garvin remembered that his pal Dex couldn't take his eyes off you and—"

"Wait a minute. Are you telling me that you think *Dexter* is somehow involved in Jake's murder?" Nell felt dizzy.

"No." He shook his head. "Actually, I don't. Not knowingly, anyway. But I think if you ask Lancaster, he'll admit that Garvin was the one who urged him to call you. You'll probably also find out that it was Garvin's idea to steer you in the direction of working for Amie and the theater. You'll also find that the theater recently received a private donation to help defray the cost of a personal assistant for its director—Amie. If you want, I'll get my laptop and show you the records that state the name of the donor. Guess who? Mark Garvin."

"But...why?" She didn't understand.

"My thinking is that Garvin was well-connected enough to know that an investigation had been started. He probably knew about the deposition Kim's wife gave, found out Jake would be handling the file. The fact that he was responsible for starting a war wouldn't have gone over real well when the time came to run for Vice President. And that's not even taking into consideration whatever despicable thing he did back in 1972—whatever Sherman was blackmailing him about. He had a lot to lose.

"Garvin was probably covering his bases by keeping track of you," he continued. "He probably suspected that you and I had something going and figured that keeping track of you could possibly be the only way he'd even remotely keep track of me."

"He must've been disappointed."

"He figured—correctly—that I would be his biggest threat if he had to take Jake out. One thing I'm still not sure of, though, is if he knew that I worked for Jake as part of the Gray Group. And if he *did* know, how did he find out?"

"I haven't said anything to *anyone,* Billy. I swear it. I wouldn't do that."

"I know you wouldn't."

He was quiet for a moment, but then he looked up at her again. "So all that—along with his message agreeing to meet me—makes Garvin look extremely guilty. I still haven't figured out what leverage he used to make Captain Lovett and the Possum sell out. But that's something I may never know."

"You'll definitely never know if you kill Garvin," Nell said hotly. "You'll never get his confession, either. And you may never find the proof you need to clear your name."

He glanced up at her. "Even if I'm cleared of all charges, my good name's gone. It'll always be connected to betrayal, no matter what I do. There's always going to be this cloud of doubt hovering over me. How much did Hawken really know? Why did he let those killers into the admiral's house?" He laughed, but there was no humor in it. "Truth is, I am at least partly responsible for Jake's death."

Nell couldn't believe what she was hearing.

"But this is all moot," he continued. "Garvin *is* going to show up here at dawn. He's not going to risk having me hunt him down—particularly since I led him to believe I'd enjoy it. And on top of that," he added, "he knows that I don't have a whole hell of a lot to lose."

He was serious. He honestly didn't believe that despite everything he'd been through, he had more to lose than most men even started with.

"If I agree to go to this SEAL's house," she said slowly, "What's-his-name's house—McCoy's—then you've got to promise me that you'll be careful."

"I'll be careful," he told her. "But…"

She looked at him in disbelief. "How can you dangle a 'but' off a promise to be careful?"

He wasn't even remotely amused. In fact, when he looked up at her again, his eyes seemed distant, his expression detached. "Whatever happens with Garvin—whoever's left standing when the smoke clears—it will mean only one thing to you. If he's the one who's still standing, then you've got to run and hide because you'll be next on his list. But I'm telling you right now that I'm going to do everything humanly possible to make sure that's not going to happen. By this time tomorrow, you're not going to have to worry about Garvin anymore."

Nell stood up, wiping the seat of her pants with her hands. "Good. Then let's make a date to have dinner tomorrow night when you come back from—"

"I won't be coming back," he said quietly.

She stared at him. "But you said—"

"There's no tomorrow night, Nell. Whatever happens with Garvin," he said again, "it won't change the fact that we have no future. *I* have no future. Even if I live, I won't come back."

Nell was aghast. Won't, he'd said, not *can't*. Even if he

lived, he *wouldn't* come back. He didn't want to come back for her. "Oh," she said, suddenly feeling very small.

He cursed. "You only wanted one more night, remember? It was sex, Nell. It was *great* sex, but it wasn't anything more than that. Don't you dare turn it into something that it's not."

She couldn't breathe. "I'm sorry," she somehow managed to say even though there wasn't any air left in her lungs. "I just…" She shook her head.

"I thought I'd made my feelings clear," he said tightly.

"You did," she whispered. He had. He'd been up-front and direct about the impossibility of a relationship right from the very beginning. "I guess I just let my imagination run away with me for a while."

He didn't look up from the work he was doing, building bombs that would allegedly protect him from a man who would go to great lengths to see him dead.

"You still have to promise that you'll be careful," she told him before she turned away.

THE COLORFUL LIGHTS OF a Christmas tree shimmered through the side window of Blue McCoy's house. It was a nice house, quietly unassuming, rather like the man himself.

Crash had driven around the block four times but had seen no sign of surveillance vehicles. He'd finally parked on a different side street, cutting through a neighbor's yard to approach Blue's house from the back.

Blue was at home—he could see him passing back and forth in front of the kitchen window. Cooking dinner. Crash hadn't known that Blue could cook.

There was a lot he didn't know about Blue McCoy, he realized, crouched there between a pickup truck and a little subcompact car that were parked in the drive alongside the man's house.

He felt Nell shift beside him. "What are we waiting for?"

Good question.

He motioned for her to hang back as he approached the back door. He could tell from one quick glance that the door didn't open into the kitchen, but rather into a smaller area—a mudroom.

The door was locked, but he had the tools to get through it in about fifteen seconds. It opened and he nodded to Nell, gesturing with his head for her to follow him.

He drew his sidearm and slipped inside the house.

Crash could smell the fragrant aroma of onions sautéing. Blue was standing at the counter, with his back to him, chopping green peppers on a cutting board.

He didn't turn around, didn't even stop chopping as he said in his deep Southern drawl, "We missed y'all at Harvard's wedding."

Crash held his weapon on the other man as he spoke from the shadows. "I sent my regrets. I was out of the country."

Blue set down his knife and turned around. His quiet gaze took Crash in from the top of his too-long hair to the tomato-juice stains on the knees of his black BDUs. He focused for about a millisecond on the barrel of Crash's sidearm, but then dismissed it. He knew as well as Crash did that the weapon was a formality. Crash was no more prepared to use it on Blue than he was likely to use it on himself or Nell.

"Ma'am." Blue nodded a greeting at Nell before he turned back to Crash. "Before I invite you in, Hawken, I've got to ask you just one question. Did you kill, or conspire to kill, Admiral Robinson?"

"No."

"Okay." The blond-haired SEAL nodded, turning back to stir the onions that were sizzling in a saucepan on the stove. "I was wondering when you were going to show up. Why don't you sit at the table? Stay low, the window's got no shade."

Crash didn't move.

"I'm guessing you're here because everyone and their dim-witted second cousin is watching Cowboy's place," Blue continued. He laughed as he added the chopped peppers to the pot and stirred the vegetables together. "Every time that boy goes anywhere, there's about four cars behind him. At first he thought it was funny, but now it's kind of getting on his nerves." He turned back to Crash. "So what can I do to help?"

"Wait a sec," Crash said. "Rewind. You ask me *one question,* and that's it? I say no, I didn't kill Jake, and you're satisfied?"

Blue considered that for a moment, then nodded. "That's right. I just wanted to hear you say what I already knew. Everyone in the Spec War business with half a brain can see as clear as day that you've been set up." He laughed in disgust. "Unfortunately it looks as if Alpha Squad is the only team with more than half a brain these days."

"You understand that by helping me, you'll be an accomplice."

"But you didn't do anything wrong. To believe that—and I do—and do nothing to help you…now, *that* would be a real crime." Blue lifted one shoulder in a shrug. "Besides, I figure you wouldn't be here if you weren't close to catching whoever did kill the admiral. Am I right?"

Crash still didn't move. He didn't lower his weapon, he didn't do much more than breathe as Blue added several cans of whole tomatoes and some spices to the saucepan.

Blue glanced at him again. "I can understand how you might be a little paranoid right about now, so I won't take that weapon you're holding on me personally. But I have to tell you that—"

"You may not hold it personally, but I sure as hell do." There, in the door to the dining room, stood a pretty, dark-haired woman wearing a well-tailored pantsuit and holding an automatic pistol in her hand, aimed directly at Crash.

"Lucy will," Blue finished.

Crash hadn't heard her come in. He'd heard no cars approaching or pulling into the driveway. He hadn't heard the front door open or shut.

But of course, she'd been home all along. There'd been two cars in the drive when he'd approached. He'd made the mistake of assuming that simply because Blue was cooking dinner, his wife wasn't home.

That would teach him to make assumptions based on gender-role stereotypes in the future. Except he didn't *have* a future.

Crash lifted his sidearm higher, holding it on Blue. "Please put down your weapon, Mrs. McCoy."

The brunette's mouth tightened. "I'm going to count to three, and if *you* don't—"

Blue moved, crossing the kitchen in two very long steps, stepping directly in front of his wife's deadly-looking pistol.

"Everything's fine," he said to her, gently pushing the barrel down toward the floor. "You can put that away. Hawken's a friend of mine."

"Everything's *not* fine! There's a man in our kitchen holding a gun on you!"

"He'll put it away."

"I can't do that," Crash said tightly.

"It looks like he can't put his weapon away right now," Blue told his wife. "I'm not sure I'd be able to do it myself if I were in his shoes." He turned back to Crash. "Can you do me a favor and at least lower it?"

Crash nodded, his eyes never leaving Lucy's handgun. As Lucy reholstered her weapon, he lowered his.

"Good." Blue kissed his wife gently on the lips before he went back to the stove. "Lucy, meet Crash Hawken. You've heard me talk of him plenty of times."

Lucy's brown eyes widened as she turned to look at Crash again. "*You're* Lieutenant Hawken?"

"Crash, this is Lucy, my wife," Blue continued. "She's a detective with the Coronado police."

Crash swore softly.

"And you must be Nell Burns," Blue greeted Nell with a smile. "On the news, they're saying you were abducted. But it looks to me like you're here of your own free will."

Nell nodded. "Billy and I both thought that I'd be safer with him—after the second attempt was made on my life."

Blue lifted his eyebrows as he looked at Crash. "*Billy,* huh?"

"Look, we're just going to turn around and walk out of here," Crash said. Blue McCoy's wife was a police detective. His current streak of dismal luck was absolutely unending.

Blue turned to his wife. "Yankee, you better plug your ears, because I'm about to ask a suspected felon to join us for dinner."

"Actually, I'm long overdue for a soak in the tub," Lucy said. "And your friend looks like he's got someplace he needs to be in a hurry." She nodded to Nell and Crash. "Nice meeting you, Lieutenant. Or was it Captain? I'm sorry, I've never been very good with names. I've already forgotten yours."

As Crash watched, she disappeared into the darkness of the other room. He could hear the sound of her footsteps going up a flight of stairs.

He could sense Nell standing right beside him, her anxiety nearly palpable. He ached to reach out and slip his arm around her shoulder, to pull her in close for an embrace. But doing that would undermine everything he'd worked so hard to do this afternoon—telling her how he wouldn't come back, making it sound as if he had a choice when the real truth was he honestly didn't think he'd live to see another sunset.

And touching her would also undermine all that he'd

done today to separate from the tornado of emotions that threatened to throw him into uncharted territory.

"Tell me what you need me to do," Blue said simply.

Crash glanced in the direction in which Lucy had disappeared.

"She's not calling the SWAT Team, I promise. She knows we're friends."

"Are we?"

Blue turned back to stir his tomato sauce. "I thought so."

Crash looked at Nell, and forced himself to detach even more completely than he had earlier that afternoon, after he'd allowed himself one more kiss. One *last* kiss. This was one of the most difficult decisions of his life, but he knew it had to be done. "I need a place for Nell to stay that's safe," he said, as ready as he'd ever be to put the one person he cared more about than anyone on the planet into another man's hands.

The blond-haired SEAL nodded as he turned back to meet his gaze. "I'll see to that."

Nell's throat felt tight. Just like that, Crash was handing her over. Just like that, he was going to walk out of the house, into the darkness. And just like that, she was never going to see him again.

"Are you set for supplies?" Blue asked. "Ammunition?"

"I could use an extra brick of C-4, if you've got any lying around."

Blue didn't blink. "You know we're not allowed to bring that stuff home."

"I know the rules. I also know that when a team is called out on an op in the middle of the night, there's not always time to go back to the base to pick up supplies."

Blue nodded. "I can spare half a block. But unless you're intending to take out more than a single house, that ought to be enough."

Nell couldn't believe what she had just heard. A half

a block of C-4 could "take out" an entire house? Crash had already used at least three entire blocks, strategically planting the bombs he had made around the edges of the clearing surrounding the cabin. If a half a block could destroy all that, then surely he'd *already* used enough to blow up the entire mountainside.

She'd realized with icy-cold shock that she'd figured out Plan B.

Crash was prepared to blow himself up if necessary, in order to take down Commander Mark Garvin.

CHAPTER SIXTEEN

THE WARM GOLDEN LIGHT of the kitchen seemed suddenly washed-out and much too bright. And Nell's ears were roaring so loudly, she almost couldn't hear as Blue said, "It's locked in the basement. I'll get it and be right back."

He vanished through the same door his wife had disappeared through earlier.

Nell fumbled for one of the kitchen chairs, nearly knocking it over in her haste to sit down. She actually had to put her head between her legs and close her eyes tightly to keep from falling over.

"Are you all right?"

Crash had crouched next to her. She could sense him, smell his familiar scent, hear the concern in his voice, but he didn't touch her. She didn't expect him to.

She shook her head no. "I'm in love with you." She opened her eyes and lifted her head slightly to find herself gazing directly into his eyes. Her words had shocked him. Her blunt non sequitur had penetrated the emotional force field he'd set up around himself. "I've been in love with you ever since that night you made me go sledding. You remember that night, don't you?"

He stood up, moving away from her. "I'm sorry, I don't."

She sat up, indignation replacing dizziness. "How could someone who's such a bad liar specialize in covert ops?"

He shook his head. "Nell—"

"Let me refresh your memory," she told him. "That

was the night you told me about Daisy coming to get you from that summer camp. Remember? That was the night you told me how it had felt to know, to *really* know that Daisy and Jake both wanted you around. You told me how strange it had felt to know that you were loved. Totally. Unconditionally."

He moved closer to the door, and she stood up, following him, angry and upset enough not to care anymore that she was making him uncomfortable. This could well be the last time she ever spoke to him. If he had his way, it would be. Because—oh God!—he believed that in order to bring down Garvin, he was going to have to die.

"Well, guess what?" she said, stepping in front of him so that he was forced to look at her. "Jake and Daisy are gone, but I'm here to carry on. I love you unconditionally. And I want you to come back to me after this is over."

To her total shock, she saw that there were tears in his eyes. Tears, and absolute misery. "I didn't want this to happen. This is *exactly* what I was trying to avoid." He ran his hands down his face, trying hard to get back into control. "If you love me, then I'm going to hurt you. And God help me, Nell, I don't want to hurt you."

Back in control was the last place Nell wanted him to be. She couldn't believe she'd managed to break through his detachment as much as she already had. She pushed, trying to see more, to get more from him. "So don't hurt me. How are you going to hurt me?"

He lowered his voice. "The odds of my surviving this altercation are low. I've known that from the start. If you love me—and please, Nell, don't love me—then I'm going to hurt you the same way Daisy hurt Jake." He met her gaze and she knew at last that she had uncovered the truth. He was doing unto others the way he wished they would do unto him. He was so terrified of losing someone he loved, he tried to keep himself from loving, he tried to shut all his feelings down. And he'd tried to keep her from loving him, to prevent *her* from being hurt, as well.

Nell reached for him, touching his arms, his shoulders. "Oh, my God, is that really what you think? That Daisy hurt Jake by dying?"

His voice was ragged. "I know she did. If Jake had lived, he still wouldn't be over her, he still would be in pain, missing her every day for the rest of his life."

"Yes, Daisy made Jake hurt. Yes, he missed her right up to the moment he drew his last breath, but think of all she gave him along with that pain. Think of all those years, all the laughter they shared. I've never known two people who were as happy as they were. Do you really, *honestly* believe that Jake would've traded all that joy simply to avoid the pain he felt at the end?"

Nell touched the unrelenting lines of his face. "I can tell you absolutely that he would not have traded even one single moment, because I wouldn't trade, either. If I could, I wouldn't choose to go back and keep myself from falling in love with you. I don't care, even if you *are* hell-bent on killing yourself."

She stood on tiptoe, pulling his head down to kiss the grim line of his mouth. "There's one more kiss I'll always remember," she told him. She kissed him again, longer this time, lingering. "One more moment I'll cherish forever."

She kissed him a third time, and with a groan, he pulled her close, kissing her with all the passion and longing and sweet, sweet emotion he'd tried so hard to keep buried deep inside.

"Please," Nell whispered as he held her so tightly she could barely breathe. "Come back to me." She was begging again. This man had the power to force her to abandon her pride, force her to her knees. "Is avenging Jake's death really worth losing your own life?"

"Is that what you think I'm doing?" He pulled back to

look at her, searching her eyes. "Don't you know I'm doing this for *you?*"

She shook her head, not understanding.

"Unless Garvin is in custody with absolute proof connecting him to his crimes, or unless he's dead, I'd never know for certain that you were safe."

She gripped his arms. "I'd be safe if you were with me."

An avalanche of emotions crossed his face. "I can't ask you to do that—to come away with me, to run and hide, to spend the rest of your life hiding."

"Try asking!"

"That's no way to live!"

She wanted to shake him. "Getting yourself killed isn't living either, in case you haven't noticed!"

He shook his head. "This way I'll know you're safe."

"So you're doing this for me?" She couldn't keep her eyes from brimming with tears. "You're telling me that you're willing to die. For *me.*"

"Yes."

"Why?"

He kissed her and she knew that he was telling her why. He loved her. He couldn't say the words, but she knew it to be true.

"If you're willing to die for me," she asked him, her heart in her throat, "then why won't you *live* for me?"

He just looked at her for several long seconds as Nell prayed her words would make him stop the chain of events he'd already set in motion.

But then he shook his head, turning away. Following his gaze, Nell saw that Blue had come back into the kitchen.

As Crash stepped back, away from her, Nell knew with a sudden wrenching pain that she'd lost. He wasn't going to stay. And he wasn't going to come back.

She pushed her pain away, refusing to stand there weeping as the man she loved walked away from her for the last time. She forced everything she was feeling, all that terrible emptiness and loss, far, far back, deep inside of her. She'd have plenty of time later on to mourn.

She'd have all the rest of her life.

She watched as Crash took the C-4 Blue had wrapped up for him and slipped it into one of his pockets. She watched as the two men shook hands. Did Blue know it was the last time he was going to see his friend? She watched, feeling oddly detached and remarkably in control as Crash paused in front of her.

Was this how he did it? Was this how he stayed so cool and reserved and distanced? It almost didn't hurt.

He kissed her again, his mouth sweet and warm, and she almost didn't cling to him for just another few seconds longer.

And when he walked out the door and vanished into the night, she almost didn't cry.

CRASH LEFT HIS CAR OUT by the main highway and traveled the last ten miles to the cabin on foot.

He sat in the darkness outside the cabin as one hour slipped into two, watching and waiting—making sure that no one had approached the area while he had been gone.

He went into the cabin cautiously, then searched it to be doubly certain he was alone up here.

He *was* alone.

In fact, he couldn't remember the last time he'd been so totally alone.

Normally, he didn't mind sitting quietly with his thoughts. But tonight, his thoughts wouldn't behave.

He couldn't stop thinking about Nell, about what she had said.

If you're willing to die for me, then why won't you live for me?

I love you, unconditionally.

Unconditionally.

When he closed his eyes, he saw her, her face alight, laughing at something Daisy or Jake had said. He saw her, her eyes filled with tears at the thought that she'd ruined one of Daisy's last sunsets. He saw her, blazing with passion as she leaned forward to kiss him. He saw her, that first time he'd seen her again in close to a year, sitting in the visitors' room at the jail, hands folded neatly on the table in front of her, her expression guarded, but her eyes giving away everything she was feeling, everything she hadn't dared to admit aloud until just hours ago.

She loved him. Unconditionally.

And he knew it was true. If she could sit there, loving him even as she visited him in jail, an accused murderer, then she truly did love him unconditionally.

As Crash got out his roll of wire and laid out his tools to rig the last of the explosives that would guarantee Garvin's death—and his own death as well—he stopped for a moment.

Because when he closed his eyes, if he concentrated really hard, he could see a glimmer—just a tiny flicker—of his future.

If he didn't die here this dawn, he *could* have a future. It might not have been the future he'd always imagined, working for the Gray Group as a SEAL until he hit his peak, then moving into more standard career as a SEAL instructor until he was too old to do the job right.

He'd always figured he'd be with the Teams, or he'd be dead.

But now when he closed his eyes, he could see a shadowy picture of himself, a few years from now, with Nell standing at his side.

Loving him unconditionally, whether he was a SEAL or working nights at the counter of a 7-Eleven. What he did didn't matter to her. And Crash realized that it wouldn't matter to him, either. Not as long as she was there when he came home.

He looked down at the C-4, at his own private cup of hemlock, and he knew in that instant, without a single doubt, that he did *not* want to die today.

He had been wrong. He *wasn't* expendable, after all.

He should have asked Blue McCoy and the rest of Alpha Squad for help.

It would've have been a whole lot easier.

Crash stood up. It was too late to contact Blue, but it wasn't too late to do a little rewiring.

He smiled for the first time in hours.

Maybe his luck was finally about to change.

NELL COULDN'T STAND IT another second.

She put down her fork, done pushing the pasta around her plate, done pretending that she had any kind of appetite at all. "He's going to die if we don't do something."

Blue McCoy glanced across the table at his wife before putting his own fork down. He knew Nell was talking about Crash. "I'm not sure exactly what it is we *can* do at this point."

In a low voice, Nell told the SEAL about all the C-4 that Crash had rigged, about the cabin, about the message to Senator Garvin, about *everything*. She didn't need to speak of the low odds of Crash's survival. Blue had already figured that out.

"There's got to be a way for Billy to beat Garvin," she said. "To implicate him in Jake's death, and to stay alive, as well. But he's going to need help. Lots of help."

As she watched, Blue glanced again at his wife.

"This sounds more like your department than mine, Superman," Lucy said softly.

"You told Billy how your squad—Alpha Squad—all thought he was being set up," Nell persisted. "Who do I have to call to ask them to help?"

Blue lifted one hand. "Whoa. Do we even know where Crash is?"

Nell's heart was pounding. Was he actually considering her outrageous request? "Yes. I could find my way back there, I'm sure of it. I could lead you there."

Blue was silent for a moment. "It's one thing for *me* to offer to help a man I personally trust," he finally said. "It's a whole other story to bring Alpha Squad in. If this goes wrong…"

"Billy spoke so highly of the Alpha Squad," Nell said. Her heart was beating so hard she could hardly speak. Please, God, let them agree to help. "If the men of Alpha Squad have even one-tenth the respect for him that he has for them, how can they refuse to help?"

"You're asking a lot." Lucy leaned forward, her brown eyes sober. "They'd be putting their careers—not to mention their lives—on the line."

Blue pushed back his chair and stood up. "I'll call Joe Cat—Captain Catalanotto," he told Nell. "I can't promise anything, but…"

He reached for the phone.

Nell held on to the edge of the table, allowing herself to dare to hope.

GARVIN APPEARED, right on schedule.

Dawn was breaking, but the west side of the mountain was still in heavy shadow. As Crash watched, Garvin drove right up to the cabin, the headlights of his car still on, still necessary.

He'd brought a half a dozen shooters with him, but they'd come in a different vehicle and parked down the road—as if they didn't think Crash would notice them, creeping through the woods, not quite as noisy as a pack of Boy Scouts on a camping trip, but pretty ridiculously close.

Garvin was a tall, handsome man with a full head of dark hair. He didn't look capable of starting a war or conspiring to kill a U.S. Navy Admiral, but Crash knew that looks could often be deceiving. As he watched, Garvin climbed out of his car, hands held out to show that they were empty, that he was unarmed.

Crash, too, had left his weapon inside the cabin. But he was far from unarmed. "Call your shooters off."

Garvin pretended not to understand. "I came alone, just as you said."

Crash stepped forward, opening his jacket, letting Senator Garvin, a former commander in the U.S. Navy, get a good look at all of the C-4 plastic explosive he'd rewired and attached directly to his combat vest. He also showed the man the trigger mechanism that he'd rigged. He'd turned himself into a walking bomb.

"Call your shooters off," he said again. "If one of them makes a mistake and shoots me, my thumb will come off this button, and this entire hillside will be one big fireball."

Garvin raised his voice. "He's got a bomb. Don't shoot. Don't anyone shoot. Do you understand?"

"There now," Crash said. "Isn't the truth so much more refreshing?"

"You are one crazy son of a bitch."

"Hey, I'm not the one who wants to be Vice President."

Garvin was backing away, slowly but surely, inch by inch.

Crash laughed at him. "Are you trying to sneak away from me? Turn around and look down the trail," he ordered the older man. "See that tree with the white marker tied around it? I tied it there, just for you. Can you see the one I'm talking about, *way* over there?"

Garvin nodded jerkily.

"That's the edge of my kill zone," Crash told him. "Start there and draw a circle with me in the middle. Anyone and anything inside that circle is going straight to hell when I lift my thumb from this trigger."

Garvin's face was chalky as he realized that edging

away wasn't going to do him much good. "You'd never do it."

Crash lowered his voice, leaning forward until he was mere inches from Garvin's face. "Is that a dare?" He raised the trigger so the man could see his thumb, started to move his thumb—

"No!"

Crash nodded, backing down. "Well, then. It seems like I've got something you want—your life. And since you've got something *I* want—the truth—I think we can probably—"

"I *do* have something you want," Garvin interrupted. Sweat was rolling down his face. "I have something you want bad. I have that girl. Nell Burns."

Crash didn't move, but something, *something* must have flickered in his eyes. Some uncertainty. Some doubt.

"Am I bluffing? That's what you're thinking right now, isn't it?" Garvin somehow managed to smile. "That's a very good question."

"You don't have her."

"Don't I? Maybe you're right. Maybe I didn't send Mr. Sarkowski into your SEAL friend's house. Maybe he didn't put a bullet into your friend's brain. Maybe he doesn't have the girl with him right now. And maybe he's not waiting for 7:00 a.m. to come—knowing that if I don't show up by then, he'll get to do whatever he wants with your girlfriend. Poor thing."

Crash didn't move. Garvin was bluffing. He *had* to be bluffing. There was no way Sarkowski could have gotten past Blue. No *way*.

"The real beauty of it is that the ballistics reports will show that the bullet that killed her came from *your* gun," Garvin continued. "So unless you disarm that bomb you're wearing—"

"No." Crash turned to look at him. "You don't know it, but by telling me you've got Nell you lost the game. I just won. Check and mate, scumbag." He kept his voice low, his face expressionless, his eyes empty, soulless. "Because if you have Nell, I truly have nothing left to lose. If you have Nell, I'd just as soon die as long as it means that I'd kill you, too."

Everything he was saying had been true. Just hours ago, it *had* been true. He could say it with a chilling believability because he knew exactly what it felt like to be ready to die.

"Here's what I'm thinking," he told Garvin. "If I disarm this bomb, you'll kill me, and then you'll kill Nell, too, anyway. Hell, if Sarkowski really *does* have her, she's probably already dead. So you see, Senator, you've just severed the last of my ties to this world. I have no reason at all not to start my search for inner peace in the afterlife right now." He smiled tightly. "And I know I'll go to heaven, because my last act on this earth will be ridding the world of *you*."

Garvin bought it. He swallowed it whole. Every last word. "All right. Jesus. I *was* bluffing. I *don't* have the girl. Christ, you're a crazy bastard."

Crash shook his head. "I don't believe you," he said in the same quiet voice. "In fact, I think you already told Sarkowski to kill her." He moved his thumb on the trigger.

"I didn't—I swear!" Garvin was nearly wetting himself with panic.

Crash reached into his jacket and took out his cell phone. "If you want to live, here's what you've got to do." With his spare thumb he dialed Admiral Stonegate's direct number. It would be after 9:00 a.m. in D.C. right now. The admiral would be in.

"Stonegate," the admiral rasped.

"Sir, this is Lt. William Hawken. Please record this conversation." Crash held the phone out to Garvin. "Tell him everything. Start with the money you got illegally in

'Nam, and the house you bought with it. Tell him about your meeting with Kim and how you killed Jake Robinson to keep it covered up. Tell him *everything*, or I'll be more than happy to escort you straight to hell."

Garvin took the phone and began to talk, his voice so low that Crash had to step closer to hear him.

He'd made over one hundred thousand dollars selling confiscated weapons back to the Viet Cong. It was a one-time thing, a temporary, momentary lapse in judgment. John Sherman had orchestrated the deal. He'd merely had to look the other way to earn more money than he'd ever dreamed of having.

But then just last year, after he'd won the senate seat, he'd been contacted by John Sherman and blackmailed. Over the next few months, he'd paid nearly five times the money he'd made illegally, with no end in sight. He'd finally gone to Hong Kong in an attempt to rid himself of Sherman once and for all. He'd worn his old naval uniform when he'd met with Kim and led the man to believe he was acting on behalf of the United States. He'd had no idea that the battle between the two rival gangs would get so out of control. He'd only wanted Sherman dead. He'd had no idea thousands of innocent people would die, as well.

He knew when word came down that Jake Robinson was looking into the matter that he had to stop the investigation at the source. He was in over his head, but it was too late to stop. He set Crash Hawken up for the fall, had the ballistics report falsified—and it would have worked, too, if Hawken hadn't been so damned hard to kill.

On and on he talked, giving details—times, dates, names. The three men who'd been part of the alleged SEAL Team assigned to protect Jake had been compatriots of Sheldon Sarkowski's. Captain Lovett and the Possum hadn't been part of the conspiracy to kill the admiral. They'd been told that Admiral Robinson had been acting oddly since the death of his wife. They were told they were being sent in to make certain he didn't harm himself or become a threat to national security. They'd been told that the three strangers on the team were psyche experts—men in white coats—who were going to restrain the admiral and bring him to a special hospital. Lovett had been ordered not to tell Crash the "real" reason they were going out to the farm. The entire affair had been a serpent's nest of lies.

Finally, Garvin handed the phone back to Crash. "The admiral wants to speak with you," he said. But then he dropped the phone, and the batteries came out. By the time he got them back in, the line had been disconnected.

It didn't matter. Crash pocketed the phone. "Tell your shooters to come forward and surrender their weapons."

Garvin turned toward the woods and repeated Crash's order.

Nothing moved.

The silence was eerie and the hair on the back of Crash's neck suddenly stood on end. There *had* been at least six men out there, he *knew* there had been. But now they were all gone. The rising sun was starting to thin out the shadows, but the early morning was misty, making it even harder to see.

The strangest thing was, Crash hadn't heard anyone leave. Yet he'd heard them all approach. It didn't seem possible, or likely, that they'd been able to leave without his being aware of it.

"Tell them again," Crash ordered.

"Come forward and surrender your weapons!"

Still no movement.

But then a man stood up, stepping from the cover of the bushes. It was as if he'd been conjured out of thin air. One moment he wasn't there, and the next he was.

It was Blue McCoy, his face streaked with black-and-green greasepaint. "We've taken care of the opposition and already confiscated their weapons," he told Crash.

We?

Crash turned, and not one or two but *five* men appeared silently from the woods. SEALs. He recognized them first as SEALs by the way they moved. But then he realized they were the men of Alpha Squad. He recognized Harvard beneath his camouflage paint. And the captain—Joe Cat. Lucky, Bobby and Wes—they were all there. All except Cowboy, who no doubt was still being trailed by FInCOM and NIS.

They moved to stand behind him in a silent show of force. And with the streaks of black and green and brown on their faces, they put on one hell of a show.

And then, damned if Nell didn't step out of the bushes, too. She was actually carrying an M-16 that was nearly as big as she was. She had greasepaint on her face as well, but as she moved closer, he saw that her eyes were filled with tears.

"Don't be mad at me." Nell wanted to touch him. She wanted to throw herself into his arms, but she was holding this huge piece of hardware, and he was still covered in C-4. "Please, will you disarm that bomb now?"

Crash looked at Garvin. "Looks like you *were* bluffing about Nell." He held up the trigger and released his thumb. Nothing exploded. Nothing happened at all. "I was bluffing, too."

He looked at Nell. "I was only bluffing," he repeated, as if he wanted to make absolutely certain that she knew that.

He took off his jacket, and peeled off his combat vest and the heavy weight of all that C-4.

Garvin stared at Crash. And then he started to laugh. "You son of a bitch."

Captain Catalanotto stepped forward, motioning to Garvin. "Let's get this piece of garbage into custody."

But Garvin stepped back, away from him. "You still don't win," he told Crash. "I disconnected that call to Stonegate before I started to talk. It's your word against

mine. You have no proof of *any* wrongdoing on my part."
He looked at the captain and the rest of Alpha Squad.
"You'll go to jail—all of you. *He's* the one you should be
arresting. He's the one wanted for murder and treason."

Crash reached down into one of the pockets of his
combat vest and pulled out a hand-size tape recorder—
one of those little things people used to record letters and
take dictation. "Sorry to disappoint you, Senator, but I've
got every word you said on tape. This game *is* over. You
lose."

The game *was* over. And Nell had won. She knew she'd
won from the look in Crash's eyes as he turned to smile at
her.

But then, as if in slow motion, Garvin drew a gun from
the pocket of his jacket.

And, in slow motion, Nell saw the early-morning sun
glinting off the metal barrel as he aimed the weapon directly at Crash.

She heard herself shout as, in the space of one single
heartbeat, Garvin fired the gun.

The force of the bullet hit Crash square in the chest and
he was flung back, his head flopping like a rag doll's as he
was pushed down and back, into the dirt.

Crash was dead. He had to be dead. Even if he *was* still
alive, there was no way they could get him to a hospital in
time. The nearest medical center was miles away. It would
take them hours to get there and he'd surely bleed to death
on the way.

She ran toward him and was the first at his side as
the SEALs disarmed Garvin and wrestled him to the
ground.

Crash was struggling to breathe, fighting to suck in
air, but she didn't find the massive outpouring of blood
that she'd expected. She took his hand, holding it tightly.
"Please don't die," she told him. "Please, Billy, don't
you die...."

Harvard—the big African-American SEAL—knelt in the dirt, on the other side of Crash's body. He tore open Crash's shirt and she closed her eyes, afraid of what she would see.

"Status?" another man asked. It was the squad's captain.

"He got the wind knocked out of him," Harvard's rich voice said. "Could be he's got a broken rib, but other than that, as soon as he catches his breath, he should be fine."

He should be…?

Nell opened her eyes. "Fine? He's got a bullet in his chest!"

"What he's got is a bullet in his body armor—his bulletproof vest." Harvard smiled at her. "Just be careful not to hug little Billy too hard, all right?"

Crash was wearing a bulletproof vest. She could see the bullet embedded in it, flattened. He *had* been bluffing with the C-4. She hadn't quite believed it—until now. He'd had no real intention of blowing himself up along with Garvin. If he had, he wouldn't have bothered wearing a bulletproof vest.

He was alive—and he wanted to be.

Nell couldn't stop herself. She burst into tears.

Crash struggled to sit up. "Hey." His voice was whispery and weak. He reached for her, and she slipped into his arms. "Aren't you always telling me that you never cry— that you're not the type to always cry?"

She lifted her head to look at him. "This must be just another fluke."

He laughed, then winced. "Ouch."

"Will it hurt if I kiss you?"

"Yeah," Crash said quietly, aware that Alpha Squad had taken Garvin away, that he and Nell were alone in the clearing. He touched her cheek, marveling at the picture she made with that war paint on her face. Nell, his unadventurous Nell, who'd rather stay home and sit by the fire with a book than risk getting her feet cold, was cammied up and ready for battle. She'd done that for him, he realized. "It's always going to hurt a little bit when you kiss me. I'm always going to be scared to death of losing you."

"You can't lose me," she said fiercely. "So don't even try. I've got you, and I'm not going to let go."

Crash kissed her. "And if I ever leave you, it won't be because I want to."

Her eyes filled with fresh tears as she kissed him again.

"I don't know where I'm going from here," he pulled back to tell her bluntly. "Even if the Navy wants me back, I'm not sure the SEAL Teams will want anything to do with me. I *know* the Gray Group won't touch me after this. Too many people know my face now. And I also know I can't handle some backroom Navy desk job, so…"

"You don't have to decide any of that right now," she told him, smoothing his hair back from his face. "Give yourself some time. You haven't even let yourself properly mourn Jake."

"I feel like I…" He stopped himself, amazed at what he'd almost revealed, without even thinking. But now that he *was* thinking, he knew he had to say it. He *wanted* to say it. "I feel like I can't ask you to marry me without making sure you realize that right now my entire life is kind of in upheaval."

"*Kind of* in upheaval? That's *kind of* an understatement, don't you…"

Crash knew the moment when she realized exactly what he had said.

Ask you to marry me…

She started to cry again.

"Oh, my God," she said softly. "I know about the up-heaval. So you can. Ask me. I mean, if you want."

"You're crying again," he pointed out.

"This doesn't count," she told him. "Tears of happiness don't count."

Crash laughed. "Ouch!"

"Oh, God, I've got to stop making you laugh."

He caught her chin, holding her so that she had to look into his eyes. "No," he said. "Don't. Not ever, okay?"

"So…you love me because I make you laugh…"

Crash lost himself in the beautiful blue of her eyes. "No." He whispered the words he knew she wanted to hear, the words he could finally say aloud. "I love you… *and* you make me laugh." He kissed her, losing himself in the softness of her lips. "You know I'd die for you."

She fingered the edge of his bulletproof vest. "I know you'd live for me, too. That's much harder to do."

"So, do you want to—" his lips were dry and he moistened them "—marry me?" He realized how offhanded that sounded and quickly reworded it. "Please, will you marry me?"

Nell made a noise that sounded very much like an affirmative as she reached for him. He held her tightly, aware that she was crying. Again.

He tasted salt as he kissed her. "Was that a yes?"

"Yes." This time she was absolutely clear.

Crash kissed her again as the shadows finally shifted, as the sun finally cleared the mountain, bathing them in warmth.

And he knew that the next leg of his journey—and he hoped it was going to be a long, long stretch—was going to be made in the light.

CHAPTER SEVENTEEN

"WHERE ARE WE?" Crash asked.

The driver didn't answer. He simply opened the door and stood back so that Crash could climb out.

He snapped to attention, and Crash realized that there was an admiral standing by the front door of the building. An admiral. They'd sent an *admiral* to escort him to his debriefing…?

Crash was glad Nell had made him wear his dress uniform. The row of medals across his chest nearly rivaled those the admiral was wearing.

The admiral stepped forward, holding out his hand to shake. "Glad to finally meet you, Lieutenant Hawken. I'm Mac Forrest. I don't know why we haven't met before this."

Crash shook the older man's hand. Admiral Forrest was lean and wiry, with a thick shock of salt-and-pepper hair and blue eyes that looked far too young for a face with as many wrinkles as his had.

"Is this where the debriefing is being held?" Crash looked up at the elegant architecture of the stately old building as the admiral led him inside. He took off his hat as he looked around. The lobby was large and pristine, with a white-marble-tiled floor. "I don't think I've ever been here before."

Forrest led the way down a hall. "Actually, Lieutenant, not many people *have* been here before. This is a FInCOM safe house."

"I don't understand."

Mac Forrest stopped in front of a closed door. "Hold on to your hat, son. I've got an early Christmas present for you." He nodded at the door. "Go on in," he said as he turned and started down the hall. "I'll be back in a bit."

Crash watched him walk away, then looked at the door. It was a plain, oak door with an old-fashioned glass door-knob, like a giant glittering diamond. He reached out and turned it, and the door swung open.

He wasn't sure what he'd expected to see on the other side of that door, but he sure hadn't expected to see a bedroom.

It was decorated warmly, with rich, dark-colored curtains surrounding big windows that made the most of the weak December sunshine.

In the center of the room was a hospital bed, surrounded by monitors and medical equipment.

And in the center of the bed was Jake Robinson.

He looked pale and fragile, and he was still hooked up to quite a few of those monitors, with an IV drip in his arm, but he was very, very, *very* much alive.

Crash couldn't speak. Tears welled in his eyes. Jake was *alive!*

"Let me start by saying that I wanted to tell you," Jake said. "But it was a week before I was out of intensive care, and nearly another week before I was even aware that you didn't know I was still alive. And then you were gone and there was no way to let you know."

Crash closed the door behind him, fighting the emotion that threatened to choke him, to make him break down and cry like a baby. Detach. Separate. Distance…

What the hell was he doing?

This was *joy* he was feeling. This was incredible relief, heart-stopping happiness. Yes, he wanted to cry, but they would be good tears.

"I'm sorry you had to go through all that thinking that

I was dead," Jake said quietly. "Mac Forrest made the decision to release the news that I'd died. He thought I'd be safer that way."

Crash laughed, but it sounded kind of crazy, more like a sob than real laughter. "This is so unbelievably great." His voice broke. As he crossed to Jake, he pulled a chair over to the bed and clasped the older man's hand in both of his. "Are you really all right? You look like hell, like you've been hit by a truck."

If Jake noticed the tears that were brimming in his eyes, he didn't comment. "I'm going to be fine. It's going to take a little while, but the doctor says I'll be up and walking in no time. No permanent damage—a few more scars."

Crash shook his head. "I should have known. It was so easy to escape after the hearing. I should have realized I was being let go."

"They gave you a little bit of help, but not much. There were only a few people who were allowed to know I was alive." He squeezed Crash's hand. "Good job with Garvin. That was one hell of a tape you made."

"I'm lucky I had Alpha Squad there to back me up."

"Speaking of Alpha Squad—you met Mac Forrest on your way in?"

Crash nodded.

"Alpha Squad's under his command. He asked me to let you know that there's been a special request made for your reassignment. Captain Joe Catalanotto's asking for you to be placed on his team. He sent a personal note to Mac along with all the paperwork. These guys really want you to work with them."

Crash couldn't speak again. "I'm honored they want me," he finally said.

"I'm glad to see you finally got a haircut. The pictures they kept flashing of you on the news were pretty scary-looking."

Crash ran his hand back through his freshly cut hair. "Yeah, Nell likes it better this way, too."

"Nell." Jake said. "Nell. Would that be the same Nell who used to work for Daisy? Pretty girl? Great smile? Head over heels in love with you?"

"Don't be a jackass."

Jake grinned. "That's Admiral Jackass to you, Lieutenant."

"Jake, I can't tell you how glad I am that you're not dead."

"Back at you with that, kid. I'm also glad you finally opened your damn eyes and saw what you had right there in front of you, ready to fall into your lap." He paused. "You *did* manage to get yourself straightened out about Nell?"

"Actually, I haven't," Crash admitted. "I'm totally tied in knots when it comes to her." He smiled ruefully. "But I'm loving every minute of it. She's crazy enough to want me, and I'm sane enough to know that I'd be an idiot to let her get away. You know, she's marrying me on Christmas. Will you stand up for me, Jake—be my best man?"

Now there were tears in Jake's eyes, but still he tried to joke. "I'm not sure if I'm going to be standing by then."

"Can we have the wedding here? There's no law that says the best man literally has to stand."

Jake held his hand more tightly. "I'd love that. It would be an honor."

It had only been a year since Crash had done Jake that very same honor.

"Daisy always knew that Nell was perfect for me," Crash said quietly.

"Daisy was…extraordinarily good at seeing the truth, even when it was hidden from the rest of the world's view." Jake looked away, but not before Crash saw the flash of pain in his yes. "God, I still miss her so much."

"I'm sorry, I shouldn't have…"

Jake looked up at him. "Shouldn't have what? Said her

name? Remembered how much we both loved her? Are you kidding?"

"I don't know. I just thought—"

"Twenty years," Jake said. "I had her for over twenty years. I would've loved forty or sixty, even. But twenty wasn't bad. Twenty was a gift." He looked up, pinning Crash with the intensity of his gaze. "Make every minute count, kid. Pay attention and really make sure you experience every step of the dance. You never know how many times you'll get to go around the floor."

Crash nodded. "I'm glad you didn't die."

"Me too, Billy. Me too, kid."

IT WAS SUPPOSED TO BE a private wedding.

But when Nell's father opened the door to Jake Robinson's hospital room in the FInCOM safe house, there were so many people there, he and Nell almost couldn't fit inside.

Lucy and Blue McCoy were there. Harvard and his wife, P.J., were there, too. Even Captain Catalanotto and his family had come. Bobby and Wes and Lucky were present, as was Crash's swim buddy Cowboy and his new wife. Cowboy was holding a baby who was his exact spitting image—and he was holding the little boy comfortably, as if the kid were an extension of his arm. It was a pretty amazing sight to see.

But it wasn't half as amazing as the sight of Nell, walking into that room on her father's arm. She was wearing a beautiful antique gown she'd found downtown in a secondhand shop. Although it was a traditional-style wedding dress, with long sleeves and a high collar, it looked incredible on her. Even Daisy would have approved.

"I thought this was supposed to be a wedding," she said, still looking around at all the extra guests with a smile, "not a surprise party."

"I called Blue to see if anyone was going to be in town,

because we needed another witness," Crash told her. "Turns out everyone was in town."

Nell looked around, and Crash knew she realized that each and every one of his friends had come here purposely to support him. Like her parents, they'd changed all of their Christmas plans to be here today.

Her father raised her veil and kissed her before giving her to Crash.

"I'm so glad all your friends could come," she whispered to him as she squeezed his hand.

The ceremony passed in a blur. Crash tried to slow it down, tried to pay complete attention to the promises he was making, but the truth was, he would have promised this woman anything. And he would fight with his last breath to keep those promises.

The pastor finally told him that he could kiss his bride, and as he kissed his new wife's sweet lips, he tasted salt.

She was crying again.

He looked at her questioningly, touching her cheek, and she shook her head.

"Tears of joy don't count," she whispered.

He laughed and kissed her again, holding her close and knowing that no matter how long they had together—one year or one hundred—he would cherish every moment.

* * * * *

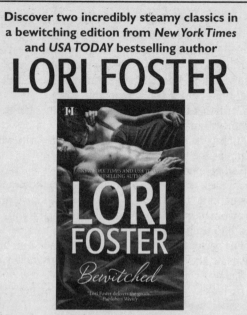

REQUEST YOUR FREE BOOKS!

2 FREE NOVELS
FROM THE SUSPENSE COLLECTION
PLUS 2 FREE GIFTS!

YES! Please send me 2 FREE novels from the Suspense Collection and my 2 FREE gifts (gifts are worth about $10). After receiving them, if I don't wish to receive any more books, I can return the shipping statement marked "cancel." If I don't cancel, I will receive 3 brand-new novels every month and be billed just $5.74 per book in the U.S. or $6.24 per book in Canada. That's a saving of at least 28% off the cover price. It's quite a bargain! Shipping and handling is just 50¢ per book.* I understand that accepting the 2 free books and gifts places me under no obligation to buy anything. I can always return a shipment and cancel at any time. Even if I never buy another book, the two free books and gifts are mine to keep forever.

192/392 MDN E7PD

Name _____ (PLEASE PRINT)

Address _____ Apt. #

City _____ State/Prov. _____ Zip/Postal Code

Signature (if under 18, a parent or guardian must sign)

Mail to **The Reader Service:**
IN U.S.A.: P.O. Box 1867, Buffalo, NY 14240-1867
IN CANADA: P.O. Box 609, Fort Erie, Ontario L2A 5X3

Not valid for current subscribers to the Suspense Collection
or the Romance/Suspense Collection.

Want to try two free books from another line?
Call 1-800-873-8635 or visit www.morefreebooks.com.

* Terms and prices subject to change without notice. Prices do not include applicable taxes. N.Y. residents add applicable sales tax. Canadian residents will be charged applicable provincial taxes and GST. Offer not valid in Quebec. This offer is limited to one order per household. All orders subject to approval. Credit or debit balances in a customer's account(s) may be offset by any other outstanding balance owed by or to the customer. Please allow 4 to 6 weeks for delivery. Offer available while quantities last.

Your Privacy: Harlequin Books is committed to protecting your privacy. Our Privacy Policy is available online at www.eHarlequin.com or upon request from the Reader Service. From time to time we make our lists of customers available to reputable third parties who may have a product or service of interest to you. If you would prefer we not share your name and address, please check here. ☐

Help us get it right—We strive for accurate, respectful and relevant communications. To clarify or modify your communication preferences, visit us at www.ReaderService.com/consumerchoice.

MSUS10R

SUZANNE BROCKMANN

77517 TALL, DARK AND FEARLESS	___$7.99 U.S.	___$9.99 CAN.
77516 TALL, DARK AND DANGEROUS	___$7.99 U.S.	___$9.99 CAN.
77471 NOWHERE TO RUN	___$7.99 U.S.	___$9.99 CAN.

(limited quantities available)

TOTAL AMOUNT	$ _____
POSTAGE & HANDLING	$ _____
($1.00 FOR 1 BOOK, 50¢ for each additional)	
APPLICABLE TAXES*	$ _____
TOTAL PAYABLE	$ _____

(check or money order—please do not send cash)

To order, complete this form and send it, along with a check or money order for the total above, payable to HQN Books, to: **In the U.S.:** 3010 Walden Avenue, P.O. Box 9077, Buffalo, NY 14269-9077; **In Canada:** P.O. Box 636, Fort Erie, Ontario, L2A 5X3.

Name: _____
Address: _____ City: _____
State/Prov.: _____ Zip/Postal Code: _____
Account Number (if applicable): _____

075 CSAS

*New York residents remit applicable sales taxes.
*Canadian residents remit applicable GST and provincial taxes.

We *are* romance™

www.HQNBooks.com

PHSB1110BL